EYES
OF THE
BLIND

ALEX TRESILLIAN

urbanepublications.com

First published in Great Britain in 2016
by Urbane Publications Ltd
Suite 3, Brown Europe House, 33/34 Gleaming Wood Drive,
Chatham, Kent ME5 8RZ
Copyright ©Alex Tresillian, 2017

A CIP catalogue record for this book is available
from the British Library.

ISBN 978-1-911129-69-1
EPUB 978-1-911129-70-7
MOBI 978-1-911129-71-4

Design and Typeset by Michelle Morgan

Cover by Julie Martin

Printed and bound by CPI Group (UK) Ltd, Croydon, CR0 4YY

urbanepublications.com

PART ONE

'Then the eyes of the blind
shall be opened…'

Isaiah 35:5

Hugo defecated by the back door and then walked nonchalantly into the lounge.

Niall groaned as the all too familiar smell drifted into his nostrils. Hugo's bowel movements were the bane of his life. Here he was, twenty-five, single, eligible, crying out for a girlfriend in fact, but doomed to be forever tied to a prolifically crapping guide dog. A dog who sat silently by the door when he was desperate instead of making some sort of useful noise to give you a hint. What could you do? Except be glad that your Mum still loved you enough to come round every week to clean the place up. And keep away from that part of the flat. As far as he was aware other people's guide dogs crapped pretty much to order, but Hugo seemed to enjoy relieving himself with gay abandon as if it were a hobby.

Dogs.

The day before, Niall had lost his job on local radio. 'Restructuring', they called it. Niall called it discrimination. They'd loved him at the beginning, loved the feel-good newsworthiness of having a blind local sports reporter: armed him with a lap-top and sent him off to some of the key matches in the Shropshire leagues. And higher. He'd covered the Shrews at the old Meadow and the New Meadow, lived and breathed the ups and downs at Telford, tipped horses at Ludlow. They couldn't say he hadn't delivered. But the novelty had worn off, the love-affair had ended, and now they had a girl with Downs Syndrome in reception they were probably easily surpassing their disability quota. Budget cuts meant restructuring, meant no dedicated local sports reporter, meant here's your redundancy and goodbye.

Sod them.

Niall thought he'd move to London. A garden flat in Telford wasn't really the centre of the media universe. It was time to make the break, get out from under his parents' feet, break his mother's heart so she could be proud of him. Apart from anything else, he wasn't meeting any girls in Telford.

He boiled the kettle, ripped the top off a Pot Noodle and stirred some water into the pot, checking the level with his finger. He'd had Pot Noodle disasters in the past, when he had totally misjudged the amount of boiling water required, flooding the kitchen floor and scalding his feet in the process. Experiences not to be repeated.

He turned the radio on and to hear an interview with a blind girl ('Patient A') who was going to have the world's first binocular eye transplant.

"Bloody blindness," he muttered. "Bloody blindness everywhere."

The interviewer brought in the surgeon who was going to carry out the operation.

"A complete, fully functional eye transplant has been the Holy Grail of researchers and ophthalmologists for decades," he said. "Indeed until very recently most – including myself – deemed it to be impossible."

"Nice one," Niall interpolated cynically.

"It was thought that the optic nerve was off-limits as far as transplant and regeneration was concerned. There were many who believed you could probably put in a real eye – as opposed to a prosthesis – but that it would never be possible to make it work. Too much blood, too many nerve endings, too difficult to get at. You'd have a monitor but you'd never be able to connect it to the computer."

Niall's monitor had started to pack up at the age of eight, although he had gone on seeing up to the age of twelve. It meant that the world was still a visual space to him; he prided himself on the fact that he still thought visually, that he could describe people and places in such a way that no-one could believe he couldn't see them. When he first went blind he refused to accept it, refused to enter the 'blind world', had ludicrous accidents because he wouldn't slow down, wouldn't shuffle about with his hand trailing along a wall, wouldn't check which way he was facing in a public lavatory. But he learnt, eventually. He didn't mind making a spectacle of himself but he couldn't bear the pity: it made him want to hit people. He'd done his fair share of lashing out at the special school his parents had fought the local authority to get him into, until finally a few good friends and two teachers he respected steered him into calmer waters. He didn't accept his blindness, he didn't think he ever would; but he saw that the way to defeat it was to build a life – a successful life – in spite of it.

And, until yesterday, that was exactly what he had been doing. He went to university and got into journalism, the career he'd planned for himself even before his lights went out - he was making a decent living. How many of his contemporaries could say that? But the truth was that, despite bottomless goodwill, the world was a sighted world, and blind people were going to be at a significant disadvantage in it.

"A Russian professor at a clinic in Bashkortostan made the initial breakthrough in the year 2000, after thirty years of research," the surgeon was saying. "He successfully transplanted a cornea and retina together into a young woman who had been blind for twenty years and was able to give her very limited vision. Mostly light and dark. Shapes. Not what you and I would call seeing. But developments in stem cell technology, tissue cloning and microsurgery have brought us from there to this point, where we are ready to dare to try. We have a perfect pair of eyes and we're ready. To perform the impossible."

"How does it make you feel when you hear Mr. Daghash talk like that?" the interviewer asked 'Patient A'.

"I just think about the possibility of seeing," she said.

"We are medical pioneers here," the surgeon said. "We truly don't know what is over the horizon. Some of my fellow professionals have called it the blind leading the blind. But let's see. This dear girl has nothing to lose by trying."

"And, Daniel Sullivan," the interviewer said to another man in the studio, "the British Association for the Blind, one of our most respected charities, is totally supporting this operation, despite its having been dismissed by many specialists in the field?"

"The possibility is too exciting to ignore," Sullivan – whoever he was – said. "A charity that exists to champion the causes of visually impaired people must pursue every avenue that may enable people to see again – to not do so would be irresponsible."

"And the cost?" the interviewer asked.

"Is this the conversation we should be having," Daghash intervened, "with this brave young woman on the verge of her leap into the void?"

Enough, Niall decided, and switched off.

Leaps into the void. Why did the whole thing sound patronising to him? Why couldn't he be thrilled by this possible breakthrough in technology? There was nothing patronising about giving somebody a new heart, or a new liver. Why couldn't he get the 'Let's help the poor blind people' tag out of his head? This wasn't offering to drag you across a busy main road when you were just stopping to get your bearings, this was medical science striving for a minority. He should be applauding. Instead he wanted to throw rotten fruit.

Why did it matter to them? Why were they doing it? Just to make themselves feel good? Boost their own egos?

He knew his reaction was ridiculous: if they were switching on parts of brains that had stopped functioning he'd be the first to call them miracle workers. It was just eyes. There was something about eyes.

He could write a piece about it, an impassioned plea for less 'precious' political correctness about disability. The one thing he'd always sworn he'd never write about. "I'm a journalist, not a disabled journalist," he always said.

But on the other hand …

Niall was never one to let the grass grow under his feet. Once an idea came to him he pursued it, totally confident that it would come to fruition. And this could be the start of a successful freelance career.

The girl was in Moorfields Eye Hospital. He had connections there. God, he'd spent enough hours of his life in the place going for meetings and check-ups and counselling. If he could find out who 'Patient A' was and get an interview with her he could sell it to the highest bidder. He knew that she'd probably made some exclusive deal with a paper for her story but that didn't put him off. He had a different angle. If he could get in first, before the 'My First Day of Seeing' spread appeared in the chosen tabloid, he'd be on his way.

His phone was in his pocket. One of his best friends from school, Simon Roberts, lived in a rented house in Chiswick with his girlfriend and a couple of girlfriends of hers, all of whom were Australian. Simon would never say no to putting him up temporarily, and then with any luck Hugo would charm the girls. He was good at that kind of thing.

"Simon, mate, how's things?" Simon was a computer-obsessive, but human with it.

"Niall, what are you doing?"

"I'm coming to London. Following up a story."

"For Radio Salop?"

"No. The fuckers fired me."

"No!"

"They've restructured. Made me redundant."

"That's shite."

"It was time to move on anyway." You had to put a good spin on these things. "I'm more of an old-fashioned pen and ink journalist. I'm going freelance until The Times beats a path to my door."

"Right."

"So I was thinking of coming to stay with you for a bit, while I do the story."

"What's the story?"

"I'll tell you when I come down."

"It'd be great to see you."

"Fantastic."

Settled. He closed the conversation before Simon had too much time to think about it, arranged to come down the next day. While he was dossing for free in Chiswick he could afford to keep the Telford place on. He'd tell his Mum he was going down to London for a week or two, get her to come over and give the place a good clean. Perhaps his step-dad could do the garden. It was the end of September, nearly time to cut everything down and put it to bed for the winter. Niall remembered the bonfires of childhood, the gathering of wood and garden rubbish with his Dad (before he was blind and before his blindness frightened his Dad off into the wide blue yonder), the splashing of paraffin on strategically placed newspaper at the bottom, his Dad leaning in to light it, singeing the hairs on the back of his hand and swearing as the paraffin caught. Crazy days. The crazy days of seeing.

Anyway. Things always fell into place when you shook them up. He woke up his lap-top and listened to its synthetic speech guiding him through buying a train ticket to London. Synthetic speech was – let's face it – crap but necessary. Irritating and impersonal, robotic but totally subservient. Whatever you typed it would say. Which could be quite amusing in a Word document but didn't help you get things done on the Internet. Niall had contemplated in his more drunken moments setting up a sex chat line where the voice was just a speech synthesiser. He felt sure it had novelty value. But he'd never followed it up.

He phoned his Mum, fed Hugo and told him a bit about what he should expect from the capital, ate his cold, congealed Pot Noodle, packed a rucksack and went to bed. This was the beginning of the future.

TWO

Susannah wondered how the journalist had got her number. She'd asked but he hadn't answered. She'd told him she'd already signed a contract with a paper and he'd made it sound like that was why he was ringing. It was all very confusing but when he told her he was blind, when he'd described how Moorfields would look the first time she opened her new eyes, she had been intrigued. Intrigued enough, at least, to agree to see him. Niall Burnet. He came from Shropshire, wherever that was.

Now that he was due any minute she wondered what he wanted to know, what he wanted to talk to her about. Up to now, hers had been the unremarkable life of an average blind girl, she thought. Cherished and protected by her family, a family who had understandably diverted a lot of her disability allowance into putting her fully sighted sister through university and helping her to become an accountant. As her parents kept saying, Amelia needed to be in a top job so that she would be able to help her little blind sister when they were gone. But now the little blind sister wasn't going to be blind any more. Maybe. And maybe she'd be able to make her parents proud.

Her door opened and a nurse whose footsteps she recognised came in.

"You've got a visitor, Susie," she said.

"Right," Susannah answered, trying to sit more upright and smoothing her hair.

"Niall Burnet," said a pleasant voice. A chocolate voice, maybe with nuts. She always characterised voices as tastes. She'd never told anybody. Her father was beef (with horse-radish when he was angry), her mother blackberry and apple. Amelia was minty – somewhere between ice cream and toothpaste.

"Don't tire her out," said the nurse. Lemon tart.

"I'm just going to chat to her. No stress, no pressure," said Niall. "Have you got such a thing as a chair?"

"Here," she said.

"Thank you." He sat down, and waited for the nurse to go out. "Hi," he said, "I'm Niall Burnet. Unless they've brought me to the wrong room as part of some elaborate joke you must be Susannah Leman."

"I am," she said smiling.

"Good," he said. "Hugo usually sorts out the introductions but he's had to stay outside. They thought he might have germs."

"Is Hugo your dog?" Susannah asked.

"You're sharp," Niall said, tongue-in-cheek.

"My parents have never let me have a dog," Susannah said wistfully. "But I suppose I won't need one now."

"Fingers crossed," Niall said. He let silence deliberately fall.

"So," Susannah said, uncomfortable with it. "You're blind and you're a journalist. That's amazing."

"Thanks," Niall said.

"I mean I never thought of blind people really doing a job like that," she went on.

"You thought basket-weaving and piano tuning were the dizzy heights of blind ambition?"

"Something like that I suppose." He heard a smile in her voice. "My parents have never really talked about me getting a job."

"They sound great," Niall said sarcastically.

"They've made so many sacrifices for me," Susannah said.

"But now," Niall said, "what are your plans? What are your dreams?"

"I don't know," Susannah said. "Actually I'm a bit scared."

"Of the operation? What've you got to lose?"

"No. Of seeing." It was the first time she had admitted it, to herself or anyone.

"What? Why?"

"Because I know my life the way it is. Because blindness is kind of safe. People look after you. People look out for you. I don't know how to be sighted."

"So why did you agree to it?"

"It was my parents really. My Dad I think. Mostly. Well, I'm sure they did ask me. But what would anybody say when offered this opportunity?"

"Why don't you tell someone how you feel?"

"Who'd understand?"

"So nobody knows you feel this way?"

"No."

Niall's story started to take shape. Whilst he tried to reassure the girl that seeing was OK, he drew out the story of a child who had had no life, had been kept in the family home like a hamster - fed, cleaned and played with, but not engaged with as a fellow human being. She had gone to the local school where the staff had no doubt been delighted by her parents' lack of expectations, sat with a teaching assistant learning next to nothing and making no friends.

The more he spoke to her, the more her sanguine acquiescence in such a pitiful excuse for a life annoyed him. He could think of dozens of blind people he knew who'd make better use of a pair of eyes than this girl, but here she was, in the right place at the right time, with a pushy Mummy and Daddy who couldn't wait to have the stigma of having produced an imperfect child between them lifted.

❧

After the blind journalist had gone, Susannah felt strange: comforted, but lonely. Nobody had ever spoken to her so directly, so personally, so challengingly. She knew some of the things she had said had exasperated him, but he was so different from her. She really liked him. He had told her that seeing would be OK, that she would soon get the hang of it, and the surprise factor would wear off, that life was genuinely better when you could see. And she believed him because she could hear pain in his voice when he said it; well-disguised, but there. Mr. Daghash had told her it would be OK, but he was the surgeon, he was bound to say that. And he'd never been blind. Niall said he was happy enough – she didn't believe him – but if he was offered it he'd take his sight back tomorrow. She was lucky. She knew she was lucky. And glad she'd agreed to see him. She wished they'd let him bring his dog in. Hugo. She really wanted to meet him.

❧

"What a stupid, fatuous, ridiculous girl," Niall said to Simon. They were in the front room of Simon's Chiswick house, which had that not-very-new-furniture rented smell about it. Hugo was asleep on the carpet, Erica (the girlfriend) sat next to Simon on a sofa flicking through a copy of *Glamour*; Simon was internet-surfing on his laptop, trying not to let Niall distract him.

"If she's the public face of blindness in the tabloids we may as well give up and go home," Niall went on.

"I am home," Simon said.

"And she's going to end up a celebrity."

"Only if the operation works," Erica said.

"God, can you imagine if it doesn't?" Niall said. "The whole nation will go into mourning for poor Susannah and the lost sight she never had."

"I don't think you're going to make a very good story out of this," Simon said.

"Fucking waste of time," Niall said. "I just wish Hugo had crapped somewhere he shouldn't."

"You could try and find out why they chose her," Erica suggested.

"You think there might be a whiff of corruption?" Niall asked. "Backhander from Daddy? Contribution to research costs?"

"Might make a story," Erica said.

"I want to find out what this operation is costing," Niall said. "My story is going to be about the thousands of blind people they could've helped in a small way if they hadn't blown all their money on this high-profile high-octane publicity stunt."

Erica said, "The eyes are the window of the soul. But whose soul will you see when you look in hers?"

"I left her my number," Niall said. "Why the Hell did I do that?"

Simon laughed. "You can't help it," he said.

"I felt sorry for her. The same way I do when I see tortured and malnourished animals on the news."

"She's a girl, so you fancied her. Remember I've known you since you were twelve."

"Could you hack into BAB for me," Niall asked, "like you once did when we were at school?" BAB was the British Association for the Blind.

"I'm a responsible adult now," Simon said.

"I just want to see if there's an email trail about this operation. I need to find out what it cost and who's paying for it."

"You're a pain," Simon said.

Hugo sighed, stretched and released an enormous fart.

"Oh for fuck's sake!" Erica said, slamming her magazine down and walking out to the kitchen.

"What about BAB?" Niall asked.

"Leave it with me. You know Lindsey Spencer works at their head office."

Niall choked on his raspberry tea.

"Lindsey Spencer?" He mimicked a strident, thin, nasal voice.

"Yeah. I'm not quite sure what she does there."

"Cleans the bloody toilets I should think," Niall said. "Probably not very well."

"I love it when your past comes back to haunt you," Simon said.

Lindsey Spencer had been in the year above them at school. She had launched herself at Niall when he was thirteen and innocent, nearly breaking his jaw with her inept attempts at French kissing. Then for two years she had managed to operate an exclusion zone around him so that no other girl and not many boys could get to spend any time with him. He had ended up despising her for it, but they had clumsily lost their virginity together, and for that alone he would always be grateful. Then when he finally had the guts to finish with her she took an overdose of paracetamol and it all got very messy. Her parents got involved, and even though they'd never met Niall they blamed him for everything. Lindsey was sight impaired but had a bit of vision and made a point of avoiding him from that time on, which suited him fine. Then he made the fatal mistake of following her down the A Level German route, and when he was in Year Twelve and she in Year Thirteen they ended up on a German blind school exchange together. Far from home on the fringes of the Schwarzwald she had cornered him and forced him into conversation.

"I've forgiven you, you know."

"Great."

"I think I'll always love you, in spite of what you did to me."

"You don't love me."

"You don't know the first thing about love."

Well maybe he didn't, but being chained to her through his middle teens hadn't helped.

"I want to be your friend," she said.

"Fine."

"You really need a good friend."

"Right." He decided the best way was to let her make her patronising speech. Get it off her increasingly ample chest. She went on for about an hour telling him things he apparently didn't know about himself, things that he had allegedly been too wrapped up in himself to find out about her; he had never realised that she had gone out with him initially because she took pity on him, or that she had wanted to end their relationship several times (and yet she would always love him) but thought that he wouldn't be able to cope.

He didn't learn a lot of German that week.

And now she worked for BAB. Which was typical, somehow. But if she was his route into head office, then so be it.

"What's BAB's phone number?"

"Haven't a clue mate. You'll have to 118 it."

Niall found out and rang.

"Lindsey Spencer please."

"One moment." The line went quiet. Niall tried to imagine what her role would be. He tried to remember if he had ever known what degree if any she had gone on to read from school. Not that that meant anything of course.

"Who's calling please?"

"Simon Roberts." The receptionist sounded as though she was on work experience.

"Simon?"

"It's not Simon actually. It's Niall. Hi Lindsey. Don't hang up."

"Niall." A pause. "Why would I?"

"I don't know. Because I haven't kept in touch."

"Which was hardly surprising."

"No, I know."

"What do you want?"

"Can I come and see you at work tomorrow? Do I need to make an appointment?"

"Yes. And no. I'm intrigued."

"Brilliant. What time shall I come?"

"Eleven? We could go for coffee."

"I don't drink coffee. What about ten?"

"Yes, OK. Do you even know where this place is?"

"Somewhere between Harrod's and the Natural History Museum."

"If you say so. I've never been to either."

"I just remember somebody telling me once."

She gave him the address and the call came to an uncertain end.

"She sounds exactly the same," Niall said.

"Yes," Simon agreed. "I heard every word."

THREE

They all sat around her bed: Mr. Daghash, who smelt of hygiene, Mummy and Daddy, Amelia, the journalist from the Mirror – Matthew somebody; a man from the British Association for the Blind and the nurse with the lemon tart voice, Beverley. Another journalist had been taking pictures, but he had gone.

"So how do you feel?" the journalist asked.

"I don't know," Susannah said after a pause for thought. "Scared probably."

"Of the operation?" Matthew pressed.

"Well – yes."

"But excited to think that tomorrow, if it all goes according to plan, when they take the bandages off you'll see the world for the first time."

"Yes." It was easiest just to say yes to him. Her thoughts were so confused and his suggestions were so logical. She knew they were what she ought to be thinking, if she could get control of herself.

"So Mr. Leman," Matthew said changing tack, "if you could say something right now to the family of the person who died and donated the eyes your daughter's going to see with, what would it be?"

"Just that we are so grateful," he said immediately, rehearsed, "that in the midst of their tragedy, they had the wonderful generosity to think of others. To make this miracle possible. They are heroes to us."

Susannah wondered if she would ever meet them: how weird it would be that they would see their daughter's/sister's/cousin's eyes looking at them out of somebody else's face. Her face. They would hate her because she would remind them of what they had lost. Nobody had even told her what colour the eyes were. She opened her mouth to ask, but the conversation had swept on without her.

"Susie will be going into theatre about three o'clock," Mr. Daghash was saying. "The operation will take several hours, and there are a number of critical points. If we pass all those critical points successfully, and if Susie has faith, then by the grace of God she will see the world for the first time tomorrow morning."

"And what are you most looking forward to seeing?" Matthew said to her.

Susannah tried to think.

"Her mother," her father said.

"Everybody," Susannah said. "Everything." Or nothing, she thought.

"But what I would like to say to you," Mr. Daghash went on, "is that when she opens her eyes none of us quite knows what she will see at first. Her brain has never processed visual data, and it will almost certainly take a little time for everything to settle down and for Susannah to see normally, as we do. At first everything may be blurred and unfocused. She will be bombarded with visual stimuli and the brain will have to figure out how to deal with it. The first few days will be critical. And then the aftercare and the anti-rejection medication are very important. We must be patient, and we must have faith."

"I never thought this day would come," her mother, Karin, said tearfully. "It's the answer to all our prayers."

"And is it right that it's all down to a commitment to fund the research from the British Association for the Blind?" Matthew asked, turning to the fourth man in the room.

"The British Association for the Blind," he said, "is committed to supporting and empowering the visually impaired, ameliorating visual impairment, and, where possible, fighting visual impairment." His voice was stodgy, but dried up. Stale treacle pudding, Susannah decided. "We have a duty to divide the money that we are able to raise through the general public's generous support between projects and services that will benefit and ease the lives of the majority of people battling sight loss, and ground-breaking scientific research that could lead to the beginning of the end of congenital visual impairment. We have supported the research into artificial 'seeing' eyes from the beginning –"

"But I am right aren't I," Matthew cut across him, "that most of the funding for this research has come from the Association?"

"Yes," said Mr. Daghash.

"The gift of sight is a wonderful thing," the Association man said.

"And what would any of you say right now," Matthew went on, "to those people who say this is playing God and it's against nature and wrong?"

"I would say today is not the day and this is not the place to be debating that issue," Mr. Daghash said firmly.

Matthew left soon after. Mr. Daghash squeezed Susannah's hand, wished her luck, and then left with the man from the Association. She was alone with her family. The family she had never seen for twenty-two years, but might see tomorrow. So many faces to learn, so many sights to see. Would her brain cope and make sense of it all? What if they wired her up wrong and everything was upside down? Would it be better to see the world upside down than not to see it at all?

"We'll be just outside," her mother said. "I won't be far away. You won't be alone."

"Thanks, Mum."

"Mum's going to stay the night with you in the hospital," Amelia said. "Dad and I are going to wait until the operation's done. Then we're going to go home and come back in the morning. It's going to be fantastic to have you look at me."

"Yeah."

She found herself wanting them to go, leave her to gather her thoughts and her courage. She thought of Niall Burnet. Whether the operation worked or not, she was going to ring him. He'd let her tell the truth.

❧

The taxi deposited Niall in Knightsbridge, outside the imposing headquarters of the British Association for the Blind.

"You've got a flight of steps and then a door that's open," the taxi driver told him.

"Cheers mate," Niall said. "Keep the change." He gave the man an absurdly generous tip, but he couldn't bear faffing about with coins. You could tell a note by its size, and by what Niall called 'wallet memory'. He used to play a game with his friends at Radio Salop where he'd get them to bet on whether he could correctly pick every item out of his wallet. He'd got it down to a fine art, and the skill had never left him.

Hugo steered him up the steps and through the door into a large reception hall, carpeted to lessen echo. Fairly standard in terms of getting your bearings, but it did mean people could creep up on you, as some woman did now.

"Can I help you at all?"

"Hopefully, if it's your job," Niall said. He meant it tongue-in-cheek, but he sensed the woman bridling, and realised that she was one of those who would never 'get' him; would think he was just rude and arrogant. It kept happening.

"I've got an appointment with Lindsey Spencer," he said.

"Oh, Lindsey," she said, thawing slightly. "I'll take you up. She's on the first floor; do you prefer lift or stairs?"

"Let's do stairs, it's good for me."

"This way then," she said.

"After her, Hugo," Niall said, and the dog, who understood his sense of humour better than most women, set off.

"Do you know Lindsey?" the woman asked.

"We were at school together," Niall said.

"Isn't she lovely?" the woman said.

"Yeah," Niall offered, trying to sound committed.

"My name's Juliette, by the way. Juliette Warwick. I work in HR."

"That's such a great phrase," Niall said.

"What?"

"Human Resources."

"It just means we look after people," Juliette said. "I like that. I'm a people person."

And I'm not people, then, Niall thought, because you're radiating dislike and we've barely met.

"What's Lindsey going to do for you?" Juliette asked.

"It's about a reunion," Niall lied quickly. He didn't want to arouse suspicion if he could avoid it, and he still didn't know what department they were going to find Lindsey in.

"I'm holding a door for you."

"Thanks. Go, Hugo."

They walked into a large office.

"Lindsey!" Juliette called loudly.

"Yes?" The voice hadn't mellowed with time.

"An old school-friend to see you."

"Let me see, let me see!" Lindsey almost shrieked, approaching. "Oh my God, Niall. Everyone, this was my first ever boyfriend, Niall Burnet!"

Maximum humiliation, minimum effort. Niall could almost have been impressed if he hadn't been inwardly squirming. He could imagine the smile of delight on Juliette Warwick's face.

"Come and meet everybody. Oh, and look at your dog! What's his name?"

"Hugo."

"That's just such a typical name for you. Mine's called Jessie. You must meet her too."

Niall met everybody, including Jessie, but he wasn't on top form and annoyingly he failed to take in their names or what they did. He seemed to be somewhere in the lower reaches of the finance department, which was promising, among book-keepers and wages clerks. It might be a short step to the information he wanted about funding, if he could regain his composure and control of the situation.

"So," Lindsey said, when she finally sat him on a not very comfortable chair in what she called 'her area', "to what do I owe this dubious pleasure?"

"Where've you been learning light sarcasm?" Niall asked. "It always used to be beyond you."

"I've grown as a person," she said.

"What do you do here exactly?" he asked, partly to avoid answering her question directly when there might be unnecessary ears listening, partly to gain control of the conversation.

"I'm not really strictly a finance person," Lindsey said. "I work with bequests."

"Isn't that finance?"

"It is when we get them," Lindsey said. "My job is to visit elderly people who are registered blind or partially sighted and talk to them about the possibility of leaving money to the Association."

"You're a predator," Niall said. "That ought to suit you."

"If you've come here to be rude to me you can just leave."

"Sorry. No. I'm really sorry." Niall cursed his tongue. He needed to open her up, not get her to close down. "Doesn't it bother you though?"

"What?"

"You're visiting vulnerable old people and persuading them to leave money away from their families. What do you think the families would say about it?"

"Number one," Lindsey said earnestly, "many of the people I go to see have no family to speak of, or if they do the family don't care about them, they just want to get their hands on their money. BAB is often the best family they've got. Number two, I don't force them into anything. I tell them about my life, about what BAB has done for me and others like me, and they know what it's doing for them. They're often delighted when it dawns on them that they can give something back."

"I hope you don't tell them too much about your life," Niall said, lightening the tone.

"I leave you out of it, don't worry," Lindsey said.

"So they say yes and what happens?" Niall asked.

"I recommend them one of our solicitors and make an appointment for them so the new will can be drawn up."

"And that's how BAB gets its money."

"Most of it, yes," Lindsey said. "We need those legacies, Niall. When the National Lottery started, regular donations plummeted. And they've never recovered. We get our share of the lottery cake but it's nothing to what we used to get. And it costs a phenomenal amount to run a big charity like this."

"That sounds like somebody else talking," Niall said.

"It's the truth," Lindsey said.

"Those old women – I suppose most of them are women – pay your wages."

"I don't think of it like that."

"Well who'd've thought it," Niall said.

"What?"

"That you'd end up as a bizarre kind of Indulgence saleswoman."

"What do you mean?"

"You know. The Middle Ages. When you could buy pardons and things that would get you into heaven. This is the same. It's playing on people's sense of guilt and gratitude."

"That's ridiculous," Lindsey said. "You always made everything ridiculous."

"Thanks. So, who decides then how all this money gets spent? I mean, once they've creamed off their salaries and paid all the minions like you, who decides what goes where?"

"Why do you want to know all this?" Lindsey asked, suddenly suspicious. "Is that why you came?"

"I came because I was staying with Simon and he said you worked here, and I was really intrigued to see you again."

"I won't go out with you," Lindsey said. "I've got a man in my life. Much more caring and understanding than you could ever be."

"I'm really pleased for you," Niall said.

"So what about you?"

"Nothing much. I'm not working at the moment."

"I could try to get you a job here!"

"Thanks. I'll think about it."

"That would be great."

"Would it?"

"Yes. I'll speak to HR." Juliette would be thrilled, Niall thought.

"I've been following this story about the eye transplant," he said, deciding to force the issue. "Have you?"

"It's amazing, isn't it?"

"Is BAB involved with that?"

"It's huge here. It's brilliant publicity. They've put loads of money into it. They think it's going to catch the imagination of the public. Every time it's been mentioned in the press donations have doubled for the week."

"Right."

"Not that that's what it's about," Lindsey said quickly. "It's a wonderful breakthrough. So much better than artificial robot eyes. Long term they're hoping to grow eyes from stem cells which will truly open it up to everyone. You might get some."

"I'll be too old by then."

"Most people don't go blind until they're old."

"True."

Their conversation went on another half an hour but Niall learnt little more of value. He used Hugo's bowels as an excuse to get away, and found his way back to the street. With a little help from Hugo and a member of the public he unearthed a bench in a nearby square and sat down. A busker was playing a flute somewhere, and, despite the obvious noise of traffic all around, it was as if London held its breath to listen.

He needed to take stock of where he was and where he was going. He was sure that if he could put together the alternative, dark side of the transplant business, the cynical use of it as a publicity stunt, he'd be able to sell his story to one of the papers that had lost the bidding war for Susannah's eye-witness account. But the story needed focus. It needed something far more selfish and scandalous than cynicism. To find it he needed to delve deeper. Perhaps he should let Lindsey swing him a job at BAB. So long as it didn't involve conning old women out of their savings.

Niall hated moments of self-doubt, but he was having one now. What did he actually know about freelance journalism? What did he know about journalism at all outside the ornamental fishpond that was local radio? Essentially he now had no home, no job, no woman, was a long way from his Mum, and was taking advantage of the kindness and gullibility of his one really good friend. He ruffled Hugo's ears.

He pressed his watch and it announced that it was eleven twenty-seven with exaggerated self-importance. He wondered what time Susannah Leman's operation was, he knew it was today; what new world awaited her, a world of colour and light, faces, trees and sunsets.

Angry at himself he stood up, but at that point his phone rang. Simon's ringtone.

"Hi Simon."

"Hi. Where are you?"

"In the middle of some square in Knightsbridge. It's nice."

"Right. I just thought I'd tell you what I'd found."

"Go ahead."

"I managed to access the system they've got for spying on staff internet use and email traffic."

"You criminal."

"I think they should look at it more often."

"Yeah, right, OK, fine, but…?" Niall tried to hustle Simon along.

"The Deputy Director General, Daniel Sullivan, has exchanged a load of emails about the eye transplant with loads of people, including someone at Moorfields."

"Who?"

"Somebody going under the name of D.Clark."

"Who is?"

"No idea. But two of the emails refer to a meeting at Number Seventeen."

"Which is where?"

"I don't know, but it's a bit weird, isn't it?"

"Why?"

"They could have met at BAB. They could have met at Moorfields."

"Number Seventeen could be a club or a posh restaurant."

"No. I Googled it. Two million hits, no London restaurant. And if it was an address, wouldn't he give the name of the street?"

"Not if it was a place they both knew."

"Sullivan also sent an internal email to the Director of Finance, John Holthouse, saying the meeting at Number Seventeen was on."

"It's flimsy, Simon, flimsy. But I suppose it might be worth a bit of digging."

"I think so."

"God knows how exactly."

"You're the journalist."

"Yeah."

"How was Lindsey?"

"Purgatory."

Simon laughed.

FOUR

Susannah became aware of darkness, and, as she did so, she wondered whether she had ever been aware of darkness before. Annoyingly, she couldn't decide. So, the operation was over. She had survived.

"I think she might be awake," she heard her mother say. "Susie?"

She had to decide whether to be awake or not. It was something you could do when you were blind. Part of her wanted a bit more solitude, but curiosity got the better of her.

"Mum?"

"Hello darling. How are you feeling? They say the operation went really well."

She started to lift a hand to her face, became aware of wires or tubes, put it down again, and as she did so felt bile rising in her throat.

"I think I'm going to be –" she vomited before she could finish.

"It's the anaesthetic, darling," her mother said. "It happens to everyone."

Nurses mopped her up, put a bucket or basin by her head in case it happened again. Which it did. Four times, and yet she'd eaten nothing for what had seemed like days.

"Poor darling," a nurse whose voice she didn't recognise said.

"What time is it?" she asked.

"It's nearly midnight, darling. You're in the Intensive Care Unit. The operation went really well apparently. Mr. Daghash's on his way. He asked to be paged as soon as you woke up."

Weird. The last thing she remembered it had been early afternoon. All those hours lost, and yet they were hours when she had been the centre of several people's attention, hours that might change her life. It was really quite scary that you could be put to sleep. For as long or as short a time as the doctor wanted. Perhaps that was why doctors frightened her.

"I think I'm a bit tired," she said.

"Try to stay awake for Mr. Daghash," her mother said. Her mother's parents – Susannah's grandparents – were Danish, and sometimes her mother's voice contained a hint of the accent still. It was the apple element in the blackberry and apple and it was always more evident when she was tired or under strain. Which she obviously was now. Susannah suddenly wondered how her parents had met, wondered why she had never wondered before. She had accepted so much of her life, in fact all of it, without question. Her family was just her family. She'd never wondered what their lives had been like before they had been saddled with a blind child, never wondered whether they had resented the way everything had had to change once she was born. It was she herself who was almost certainly the cause of the strain she was so often aware of in her mother, the anger she so often heard in her father. No wonder they had been so keen to put her forward for the operation. It was for her, but it was also for them.

The door opened and she smelt Mr. Daghash.

"Susie!" He came to the bed and squeezed her hand. "My brave girl." Mr. Daghash would be a kind father to his children. If he had any. "Everything has gone extremely well. The neurological tests suggest that everything is working as we would want it to be working, and in the morning, after you have rested, we shall unveil your new face. Then you must start to learn to use the muscles that will make you see properly."

I've got two foreign bodies in my head, Susannah thought. Two eyes that spent years seeing for somebody else who had a life that was tragically cut short, and now they're starting a new life with me. What dreams, what visions will they bring with them from their past?

"You're sleepy, I know," Mr. Daghash said. "I will leave you to rest. I just had to see you to tell you how it had gone, how it couldn't have gone better."

"Thank you," she said.

"Thank you," he said. "For your courage. For your determination."

What courage? What determination? They had changed her life and yet they knew nothing about her.

Three times that night Lindsey had rung Niall. He had seen with Erica's help that it was her and let it go to voicemail. Then refused to listen to it. Endured Simon's exaggerated hilarity at his discomfort.

"You couldn't resist giving her your number then?"

"She asked for it. She's a potentially useful contact. She said she had a life and that life had a man in it."

" 'Niall, I will always love you,'" Simon squawked nasally. "You walked back into her life and turned everything on its head."

"I don't believe it," Niall said. "She seemed so much more together."

"It's the power you have over women," Simon said.

"Why is she the only one that feels it then?" Niall asked.

"Because you were meant for each other. Soul-mates."

"Stop it," Niall said angrily.

His phone rang again. Erica had gone to bed.

"It's her," he said.

"It's one a.m.," Simon said.

"Why the Hell isn't she in bed?"

"Perhaps she is."

"Shut up."

"Just answer it. You're not going to get any sleep until you do."
Niall growled.

"Hello?" he said, trying to sound as if he had just woken up.

"Niall, thank God." It was Lindsey. Upset.

"What?"

"Did you get my messages?"

"Sorry, no, there's a problem with my voicemail. Lindsey, it's the middle of the night."

"I'm getting the sack." She sobbed.

"What? What are you talking about?"

"I'm sorry Niall. I realise you were asleep but I just didn't know who else to talk to."

"OK, OK." Niall settled himself more comfortably into the sofa. "What about loverboy?"

"He can't be here tonight."

"Right."

"This is just as humiliating and embarrassing for me as it is boring for you I can assure you."

"No, Lindsey, I'm sorry. What's happened?"

"At the end of the day HR asked to see me. They told me that one of the people I visited had made a complaint about me. And I was going to be suspended while it was investigated." The tears were making her voice break up. It was quite difficult to hear what she was saying.

"What's the complaint?"

"They won't tell me."

"So how are you supposed to defend yourself?"

"Niall, whatever it is, I've never done anything. I've visited people, I've done the job and I've left. I can't even begin to imagine what I might have been accused of, because I've not done anything wrong. Almost in my entire life. You know me."

"You had under-age sex with me."

"Niall this is serious."

"I know. Lindsey, I'm – flabbergasted. I'm speechless, and you know that doesn't happen often."

"Apparently, they have to investigate it and then decide if it's serious enough to need a disciplinary hearing."

"So maybe it won't."

"It was just the way Juliette looked at me. It was almost like she was giving me the opportunity to resign."

"Not Juliette Warwick?"

"Yes. She's the one who's doing the investigation. She said she was sorry."

"The people person."

"Mm?"

"Nothing. Lindsey, I'll come over tomorrow. Where do you live?"

"In an annexe of my parents' house in Harrow. I can't tell them though."

"Don't be silly."

"It would break their hearts."

"They'll support you. They'll believe in you."

"Niall I can't. They're going on holiday in three days' time. I've just got to go through the motions for three days. When they come back maybe I'll've found something else. Or moved out. Or killed myself."

"No, Lindsey. No. How long are they going for?"

"Three weeks. Cruising somewhere. Alaska or something."

"OK. Come here in the morning. Simon would love to see you."

"What?" Simon interjected, but it was too late. With profuse thanks Lindsey let Niall 'go back to sleep' and rang off.

"Now how weird is that?" Niall said.

"What?"

"I go to visit her, we talk about the eye transplant, who knows who was listening, and by the end of the day they've got her out of the place."

Niall explained the circumstances to Simon.

"Maybe she has done something stupid," Simon said.

"Can you really imagine it? Lindsey not doing everything by the book? And it's just the coincidence. I don't believe in coincidence," Niall said decisively.

"But you'll never find out who was listening."

"Lindsey's got some sight," Niall said. "She might be able to remember who was close by. She'll know what part of the office we were in at least."

"But that'll mean telling her about your story."

"Yeah, maybe I'll have to," Niall said thoughtfully. "But this has made it all a lot more interesting."

"You heartless bastard."

"No, but it's decidedly suspicious."

"I'd say it was flimsy," Simon said. Niall threw a cushion at him. Shortly afterwards, Simon went up to bed, Niall undressed, fished out his sleeping bag from behind the television, and stretched out on the sofa to think things through. He fell asleep.

Lindsey arrived at half past eight the next morning, causing a certain amount of consternation in the household. Niall had quickly realised that until the three working women had left the building it was best to lie still and pretend they hadn't woken him. Hugo hadn't worked that out and he seemed positively to enjoy getting under their feet in the kitchen until one of them locked him out in the back yard. Between swearing at the dog, swearing at the time, thundering up and down stairs, swearing at hair straighteners, mirrors and other inanimate objects whose fault it obviously was that they hadn't got enough time to get ready, there was really very little likelihood of sleeping through the girls' breakfast.

Lindsey's ring on the doorbell provoked another volley of swearing, and then Erica burst into the lounge.

"Niall, there's a girl and a dog at the door. You need to wake up and deal with it." Her heels clopped into the kitchen and one of them said something about not choosing to live in a hostel for blind people.

"Niall?" He heard Lindsey calling from the hallway. He was only wearing boxer shorts and that was not how she was going to see him. He groped around for his jeans, located a t-shirt, pulled that on, found the jeans under the coffee table, scrambled into them and stood up as Lindsey called him for the third time.

"I'm here. Come in. Door on the left."

Jessie brought her in.

"You found it all right then?"

"Of course."

"I'll get you a drink in a minute, when the girls have gone out."

"Trust you to be living with three girls."

"It's Simon, not me." Niall started to gather his thoughts, realising that his breath probably stank as he hadn't cleaned his teeth and his hair was sticking out ludicrously because he hadn't had a chance to deal with it. "I didn't realise you'd be quite so early," he said.

"I had to leave the house at the normal time," Lindsey said. "Otherwise my parents would've known something was wrong."

"You should tell them," Niall said again.

"I don't need the stress of knowing they're worrying about me all the time," Lindsey said.

There was a cacophony of shoes on the hall floorboards and the workers left the house, without saying goodbye, slamming the door behind them.

"I blame Hugo," Niall said. With the freedom of the kitchen he made her a coffee, sat her down, asked for ten minutes to make himself presentable – which she laughed at – and then, with his dog fed and watered and he himself cleaned up, he sat down with Lindsey to 'work on her problem.'

"We can't do anything until we know what I'm accused of and by whom," Lindsey said.

"Yes we can," Niall said. "Because we can guess that they're going to get some old biddy to say you intimidated her or threatened her or behaved improperly in some way."

"I never, ever –" Lindsey began.

"I know that," Niall said. "But there are two possibilities. One is, that somebody you went to spoke to their family and the family were really angry because they saw their inheritance slipping away; or maybe the old biddy herself suddenly thought better of it and decided in her head that you'd tricked her."

Lindsey started to cry.

"Or," Niall went on ignoring her, "for some reason BAB want to get rid of you and they've persuaded someone to make a complaint."

"That's ridiculous," Lindsey sniffed.

"Maybe," Niall said patiently. "So let's consider the first option. Don't cry, there's no point."

"You'd cry if you'd just lost your job."

"I did. Three days ago."

"God, why didn't you say something?"

"It wasn't important. And it wasn't like this. And you haven't lost your job yet. Have BAB been pleased with your work?"

"I thought they had."

"Juliette Warwick told me you were lovely," Niall said. "So if they all rate you, they're going to defend you. They're going to back you and not the person making the complaint."

"I don't know," Lindsey said.

"Can you think of anyone, ANYONE you've been to see in the last month who maybe was a bit iffy, or sent you away with a flea in your ear, or seemed like they didn't want to be persuaded to part with their money?"

"No," Lindsey said quickly.

"You didn't think," Niall said.

"I've been thinking all night," Lindsey countered. "There's no-one. Everybody's always absolutely lovely. And I always do it by the book."

"OK," Niall conceded. "I believe you. Anybody say 'I'll need to talk to my son or daughter about it?'"

"Maybe. I can't remember every session word for word."

"You should record the conversations."

"We're not allowed."

"But that'd give you evidence. They shouldn't let you go on your own."

"They didn't at first," Lindsey said. "We used to go in pairs. But then the man I worked with left and they didn't replace him."

"Why did he leave?" Niall asked.

"He retired. I think he was ill, but he never said."

"OK," Niall said. "Lindsey, I want to tell you my theory and I don't want you to scoff and switch off until you've heard it all."

"Go on then," she said.

He told her about his interest in the transplant case, about his visit to Susannah Leman, his curiosity about the funding, about the emails Simon had found.

"Don't be offended, but when I came to talk to you it was because I wanted to find out more about the funding for the transplant surgery. I asked you about it and you talked quite openly about what good publicity it was. Who could've overheard that conversation?"

Lindsey was quiet. He wondered which bit of what he'd said had upset her the most and how she was going to lash out.

"I don't really understand," she said finally.

"OK," Niall said, trying to be patient. "What if it got out that BAB's main interest in this transplant research was because it was good publicity? Because it actually raised more money than they gave to the research? How would that look? What if the girl who's had the operation was only chosen because she had a rich Daddy who paid BAB for the privilege? What if they've diverted funds away from some of the important services they provide just to fatten up the goose that lays the golden egg?"

"I'm being stupid, I know, but –"

"Let's say, for sake of argument, that something that might look dodgy is going on. They find out that I was at Moorfields talking to the girl. The next day I show up in Knightsbridge and talk to you. We're overheard talking about the transplant. They think I'm in danger of getting somewhere and they decide to close down my channel of communication: i.e. you. It makes sense."

"I think you've been watching too much television."

He could tell that Lindsey didn't buy his story any more than Simon did, and yet the more he thought about it, the more certain he became that he was on to something. 'Journalist's nose', he called it. BAB was a sleeping dragon. He was a fly on its face. He had irritated it and it had soporifically attempted to swat him away. But flies could be infuriatingly persistent.

FIVE

Susannah woke and lay deliberately still, listening to the sounds of the hospital outside the ICU. They were distant, dreamy, which meant that a door must be closed. Was her mother in the room with her, or just outside, or had she sneaked off for breakfast, or one of the cigarettes Susannah wished that she wouldn't smoke? This morning, if the operation had worked, she was going to see. Maybe not much at first, but she believed in Mr. Daghash, his gentle certainty, and she believed, even though a part of her mind told her that she shouldn't, that she was eventually going to see properly. The concept was almost too much to take in. She would see this room, see the family she had loved by touch and sound alone, and that might be weird. She would see herself. She had no idea what she looked like. Whenever she had asked the question the answer had been a patronising, meaningless 'You're beautiful,' which told her nothing. And yet there had been times, particularly during her adolescence, when she had been obsessed by her appearance, had wanted to lock herself in her room because she couldn't be sure of how she looked. Perhaps she should get used to herself in photographs before she faced the mirror. Photographs, mirror – the epic vastness of the world that was opening up before

EYES OF THE BLIND

her was just … mind-blowing. Sight, that so many millions took for granted and probably barely appreciated, that had been denied her since birth, was now waiting for her. Just waiting for her to open her eyes.

She heard Amelia's voice outside, and her mother's, and then the door opened and her family came in with a nurse.

"Hi," she tried to say, but only a strange croak emerged from her parched throat. She wondered if she could have a drink. She had an excruciating pain in the front of her head and a feeling she described to herself as general fuzziness. Conversation was the last thing she wanted, but they were here for her. She had to try.

"What a load of drips and tubes!" Amelia said. "That's impressive, Susie."

She smiled weakly. The nurse – at least she presumed it was the nurse – pushed some contraption into her hand.

"If the pain gets too much," she said, "just push this. It increases the pain relief. But try to deal with it if you can."

Susannah tried to deal with it, but her head really hurt.

"My head hurts," she croaked. "And I'm thirsty."

A straw was pushed between her lips. Or it might have been a tube.

"Water," the nurse said brusquely. At least, it felt brusque in her fragile state.

"Matthew Long's outside. The journalist," Amelia said. "He's quite fit, Susie." Susannah smiled again. "He's going to come in for a bit once you've seen all of us."

"I might not see anything today," Susannah said.

"Of course you will," Amelia said.

A doctor came in and introduced himself to the family. Doctor Clarke. His voice was liquorice toffee. He said he was the consultant in charge of the after-care medication and support.

"Mr. Daghash's the genius who put it all together," he said. "I'm the one now who has to make sure it works and goes on working."

Like some kind of remote control toy, Susannah thought. He had obviously met her father before and the two of them fell into conversation in subdued tones, as if loud noises might damage her. She realised they were waiting for Mr. Daghash, and with every minute that passed the tension increased. Her mother kept blowing her nose, which meant she must be crying already. Amelia reminded her of times when they were children and Susannah had pestered her elder sister to describe colours to her.

"I wonder if you'll recognise them from my descriptions," she said. It was funny what had been important as a child. Because she heard other children say 'What's your favourite colour?' she had needed to have an answer and settled on green, though she didn't know why. Maybe the word had a gentleness, a freshness about it. She hadn't thought about colours for years. Between them her mother and Amelia had guided her clothes shopping so that everything toned – it didn't really matter what she wore. Now colours were going to launch themselves at her, cry out for recognition and understanding. Green grass, blue sky, white clouds.

"Susie!" Mr. Daghash arrived. "Good morning. It's a beautiful morning. You'll need sunglasses if you go outside."

"Am I going out today?" Susannah asked.

"Not home today," Mr. Daghash said, "but maybe this evening a little walkabout in the hospital. We don't want to risk any infections. You're very vulnerable just now. The anti-rejection medication reduces your body's ability to fight infections. And the London air isn't good for eyes."

She felt hands on her head.

"Now, Susie," Mr. Daghash went on, "I'm starting to take the bandages off. I don't want you to try to open your eyes until I tell you."

I don't know how to open my eyes, Susannah thought. She felt the bandages removed, and she sensed light flooding into her head. It was weird. She thought it might be like dying, the light at the end of the tunnel.

"Nurse," Mr. Daghash said. Then she felt something cool and moist rubbing around where the bandage had been. "There's a little encrustation," Mr. Daghash went on. "We're just wiping it away. Now..." She felt his fingers laid very gently, one on each eyelid, and as she did she became aware that there was something in each eye-socket which had not been there before. Something that was aware of the pressure from Mr. Daghash's touch. "I'm touching your eyelids, Susie," he said. "If you can, I'd like you to open them now, and then tell me exactly what you can see."

Susannah raised what she thought were her eyelids, but nothing happened.

"That was the skin above your eyes. You're raising your eyebrows at us," Mr. Daghash said. He touched the eyelids again and something clicked inside Susannah's brain. She opened them.

She heard a gasp and a sob from her mother, and various reactions of astonishment and appreciation.

"Well done. What do you see?" Mr. Daghash asked earnestly.

"Light. Shapes. Dark bits. I don't really know." Susannah started to cry.

"OK," Mr. Daghash said patiently, kindly. "It's a shock to your system. Now open your eyes again." Susannah hadn't realised she had closed them. "Can you see a dark shape straight in front of you?"

Susannah stared in front of her. "Two. I can see two shapes."

"Right. That shape is my face. I'm right in front of you. I want you to try to concentrate on my face. Concentrate on that shape."

"Which one?" Susannah asked.

"Either. They're both me."

"Have you got two heads?"

"No." Mr. Daghash laughed. "You have two eyes."

"So will I see everything twice?"

"No. You are experiencing what is called double vision. When you are more in control of the muscles in your eyes you will be able to pull them together and make one three-dimensional image. We hope."

Susannah concentrated hard on the shape to the exclusion of all else and gradually she became aware that there were details on it that she hadn't seen at first.

"Have you got dark hair?" she asked. Her mother sobbed again.

"I have," Mr. Daghash said gently. "It's very dark brown. Some people would say it was black. Ladies and gentlemen", he went on to the room at large, "the eyes are talking to the brain. The optic nerve is working. One of mankind's giant leaps has been made." He kept still, letting her focus on his face. She tried to turn the two images into one, she felt sure that if she could do that the whole room would make sense, but the shapes came and went. She closed her eyes again.

"It's tiring, isn't it?" Mr. Daghash said.

"I just feel I need to practise opening and closing," Susannah said.

"Fine," Mr. Daghash said. "Whatever you feel." She opened them again, and this time she thought she saw features on Mr. Daghash's face. But it could have been her imagination.

Once more, Hugo and Niall climbed the steps to the front door of the British Association for the Blind. He had rung, said he was researching a PhD in Attitudes towards Disability in Disability Charities and asked for an appointment with someone to go through a questionnaire with him. He had called himself Jamie Williams, the name of a boy he had detested at school, just in case, as Niall Burnet, his card was already marked. Lindsey thought he was being stupid, Simon asked him perfectly reasonably what exactly he thought he was going to find out. All he could say was that he needed as much inside information on BAB as he could get, and the only way to get inside information was to get inside. He had wanted to say that the PhD was about funding, but the others had convinced him that that might have put whoever was delegated to see him on their guard. He just had to hope that he didn't bump into Juliette Warwick when he walked through the door. Lindsey had said if he got found out it would only make things worse for her than they already were. Niall had replied, unhelpfully, that that was impossible.

And now he was inside, visible, vulnerable. Hugo seemed uncertain as to where to go but Niall kept urging him forward. Finally, he was relieved to hear a man's voice asking him his business.

"Hello, yes. My name's Jamie Williams. I rang and made an appointment to speak to somebody about my PhD. Somebody in public relations, I think they said."

"Just a moment, Jamie," the man said. Niall knew the blind world was a small world. Lindsey Spencer had a job at BAB. How many other people that he had known at school might be inches from him now? Sometimes he wished he didn't have a habit of rushing into things – they always seemed simple, sensible and virtually inevitable at the planning stage, luring him into following them through without fully considering the risks or the likely outcomes.

"You've got an appointment on the third floor," the man said, returning.

"Is that good or bad?" Niall asked. The man laughed by way of answer, and led him towards the lift. He hoped the third floor was a long way from HR, but he was a little disconcerted as to how far he would be from the main entrance and escape. The lift doors seemed to take an age to close (probably deliberately, to let the poor blind people blunder in and get their bearings) and then the contraption laboured asthmatically on its upward journey before announcing in a welcoming female voice, "Third floor. The doors are now open." It was the first time in his life that Niall had felt patronised by a lift.

It was quiet on the third floor, and their nameless guide led Hugo and Niall down a corridor into what felt like the depths of the building. If Niall hadn't felt the lift rising, he could have believed they were taking him to a dungeon.

"Here we are," the man said pleasantly, opening a door, "there'll be someone to see you in just a moment." He left without explaining the layout of the room at all.

Which might just have been an oversight, but seemed deliberately inconsiderate. Niall explored, found a desk, a chair, a water dispenser, more chairs. He sat on one, and Hugo came and sat by his side. It was very quiet. What was he going to ask? What was he going to find out? Some general questions about disability, political correctness, positive discrimination; then maybe some teasers about money raised on people's goodwill, on nudging their consciences and making them feel guilty for having five functional senses; then bring it round to the transplant. Attitudes towards such a high-profile, expensive operation. Did they think supporting the scientific battle against disability (of any kind) was the same as supporting the disabled? To raise people's hopes of a future without blindness was not the same as helping them to cope in the world as blind people, convincing them that they had worth even without sight. Surely it sent a message that blindness was such a handicap that the best thing to do was to get a new pair of functioning eyes.

And how would the answers get him any nearer finding out if there was skulduggery going on? OK, they probably wouldn't. He was new to this. But he might get lucky, he might catch someone unawares and realise from something in their tone that they were covering something up.

What? What did he really think was going on? It wasn't a crime to support medical research, even if your motives were essentially selfish. He felt that the eye transplant operation had been stage managed. Which came first, the patient or the eyes? How was she chosen? Why a twenty-two-year-old girl and not a forty-year-old man? Or a fifteen-year-old boy? What about the family who had donated the eyes? Had they known what they were doing? But all the same, would anybody in the world see any of this as wrong? It had to be somebody, why not Susannah Leman? He would just sound jealous and bitter if he wrote about that. He was looking for a story that maybe, if he was going to be completely honest with himself, just wasn't there. He should ditch blindness, leave BAB to its own arcane ways, go back to sport. Maybe there was a Doping in World Tiddlywinks scandal just waiting to break. He could bring it to light.

But Lindsey had been suspended. Suspended, he was absolutely convinced, for talking to him. And that was bizarre.

He heard footsteps in the corridor. He was Jamie Williams. He was researching a PhD. Hugo stood up. The door opened.

"Hello," he said.

A pause.

"Niall Burnet. How extraordinary. I was expecting Jamie Williams."

☉

Susannah lay in bed after one of the most difficult mornings of her life. She was alone, and she was in tears. Because everybody had expected so much, looked to her for so much, and maybe she had too, and their disappointment at her failure to deliver had rolled over her like a tsunami. She had seen, but not clearly, and nobody seemed to understand why she found it easier to do things with her eyes shut, obey the instincts of a lifetime. Her mother's euphoria had turned to painful despair, her father had been brisk and frustrated; Amelia silently disappointed. Only Mr. Daghash and Dr. Clarke seemed to have any hope left that her sight would improve. They said what was going on would be like an earthquake inside her head, that it would be stressful for her brain and it would take time for the dust to settle. It would take time for her to learn the habits of looking and seeing and living in a sighted world. She thought how much better it would have been if they had given the eyes to someone like Niall, someone who knew how to see.

Then Matthew the journalist had come in, hungry for a story of triumph and new worlds to go with a picture of her smiling sighted face. His photographer had stood in front of her and there had been a blinding flash which made her wince. Mr. Daghash had got cross, saying that he had specifically stipulated no flash photography. Everybody had gone away miserable and deflated, sent away by Mr. Daghash so that she could rest.

For months, this day had been the focus of her family's attention, the focus of her own fears and anxieties. Now it had come. The operation was over. How successfully, it was too early to say, but she could certainly see, and that meant her life would change. She had to plan a future, think about maybe getting a job. What, though? She thought perhaps she'd like to work with children. Disabled children, because she knew what it was like. So how did you go about it? She would have to get qualifications, prove herself. She'd never found anything like that easy, and she didn't think being able to see was going to make much of a difference. Presumably she'd stop getting her disability allowance because she wouldn't be disabled any more. What would she live on? Her parents would expect her to go out into the world as Amelia had done. She couldn't see what she had to look forward to. She picked her mobile phone off the bedside cabinet. With her heart pumping she rang Niall Burnet. He didn't answer, and she was too scared to leave a message.

❦

"I don't understand the need for deception."

Niall was thinking furiously. Vivien Loosemore. The former principal of his old school. They had cordially detested each other for the best part of seven years, and now she was at BAB. The Blind World was even smaller than he thought.

"You left school then," he said.

"They asked me to head up the Education Division," she said. "That's why I agreed to take time out to see Jamie. As a research degree is an educational matter."

"And you always thought the sun shone out of Jamie's arse," Niall said.

"So, Niall, what's going on? What is it you want?"

"I want to know why Lindsey's been suspended," he said. It

came to him in a flash as the only possible camouflage.

"And why not come openly, as yourself?"

"I don't know. Call it a whim."

He remembered the ill-disguised hostility of their battles when he was a sixth-former using every ounce of his intelligence to challenge the system, and she was – as they had all thought – an inept principal trying to assert her authority.

"I can't talk to you about Lindsey," she said in her irritatingly superior way.

"You know about it then," he said.

"Yes," Vivien Loosemore conceded, "and it shocks and saddens me."

"Except that you know it's impossible," Niall said.

"I know that a complaint has been made."

"So why not defend her? You know what she's like."

"If Lindsey wants to call me as a character witness, I shall be happy to speak of what I knew of her when she was at school," Loosemore said.

"You're thinking there's going to be a disciplinary then?" Niall said.

"Lindsey could spare herself any unpleasantness if she chose to resign. HR would give her an excellent reference, I'm sure."

"So one minute they want to take her to a disciplinary, and the next they'll give her a glowing reference. Come on, Vivien."

He sensed her stiffen at the use of her Christian name, enjoyed the moment. They weren't principal and student any more.

"I didn't realise you were still so close to Lindsey," she said.

"She rang me sobbing in the middle of the night."

"After you'd been to see her the day before."

"How did you know about that?"

Silence. Vivien had blundered. He knew it, she knew it. He also knew from experience that once she was flustered she could dig a deeper and deeper pit for herself.

"Juliette Warwick mentioned that she'd shown you up."

"I bet you enjoyed her description of me."

"She described a man I recognised immediately."

"And then Lindsey was suspended," Niall said.

"Lindsey was suspended because of a very serious complaint," Loosemore said.

"And no-one will even tell her what it is."

"That's standard procedure."

"It's ridiculous, and the whole thing is a fraud. As you well know," Niall said.

"Niall, I strongly recommend you to leave this alone," Vivien said.

"You know that saying that will make me do just the opposite."

"You won't help Lindsey. You can't help Lindsey."

"Tell me what she's been accused of."

"I can't."

"Intimidating one of her 'clients'."

"She has a very sensitive job."

"And she was doing it to everyone's satisfaction."

"Niall!"

"What?" He heard her sigh. "Who are you going to report this conversation back to?" he asked.

"I shall say nothing about it."

"Lindsey's going to fight all the way," Niall said. "I'm going to defend her."

"That is both sad and foolish," Vivien said. "She could have done with some better advice around her at this time."

"And all because I happened to ask her about the eye transplant."

"What?" Vivien sounded genuinely astonished.

"Susannah Leman's new eyes. She must be looking out of them now."

"What on Earth has that got to do with anything?"

"Big business at BAB."

"You've lost me completely, Niall. As always, you appear to inhabit a totally different world to the rest of us."

"I wonder," Niall said.

Daniel Sullivan lay in a deep bath, watching his nipple hair rise and fall like seaweed at the mercy of the tide. The Fourth Mrs. Sullivan was slaving over a hot stove preparing dinner; where women, in Daniel's opinion, really wanted to be. He didn't consider himself a misogynist – anything but. Women had been placed on Earth according to the book of Genesis to be man's helpmeet and companion, to meet his needs. Deep down, it was what they wanted. Daniel's needs were crystal clear: domesticity and sex. During his naive twenties, he had believed he could find both in one woman. Now he didn't even try. When he got out of the bath he would tell her that he was going out. It was a Number Seventeen night.

He soaped his penis and thought about Susannah Leman. He wondered how easy it would be to seduce her. She was presumably totally inexperienced, sexually. He had found over the years that being a significant figure in a major charity intrigued and attracted the vast majority of women. A bit of judicious name-dropping usually did the rest. Encounters with the Prince of Wales ('HRH' in Daniel's parlance) and both of his sons went down well, and the

EYES OF THE BLIND

beauty of it was that he really did meet them, and he was able to turn those meetings into sexual capital.

The young Miss Leman would certainly be a project, and he liked to have a project on the go. He would have to make it look as though his interest in the outcome of the operation was what kept bringing him to her bedside. Then he could offer her a guided tour of BAB, and maybe follow it with a tour of London sights. Bowl her over by making time for her in his exceptionally busy schedule. Then gently introduce her to the mysteries of the flesh. He would open her book of sex and write a first chapter that would be a hard act to follow.

He smiled at the thought and wondered what life would consist of without these diversions. If he spent his working days thinking of nothing but work and his evenings passively soaking up television and good dinners with the Fourth Mrs. Sullivan. He remembered a Dylan Thomas poem from his distant schooldays – "Rage, rage against the dying of the light": he was raging already and his light was a long way from dying.

◉

In the Intensive Care Unit at Moorfields Eye Hospital, the only place on Earth she had ever seen, Susannah lay in bed talking to Mr. Daghash and Dr. Clarke. Talking to them was better than talking to her family. Not so emotional. They were talking about her eyesight, asking her what she saw and how it felt. Nothing she said seemed to surprise them. She described shapes and light and shade and – to their great delight – colour. Colour seemed to be a big thing to them. Her head wasn't hurting as much as it had done, but the fuzziness – which Mr. Daghash explained was caused by the pain-killing medication – was the same. She was trying to get used to living with it.

"Put your hand up in front of your face," Mr. Daghash said. "Your right hand – not the one with the tubes." She did. "Now open your eyes and take a look."

She opened them. She found that they closed of their own accord. She was going to have to get into the habit of keeping them open. Before her was a shape, a pale shape.

"What do you see?" Dr. Clarke asked.

"I can see that something's there in front of my face," Susannah said.

"That's great," Mr. Daghash said. "Now, will yourself to see it. Imagine that you're a baby and you're trying really hard to see the detail on it."

She tried, and suddenly the fog cleared and there was her hand – five pale, bony fingers and a hand.

"I see it!" she said excitedly. "I see it!"

"Bravo!" said Dr. Clarke.

She turned to look at the two men but as she did so it was as if a switch had been thrown and the fog returned.

"Oh," she said, disappointed.

"Little steps," Mr. Daghash said. "One little step at a time. You focused. You managed to focus your new eyes and the brain decoded the messages. This is fantastic Susie. Truly fantastic."

She turned back to her hand. Yes, there it was again. And there were the nails her mother had stopped her from biting when she was thirteen.

"If you never see any more than just in front of your face you could get a job at a fair reading palms," Dr. Clarke said.

"I'd have to learn how," Susannah said.

"He's joking Susie," Mr. Daghash said. "We both know you're going to see a lot more than that. When we've gone just keep practising. Keep looking at things. Look at your hand close up. Practise focusing. Look around the room, try to see things a bit further away."

"Would you think it was pathetic of me if I asked for a mirror?" Susannah asked. "I really want to see what I look like."

"It's only natural," Mr. Daghash said. "Of course. We'll get a nurse to see if she can find one." She heard Dr. Clarke get up and go out.

"But I should warn you," Mr. Daghash went on, "you're not looking your absolute best. Anyone who didn't know better would think I'd been punching you in the face."

"That's OK," Susannah said. "The nurses say I look like I've gone ten rounds with Frank Bruno. Whoever he is."

"Tomorrow, Susie, we're going to move you back to your room. You're doing really well and so long as we manage the environment in the room properly it'll be better for you than being in here. You'll be able to have fruit and flowers. Things to look at."

"Yeah. Thanks." Susannah didn't really know what to say. At the moment, one room was much the same as another. And she was less available to visitors in the ICU and being alone was less stressful than being in company.

"Then I want you to meet with one of our counsellors," Mr. Daghash was saying. "Faith Hodgkiss. She's absolutely lovely and has worked here for ever. I'm hoping she's going to be a key point of contact for you when you go home and start putting your life back together. You'll be able to tell her everything."

Not if I don't want to, Susannah thought. She thought about the life she had to put back together and realised that it really amounted to nothing. In any case, that life was over now. It was a case of starting from scratch.

"Then I've arranged with your family for a kind of general council around your bed at ten o'clock. If you don't feel up to it when the time comes then that's fine. We'll go somewhere else and leave you in peace. But I want Dr. Clarke to explain to you and your parents what life is going to be like for you and them following the transplant. He needs to explain the medication, you need to decide who is responsible for it – ultimately, of course, Susie, it has to be you, if you want an independent life."

"Will I always have to take medication?" Susannah asked.

"Yes, almost certainly," Mr. Daghash replied. "You will have to maintain some anti-rejection medication, but hopefully the dosage in the end will be quite small. You certainly won't always be as vulnerable and susceptible to infection as you are now."

Susannah smiled. She didn't know why.

"Now is there anybody else," Mr. Daghash went on, "apart from your family, that you would like to have at that meeting tomorrow? Any special friend that you'd like to hear about your medication and how life's going to be for you?"

Susannah pretended to think. The truth was, she didn't really have any friends. Not ones who would help her lead a full and independent life by taking responsibility for her own medication. And then it came to her, as a way of seeing him again. He should be interested – he was supposedly writing something about her case.

"Yes," she said. "I've got a friend called Niall. Niall Burnet. I'd really like him to be there."

"That's fine," said Mr. Daghash, not showing the surprise that he felt. Susannah Leman was a darker horse than he had thought. "The meeting will be at ten o'clock. You can call him and tell him."

"Actually do you think you could call him?" Susannah asked. "I've got the number in my phone. You could explain what it's all about much better than I could."

Surely Niall wouldn't refuse a call from the surgeon who had performed her operation?

The door opened. She assumed it was Dr. Clarke returning with the mirror and turned expectantly in his direction.

"Jamal," a very different voice said.

"Duncan," Mr. Daghash replied. "Susie, this is Mr. Clark. One of the senior consultants here. Not to be confused with our Dr. Clarke. Duncan Clark, Susannah Leman."

"How do you do, Miss Leman?" Duncan Clark said. His voice was quite a sharp fruit – redcurrants or the wrong sort of strawberries. His greeting felt as if he had added a spoon of sugar to mask the sharpness. "Is Mr. Daghash busily describing what you can see to you?"

Susannah looked puzzled.

"Mr. Clark doesn't believe what we have done is possible, Susie," Mr. Daghash said. "He has written a very learned article about it. But luckily the field of medical science is a broad church, or you might not be here today, seeing even as much as you are seeing."

"And what have we seen?" Mr. Clark asked.

"My hand," Susannah tried to say, but her voice gave up on her.

"I wonder," Mr. Clark said.

"One day soon, Duncan," Mr. Daghash said, "you will have to accept the truth of what we have accomplished."

"I've never had a problem with truth, Jamal," Mr. Clark said. "Miss Leman, I wish you joy of your contract with a tabloid newspaper, and the life of a celebrity upon which you are undoubtedly now embarked. Good evening." And with that he was gone. Susannah found she was shaking. Mr. Daghash took her hand.

"I'm sorry about that, Susie," he said. "I don't know why he came in. Duncan Clark has been against us from the start. He didn't believe the operation was possible, he thinks it's a scam and a publicity stunt, and he didn't want Moorfields to have any part in it. He was voted down by the trustees and has been rude to me ever since. But I didn't think he'd stoop so far as to confront you. I'm so sorry."

"It's OK," she said. "I suppose I need to get used to people being negative."

At that moment Dr. Clarke returned with a nurse.

"It's only one out of my handbag, love," the nurse said. "But you're more than welcome."

She put a small circular object into Susannah's hand.

"Thanks," Susannah said.

"And on that, Susie," Mr. Daghash said, "we will leave you. We will leave you alone with your face. But remember – it will get better."

"I will," Susannah said.

"And I'll call your friend."

"Yes. Thanks."

"Is he in London?"

"I think so. Yes, I'm sure he is."

Still further puzzled, Jamal Daghash bid Susannah goodnight. Dr. Clarke did the same, and the two of them withdrew.

'Alone with her face'. Susannah opened her eyes and focused on the disc in her hand. Sure enough, there it was. Close up, things were getting easier. It had a pattern on one side that might have been flowers, but on the other she saw the glass surface. She held it up to her face and studied her reflection.

This was the face she had felt who knows how many times, the cheeks, the lips, the nose. She had wondered so much about noses, and this was hers. But in amongst the purple bruising (they told her it was purple) were two things that were not hers. Two eyes that belonged to somebody else. Except now they were hers. For the rest of this life they were hers, and a part of who she now was. This wasn't Susannah Leman's face – Susannah was a blind girl she had known and loved but that girl was gone. This was a new girl who needed a new name. Even as she thought it she wondered whether anyone would understand. She had been born Susannah Miranda Leman. Susannah was gone. She would be Miranda now. This was Miranda's face. These were Miranda's eyes. Those eyebrows were Miranda's eyebrows and Miranda was going to ask someone to pluck them for her in the morning. She remembered Amelia plucking her eyebrows once: it had hurt and she hadn't enjoyed it but Amelia had said that stylish girls and women all plucked their eyebrows. Looking at the dark lines above her eyes, Miranda resolved that she would be stylish, even if it cost some pain. It would be nothing to the pain she had felt earlier in her head.

She tilted the mirror so she could see more of her hair. 'Light brown' people had always described it. So that was light brown. It was a difficult colour to describe. Actually the eyes – no, her eyes – were similar. Maybe a little darker. She looked at the skin on her face. White. People talked about being white but if the sheets on her bed were white then skin really wasn't white at all. The world of colour was a world of confusion. Blindness had been so simple.

And suddenly she cried. Cried for blind Susannah who was lost for ever. She saw wet tears run down her face. They had no colour at all.

Niall was very annoyed with himself. He had had Vivien Loosemore on the ropes and then he had let her get away from him. Losing his touch. Was he too direct? Or pressing the wrong buttons? She definitely knew something. And he had failed to get it out of her. Hardly premier league journalism.

"I'm just so pissed off," he snarled into a beer at Simon's nearest pub.

"Why?" Simon asked obligingly.

"Because I had her. She was starting to go. The legs had gone. Two good punches would have finished her."

"Did you actually fight her then?" Simon asked.

"Sporting metaphor, you cyber-moron," Niall said. "I didn't go in for the kill when I knew she was down."

"Would that be a hunting metaphor?" Simon asked. Niall threw a pork scratching in his direction.

"I'm missing something," he said.

"Because you don't know what it is," Simon suggested.

"Thanks, Einstein."

"No," Simon went on defensively. "What I mean is, I think that maybe – don't ask me why I think it but maybe – you're right that something's not right at BAB, and Lindsey's suspension is connected with it. The problem is, you really don't have a clue what it is."

"Thanks."

"I'm saying you're right, you fucking arsehole."

"It's not helping."

"When we were at school," Simon enlarged after downing the last third of his pint, "you knew what was going on. Between us in the Sixth Form we knew everything. So when Vivien Loosemore made one of her little slips you could pounce on it and make things worse for her. This time she knows everything and we're in the dark."

"She won't know everything," Niall said. "Not unless whoever's running this show has no idea what a headless pelican she is."

"Think about the leads we have got while I get another round in," Simon said. He got to his feet and turned towards the bar. The regulars were used to him and helping hands ferried him forward.

Niall reviewed his leads for all of ten seconds before deciding he hadn't got any and relapsing back into self-pity. When Simon returned it was to find him telling Hugo that he should 'get a new retard to pull around'.

"Niall get a grip," Simon said. "The fact that Loosemore nearly fucked up in front of you shows that she had something to fuck up about. It's the first thing that's convinced me that there's anything in this so-called story of yours. That's progress."

"Convincing you wasn't really the main criteria for success," Niall said.

"Thanks. But I'm on board with it now. We've got Number Seventeen to get to the bottom of, Lindsey's disciplinary, and the girl."

"What girl?"

"The eye girl, you fuckwit," Simon spluttered. "That's where all this began."

"There's no story there," Niall said.

"Because you didn't like her."

"Because she just –" Niall searched for words that wouldn't come.

"She can see now," Simon said. "Bye bye, Blind World."

Niall was silent.

"Now I get it," Simon said. "You're bitter. You're jealous of her. You wish it was you and that's why you don't want to follow it through."

"Crap," Niall said.

They drank.

"All right it isn't crap," Niall relented finally. "I thought it was crap but it isn't. I do want my sight back. What the fuck can a blind freelance journalist ever fucking accomplish? You know, we kid ourselves that it's all going to be OK and we're going to have a great life and people think we're fantastic for being so up-beat and making a go of things, but the truth is we're fucked from the start. The so-called Blind World is just something we've invented to try and make out we've got something special that's just ours and nobody else can have. But it's shite. It's total fucking garbage. The real world, the only world, is the sighted world, and we can't fucking compete."

Simon didn't respond.

"Unless you're a fucking computer nerd of course," Niall added.

"That's right," Simon said. "I'm on the cutting edge. That's why I've got such a high-flying job. Not."

They sat for a while, drinking in companionable silence.

"Did you ever have sight?" Niall asked eventually.

"No," Simon said.

"I think that's the difference."

"It's a difference," Simon acknowledged. "Or you might say you were the lucky one because you had it for a while. You've got real pictures for your dreams."

"No, to have it and to lose it. That's the worst."

"Of course, mate." Niall threw a beer mat. "Don't get me chucked out. This is the only decent pub round here."

"That would just about top off my trip to London," Niall said. "I've got your flatmates pissed off, I've lost Lindsey her job, and now I'm going to get you barred from your local."

"You don't care about Lindsey anyway."

"No but she didn't deserve this. The best thing I can do is piss off back to Shropshire. Collect my DLA and write some fucking awful novel. Publish it on the internet."

"I'd read it," Simon said.

"I'm serious."

"I know."

There was a pause. Niall's phone rang.

"This is a mobile free pub," Simon said.

"Shit," Niall said, and answered it quickly. "Hello?"

"Hello? Is that Niall Burnet?"

"Yeah, speaking."

"My name is Jamal Daghash. I'm a surgeon. I'm the surgeon who carried out Susannah Leman's eye transplant."

"OK."

"Is this a convenient time? Do you have a moment?"

"Yes. Yes. Fine."

"Susannah has asked me to call you. You're a friend, I understand. There's a meeting at Moorfields tomorrow at which all her after-care medication is going to be explained. She has asked if you could attend the meeting."

"I – I – me?" Niall struggled for words. "The operation was successful then?"

"It seems so, thus far," Daghash said. "Susie hasn't called you?"

"I've been busy," Niall lied, still trying to get his head round the conversation. "Away from my phone. And she wants me to be there?"

"It seems very important to her," Daghash said. "I don't have to tell you she's in a very fragile emotional state. Any support that any of us can give at this time is worth its weight in gold to her. I appreciate it's short notice – "

"No, no. I'll be there," Niall interrupted. "What time?"

"Ten o'clock. At Moorfields Eye Hospital. City Road. Someone will direct you when you arrive."

"Thanks. Thanks."

"No, thank you. I know she'll be pleased."

"OK."

"Goodbye, Mr. Burnet."

"Goodbye."

Niall hung up and sat in silence, staring sightlessly straight ahead.

"Are you going to enlighten me?" Simon asked.

"I need another beer first," Niall said.

❧

The taxi pulled up outside 17 Cardew Crescent. Rebecca Blackford blamed the government. Not for the taxi but for the fact that she was in it. The fact that all three of them were in it. Her housemate Penny from Cardiff who had started it all, Penny's fellow nursing degree student Beth, and her. Two years into her BA (Ed.). A respectable primary school teacher in the making. But how were you supposed to exist as a student in London? When you needed a loan for a night out, never mind tuition, rent and just – well – life.

Typical of Penny to have taken the plunge. She was game for everything; had tried more things in twenty-one years than most people would get through in a lifetime. Rebecca couldn't decide whether she had no self-respect, or so much that nothing could touch her. Whichever it was, she loved her for it.

She hadn't known at first, because Penny had been using B&Bs and cheap hotels, but eventually the economic imperative drove her to confess, and start bringing the men to her room. They had a heart-to-heart over a bottle of wine in the kitchen.

"Penny I don't think I believe you," she said.

"Then where do you think I got these from?" Her Welsh brown eyes twinkled as she pulled four fifty pound notes out of her purse.

Instinctive moral outrage rained down on her poor housemate for about twenty minutes.

"Worse than my mother," Penny said. "Look, Becky – " Nobody in the world called her Becky apart from Penny. She was Rebecca or Reb. "It's not what I'd've wished for myself when I was playing with My Little Pony Dream Castle but it is only sex. And it's better than trying to live the rest of your life with one hand tied behind your back paying off student loans for ever. I shall stop it when I get a proper job."

"If you haven't caught AIDS or got killed by some pimp because you're on his territory," Rebecca had said.

But Penny hadn't caught AIDS, and she hadn't got killed or beaten up; instead she had got into the very expensive car one day of a gross man who thought the sun shone so brightly out of his own arse that it could blind you without proper protection. Penny had had her in hysterics with her description of him. And he had taken a Pretty-Woman-ish shine to her (but in a totally repulsive and unromantic way) and offered her stupid sums of money to work exclusively servicing him 'and some of my intimate friends and business colleagues'. 'Think of yourself as my paid courtesan or geisha' he had apparently said.

"And that's a top profession in Japan," Penny said proudly.

"Oh but Penny he's revolting," Rebecca had said. She had seen him arrive with her when she had dared to peer out of the top floor window. If she wasn't actually out she had to pretend to be during one of Penny's 'client visits',

" – because if you're not careful they'll be after a threesome and will wonder why you're not up for it."

It suited Daniel (his name was Daniel) that Penny was a student – a cut above the average prostitute – 'clean, respectable and intelligent' were his exact words, and Penny was more than pleased to give up random clients.

"It's a safe arrangement that suits everybody," she said, and Rebecca had to admit to herself in darker moments that she was more than a little envious of the money Penny was earning. It made her pittance from waitressing look particularly feeble.

Then Daniel had asked Penny to recruit a couple of friends – 'same terms, no questions asked, and a bonus for you each time they come'.

"I hope he didn't actually mean 'come'," Penny said, "because I'd never get the bonus then."

Daniel wanted to develop 'Roman-style soirees' in which 'high quality women eat with and give significant attention to some of my closest friends.' Penny seemed to take great delight in quoting his exact words when she regaled Rebecca with each new development.

And of course she had asked her.

"Go on Becky. It'll be fun. Think of the money. Then we can come home and tell each other what a bloody awful night we've had and make each other laugh."

She had been tempted. But her upbringing saved her. Penny was disappointed but found some other volunteers who didn't share her scruples.

Then Rebecca's brother died in a car accident. Her little brother whom she had loved and nurtured and played with all through their shared childhood. And nothing felt the same. He had been a passenger in his best friend's car. Somehow he was still holding his dead girlfriend's hand when they found him (or so somebody had said). He survived the crash but died in hospital. Her parents signed away his organs as if they were stale buns on offer from a supermarket bakery. And she had to pick up her life and make sense of it.

People expected her to take time out, to ditch her course and go home. For what? If he'd been paralysed there'd've been something to go home for: to be with him and make him laugh. But he was dead. Gone. That book was finished. There was no more Joe. No sequel. No remake. Nothing. She actually didn't want to be there because there were too many good memories and she wasn't ready for them. Wasn't ready to consign him to the past and certainly wasn't ready to cope with her parents' grief. Which sounded heartless but was true.

So instead of going home to help with the funeral arrangements she was going to have sex for money with rich men she didn't know. Was it any worse than trying to lure a millionaire husband? Because, to paraphrase her favourite of all heroines Scarlett O'Hara, nothing was ever going to hurt her again.

The three girls stepped out of the taxi and walked up the path to the front door. 17 Cardew Crescent was an imposing London house, still intact where others nearby had been carved up into flats. They rang the doorbell and it was answered by a woman with iron-grey hair and a rather distracted expression.

"Come in, come in," she said.

"This is Mary," Penny said to Rebecca. "At least it's not really, because we all have fake names here, but this is her house."

"What's my name then?" Rebecca asked.

"You'll pick one out of a box. I'm Tanya. Isn't it a laugh?"

Mary took them upstairs to what was obviously her bedroom. She told them to make themselves at home and excused herself to see to the dinner.

"So what's her role in all this?" Rebecca asked.

"I don't really know," Penny said. "It's her house and she sorts out the catering. I think she buys it all in, just has to heat some bits up. But WHY she does any of it, well, that's a total mystery.

Perhaps she gets turned on watching young girls in underwear feeding middle aged men. Perhaps she watches the sex on CCTV."

Rebecca didn't want to think about it. As the hour crept closer she felt more and more like making a bolt for freedom. She wanted to tell Penny it had all been a big mistake. But now she felt trapped.

She realised Penny and Beth were stripping down to their underwear. Trying to detach herself from her body and find a happy place to escape to, she did the same. It was very warm in the house, probably deliberately.

Then there were men's voices in the hall downstairs. The 'Roman-style soiree' had begun.

SEVEN

Lindsey called Niall as he was travelling to Moorfields for Susannah Leman's medication meeting.

"Hi Lindsey, how're you doing?"

"Juliette just called. I've got my first interview with her this afternoon. Three o'clock."

"God, they're not wasting much time."

"Can I come and see you first?"

Niall cursed.

"Lindsey I'm kind of in the middle of something," he said. "I could see you after."

"This is my life we're talking about. And there's no-one else I can talk to."

"What about the man in your life?"

"I can't," she said. "He wouldn't understand."

"So you're lying to him too?"

"No. Niall. Stop it. Stop it."

"OK, OK, I'm sorry. Look I know it's tough. But you need a solicitor with you. Or someone at least. You shouldn't go in on your own."

"They told me I can take someone but I haven't got anyone."

"Then for God's sake tell them you're not ready. You have rights, you know."

She went quiet.

"I've promised to be somewhere else this morning," Niall said. "I gave my word. I can't get out of it. But I'll call you as soon as it's finished."

Still nothing.

"I swear, Lindsey. I'll call you."

"OK."

She hung up.

"Fuck it," Niall said, to the amusement of the taxi driver. Hugo's ears twitched. It was an expression he'd come to recognise over the years.

They were almost all here now. When Susannah had woken that morning her eyesight was much clearer, and it had filled her with amazement. They hadn't allowed her to get up – they still wanted her to keep her head as still as possible – but they had wheeled her out of the ICU and into the corridor, and the sheer scale of what eyes could see overwhelmed her. She felt as though the whole concept of seeing was like a hurricane around her head. Coming back to her room had felt like coming home. She recognised the sounds and the smells but now she saw it for the first time. Susannah had left this room, but Miranda had come back to it. She wanted to laugh and cry.

Then Faith Hodgkiss had come to see her. She liked Faith's face. She thought she had grey hair. They hadn't talked about much but she felt as though they liked each other. She'd told Faith that she wanted her eyebrows plucking and Faith had laughed. She'd said the whole area was still a bit tender and she would have to cope without vanity for a bit. Which was disappointing but OK. Between them they had brushed her hair and made her feel a bit more presentable.

Everyone was looking at her, which made it hard to really look at them, because it felt strange, and she had to keep reacting, reflecting smiles back to the people who gave them to her.

Amelia had helped the nurses bring in extra chairs and was perched near the door. Her mother had a note-pad and pen in her hands. She was fidgeting with the pen to take her mind off the desire for a cigarette. Susannah used to hear her fidgeting; now Miranda saw her. Her father sat very still, saying nothing, probably hating the fact that he'd had to give up a morning's work to be there. She was trying hard not to stare, but it was difficult when you were discovering for the first time what your parents looked like.

The inevitable Matthew Long was there, which pleased Amelia far more than it pleased her. She was fed up with his questions, fed up with his hanging on. She wondered how long he was going to have to remain a part of her life, what her father had signed and condemned her to.

Which meant that, by her reckoning, they were now only waiting for the doctors and Niall. He had promised to come. He wouldn't break that promise. And he was a journalist like Matthew, so presumably he would want to be there. She was going to see what he looked like. What a blind person looked like. But even if he was ugly it wasn't going to change the way she felt about him. What did they say? 'Beauty is in the eye of the beholder'. She would make up her own idea of what was beautiful and what wasn't. She certainly saw nothing to get excited about in Matthew Long. Sight really complicates things, she thought.

A nurse came in and said that Mr. Daghash was very sorry, but he wasn't going to be able to attend the meeting. He had been called to an emergency admission. That was a disappointment, as was the totally unexpected arrival two minutes later of a large man whose treacle pudding voice she instantly recognised as the man from the British Association for the Blind. He asked everybody but her whether they minded him attending and everybody but her said no.

It was ten past ten. Dr. Clarke walked in. He seemed slightly put out by the number of people present, but he collapsed his tall frame onto the one remaining chair and opened his briefcase.

"So," he said. "Sorry I'm a little late. I think we're all here?"

"Yes," said Susannah's father.

"No, actually," Susannah said, amazed at her own confidence. "My friend Niall's coming. Mr. Daghash spoke to him last night."

"Your friend Niall?" her father asked incredulously. Her mother just looked puzzled.

"Susie!" Amelia said from across the room. "What haven't you been telling me?"

And then she heard a chocolate 'thanks – he shouldn't be any trouble' in the corridor and a blind man entered the room.

"Sorry we're late," Niall said. "Hugo has this thing about keeping people waiting. He thinks he's some kind of celebrity. He's a bit cheesed off they're not letting him in."

Susannah thought of the expression 'You could cut the atmosphere with a knife'. It certainly applied here, and for the first time she could see how it looked.

"I'm over here, Niall. Hello," she said.

"Hi. How's things?" he replied.

"Take my seat, Niall," Faith said, getting to her feet.

"Faith! Is that you?" Niall seemed genuinely pleased.

"Do you know each other?" Susannah asked.

"I've known Niall since he was eight years old," Faith said with warmth and a smile in her voice that gave it the distinct flavour of Christmas Pudding with a lot of brandy butter.

"Susannah, who is this?" her father asked irritably.

"My friend," Susannah said.

"Niall Burnet. Pleased to meet you," Niall said, ignoring the hostility.

❧

Rebecca Blackford sat in a seminar on Emotional and Behavioural Difficulties in Early Years Schoolchildren but her mind was processing the events of the previous night. She had wanted to take the day off, plead her brother's death, but Penny had bounced into her room and convinced her the best thing was to get on as if nothing had happened.

"Keep your real life going and keep it separate," she said. "That way you'll keep your self-respect."

So she had got up, showered, dressed, tried to make herself feel normal, and gone in to university. How she would've coped if she'd been in the middle of a teaching placement she had no idea, but that didn't start until after half-term.

The night had been beyond all imagining. It had a dreamlike quality about it now that made her wish that it *had* been some nightmare. But it had been real. She had the money to prove it.

The girls had gone downstairs in their underwear. 'Mary' had offered her the box of names and she had picked one – Megan. She had been Megan from that moment on.

They walked into a lounge with a fake flame gas fire. Richly furnished, large enough for three two-seater sofas and a man on each of them. The men, Rebecca thought, had not – apart from Daniel – entered into the spirit of the evening. He at least was wearing a jacket and tie. The other two were surprisingly casual. Although why should she have been surprised? She had no idea what men wore to have sex with prostitutes. But she felt that this was meant to be a kind of up-market event. There should have been a dress code for the men.

The other two men were younger than Daniel – whose name for the evening was Gordon. She thought it was funny how Penny knew his real name. Everybody else was completely anonymous. There was a dark, quite handsome man, probably forty-something, with a sharply cut beard ('Adrian') who was clearly expecting Beth, and then 'Richard', who was her partner for the evening. Richard was tall, maybe middle to late thirties, and looked as uncomfortable as she was. He was wearing jeans and a polo shirt.

She was introduced and said 'hi', and then followed a surreal 'meal' in which the men talked about cars and sport and money as if the women weren't in the room, while the three women collected plates of food for them, topped up their drinks, and sat beside them like trophies. If it hadn't been revolting it could almost have been comic.

It was as if they were too insignificant to have an opinion worth hearing on any topic. Not, Rebecca thought, like Japanese geishas at all. As for the women at Roman orgies, she had no idea. But she was absolutely certain that a Roman orgy had felt nothing like this, that a group of Italian middle-aged men would have found this strange set-up pathetic and somehow incredibly English. Surely only English men could hold a name- and bank-balance-dropping conversation as if three practically naked and, though she said it herself, attractive young women weren't really in the room. Daniel did occasionally look at Penny with undisguised lust, but it was only when she was getting him food from the two low tables in the centre of the room. He never met her eyes. Adrian barely seemed to notice Beth. He was one of those men who couldn't take part in a conversation without having to trump whatever had just been said. She was quite glad she hadn't ended up with him. Richard was no trouble: said less than the other two and didn't eat much either. Although he did drink rather a lot of red wine.

"Bordeaux – the only real wine," as Daniel fatuously said. Adrian checked the label and vintage and announced that another, more expensive claret that he had drunk recently was the wine to end all wines.

She had watched the food go down and prayed that all six of them were not expected to do it together in the same room when the meal was over. That particular prayer had been answered. Daniel had announced, "I don't know about you, but my plans for dessert belong behind closed doors" and he had taken Penny off with him, presumably to a bedroom. The others had stood up at that point and 'Mary' had escorted them back upstairs. Beth and Adrian were left at one door, and then she and Richard were taken up again, to the second floor – a long way from escape, she had thought – and let into a medium-sized double bedroom with a large half-tester bed in it.

"If there's anything you need, let me know," Mary said incongruously, and left them. At that point Rebecca had realised that she was probably supposed to take the lead. She walked up to Richard, who was standing in the middle of the room, and started to undo the belt on his jeans.

"No, I'll undress myself if that's OK," he said.

"Fine," she said.

"You can just get into the bed, that'll be fine," he said. "I don't want any fancy stuff."

"Fine." With her back to him she took off her underwear and got into the bed. She lay there, not watching him, and a minute later he climbed in beside her. She noticed he was still wearing his boxer shorts.

It dawned on her then that prostitution – as well as being disgusting – was also a skilled job. It probably required training. She didn't know now whether she should make a move or wait for him to make one. And she didn't know what that move should be. Should there be any foreplay? Should she touch him? She knew that prostitutes didn't kiss and she was glad about that, but that was the beginning and end of her knowledge.

In the end, Richard answered the question for her. He made a grab for her breasts and then clambered straight on top of her. But she knew immediately that he had no erection and nothing was going to happen. He tried desperately for a while and then rolled off her with a groan.

"Don't I turn you on?" Rebecca asked. It was the first full sentence she had actually spoken to him.

"You're beautiful. You're sexy, Megan. I'm sorry. It's me," Richard said.

"It's OK," she said.

"I'm happily married. I've got three kids at home. I don't know what the hell I'm doing here."

"You were invited, I guess," Rebecca said.

"What are you doing here?" he asked. "I'm sorry, it's none of my business. But you seem like a really nice girl."

"I need the money," Rebecca said.

"Oh God," Richard said. They lay in silence for a while.

"I don't know what I thought," Richard went on at last. "I don't know what I expected. Something rather sordid. I just –. I should be at home with my family. But I'm under a lot of pressure at work.

And Theresa's at work as well. We don't see each other. I just needed – something. I thought I might just get – relief. I'm so sorry."

She had felt she needed to do something. She didn't want there to be any quibbles about whether she had delivered value for money. She had taken hold of his penis. He had groaned and said she didn't have to do it. And she had tossed him off as quickly as she could, thinking of Bloom's Taxonomy.

There had been a further storm of apologies. He had got dressed. Mary had come to the door to say that it was time to go. She had given Rebecca her clothes, and ten minutes later the three girls had been on their way home. None of them said much. Rebecca promised herself with a secret, sacred vow that she would never do it or anything like it again.

❦

Dr. Clarke was trying to make it sound simple, but it wasn't. Acute rejection, chronic rejection, immunosuppressants, T-cells, cyclosporin, Rapamune, Imuran, Prednisolone. Her mother frantically writing it all down. Miranda's head was starting to hurt and her vision was going blurry. She wished the meeting would end. If Niall somehow escaped without speaking to her she would send Faith Hodgkiss after him. She'd said she wanted to help.

"So," Dr. Clarke said at last. "It's all about sensible precautions. If you're sensible, you'll be able to lead a full and normal life."

"Incredible," the man from BAB said.

"In terms of time-frame," Dr. Clarke went on, "we'd like to keep you here for another week, if you can bear it. It'll take a week for the acute rejection to really kick in and we'll know then what we're dealing with. But we'll get you up, we'll get you moving, and your family can start getting things ready for you at home."

"OK," Susannah said.

"One thing," Dr. Clarke added. "In a week most of your swelling and bruising will have gone down. You'll be looking a lot better for those front page pictures."

"What pictures?" Susannah asked.

"You're a big news item, Susannah," he replied. "There'll be people waiting for you the day you walk out of here."

"I thought Matthew – Mr. Long – was my journalist."

"I've got exclusivity on your personal story," Matthew explained. "But we can't stop the rest of the media altogether. People are going to want to know about you. You're on your way to becoming a celebrity."

Which was exactly what the scornful Mr. Clark had said last night. And he thought that was what she wanted. Perhaps they all did.

"My sister the celeb," Amelia said. *"Hello Magazine here we come."*

"You may need someone to act as an agent for you," the BAB man said. "I'm sure BAB would be able to help in that regard."

"Got a lot of experience of representing celebrities, have they?" Niall asked dismissively.

"We are a large charitable organisation with a long reach," the man answered, which made no sense to Susannah, but Niall didn't follow it up.

"Right," Dr. Clarke said, bringing things to a close. "I'm going to give each of you my card, with my phone number on it. Once Susannah's back home, feel free to call me day or night, wherever you are, if you think there's any problem. Don't hesitate. If anything should happen to go wrong, we'll need to move fast to make sure any damage isn't permanent."

He passed out his cards, putting one in Susannah's hand. She had closed her eyes. They were too tired to work properly and it was comforting to revert to the sensory world she knew. She hoped when Dr. Clarke left the others would take their cue as well.

She sensed a presence close to the bed and opened her eyes again. It was Niall.

"Hello," she said.

"Hi. I've come to say goodbye actually. I've got to make a move. Promised I'd meet someone as soon as we were finished here."

"Oh. I really wanted to talk to you. About stuff."

"OK." Niall was surprised. And pleased, in spite of himself. "I could come back tomorrow."

"Yes. Come tomorrow evening." She dropped her voice to a whisper. "Everyone else will have gone home then."

"OK," Niall said. "You take care. How's the seeing going?"

"It's weird. Different. I'll tell you tomorrow."

"Right. 'Bye Susannah."

"Bye."

She heard him chatting to Faith Hodgkiss who was presumably escorting him to the door. Then the man from BAB loomed over her.

"Susannah, we've never really had much of a chance to talk one to one," he said. "Daniel Sullivan. Deputy Director General of the British Association for the Blind."

"Yes," she said.

"I want you to know that we shall always think of you as one of ours, even when you have perfect sight. We've been together with you in this from the beginning. If you're looking for a career in the future I'm sure you could make one with us. I would support any application that you made."

"Thank you," she said.

"Delighted that the operation has been such a success," he said.

"It's early days."

"It's a triumph, my dear. You're a triumph." And he squeezed her hand. Held it for about five seconds before he let it go. Then he was gone.

❂

Niall trailed slowly up the corridor hoping to find a nurse who could point him in the direction of Hugo. His insistent independent streak had forced him to parry all offers of help from Faith, for all that he was totally devoted to her and had been for years, and the consequence was that he was making unnecessarily slow progress and he was lost. He heard footsteps some way behind him, stopped and half-turned.

"Mr. Burnet." It was Susannah's father.

"Hello." Niall stood still and waited for the other man to meet him.

"Roderick Leman," he said. Niall offered his hand but it wasn't taken. "I have one thing to say to you, Mr. Burnet, and one thing only. I don't know who you are, I don't know where you've come from, I've absolutely no idea how Susannah met you, but you're to stay away from her. Do you understand? Stay away from my daughter."

"Any particular reason?" Niall asked. "Since, as you say, you don't know who I am. Or is it just because I'm blind?"

"How long have you known her?"

"Oh no," Niall said. "You said you had one thing to say to me and you've said it. That wraps it up as far as conversation's concerned." And he turned to find the wall and continue walking away.

"You …" Roderick Leman began, and then stopped. "Just do as I say. I'm absolutely serious."

"Lucky you," Niall said.

"I beg your pardon?"

Niall started to walk away. He heard footsteps coming towards him.

"Nurse?" he said hopefully.

"Yes?"

"I've got a dog here somewhere, and then we'll be looking for the way out."

"Come with me," she said. He took her offered arm.

"It's just so weird," Amelia said. "I've got a seeing sister. And she's gorgeous."

"Stop it," Susannah said.

"She's right," Matthew ('Call me Matt') said.

"I feel awful. Everybody says I look as though I've been in a fight. Where's Mum?"

"I think she went out for a cigarette."

"Dr. Clarke said I have to keep away from smokers and smoky environments."

"Mum's not really a smoker."

"Susannah."

It was her father. Where had he been?

"So tell us about Niall Burnet," he said. "Where did you meet him? How long have you known him?"

"Why does it matter?" Susannah asked.

"Of course it matters."

"She's twenty-two, Dad," Amelia said.

"She's got the emotional intelligence of a child," her father said. "You know that as well as I do. What other little secrets and surprises have you got for us?"

"I've got a friend," Susannah said. "I haven't known him long – "

"I knew it," her father interrupted. "You're going to have to get used to this, Susannah. You're going to be somebody everybody knows about for a while. People are going to want to know you for the wrong reasons. Not because they really want to be your friends but because they want to exploit you and get control of you. They'll know you've got money and they'll be trying to get their hands on it."

"Have I got money?" she asked.

"You will have."

"And what if you're totally wrong about Niall?"

"You don't need a blind friend, Susannah. You can leave all that behind. Blindness is history for you now."

❂

Niall called Lindsey and arranged to meet her outside the main entrance to the Victoria and Albert Museum. He didn't know what prompted him to suggest it other than that it was an easy destination to give a taxi driver, and it wasn't too far from BAB, where Lindsey's 'interview' was taking place at half past three.

"It should've been on neutral territory," Niall said.

"I didn't have anywhere to suggest," Lindsey whined.

Hugo did a good job of flagging down a taxi and they were soon on their way.

"All these cabs are costing me a pretty penny," Niall confessed to the dog. "If we stay in London much longer we're going to have to get our heads round the tube."

Hugo gave no indication that he was impressed at the prospect.

"What was all that about, up there?" Niall went on, forgetting that Hugo had missed it all. "The girl suddenly wants to talk to me and the Dad warns me off. Do you think he's got something to hide and he's terrified she's going to tell me? In which case, surely he should be more worried about the guy from the *Mirror*. Or maybe he's bought him off. It's all good fun anyway, eh? Means more trips to Moorfields, more expense. And I can't stay in Simon's lounge for ever. We're totally unwelcome as it is."

They arrived very early at the V & A, and settled down to wait. Niall wished he could have ten pounds for every time he had to say 'I'm just waiting for someone'. He knew people meant well, he knew blindness did bring out the helpful streak in people, but he did wish they'd just leave him alone. Some of them only wanted an excuse to meet Hugo, but others were really irritating.

It was a relief when Lindsey's less-than-dulcet tones broke across his contemplation.

"You said half an hour," she said.

"I know. You're fine. I was early."

"So this is the V & A," she said, astonishing him.

"You work near here," Niall said.

"Do I?"

"Unbelievable."

With help from a number of passers-by they found their way to a coffee shop and Lindsey ordered a skinny latte. Raspberry tea wasn't on the menu so Niall had to make do with peppermint.

"Every cafe in Shrewsbury serves raspberry tea," he said to the girl behind the counter. It was almost certainly not true, and as she sounded as though she had only been in the UK for a week she probably had no idea where Shrewsbury was, but it made him feel better saying it. Indulging himself in a little justified outrage.

"So," he said, when they were safely ensconced at a table. "What's up?"

"You know what's up," Lindsey said.

"What's going to happen then? At the meeting."

"I suppose Juliette's going to ask me about the allegations."

"And you still don't know what they are?"

"No."

"It's outrageous." Niall raised his voice.

"Ssh! I don't want people listening to us."

"No. OK. Sorry. But it is. They're holding all the cards. You can't prepare any kind of defence because you don't actually know what you've got to defend yourself against."

"There's no point getting angry, Niall," Lindsey said on the verge of tears. "It won't change anything and it won't help."

"OK. OK. I'm not angry."

"Juliette did say I could bring someone with me if I wanted."

"Because she had to. Because she's making damn sure she's playing this by the book."

"But I don't know anyone," Lindsey said helplessly.

"What about this man in your life?" Niall asked. "Can't he support you? He bloody well should."

"He would if he could but he works at BAB so it's really awkward."

"Oh no. What does he do?"

"It doesn't matter what he does," Lindsey insisted angrily. "Just leave him out of it. He hates what's happening to me but we can't risk both of us losing our jobs over this."

"Over what?" Niall said exasperated.

"I'll find out this afternoon," Lindsey returned in the same tone.

They sipped coffee and mint tea. The dogs dozed under the table.

"I was hoping you'd go with me," Lindsey said at last.

"Me?" Niall spluttered, incredulous.

"You won't let her walk all over me."

"God I'm in demand at the minute," Niall said.

"What do you mean?"

"Nothing. Lindsey, look, yes, I will go with you if it's what you want, but seriously – I don't think it will help you if they know I'm in your corner."

"I don't know what will help me," Lindsey said. "I just can't face this on my own."

"OK. It's a deal. Who'd've thought it?"

"What?"

"Lindsey and Niall. Together again."

"We're not together."

"No. I know."

Daniel Sullivan illegally made a call on his mobile phone while driving.

"Hello?"

"Daniel," he said, by way of introduction.

"Yes," confirmed his interlocutor.

"The irritant is still in evidence."

"Frankly I don't consider it a problem."

"It's annoying," Daniel said. "Unnecessary."

"We're secure. We'll monitor the situation closely. If it becomes necessary to unleash the pit-bull, then we will."

"OK," Daniel said. "Just thought you should know."

He rang off without ceremony and gave his attention back to the road.

Lindsey and Niall arrived at BAB at three fifteen. Niall was nervous, but alert. Part of him didn't want to be so obviously on BAB's radar at the moment, but part of him did. He wanted to redeem himself in his own eyes following the debacle of his interview with Vivien Loosemore. And there was still the fact that Lindsey's suspension was phoney. Somehow a nerve had been touched. He wasn't even sure if it had been by him. He was certainly no longer convinced that it had anything to do with the transplant. But people at BAB were running scared of something and lashing out. He needed to start being calm, collected and inspired. No more mistakes. Full concentration.

Lindsey introduced herself at reception, said that she had brought somebody with her. Niall concentrated on listening to the tone of voice of the staff members who greeted her. He sensed shock, sympathy, collective disbelief. These people were going to struggle to accept her guilt. He wondered whether the shadowy masterminds behind this ploy had considered that.

They were shown to a room and told that 'Ms. Warwick' would be with them shortly. Lindsey took a seat at one side of a large table and called Niall to sit beside her. The dogs settled down beneath them.

Niall wondered whether the word would have got out that he was with Lindsey, whether someone had recognised him on their way through the building and primed Juliette Warwick. He hoped not. If he could at least cause her a moment's discomfort when she walked in, that would go down as a small victory. Something to build on.

Half past three came and went. Niall could tell that Lindsey was getting more and more uncomfortable and he cursed Juliette Warwick for, as he saw it, playing deliberate mind games. But he had promised Lindsey he would be calm and supportive, so he said nothing. They both said nothing. The only sounds they heard were muffled voices in other rooms or corridors nearby.

Finally, just before a quarter to four, the door opened and two people came in.

"Hello, Lindsey. Sorry I'm late," Juliette Warwick said. Niall recognised her voice and tried to stare unsettlingly in her direction.

"This is Jane Thompson, from the legal department," Warwick went on, introducing her side-kick.

"Right," Lindsey said. Niall felt her shudder. "This is – well, I expect you remember Niall Burnet."

"I do," Juliette Warwick said. "I did tell you you could bring legal representation to this meeting."

"I know," Lindsey said.

"How do you do, Lindsey. How do you do, Niall," Jane Thompson said. She seemed oblivious to any tension in the room.

"Hi," Niall responded.

"Now," Juliette Warwick said, sitting down. "This is a very awkward and uncomfortable situation for all of us. As you know, Lindsey, an allegation has been made of unprofessional conduct, and you have been suspended pending an investigation of that allegation, and this meeting is the first step in that process. I have already had a meeting with the complainant, and now this will be your opportunity to answer some of the points raised."

"Yes," Lindsey said.

"I'm going to start by explaining the process of what we're doing," Juliette Warwick went on. "The first step in following up a complaint of this nature is to undertake an investigation. You will be given every chance to contribute as fully and comprehensively as you like and as you can to that investigation. We're not in a trial situation. On the basis of the findings of the investigation, the Association will then decide whether to move to a disciplinary."

"Or exonerate and reinstate," Niall said.

"Yes," Jane Thompson said.

"Although you are suspended," Juliette continued, "that is merely an automatic response to a complaint having been made. It does not indicate a presumption of guilt."

"OK," Lindsey said.

"I'm going to ask you about a visit you made on 13th July to a Mrs. Ingrid Besser."

Niall felt Lindsey go rigid beside him. For the first time he wondered whether there was something Lindsey hadn't told him, whether there was in fact substance to the complaint.

"Do you remember Mrs. Besser, Lindsey?"

"Yes," Lindsey said, but without any great confidence or certainty.

"I'd like you to tell me in your own words everything you can about how that visit came to be arranged, and what happened when you were there."

"It was four months ago," Lindsey said unhappily.

"I know," Juliette Warwick said.

Lindsey stumbled over her story. Yes, she remembered Ingrid Besser. An old lady with a thick Germanic accent, cataracts and macular degeneration. She had got her name in the usual way, passed on to her from the department that Mrs. Besser had herself contacted – or her family had contacted – for support. It was the accent she particularly remembered. She had called her and asked if she could visit. Juliette Warwick interrupted.

"Did you explain why you were arranging to see her?"

"No, not exactly," Lindsey said.

"Why not?"

"Because when I was first employed I was told that I shouldn't."

Juliette Warwick drew air in noisily through her teeth.

"Who by?"

"By Michael Carstairs I expect."

"Would he back that up?"

"I've no idea."

"Sorry," Niall interrupted. He sensed astonishment and irritation from Warwick, "who is Michael Carstairs?"

"He was the man I used to work with," Lindsey said.

"He retired early on health grounds," Juliette Warwick said.

"And was never replaced," Niall said.

"No."

"Is that OK with the legal department?" he asked Jane Thompson. "Sending one person alone to people's houses on this kind of work?"

"Well …" Jane said.

"You'll have ample opportunity to make any points and raise any questions you see fit at a disciplinary, should it come to that," Juliette Warwick said, talking over the other woman. "At present we are here to explore the complaint made against Lindsey."

"Fine," Niall said.

Lindsey went back to her account of what she remembered of the visit. She had arrived at the flat in Hamilton Terrace. Mrs. Besser had a companion, Friedl, who had let her in. She didn't know Friedl's other name. They had had tea and Battenberg cake. She had told Mrs. Besser about her eye condition. Mrs. Besser had appeared very interested. She had told her about BAB, gone through everything exactly as she always did, talked about the importance of what they did for people, of what they could continue to do for Mrs. Besser. She was 'as sure as she could be' that Mrs. Besser had herself asked the question about how BAB managed for money. This was what she had been trained to try to wait for. Then she had explained about legacies, talked about the damage the National Lottery had done to BAB's income, left some large print leaflets and her telephone extension number. That was all she remembered.

Niall wondered.

"Thank you, Lindsey," Juliette Warwick said. He had heard her making notes throughout. "Now I'm going to ask you some questions that stem directly from the complaint that has been made."

"OK."

"When you contacted Mrs. Besser to make the appointment, did you at any point in that conversation say that she could have another member of her family present if she wished?"

"I expect so. It's part of what we're supposed to say. I don't exactly remember."

"So it's possible that you didn't say that?"

"I'm pretty sure I would have."

"But it's possible that you didn't?"

"Well – yes, I suppose."

"You don't have a list of questions and information points that you go through when you call somebody like Mrs. Besser?"

"I do have one. But it's what I do every day. I sort of know it by heart."

"So you don't always have it in front of you?"

"No. Nobody does."

Niall heard the pen making copious notes. If he had been a solicitor, and this had been a police interrogation, he would be advising Lindsey to stop incriminating herself. But, under the guise of 'information-gathering', there were no legal protocols to defend the accused.

"When you arrived at Mrs. Besser's flat, did she let you in?" Juliette Warwick asked.

"Well, no. Her companion, Friedl, did."

"You introduced yourself? You were invited in?"

"They were expecting me. We had an appointment."

"Mrs. Besser's niece claims that she called and cancelled your appointment that morning."

"No."

"She says she called the Association, was put through to you, and told you that under no circumstances were you to visit her aunt."

"She did call me," Lindsey admitted. "I do remember that."

"To ask you not to visit."

"No. Just to ask me what it was about."

"And you told her."

"I told her that I wanted to meet Mrs. Besser to tell her more about BAB, as she had expressed an interest in our services."

"She says you were off-hand and rude. Did anyone else hear the conversation?"

"I don't know. Why would I have gone there if they had cancelled the appointment?"

"Because of your misplaced zeal to do the best you could for the Association."

Niall snorted.

"Mrs. Besser's niece says," Juliette Warwick went on, "that after you left her aunt was very upset and rang her immediately. She said she had felt intimidated and bullied."

"So why wait four months to make a complaint?" Niall asked.

"That's a question that I put to her," Juliette Warwick responded.

"And?"

"It's my job to gather information at the moment, not answer questions," she said.

"It's quite clear what you're going to end up with," Niall said.

"Lindsey's version of what happened, and Mrs. Besser's niece's version. Nobody's going to be able to prove anything one way or the other."

Juliette Warwick ignored him. She asked Lindsey some more questions relating to her behaviour during the appointment in Hamilton Terrace. Lindsey attempted to answer but was clearly stressed and panicking and her answers became increasingly vague and contradictory. Eventually, with the clock showing nearly five, Juliette Warwick declared that the 'interview' was over. She explained that she would now have to make further inquiries and then pass her findings on to a higher authority. Lindsey should expect to hear something in writing within a fortnight. In the meantime she was not, under any circumstances, to attempt to make contact with Mrs. Besser or her niece. If she wanted to discuss anything regarding the case, she was to contact Jane Thompson.

Lindsey was crying by the time they emerged from the portals of BAB. It was also raining. They took a taxi as far as Simon's local pub, and Niall called him to ask him to join them there.

"Tomorrow morning we get you a lawyer," Niall said.

"How?" Lindsey whined.

"Citizens Advice. We'll call them and make an appointment."

"I won't need one if they decide everything I did was OK."

"Lindsey, they're not going to. You know that. I know that. It's a fit up. So why don't you tell me what really happened with this Mrs. Besser thing?"

"What do you mean?" Lindsey asked.

"Hi guys," Simon said.

The conversation shifted gear, and Niall never got his answer.

Katrina Masters prepared a large bowl of green salad tossed in a dressing of her own devising. She had two swordfish steaks prepared and waiting for the griddle, and a bottle of Chilean Sauvignon Blanc open in the fridge. She loved, on her day off, to have the meal ready and waiting for when her partner came through the door. It just made the perfect start to the evening.

She worked as a pastry chef at Arvo's, a restaurant with a growing reputation not far from her home in Kilburn. She knew that the irregular hours she worked placed a strain on her relationship, and that relationship had been going through a sticky patch, so she always tried to make as much as she could of the evenings she was home.

She heard the key in the door and her partner came in. Katrina could tell, just from the way she came through the door and took off her coat, that it hadn't been a good day. She took the wine from the fridge, poured two glasses, and stood with them in her hands waiting for Juliette to come into the kitchen. She didn't. She went straight into the downstairs cloak-room. Katrina put the glasses of wine down on the kitchen table.

Juliette emerged two minutes later, came into the kitchen, kissed her perfunctorily and took a long slug of the wine.

"Not good?" Katrina asked.

"Mm? Oh. No. Not good. Not good at all."

Juliette took her wine and walked out. A moment later Katrina heard the television on in the living room. It was going to be another 'dinner-on-trays' evening. She sighed and lit the gas under the griddle. She took a lemon out of the fruit bowl and quartered it. Juliette's moods were increasingly taking over their life. She felt as though she was bending over backwards to be accommodating and she was getting nothing in return. Tears pricked at the corners of her eyes but she fought them back.

Even down to this business with her aunt.

She cooked the swordfish feeling desperately lonely. She was an only child. Her parents were dead. She seemed to have no friends other than Juliette's friends. She was about to be forty and what had she got in her life? Her job. She had given up her position in a building society three years ago to follow her dream of a career in catering. Juliette had supported her at the time, but then at the time their relationship was very new. She had trained and qualified and worked her way up to a good position, but from day one of the reality of working restaurant hours Juliette had disliked and resented it. Although she wasn't really sure whether it was the hours Juliette objected to or the fact that she was doing something interesting for herself by herself. Juliette did like to dominate her.

Katrina arranged salad on two plates, positioned the griddled swordfish, seasoned them lightly and added the lemon wedges, put the plates on trays and carried Juliette's through to her. She came back to the kitchen to get her own and to fetch the bottle of wine. Then she joined Juliette in front of the television.

"So tell me," she said.

Juliette chewed a mouthful of fish and salad and washed it down with wine.

"I'm angry," Juliette said. Katrina said nothing. "I'm angry with the people that contrived this situation and I'm angry with the stupid woman who's allowing herself to be destroyed by it."

"Are you angry with me?" Katrina asked.

"I'm angry with everybody," Juliette said dismissively. "Ignore me. It's a pity it's not a work night for you."

Katrina thought back through the whole saga of her ailing aunt's dealings with the British Association for the Blind. It had been Juliette who suggested that the Association might be able to offer her support of one kind or another when Katrina had told her about Aunt Ingrid's eye problems. Aunt Ingrid was Katrina's only living relative, as far as she knew. She and her much younger sister Liesel had come to England with their mother, running from the Nazis at the beginning of World War Two. Liesel, Katrina's mother, had been much too young to remember anything of the life and family they had left behind in Vienna, but Aunt Ingrid had shown her photographs of her grandfather and great uncles – even one uncle – who, to the best of Ingrid's knowledge, had all died somewhere at the whim of the Third Reich. Ingrid had never married, and Katrina had sometimes wondered if she had inherited her sexuality from her, if such a thing were possible. Although she didn't believe the relationship between her aunt and Friedl, who lived with her, was anything other than companionship.

When Aunt Ingrid had called her that afternoon in July to tell her that a woman from the British Association for the Blind was coming to visit her the following day Katrina was instantly suspicious and protective. Her aunt was a very old woman who had clearly been confused and upset by the conversation. Katrina had demanded from Juliette an explanation of what the appointment meant. Juliette had been unusually defensive and they had had one of the very rare rows in which Katrina did not come out feeling totally humiliated. Instead she wrung a concession from Juliette that, if she called the woman in the morning, she would get the appointment cancelled.

And she had called. She had been, admittedly, aggressive, and the woman – Linda or Lynne or Lindsey Spencer or Spence or Spicer or some such name – had met fire with fire. It had astonished her, and in her astonishment she was unable to recall whether she had insisted that the appointment was cancelled or not. But she knew that was the reason for the call, so she couldn't believe that she hadn't said it.

Then Aunt Ingrid had phoned her later in the day to say how lovely the woman had been and how she was silly to have worried about it. She said she thought the woman was probably hoping for a large bite of Katrina's inheritance, 'but as you know, my dear, I have very little to leave, and what I do have will all be yours.'

Katrina had been ready to make an official complaint. Juliette had talked her out of it. Had told her what a lovely person this Lindsey was. That she was doing a difficult job very well. That she had tunnel vision, and even that might go in time. Made Katrina feel sorry for her. And there had been no harm done. Aunt Ingrid had not been tricked into anything. The whole incident had passed into history.

And then this week Juliette had telephoned her from work and asked her to make the complaint. Said that there was too much going wrong in that department and it would be helpful for everybody if it could all be brought out into the open. "Lance the boil," she had said. Katrina hadn't enjoyed the image.

"What really annoys me," Juliette said suddenly, bringing Katrina back to the present, "is when women fall apart. Lindsey was essentially a good woman doing a decent job. Is she standing up for herself? No."

She put her plate down on the floor. Katrina noticed that she had barely eaten half the fish and left almost all of the salad.

EIGHT

The Citizens Advice Bureau in Harrow was near Harrow and Wealdstone station, not very near to where Lindsey lived and a long and expensive taxi ride out from Chiswick. Lindsey tried to persuade Niall to use the rail network, but once they had called and made an appointment to see one of the legal people Niall insisted there wasn't time.

Their arrival provoked the flurry of attentive concern and fascination that was all a part of being blind, and they were escorted without delay into an office where the smell declared that – even though it was a no-smoking building and no smoking had taken place in the room – its occupant was clearly a smoker.

"Hello," he said cheerfully, in an accent that was anything but Harrow. "Charles Taylor."

Charles Taylor came round from behind his desk, organised chairs for Lindsey and Niall, asked at the door for some water to be brought for the dogs, which impressed Niall, and then settled down.

"You like dogs?" Niall asked, when the introductions were over.

"Proper dogs, yes," Charles Taylor said. "I've got two Great Danes that keep me permanently overdrawn. I can't be doing with dogs the size of hamsters."

"You're not from London?" Niall continued.

"No. Plymouth born and bred," Taylor replied. "The sea's in my blood. That's why I live in Harrow."

"So why do you live in Harrow?" Niall couldn't help asking, appreciating the irony in Taylor's remark.

"Well, I could answer that," Taylor said. "But time is money, even though in this instance it isn't yours, so why don't we get down to why you're here?"

Between them, Lindsey and Niall painted as clear a picture as they could of her situation.

"Basically we're here," Niall finished up, "because I'm not a lawyer and Lindsey needs one. They've got people who know all the rules and we need someone in our corner who knows them too."

"Yes, right, yes," Taylor said. It wasn't the incisive immediate response that Niall had been hoping for. Maybe this was why Charles Taylor had ended up at the Citizens Advice Bureau, and not in some excruciatingly expensive law firm. "Are you two an item?" he asked at last.

"No!" Lindsey stormed, at the same moment as Niall was asking "Is that relevant to the case?"

"Well," Taylor said, "you suspect dirty tricks. We need to know how many dirty tricks they have up their sleeve. We want to have all the bases covered."

"I don't see how bringing me into it will help them," Niall said.

"According to you," Taylor replied, "it was you walking in to speak to Lindsey that set this whole thing in motion."

"I did think that," Niall said.

"But - ?" Taylor prompted.

"I'm not sure now. It comes down to the phone call."

"Phone call? I'm supposed to be your solicitor. You've nothing to gain from being obscure with me."

"The phone call between Lindsey and the niece," Niall said, looking in Lindsey's direction. There was a short pause.

"She shouted at me," Lindsey said suddenly. "She shouted at me and then I shouted back."

"OK," Taylor said. "Can you remember any details?"

"It was the first time it had ever happened to me. I'd been warned when I started that sometimes relatives took an aggressive stance but it had never happened to me and I wasn't expecting it. She accused me of being irresponsible, of terrifying a vulnerable old lady who'd lived through more horrors than I was ever likely to. So, then I told her about the horrors of being blind and – well – I honestly can't remember everything I said. It was awful. But she was just as bad and she started it."

"Did anyone overhear the conversation?"

"Yes. Three or four people in the office."

"And they were all on your side?"

"They all agreed they'd keep quiet about it. They knew I shouldn't have spoken like that but they knew me and they knew it was out of character, so I must have been provoked."

"OK." Taylor thought for a moment. "The real question is, 'Why now?' If the niece had made her complaint that day, or the next day... Why did you go to the house, incidentally?"

"Because I was damned if that woman was going to speak to me like that and get away with it. I mean, who did she think she was? I'd been perfectly pleasant to her aunt, I'd done everything by the book, and I was absolutely determined to keep the appointment."

Niall interrupted. "So when you were first suspended, and called me in the middle of the night, and told me you'd never done anything wrong, you already knew this had happened and you must've guessed that it was involved in some way."

"It was so long ago," Lindsey said feebly.

"You lied to me," Niall said. "You told me you'd been thinking all night and you couldn't think of anything."

"There wasn't anything."

"You abused a woman on the phone."

"She abused me."

"You must have known."

"I realised that it might be something to do with that. I just was sure it couldn't be because it was so long ago."

"OK, OK," Charles Taylor interrupted. "Now, we're going to have to sit out the two weeks until we find out the next step. Chances are, though, that employment law being what it is, whatever happens you need to be looking for another job."

"But …" Lindsey tried to say.

"They will argue that the relationship of trust between employer and employee has broken down, and will therefore be able to terminate your contract, with or without a finding of professional misconduct. You could fight it through industrial tribunal and all the way to the European court on the basis of unfair or constructive dismissal, but it would take years and you still wouldn't get your job back."

"So what are you saying?" Lindsey said.

"I'm saying if they offer you a chance to resign it'll look better on your CV."

"One mistake," Lindsey screeched. "One mistake. Aren't I supposed to get a warning or something?"

"You've got no witnesses to the phone call in which you first spoke to this Mrs. Besser. If they claim you were abusive to her, you'll only have your own denial to fall back on. That's compromised by the fact that there are witnesses to the conversation the next day, and rest assured they'll come forward when push comes to shove, not thinking they're doing any harm and absolutely sure that you were provoked, but all the while proving that you are well capable of losing it on the phone. If you did it once you can do it again. By your own admission you don't know what you said to the niece, and then you went ahead with the visit after you were expressly told not to. I don't know all the red tape surrounding your job but that may very well be illegal. The only witness to what actually took place between you and the old woman is the woman herself or her companion, and they'll be very unlikely to call them. They'll just use the niece, who's very angry. Then you've got the fact that a big national charity like BAB is going to want to be seen to be keeping its house in order. They won't want to risk embarrassment or bad press."

"I thought lawyers were supposed to help you," Lindsey said stubbornly.

"There are lawyers out there who'll take your money and dishonestly tell you there's a case worth fighting. I'm here to give you free advice, and that's what I'm doing," Charles Taylor said.

"Appreciate it," Niall said. He found himself liking Taylor, despite the uncompromising nature of his advice.

"If they give you a chance to jump, take it," Taylor went on. "They're not going to want to go to disciplinary if they can avoid it."

"They could just move me to another department," Lindsey said helplessly. "I could promise never to answer the phone again."

"You can always suggest it," Taylor said. "You need to wait for them to make the next move. I know that's difficult. But then you need to have your plans ready for when they do. If they say the decision's a disciplinary, then you can say 'What if I resign?' or 'Couldn't I move to another department?', but you need to know for sure what you're prepared to do. Just remember that getting a job when you're visually impaired is no joke, and having a dismissal for professional misconduct on your record isn't going to make it any easier. Try to get a reference out of them."

"I don't believe this." Lindsey started sobbing.

"But why now?" Taylor mused, ignoring her. "That's the only curious thing."

"Do you think it could have anything to do with the questions I was asking about the transplant?" Niall asked.

"Hard to say. Have you found anything out?"

"No."

"I suppose you wouldn't tell me if you had. Journalists."

"That's right," Niall said, glowing internally at the fact that someone was considering him on his own evaluation – a journalist, not a blind journalist.

"I'll give you my number," Taylor said, "in case you find yourself needing a solicitor."

"I don't live in Harrow," Niall said.

"I do private work as well," Taylor said. "And this does sound interesting."

"Oh and I don't," Lindsey said suddenly.

"If you decide to go to disciplinary, call me," Taylor said. "But don't say I didn't warn you what would happen."

It was six thirty pm when Hugo, exhausted, dragged Niall once more through the portals of Moorfields Eye Hospital. It had been a long and expensive day, the final expense being the rail ticket back to Telford that Niall had bought online for the following morning. After the good old-fashioned row that he had had with Lindsey to the astonishment of the passers-by on Station Road in Harrow, he had reached some decisions in the back of the cab that returned him to Chiswick. Firstly, the case that his imagination had built up around the eye transplant had collapsed. The one really suspicious event, Lindsey's suspension the same day that he had met her at BAB, turned out to have a real, logical explanation. His conspiracy theory was now too 'flimsy' even for his own wildly creative mind to run with. There were still some curious anomalies, but nothing that proved anything or even provided a stepping stone towards something else. There was no chain, no progression, no developing investigation. So it was over. He would do his final good deed, pay this promised visit to Susannah Leman, and then close the book.

He also needed to get out of London. It was costing him a fortune and that was without paying rent. He had put Simon's relationship with Erica under pressure by out-staying his welcome in the house, and Hugo wasn't making friends there either.

He needed a future and this was not it. Once you got on the right path it was amazing how things that would normally seem insurmountable just fell away. London obviously wasn't the right path. He should've read the signs when the path he chose led to the feet of Lindsey Corncrake Spencer. It had all been entertaining for a while, but it was not leading towards a job. And that was what he needed, a job and a life.

Leaving Hugo where he would be well looked after, he allowed himself to be guided to Susannah's room.

"Another visitor," the nurse said, bringing him in. "Somebody's popular this evening."

"Hello Niall," he heard Susannah say. "I'm so glad you've come."

"Hi," Niall said. "Got company?"

"Yes, Mr. Sullivan from the Blind Association."

"I told you to call me Daniel," Sullivan said.

"OK," Susannah said uncomfortably.

It was another twenty minutes before they managed to get

Sullivan to leave. Twenty minutes of roundabout conversation, inconsequential remarks loaded with sub-text, and Sullivan determined not to take the hint. In the end Susannah, desperately worried that Niall would make some excuse and leave before she had a chance to have her proper conversation with him, took the bull by the horns and told Daniel that she needed to talk to Niall in private. He was clearly unimpressed, but left with as good a grace as he could muster.

"What did he want?" Niall asked.

"You don't like him, do you?" Susannah said.

"I don't really know him. He sounds a pompous ass."

"He's being very kind to me."

"Oh yeah?"

"Yeah."

The conversation ground to an uncomfortable halt.

"How do I look?" Niall said at last.

"Do you hate me?" was Susannah's response.

"What? No. Why?"

"For seeing."

"I don't hate you."

"You were the one who gave me the courage to face it."

"Rubbish."

"No, really. All the sighted people, talking about sight as if it's the most wonderful thing in the world and 'Oh you must be so excited', 'Oh it's so thrilling' and they had no idea. That from where I was it wasn't wonderful, it wasn't thrilling. It was just scary. Still is. I had a life and it made sense. Pathetic compared to yours, I know, but it was mine and I was at ease with it. Now I have to start all over again. Mr. Daghash even says I'm going to have to learn to walk again. To stop walking like a blind person. Can you imagine that?"

"Yes," Niall said. "It's what happened to me, but in reverse. Believe me, I'd rather be where you are."

"But I'm not me anymore."

"Yes you are."

"No. I feel different. I've changed my name."

"What?"

"Nobody else knows. But I'm not Susannah any more. She's dead and gone. I'm Miranda now."

"Admired Miranda," Niall said, instinctively quoting A Level Shakespeare.

"Do you think that's crazy?"

"No. I think it makes a Hell of a lot of sense."

"I knew you'd understand."

"And what's Miranda going to do with her life?"

"I've absolutely no idea."

"Well if she fancies a future in sunny Shropshire, just give me a call. I'm going back tomorrow."

"Oh." Niall hadn't heard that much disappointment in a woman's voice for a very long time. Certainly not at the prospect of him going away.

"Where is Shropshire?" Miranda asked.

"In the middle," Niall said. "Between Birmingham and Wales."

"Is it nice?"

"It isn't exactly the centre of the universe, but – it's home." A good place for failures and no-hopers to grow old, he wanted to add, but it would have spoiled the moment.

"And you live in - ?" he asked instead.

"Surrey."

"Of course."

"What do you mean?"

"Nothing. It's not your fault. It's just kind of – predictable."

"You think I'm a poor little rich girl, don't you?"

"Now that's Miranda talking," Niall said with a smile. "I think I'm going to like her."

"I hope you do," Miranda said. "She likes you."

"Because she hasn't met enough guys yet to know better."

"What do you mean? I've met Daniel Sullivan."

"Of course."

"And Matthew Long."

"Oh yes. Mr. Tabloid."

"My sister thinks he's fit."

"Right."

"This is so strange. I have the kind of conversations with you that I have with me in my head. It's weird."

"Weird."

"I've never talked like this to anyone before."

"Look, Miranda," Niall felt it incumbent upon him to say, "don't build it into something it's not. I have to go back to Shropshire. You have to go and see Surrey. And meet the press. And be famous. We're moving in opposite directions."

"Are you still going to write your article about me?"

"Yeah, yeah – sure."

"So you might need to interview me again."

"You've signed a contract."

"Do you know what? Come closer, I want to whisper something." Niall walked up to the bed. She took his arm and pulled his head down to hers. "Fuck the contract," she whispered, and laughed. "Do you know," she went on, letting go of him, "that is the first time in my life that I've said that word."

"I think you had a personality transplant along with the eyes," Niall said appreciatively.

"Do you think that's possible?" Miranda asked, suddenly

serious. "The eyes have brought some of their old owner with them?"

"No," Niall said. "They've just given you the confidence to step outside the box your parents put you in."

Half an hour later Niall left. He promised to keep in touch but he knew as he said it that it was a promise he wasn't going to keep. The only thing that surprised him was the sense of loss that he felt as he walked out of Moorfields with Hugo.

Being blind, he didn't notice the silver BMW that followed him back to Chiswick, and again from Simon's to Paddington station the next morning.

PART TWO

'I once was lost, but now am found
Was blind but now I see...'

Amazing Grace

NINE

In the dream, Rebecca was back in the room at the top of 17, Cardew Crescent. She was naked, and so was the man who wasn't Richard (but whose face was a blur). He started to touch her and in spite of herself she started to feel turned on. Knowing she didn't really want to, she nevertheless lay down on the bed and spread her legs. Instead of getting on top of her though, he just smiled (but how can a man smile if his face has no features?) and guided her hand to his penis. She didn't want to do it, but she did. Gently at first, rhythmically, and then gathering momentum almost into a frenzy until she felt the explosion that told her it was over. He relaxed. She relaxed. She looked at his face and it was her brother Joe.

Rebecca woke up shaking. Her sheets were damp with cold sweat. She was a wreck. She had been a wreck since the night of the 'adult soiree'. The whole sordid experience had messed with her mind and she hadn't been able to move on from it. She couldn't concentrate on her work, her relationship with Penny had become complicated, and her nights were racked by terrible haunting dreams. She was losing it, and everybody was so understanding because they said it was delayed grief for Joe: her body had gone into shock at first, but now this was the next phase in coming to terms with it. And she just wanted to shout at them and throw things at them because it was nothing to do with that. Well maybe partly, but that wasn't what it was actually about. It was her total disgust at Daniel's sex party, the sex act she had performed, Penny's prostitution, Daniel, "Adrian", "Richard", "Mary", Penny, Beth, herself and anyone and everyone who had ever done anything sordid in the sexual line. She felt as though she would never get into bed with another man ever, for as long as she lived.

"You've got to get over it, girl," Penny said, trying to joke and jolly her out of it.

"I can't," Rebecca said. But why couldn't she? If Penny was OK with it, and Beth was OK with it, and hundreds of thousands of women throughout history had coped with it, why was she incapable of rationalising it and putting it in perspective? Her body had not been violated thanks to Richard's failure to perform; but part of her felt it would have been easier to excuse if it had been: she could have allowed that to feel a bit like rape, something she had unwillingly succumbed to. Instead of leading him by the prick to somewhere he was really too embarrassed to go. Why the Hell had she done it? Every time she stood at the basin in the bathroom she was Lady Macbeth, frantically scrubbing at her right hand in a pathetic and doomed attempt to cleanse it.

Her tutor had offered her the chance to defer her studies and start the whole year again the following September. It had felt like the last thing in the world that she wanted or needed to do at the time, but now, maybe – To get out of London, away from Penny and everything she now stood for, even if only for a while, might help to clear her head. Let her breathe again. Rebuild whatever part of her had collapsed. Perhaps her parents did need her. Perhaps she needed to be needed. To feel a cleansing winter wind blow through her on the Sussex Downs. Let the New Year come and open the door to a better future.

She made a decision. She would go home.

❧

By December 10th Niall had had enough of Christmas. He had eaten all the chocolates in the Advent Calendar his mother had bought him, heard more than his fair share of Christmas music, and endured a visit from some Bible-basher who had knocked on his door, offered him a mince pie, and then proceeded to ask him whether he ever thought about the spiritual side of Christmas. Admittedly his answer – 'Not really' – had probably not been the smartest thing he had ever said, but at the time he had been trying to keep Hugo's nose out of the woman's mince pie tin.

Life as one of Telford's unemployed had brought few excitements since his return from London. The phone that had seemed red hot back then with calls from Lindsey Spencer and Susannah Leman's eye surgeon was now stone cold and almost completely dormant. He had dropped off the map, fallen off the carousel, become part of the two-dimensional background of life. Sometimes he minded, and sometimes the softly-sprung ease of it all reached out and lured him in.

He assumed that silence meant Lindsey had either heard nothing, or heard something but decided she didn't want anything more to do with him, or been reinstated following the delightful Ms Warwick's investigation, or sought refuge with the man in her life who might or might not actually be a myth.

He assumed that silence meant that Susannah or Miranda had

walked out into the sighted world and forgotten all about him. He had picked up a news item on the day she left hospital, but after that the trail had gone cold.

He assumed that silence meant that Simon had not yet forgiven him for the disturbance he had caused in his domestic affairs.

All in all, this was going to be a year to forget. Roll on January 1st. He presumed he'd go to his mother and stepdad's for Christmas – or at least that was what she presumed – but New Year's Eve was a time for solitary reflection with a congenial guide dog, some Guinness and a couple of spicy Pot Noodles.

Then his doorbell rang. After his experience with the rabid Christian he decided to employ a caution that was altogether foreign to his nature. He couldn't pretend to be out, because Hugo had already given the game away, but he could at least act the part of the poor defenceless blind person if it turned out to be someone after money or his soul.

"Who is it?" he called, without opening the door.

"Niall! That's not like you."

The voice was maddeningly familiar. He just needed a second to –

"Faith? What on Earth are you doing here?"

And he opened the door.

"Well I've come to see you of course," Faith Hodgkiss said. "It's a bit wet out here. Are you going to ask me in?"

"Of course, of course." Niall backed away from the door and the counsellor who had nursed him through every crisis since he first started to go blind stepped into his flat.

"This is a nice place, Niall," she said appreciatively.

"How did you find it?"

"I treated myself to a SatNav," Faith said, in a voice that managed to sound both gleeful and apologetic. "It's been a great investment because it makes me laugh and it helps me get to places. I was never very good with maps, especially if I wasn't going from the bottom in the direction of the top."

"I can offer you raspberry tea, Guinness, ordinary tea, or there might be some lager," Niall said.

"Difficult choice," Faith replied. "I think ordinary tea sounds good under the circumstances."

"Actually there might be some Earl Grey or something that my mum put in the cupboard for when she comes round," Niall added on reflection. "Come into the kitchen and have a look."

Between them they furnished Faith with a cup of Earl Grey and Niall with his inevitable raspberry, and then he led the way to the lounge.

"I'd've tidied up if I'd known I was expecting visitors," he said.

"No problem," Faith said, making space on the sofa and sitting down.

"So," Niall said. "You've never done this before, dropped in unannounced, so what's the occasion?"

"Well," Faith said, "partly I was concerned about you, knowing you'd been made redundant and wondering how you were coping. But I could have rung you to talk about that. But more importantly, I think your help is needed, and I feel responsible on two counts, and you are too, and I thought it would be better to discuss it face to face."

"Wow. Must be serious," Niall said lightly.

"It is," Faith said. "It's about Susannah Leman."

"Susannah Leman." Niall was both astonished and curious.

"Yes, or Miranda, as she calls herself now."

"Did she really go through with that?" Niall said, appreciatively.

"You have no idea what she's gone through."

"I hardly know her," Niall said defensively.

"No," Faith replied, "and she hardly knows you, but she's built you up into something very special inside her head."

"Oh no," Niall said. "I really didn't try to –"

"Niall," Faith cautioned, "I know you too well."

"Honestly. I didn't even like her much at first."

"Well, one way or another it happened."

"And that's why you're here?"

"Partly. But not on her behalf. She has no idea where you are and it's not for me to tell her. But as it was me who put you onto her in the first place because you were so insistent and I thought it might help both of you, I feel a sense of responsibility. And so should you, because you were the one who rang me to try to get enough of the inside track to wangle your way in."

"OK," Niall said. "Responsibility for what?"

"For her," Faith said. "For everything she's going through and everything that's happened to her. She's back in hospital you know. They think she may be getting chronic rejection of the new eyes. And I really think you can help her."

"Why?"

"Because she's in a very lonely space and she trusts you," Faith said. "For whatever reason. And the other people around her all seem to have an axe of their own to grind."

"I can't go back to London," Niall said. "Simon won't put me up again."

"We'll cross that bridge later," Faith said. "I just think first of all you need to hear everything that's happened to that poor girl since she came out of Moorfields."

"OK. I'm all ears. So's Hugo."

"Dear Hugo," Faith said, stroking him. "He was the perfect dog for you. Intelligent, individual, with a charisma that you can't quite put your finger on."

"He's a good mate," Niall said.

"I spoke to Susannah a couple of times before she came out," Faith began in earnest. "I could tell she was very nervous. She'd been upset by one of the consultants, Duncan Clark, who had accused her of just wanting to be a celebrity. I've known Duncan for years and he's a brilliant man who knows more about eyes than almost anyone on the planet, but he's never believed that what Jamal and his team have been doing in relation to the transplant was possible. He's like a paid up member of the Flat Earth Society. Somebody could sail round the world in good faith and come back into Portsmouth, and he would claim the whole thing was a stunt. Because his mind just can't go there. It goes against everything he's ever known, ever learnt and ever done. And he can be very cutting when he puts you down. I suppose he went to see her out of curiosity, and dismissed her out of hand. It really upset her. You know her, you know that being a celebrity is hardly high on her list of priorities."

"You never know," Niall said. "It's supposed to be every young person's ambition nowadays."

"I think the ambition is all on her parents' and her sister's side," Faith replied. "It was her father who pushed her to the front of the queue, and her sister was positively lapping up the media attention. Anyway, back to the plot. Susannah shared with me a lot of her early seeing experiences. Her anxiety about seeing, about knowing how to see and how to live in the sighted world. I know she said the same stuff to you because she told me so. She was worried about letting her family down, worried about who she was. All very understandable stuff except nobody around her was in a mood to be understanding.

"The day before she came out that clown of a journalist said something about being a new person and Susannah – Miranda –

just came out with it. Told her assembled loved ones that Susannah was gone and they should call her Miranda from now on. You've met her family, you can imagine the response. Roderick Leman doesn't compute emotional trauma. He told her to stop talking rubbish. She cried. Her mother cried. Then her sister weighed in with the fact that she thought she'd've been more grateful for everything that everyone had done, instead of wallowing in self-pity. She'd had an operation that nobody else in the world had had, and the 'right reaction' as she put it, was to be thrilled about it. Idiot journalist doesn't know which way to look. Not sure if this is good copy or whether it gets in the way of his feel-good happy family story."

"You were there?" Niall interposed.

"I was there. Shocked into silence, if you can imagine that."

"No, but I know how you can be silent when you want other people to talk."

"Except that what I really wanted was for them all to shut up and listen to her. But it just doesn't seem to be about her at all."

"I got that impression when I was there," Niall said. "Does make you wonder how she came to be chosen." The story that had never quite been a story stirred and shook itself at the back of his mind.

"I imagine blood group will have had a fair amount to do with it," Faith said. "But I agree with you that there must have been a shortlist and there's no way Susannah would have got herself on it."

"There had to be money involved," Niall said.

"Sad but true," Faith said. "And that presumably was what you were trying to discover."

"Yes, but I realised I didn't really know where to start," Niall admitted.

"So the next day she emerged like some frightened animal coming out of hibernation. But the thing is, Niall, she's not a frightened animal. She's a plucky little fighter who has suddenly been given the means and opportunity to see that her family have abused her her entire life and she has a right to a personality."

"Abused her?" Niall asked.

"Not physically," Faith replied. "Just by treating her as a poor little second-class citizen who wasn't entitled to opinions or an independent life."

"I did wonder about the dad," Niall said.

"Vile but I don't think he's an abuser," Faith said. "I have a bit of a radar for that, but, well – no, I don't think so. Jamal took a lot of the pressure off her in the media scrum outside Moorfields, and then, having survived that, you'd have thought she might have gone home to quiet recuperation. But of course that wasn't what any of them really wanted."

"No." Niall slurped raspberry tea.

"She wanted to manage her own medication but her mother didn't think she was capable. The father, would you believe, employed an agent for her. I think he has visions of her being on every reality TV show going and BAB really aren't that far behind him. I've been totally sickened by the whole thing, believe me."

"Poor kid," Niall mused.

"I told her she could call me day or night if she needed to, and I'm very glad I did. If I hadn't, I wouldn't have found out that they confiscated her phone."

"Unbelievable," Niall said.

"She called me a few times, always late at night, when everyone was in bed, just to go through the events of the day really, tell me how she was feeling. It was the third or fourth call when she told me for the first time that she thought her sight was failing. She was getting moments of complete blackout and others where things were just losing focus. She mentioned that more in passing than anything, because she was far more upset about the way her family were treating her. They really didn't want her to be any more or any different from what she'd always been. They vetoed any kind of independence. She had a stand-up row with her mother, and the sister got it into her head that she was using her phone to call you and that you were putting all this attitude into her head. I only found that out much later when I saw her at Moorfields.

"So the sister started listening in secret outside her bedroom door at night, and she heard her talking to me, only she thought it was you. The next day she and the mother launched a commando raid and took her phone off her. We think her father has it locked in an office at work, if he hasn't thrown it away. But it still rings when you call it. I think they're hoping you'll keep ringing and ringing and she won't answer and in the end you'll get the message."

"Hysterical," Niall said.

"The first couple of days I thought nothing of it. Thought – hoped – that the reason she wasn't calling was because things were getting better. But on the third day, when I hadn't heard anything I phoned the house and spoke to the mother. She told me everything was fine but they were a bit worried about Susannah's eye-sight. I said she had stopped calling me and I could tell straight away that the woman was flustered. She said something about losing the phone or the signal not being very good or there being something wrong with it. Changed her story three times in the space of a minute and seemed to be totally unaware that I'd ever had the number.

"Well, you know me, Niall. Next day I went down to the house. It's why I bought the SatNav actually. I don't know my way round Surrey. I arrived to find them bundling her into an ambulance because she'd woken up blind and I think they panicked that all their new-found fame was about to desert them.

"I think she's happier in hospital. She gets some peace there."

"So how is she now?" Niall asked. "Has her body rejected the eyes?"

"No," Faith replied. "She's lying in bed not getting up, they're monitoring her medication, and the sight's come back. The hospital staff all think someone screwed up the medication at home, and I can't help fingering the sister. She's a spiteful cow, pardon my French."

"On purpose, you mean?"

"Yes. All that attention on your younger sister when you're used to her just being part of the wallpaper."

"That's evil."

"I'm afraid there is evil in human nature, Niall," Faith said.

"So what are you planning?" Niall asked. "And how does it involve me?"

"Ah, well, yes," Faith prevaricated, "now then. Miranda is – legally – an adult. I want to persuade her to come and stay with me when she comes out this time. The family will set up a hue and cry but – well – bugger them, frankly. They can't stop her, if she chooses to do it. And she'll be far more likely to choose to do it if she thinks you're going to be there."

"And the family will be even more pissed off," Niall observed.

"Well yes," Faith conceded. "I can't deny that. But she can spend time with you, get to know Hugo, get to know who she is away from all the stress. It's got to be for the best. And if you're staying with me it won't cost you anything and you won't have to go back to Simon's. We're the only real back-up team she's got, Niall. And she needs us. Come down for Christmas – I'm going to be on my own – and then stay on for a bit. What do you say?"

Niall thought for a moment.

"How can I refuse?" he said. "It's a bloody generous offer and you're great company. You'll soon get fed up with having me around, though."

"We'll see," Faith said.

"My Mum won't be pleased," Niall went on. "She thought I was going to hers for Christmas."

"She could come down for a few days. I've got enough room."

"Live in a palace, do you?"

"Not exactly, Niall, but it's a big old London house with plenty of floors."

"Well," Niall said, "you are a woman of mystery."

"Not really," Faith said. "I don't expect you to drop everything and come with me now, but if you let me know what day you're planning on coming down I'll come and get you. You can give me something towards the petrol – it'll be cheaper than a train ticket."

"OK," Niall said. "But you've come all this way. Are you just going to turn round and go back?"

"No, I've got some friends who live near Monmouth, and I'm going to stay with them for a couple of days. It's a nice run down the A49 from here."

"Won't need your SatNav for that then?" Niall quipped.

"Only to get me out of Telford," Faith retorted. "It's worse than the labyrinth at Cnossos."

❂

On the 20th of December Niall found himself travelling down to London with his mother. She had agreed to drive down, stay until Christmas Eve, and then go back up to Telford to her husband, leaving Niall behind. She had appreciated Faith before Niall had been able to, and a friendship had grown up between the two women that had continued throughout Niall's childhood and adolescence and into the present time.

Niall sat in the car letting his mother's Motown music wash over him, reflecting on what he was going back to in London. Miranda Leman. To his surprise, he found he was excited at the prospect of seeing her again. In fact, he had been able to think of little else since Faith's visit. Having any kind of admirer was such a rare event for him he really had to make the most of it. He was excited at the thought of crossing swords with her father again. And in a part of his mind he was reviewing what he recalled of his research into BAB. Perhaps he hadn't been wrong. Perhaps what he'd identified as suspicious circumstances actually were suspicious.

Which led him to thinking about Lindsey Spencer. He ought to call her. Tell her he was back in town. Find out what had happened. But after the manner of their last parting he wasn't at all sure that he could face it.

Then there was Simon. They could go out for a Christmas drink and put any residue of awkwardness from his autumn visit behind them.

All in all, things were looking up.

TEN

Daniel Sullivan was enjoying a three-course lunch with BAB director of finance John Holthouse. In due course they would ask for two copies of the bill and both of them would put it through their expense accounts. Daniel loved eating in expensive restaurants, although he had no real palate for fine food. He delighted in committing culinary heresy by making a point of asking for tomato ketchup with the chef's signature dish or a portion of frozen peas on the side. After showing himself up some twenty-five years ago with the cardinal wine faux pas of asking for red Liebfraumilch, he had made a point of studying enough to sound knowledgeable and order more or less what Hugh Johnson would recommend with every dish, whilst at the same time believing that the whole fine wine charade was a scam, and not being able to taste the difference between one and another. Price was generally an infallible guide.

"So how's the little project?" Holthouse asked as the mains were cleared away and they both opted for cheese to finish their bottle of Chateau Talbot.

"It's ongoing," Daniel said. "Not helped by the fact that she's flat on her back in a hospital bed, but I'm working round it."

"I thought you wanted her flat on her back," Holthouse said, smiling.

"I'm not going to shag her in Moorfields," Daniel said. "I've only once had sex in that place. Tiny Filipina nurse who was so hot I couldn't wait to get her somewhere more appropriate. Phenomenal energy. Phenomenal flexibility. I can see the attraction in these South Asian brides."

"Russian girls," Holthouse said. "They're the best."

"But Susannah," Daniel said, reverting to the original topic because he liked talking about it, "is going to require a lot of patience. A lot of mise-en-scene. At the moment I'm just a kind man about the same age as her father. I'm not sure she even knows that sex exists. I shall have to educate her. I'm thinking Covent Garden. Use the DG's box. All girls are barmy about ballet and she'll've never seen one."

"And she won't see much of this one if all goes according to your wicked plan," Holthouse said laughing.

"The lesson in sex will be strictly post-theatre," Daniel replied. "Performance post-performance."

"And talking of performance," Holthouse quipped, "any Christmas Specials at Number Seventeen in the pipeline?"

"Number Seventeen nights may have to be moth-balled temporarily," Daniel said.

"Disappointing," Holthouse said. "Why?"

"Our hostess is entertaining other visitors over the Festive Season," Daniel replied.

"Damn," Holthouse exclaimed. "How inconsiderate."

"You'll have to fall back on Old Faithful," Daniel said. Holthouse groaned.

"And you'll have to be Father Christmas for the Fourth Mrs. Sullivan," he retorted, "and give her a Christmas Night to remember."

"Not if Miss Leman has been discharged," Daniel said.

"We're a couple of lovable rogues, aren't we Sullivan?" Holthouse said. "They should turn our lives into a TV show."

The cheese selection was brought to their table by the manager. They thought it was on account of their being considered important customers. In reality it was because all three of the waitresses working the shift, tired of being subjected to suggestive remarks and wandering hands, had refused to go near their table again.

❧

"You've got visitors."

Miranda looked up from a magazine. She had only just started to face up to the fact that she would have to learn to read all over again, and was mostly looking at the pictures as a way to flood her mind with new visual images that could be processed and help to make sense of her new world. If that new world was to be permanent. The return to Moorfields had made her realise how fragile her sight was. What an irony, she thought, that having lived in the blind world cotton-wool-cocooned by her parents, the price of continuing sight might be to live in a cotton-wool cocoon.

'Visitors' meant either her family or Daniel Sullivan or Matthew Long, so it was with no enthusiasm that she looked towards the door to see Faith ushering Niall into the room.

"Surprise!" he said.

"Wonderful surprise," Miranda responded, her face transformed. "Christmas wish in fact. Why didn't you let me know you were coming?"

"They told me your calls were being monitored," Niall said smoothly.

"They were," Miranda said, "but Faith went out and bought me an iPhone and none of them know I've got it. Yours and Faith's are the only numbers I've programmed into it," she admitted.

"You memorised my number?" Niall asked, surprised.

"I remember numbers," Miranda said unabashed.

"Bloody Hell, Faith," Niall said. "iPhone. What was it? Big win on the geegees?"

"I don't win anything on the geegees since you stopped giving me tips for Ludlow," Faith retorted.

"So how's it going?" Niall asked, when Faith had settled him in a chair.

"Not so great," Miranda said. "Faith's probably told you."

"She told me celebrity's not all it's cracked up to be."

"I'm just Celebrity Cash in the Attic as far as my family's concerned."

"That must be so tough," Niall said, "when you thought your family really loved you."

"I don't think they don't love me," Miranda said. "They just don't want to try to understand me. They thought when I got eyes it would be like flicking a switch and I'd be normal. They'd have a normal family. But at the same time they hadn't bothered to think that I'd actually be different. I wouldn't need their claustrophobic caring for me in the same way anymore. Then when it all started to go wrong they really panicked."

"Why do you think it went wrong?" Niall asked. "Was it the medication?"

"That's what they think here," Miranda answered, "but they're wrong. We fought over who was going to manage my medication but between all of us we never made a mistake. They've altered the dosage slightly since I've been back in here, but I think it was mostly stress."

"You certainly don't need that right now," Niall said.

"I'm sure that's why they haven't sent me home," Miranda said. "There's nothing the matter with me now. My eyesight's the best it's been yet. They say they're monitoring me but I think they're just keeping me away from my parents."

"Which is why we're here," Faith said. "Well, one of the reasons."

"You've come to take me home?" Miranda said, without any hope in her voice.

"We've come to offer you my home as a place to convalesce," Faith said. "Don't say anything now. Just think it over. You're an adult, you are not obliged to go home to your family if you choose not to. You need to be somewhere where you can relax, start to enjoy life, build yourself up before you put yourself into the public eye. All this nonsense of the last few weeks was too much too soon, and hopefully your parents will realise it. I'm offering you a safe haven in which to get well. Niall's staying with me at the moment and he'll vouch for the fact that it's not a bad place to be, I'm sure."

"It's brilliant," Niall said.

"You're so kind," Miranda said, tears starting in her eyes.

"Jamal – Mr. Daghash – wanted me to look after you and be there for you when you went back out into the world," Faith said. "I'm just trying to carry out his wishes."

Faith and Niall stayed for an hour, and then left, promising to return on Christmas Eve to take her away, if that was what she wanted. Returning to Faith's north London home Niall asked her about Miranda's prognosis.

"Nobody really knows," Faith said. "She's a pioneer. Jamal certainly hoped that her body would accept the eyes with the right medication and she would then have normal vision for the rest of her life, subject to the usual deterioration. The spectre of chronic rejection was something that was always out there, but we all rather hoped it wouldn't happen. Jamal was so disappointed when she was re-admitted."

"But it wasn't chronic rejection," Niall said, "because now she's seeing again."

"So it seems," Faith said. "And we all have to hope that this time things go better."

Walking into the house Niall asked, "So how much did this pile set you back, Faith? Must have cost a fortune, a house this size in London. Didn't realise counsellors were so well paid."

"Niall," Faith replied, "although I know almost everything about you, there is still a great deal you don't know about me." She saw Niall's mother coming out of the kitchen to meet them and winked at her. "For example, once upon a time I was married to a consultant surgeon who earned a great deal of money. We bought this house together, although in those days houses round here were a lot cheaper – relatively speaking – than they are now, because the area hadn't 'come up in the world'."

"And now it has?" Niall asked.

"I like to think it was Graham and I moving in that started it all off," Faith said, grinning.

Niall processed this information as he and his mother fixed Hugo up with some water and Faith made tea.

"So what happened?" he asked at last. "Where's Graham?"

"Niall," his mother interposed, "don't be so direct."

"I'm a journalist, mother," he replied, "direct is what I do."

"Our Graham is Stateside now," Faith said, "lured by the mighty dollar and an earnest young American woman. I don't miss him. We'd grown out of each other. It was all very amicable. We still send each other birthday cards."

When they had settled in front of the fire in Faith's capacious lounge she said,

"And talking of being a journalist, Niall, I've got some information for you."

Niall's head shot up.

"Yeah?"

"Yeah. I asked Jamal some questions about the transplant. I thought as you were helping me out it was only fair if I could do something for you. Anyway, I was wrong about there being a number of possible recipients for the eyes. Susannah was the only one. Exactly how her name came to the top of the pile I don't know, but Jamal said he negotiated it all through Daniel Sullivan at BAB, and in due course Susannah arrived for a preliminary medical exam. Apparently, she ticked all the boxes and then it was just a case of waiting for the right pair of eyes."

"Sounds sick when you put it like that," Niall's mother said.

"That's the truth of the transplant business, I'm afraid," Faith said. "Forever waiting and hoping for somebody else's tragedy."

"When you think of the thousands they must have had to choose from," Niall said.

"Don't blame her, Niall," Faith said. "She never asked."

"I reckon it was carefully planned," Niall said. "They wanted a girl because girls are somehow more vulnerable. BAB stage-managed the whole thing to give them maximum positive exposure."

"I did ask Jamal what he knew about the funding," Faith added, "and whether the Lemans had contributed. He said he really didn't know, and I believe him. He's just not interested in mundane things like that."

"But they must have," Niall said. "Leman must have made some deal with Sullivan, unless they were at school together or are both in the masons or something. I think I may have to contrive a meeting with the guy."

"Leave it till after Christmas," Faith pleaded. "Leave it until

Miranda's made her choice about where she's going to spend the next few weeks of her life."

"I will, don't worry," Niall said. "By then he might be quite keen to see me," he added mysteriously.

"Why?" Faith asked.

"He's already warned me once to stay away from his daughter."

"I wish you'd told me that before," Faith said.

❀

After the rare luxury of a night spent in his own bed, Matthew Long pounded the better-lit areas of Wandsworth Common in the early morning dark of Christmas Eve. Not that he felt unsafe – muggers weren't early risers on the whole. A light drizzle was falling but it still felt good to be in the open air, back in the running groove. He wondered whether the fact that he had started sleeping with Amelia Leman was going to be a good or a bad thing, as far as his reporting of her sister's story was concerned. On the one hand it would give him another perspective on the family and the situation that he could never have expected otherwise to obtain. On the other, the whole point of his assignment was that it was Susannah's perspective, and as far as that was concerned Amelia's insights, which were not entirely complimentary, were unhelpful. His editor had given him the job knowing that girls were attracted to him, in the hope that Susannah might become smitten and provide better copy as a result. What was it someone once wrote about the best laid plans? He'd never been that interested in literature.

He had accepted Amelia's invitation for a drink one evening as they were emerging from Moorfields not long after Susannah's operation. She was an attractive girl and he was currently unattached, having finished with his previous girlfriend three weeks earlier, largely because they'd been together for almost a year and it was starting to feel like a commitment. Saved himself the expense of any anniversary gift in the process.

He and Amelia had gone to a nearby wine bar and after they had both enjoyed a glass he suggested they share a bottle, which she readily agreed to. They talked about – he couldn't really remember what - and then she invited him back to her place. They rode the tube to Archway, where Amelia had a small flat. Once inside she offered him vodka instead of coffee, and a few shots later he had kissed her – or she had kissed him. That had led to pretty serious groping on both sides and then she had suggested he stay the night. It was fair to say he hadn't been slow to take up the suggestion. They had made love with drunken vigour and – on Amelia's part – a great deal of noise, and in the aftermath she had astonished him by reaching for her handbag, pulling out a notebook, and drawing what appeared to be a large erect penis.

"What are you doing?" he asked. "What is that?"

"It's a normal curve," she floored him by replying. Then, at the penis's tip, she drew a vertical line and the date.

"You've lost me," he said.

"I thought that was pretty amazing sex," she said. "What did you think?"

"Yeah – pretty amazing," he agreed.

"So that's our benchmark," she went on. "Every time we make love we can rate it against what we just did."

"Why?" he asked.

"I'm an accountant. And a statistician. These things matter. And because it's fun," she said. "And it's good to talk about it. Then, after a week or so, we can look at the distribution and see whether we need to try harder."

He really didn't get it. Decided it was something she must have read in a magazine. Why did girls have to analyze everything?

"We want sex to be that good every time, don't we?" Amelia continued. He was ready to sleep.

"Yes," he said.

"So that's what we strive for," she said. "Sometimes we'll make it, sometimes we'll exceed it, sometimes we won't. But what we won't do is clam up about it."

Clam up. She was the noisiest lover he'd ever had. Talking, moaning, swearing the whole time if his mouth wasn't pressed on hers. But he had to admit that the sex was unforgettable, and laughing about 'placing it on the prick', as he christened it, did allow them to relive every moment and describe it. On two occasions Amelia's descriptions of what she had felt had turned them both on so much they had had to drop the chat and do it all over again.

Then one morning she had creased him up at work by emailing him a beautiful graphic she had worked up on her tablet.

But all this was moving him further and further from a sympathetic interest in Susannah. Quite apart from anything else, Amelia had seriously fallen out with her sister since the operation, and he found himself taking his lover's part where he should professionally – have been taking Susannah's. In fact, Susannah was not turning into good copy, full stop. She didn't want to share any thoughts and feelings, had had a kind of mental collapse in which she seemed to think she had had a personality transplant and become a different person with a different name, was resisting attempts to bring her into the public domain, and now, to cap it all, was back in hospital and it looked as though the whole operation might have been a failure. His editor had told him to 'put her on the back burner without ever for one minute letting her out of your sight', which was the kind of instruction he was used to receiving. It was possible to argue that sleeping with her sister was keeping her in sight, but he wasn't entirely sure that his boss would agree.

Since that first night back in November he had slept at Amelia's far more than he had slept at his own place, which wasn't exactly a problem, but he did miss some of his routines, and running in the morning was one of them. But now Amelia had gone down to Surrey until after New Year and he didn't want her parents to realise that the journalist who was supposed to be covering one daughter's life was busily employed covering the other. The writer in him enjoyed the pun as he thought of it. Amelia seemed to agree with him as far as her parents were concerned, and they had parted the day before with much kissing and touching of body parts. He had told her to expect to see him at the hospital on Christmas Eve for Susannah's second homecoming, but she had told him that she wasn't planning to be part of the welcoming committee this time round.

So unless he went down to the house he wasn't going to see her for more than a week. Which he wasn't sure he could manage. But on the other hand, did he want to see her and not have sex with her, which would be the order of the day at the family home? No. Bugger.

He stopped running and sat on a wet bench.

He thought back to the media interest the day Susannah had come out of hospital the first time. It had been a dry but dull day, and the pavement outside Moorfields had been a mass of photographers, journalists and curious bystanders, most of whom must have thought some ready-made celebrity was expected instead of a girl whose celebrity status was all ahead of her. Susannah's new eyes were hidden by dark glasses as they all posed for photographs – people seemed happy to include him in the group as if he was family, which was ironic if you thought about it – and then came the calls for her to take the glasses off and show the world what so far only his readers had seen. Jamal Daghash gave the all clear and she took them off, revealing two blinking, beautiful deep brown eyes.

"Two minutes," Daghash had said. "London air's not good for eyes." And the shutters had clicked. There had been statements from all the key players and all in all it had taken the best part of half an hour to get into their cavalcade of cars and away.

Today he imagined the steps of Moorfields would be deserted, and Susannah would step without fanfare, almost anonymously, into the world once more. If she didn't get onto This Is Now or breakfast television soon she would be completely forgotten, and the over-generous sum that had been paid by his employers to the family for exclusive rights to her story would go down in history as one of their biggest ever gaffes. He imagined even heads might roll, just hoped his wasn't one of them.

He got to his feet and started walking slowly back home. The Lemans had told him they were planning to pick Susannah up at eleven. There was no hurry.

◉

Miranda looked at her new, 'sighted' watch – an 'early Christmas present' from Daniel Sullivan. She still had to resist the urge to press it to have it tell her the time. It was just before ten o'clock. Faith had promised that she and Niall would get to Moorfields by ten, so that there was no chance that her parents, who were due at eleven, could spirit her away before they arrived. Miranda had made the decision very quickly that she did want to stay with Faith and Niall (he would have described it as a 'no-brainer'), but she was dreading the scene that would follow when she told her parents, and hoped that she really did have the courage to stand up for herself and go through with it. She knew that Susannah would not have done. She hoped and prayed that Miranda did. Not least because Niall would think less of her if she backed down under pressure, and Niall thinking less of her was not to be borne.

Then there was the complication of last night's visit from Daniel Sullivan, following up his early Christmas present with an offer to take her to The Nutcracker at Covent Garden the day after Boxing Day. The idea of going to the ballet thrilled her; the idea of spending an evening with Daniel Sullivan did not; and she could already imagine what Niall would have to say about it. But how could you say 'no' when somebody made an offer like that? He had tickets for a box. Goodness knows what they must have cost. She wanted to believe he was motivated only by kindness, but she had watched enough television drama, even before she could see, to know that people's motives were rarely innocent.

Susannah's life had been simple, anonymous and safe. Niall would say it was dull. Miranda's was the opposite. She just hoped she was ready. And strong enough.

She was dressed and packed when Faith and Niall arrived at ten fifteen. "Problems on the tube," Faith explained. Miranda told them her decision, but said she was going to need their help with her family.

"For sure," Faith said.

Faith had hoped that Jamal Daghash would be there to second the idea of convalescing with her, but he was abroad, so only Dr. Clarke would be on hand to put the medical argument. She hoped he would be sensible and support the patient's wishes.

"I wish we could leave now and just run away before they arrive," Miranda said.

"That wouldn't be the right way," Faith said. "Sometimes things have to be faced head-on."

"I know," Miranda said sadly.

"Do you think it would be better if I was out of sight?" Niall asked. "I just think knowing I'm involved could make things worse as far as your Dad's concerned."

"No please stay," Miranda said quickly.

"I'd rather he knew," Faith said. "I don't want any accusations of half-truths or dishonesty."

It was just before eleven when Dr. Clarke, Roderick and Karin Leman, and Matthew Long arrived. Their welcoming smiles died on their faces as they saw Faith and Niall.

"What's this?" Roderick Leman demanded, looking at each of them in turn.

"Good morning Mr. Leman," Faith said calmly.

"Good morning," he responded grudgingly. "Have you come to see Susannah off?"

"No," Faith said. "Miranda?" She looked at her expectantly.

"Please can we drop the Miranda nonsense," Roderick snapped.

"Faith's invited me to go and convalesce at her house," Miranda said in a trembling voice.

"No," Roderick said loudly. He turned on Faith. "Interfering woman. This is none of your business."

"On the contrary," Faith said, not in the least intimidated. "It is entirely my business. I am a professional charged with Miranda's wellbeing. In my professional opinion, after the fiasco last time, it would be medically advisable for her to stay somewhere secure and free of emotional trauma while she attempts to recover from her operation. Jamal Daghash would agree with me if he were here."

"I forbid it," Roderick said, looking to Dr. Clarke. "This is my daughter we're talking about."

"Your daughter," Faith replied, "is twenty-two years old. She has an absolute right to make her own choice. Once made, you have no right or power to overturn that choice."

"Say something Clarke," Roderick barked. "This is an outrage."

"I can't disagree with Miss Hodgkiss," Dr. Clarke said.

"You bloody ass," Roderick snarled.

"Don't Roderick," Karin Leman interposed, touching his arm.

"And what's Blind Pew to do with this?" Roderick Leman went on, looking at Niall.

"Niall is staying with me over Christmas," Faith said quickly before Niall could rise to the bait. "It'll be nice for Miranda to have someone her own age to talk to."

"If you go through with this," Roderick threatened, "you can expect to hear from my solicitor. This is tantamount to kidnap."

Faith smiled. Roderick Leman turned to his daughter.

"And you, young lady," he said, saliva showering from his mouth as he spat out the words, "if this is what you want, to deny your own family after everything we've done and sacrificed for you since the day you were born, well so be it. Don't ever darken our doors again. I won't want to see you. I won't want to hear from you. As far as I'm concerned you won't even exist."

Miranda started to cry.

"That's right," he went on, "the woman's ploy. If in doubt, turn on the waterworks. You're an ungrateful little cow and I have no sympathy. You'll break your mother's heart; Amelia just won't understand, as indeed I don't. I don't know what's happened to you. As far as I'm concerned this operation has been a disaster. It's the worst thing that's ever happened to you in your entire life."

"Shame when it cost so much money," Niall couldn't resist saying.

"I beg your pardon?" Roderick Leman blustered. "I strongly

suggest you keep your mouth shut if you want to go home with any teeth at all."

Niall was about to answer but Faith put a hand on his arm.

"Mrs. Leman," Faith said, ignoring Roderick. "Karin, this is just temporary. Just to give her a chance for a calm, quiet convalescence."

"Our house is calm," Karin Leman said.

"You think we fucked up the medication," Roderick said, turning on Dr. Clarke again. "This is your way of saying we're incompetent. We can't be trusted to look after our own daughter. For fuck's sake!"

"Please don't start swearing Roderick," Karin said.

"Where's Daniel Sullivan?" Roderick blurted out. "The British Association for the Blind should have a say in this."

"It's actually nothing to do with them," Faith said quietly. "But in any case, I do a lot of work for the Association, so you can work on the assumption that I represent their views in this matter."

"What did we do wrong?" Karin Leman asked sadly.

"It's not about right and wrong," Faith said, although privately she thought keeping the girl like a prisoner and confiscating her means of communication with the outside world were considerable wrongs. "Understandably, you were all very emotional when Susannah Miranda came home. Emotion on all sides causes stress. That stress may have been a factor in her deteriorating sight. We don't know. But I'm not her mother, so I won't be emotionally involved in her recovery, whether it goes well or badly. My home is just a safe haven. A half-way house. I'm not trying to steal her from you."

"You're a fucking smooth operator," Roderick Leman said. "I'll give you that."

"Please don't swear," Karin said again. "It doesn't help."

"Now my wife's trying to tell me what I can and can't say," Roderick sneered. "It's a fucking female conspiracy."

"What's it to be then, Miranda?" Faith said, turning to her. "No point prolonging the pain."

"I'd like to come with you," Miranda said, her voice a croaking whisper, tears running down her cheeks. "It's not your fault, Mum. It's nobody's fault. It's just – what I want. I'm not leaving you for ever."

Karin Leman threw her arms round her daughter and both of them sobbed.

"I'm sorry, darling," Karin managed to choke out.

"Don't be sorry," Miranda said. "You don't need to be sorry."

"Unbelievable," Roderick Leman scoffed. "This isn't over," he snapped as he turned on his heel and left the room.

Matthew Long stood, mouth agape like a haddock, wondering whether his editor would be interested in an account of what had just transpired in front of him. Amelia certainly would be.

❦

As they rode the tube home Niall and Miranda kept showering Faith with praise for the way she had managed things at Moorfields.

"'If you can keep your head when those around you are losing theirs,'" Faith said.

For Miranda, it was her first sighted experience of the London Underground. Niall was wrestling with an ethical dilemma. Yes, he wanted to help Miranda: he had promised Faith that he would. But he also wanted to pursue his investigation into the funding of her operation. The more he thought about it, the more convinced he became that Daniel Sullivan had accepted some kind of bribe or 'donation' from Roderick Leman which had pushed Miranda to the head of the queue for the eye transplant. Had that donation gone into the coffers of BAB, or had some of it – or all of it – found its way into Sullivan's own pocket? Somehow, he had to find out. But the big question was, could he tell Miranda what he was up to? Could he maybe even enlist her help? Or was that, under the circumstances, bordering on the insensitive?

ELEVEN

On Christmas morning Faith sent Niall, Miranda and Hugo out for a walk while she prepared Christmas lunch. Gifts, according to her own family tradition, were not opened until after the main meal. It was a mild, dull, but dry day, and the streets were more or less deserted.

"Don't get us lost, will you?" Niall said to Miranda.

"I'll try not to," she said, "but you may be better off relying on Hugo."

Hugo's ears twitched at the sound of his name, but he made no obvious response.

They walked the length of Faith's road and then discovered a small park at the end of it.

"Park or street?" Miranda asked.

"Park," Niall said. "There might be somewhere to sit down."

"We're supposed to be out for a walk," Miranda said laughing.

"Exercise is totally over-rated," Niall said. "You wait – in a few years scientists will prove that it's bad for you and slobbing around on a sofa makes you live longer."

"If you say so," Miranda said. "I like walking."

"Makes a difference when you can see where you're going," Niall said.

"OK. I'm sorry," she replied.

"No that's not what I meant," Niall responded quickly. "Look I really am pleased for you about your eyes."

"Yeah," Miranda said thoughtfully. "I tried to figure out what I felt that day when I woke up blind again. It was like I was being offered the chance to go back to the life that I'd had, the life that I knew and understood. If someone had asked me the day before, I'd've said that I would have been happy to take it. But when it came to it I wasn't. I was at the beginning of this incredible seeing adventure and I wasn't ready for it to end. I really really really do want to see."

"I knew you would," Niall said.

"But I am terrified that I'll lose it again."

"Yes. Now that is a place I have been."

They walked three times round the park sharing blind and sighted memories. Niall took Miranda's arm and let Hugo off the lead.

"Now you can find out what it's like being a sighted guide," he said to her.

"I expect I'll be rubbish," Miranda said. She attempted to describe the park to him and he attempted to fill in gaps in her own knowledge from his own store of sighted memories.

"How did you first find out there was a chance you were going to have the operation?" Niall asked, trying not to sound as if he was probing.

"I can hardly remember," Miranda said. "I was sitting having tea in the kitchen and my Dad came in and said how would I feel about being able to see, if there was an operation that could make it happen."

She paused, trying to remember the details.

"Then my Mum said there wasn't and my Dad said yes there might be. He'd been speaking to someone who knew a lot about these things and they were really close to an eye transplant operation. My Mum sort of burst out crying and said how wonderful if it could be me. My Dad said he was going to do his damnedest to see that it was me."

"And what did you think?"

"You know what I thought. But I'm glad now. Even if my body does reject the eyes eventually. I'm glad I've had the chance to see, even if only for a few weeks, and I'm glad because if I hadn't had the transplant I'd never've met you."

"You're going to have to learn that being honest can leave you extremely vulnerable," Niall said.

"I've always been vulnerable," Miranda said. "I just never realised how much until now."

"So anyway," Niall went on, getting back to his theme, "what was it that your Dad did that was 'his damnedest'?"

"I don't know," Miranda replied. "Next I knew I had an appointment at Moorfields for a preliminary medical to see if I was a suitable candidate for the operation."

"What does your Dad do for a living?"

"He's an architect. Works with a big London firm who do a lot of work in the middle east. He goes to Dubai and Doha a lot."

"Have you ever been?"

"No. Why all this interest in my Dad all of a sudden?"

"You have to get to know your enemy," Niall said with a smile in his voice.

"Oh Niall."

"He hates me," Niall said. "He told me to keep away from you."

"And you ignored him."

"Too right."

"But I thought you hadn't," Miranda said. "You went back to Shropshire and you never called."

"I know. I'm sorry."

"Did you ever finish your article about me?"

"No."

"Oh."

They walked in silence for a while.

"What ever happened to that bench we were going to sit on?" Niall asked.

"They're all covered in rain from yesterday," Miranda said.

"OK. No problem. We don't really want to sit down to Faith's Christmas lunch with a wet arse."

They talked about their experiences of Christmas from childhood onwards. Niall told her about sighted Christmases and blind Christmases. Miranda talked about Christmases that had been big family affairs, something Niall had never known. They talked about plans for the rest of the week. Faith had already announced that as soon as Miranda felt up to it they would 'hit the sales' so that she could get her first experience of London's Christmas lights. They also had to get her something to wear for Covent Garden. Niall had felt a surge of irrational jealousy when Miranda had told them about Daniel Sullivan's invitation. He had tried to persuade her to back out, but Faith had stopped him.

"I'm sure he means kindly," she had said, "And what a wonderful opportunity. I'll go if you don't."

Niall's dire warnings that Miranda should be on her guard because Sullivan was a 'lecherous old goat' had been ignored.

Getting cold and hungry they called Hugo, who had been chasing birds, 'retrieving' anything that he could pick up in his mouth, and getting covered in mud, put him on the lead and set off back to the house.

"Here we are," Miranda said as they reached the gate. "Number 17. I didn't get us lost."

"What number?" Niall asked sharply.

"17. It's Faith's house number. I checked when we started."

❦

"Susannah. You look beautiful." Daniel bore down on her outside the imposing portico of the Royal Opera House. She didn't feel particularly beautiful, she felt cold, having refused to hide her new Top Shop dress under the only scruffy coat that she owned.

"Please call me Miranda," she said. She had spent several hours the day before with Faith and Niall, shopping and trying on, exhausting herself and testing Niall's patience to the limit in the process. Finally she had settled on a dress and a pair of River Island shoes which were starting to rub blisters on her heels. Shopping had been a lot easier when she couldn't see.

Daniel Sullivan sighed.

"That makes you Caliban, I suppose," Faith said smiling. She had insisted on escorting Miranda to Covent Garden.

"Thank you, Miss Hodgkiss," Daniel said. "Always a pleasure."

They left Faith and went inside. While Miranda tried to take in the people and the surroundings, Daniel steered her towards the Perrier Jouet Bar, where he bought a bottle of champagne.

"No point in going to the ROH if you don't do it in style," he said.

Miranda watched the bubbles rising in their columns, fascinated by the way they seemed to start from nothing. She had drunk champagne before – once – and remembered the feel of it on her tongue, but seeing it, watching it, was magical.

"Thank you so much for this," she said.

"The pleasure is all mine," Daniel said. "You've got a lot of experience to catch up on. Anything I can help with I will be happy, no, I will be honoured to. Just say the word." He downed his first glass and refilled it.

"You need to drink up," he said. "Show starts in twenty minutes."

Dutifully Miranda drank, although she found the wine very dry and the bubbles made gulping it down difficult. As soon as her glass was empty, Daniel filled it again.

"Enjoy being anonymous while you can," he said. "In a couple of months you won't be able to sit in a bar without being recognized."

"Why?"

"As soon as everybody's sure your sight has stabilized we need to get you out there and shout it from the rooftops. You're a lovely looking girl, and what's happened to you is not much short of miraculous. You can't hide. Can't hide this beautiful face." He put the palm of his hand on her cheek. She didn't like it, so reached for some more champagne.

"Good girl," he said.

They finished the bottle as the final call was made for them to take their seats. Miranda stumbled as she got to her feet, and Daniel took hold of her, steering her to their box. She would have liked to have visited the bathroom, but there wasn't time. She barely had an opportunity to open the programme Daniel had bought her and look out over the sea of people in the stalls before the house lights started to dim and she became aware of the orchestra in the pit. She felt bombarded by visual stimuli and the champagne in her head was giving everything the mixed up, random quality of a dream. The conductor was applauded to the podium and then the music began, spiriting her away into Tchaikovsky's world, the bright colours and costumes a kaleidoscope of magic in her head.

◉

There was nothing kaleidoscopic about Simon's local in Chiswick, but it was there that Niall had arranged to spend the evening to take his mind off Miranda in the clutches of Daniel Sullivan. Simon had been initially cagey until Niall had made it clear that he was staying at Faith's, so wasn't on the look-out for unsuspecting hospitality. Once that was clarified he had been enthusiastic. "Got things to tell you," he had said.

And so Niall, early, courtesy of his inevitable taxi, sipped his beer and considered the shifting landscape inside his mind. Faith lived at number 17. OK, it could be a coincidence, but who was he kidding? Faith knew people at Moorfields, Faith knew people at BAB. She also had no idea that he knew anything about the meetings at number 17 because he had never mentioned them when he had discussed the story with her. To be honest, he had all-but forgotten them himself until Miranda had dropped the bombshell on Christmas morning. What did all that mean? If the meetings at number 17 were connected with whatever wasn't kosher about the eye transplant, then Faith was involved in it. In which case, was there something sinister in her exerting herself to get him and Miranda under her roof? Then, she knew he was curious about aspects of the eye transplant, especially the financial aspects – was she keeping him where she could see him and monitor what he was up to? Feeding him information which was designed to steer him away from the truth, whatever that truth was?

But could he believe that Faith, whom he had known and cared for, if not loved, for nearly two decades, was involved in something shady? Surely not. Surely not? It was too depressing to contemplate. And now, like the witch in Hansel and Gretel, she was fattening him and Miranda up to eat them later on. He mustn't, under any circumstances, give her occasion to suspect that he knew. That way he maintained a position of strength. He could observe her closely while she thought she was above suspicion, treating any information that she did push his way with a healthy degree of scepticism. He would have to go through the motions of following up any leads she gave him, but not to the extent that he took his eye off the ball. The ball which had landed so fortuitously in his court.

"Niall?" Simon arrived with the assistance of a barman who promised to courier them a couple of fresh pints.

"Hey. Happy Christmas. How's it going?"

"Good actually," Simon said.

"Great," Niall replied. "Erica OK?"

"Erica's fantastic. You frightened her friends back off to Oz so we've got two new girls living with us."

"Hm, sounds like I should come round."

"Forget it. You did enough damage the first time."

"OK. OK," Niall conceded. "So. You said you had things to tell me?"

"Did I?" Simon said vacuously. "Yes. OK. I've got a job."

"You've what?" Niall spluttered.

"I've got a job," Simon repeated. "Possibly not what you'd call a proper job, but I'm getting paid for it."

"That's fantastic," Niall said. "More than I've got."

"You could get one if you stopped fannying about and applied for one," Simon said.

"Suddenly you're the expert."

"Yes." Their beer arrived and they toasted each other before Simon went on, "It's a new charity – Victory it's called. The V I stands for V.I. and the C stands for computers, but I don't think the Tory stands for anything. They just got as far as VIC and they couldn't think of an acronym to finish the word off."

"Nothing to do with the Conservative Party?" Niall asked.

"Definitely not," Simon said. "It's a charity that gets laptops and technology to blind kids in mainstream schools and trains them up on how to use them. I'm one of the trainers."

"Brilliant, man," Niall said enthusiastically. "That is a perfect job for you. And it sounds like a good charity as well."

"Yes. It's new," Simon explained. "Set up by a couple who had a blind kid and decided they wanted to embrace the blind world."

"Good for them," Niall said.

"So what have you got to tell me?" Simon asked, picking up his beer. Niall brought him up to speed on his return to London.

"The transplant was definitely dodgy," he finished. "I've never been more certain of anything. And Faith lives at number 17."

"No!"

"Yes. I'm staying in the actual house that holds part of the key to the whole mystery."

"They say walls have ears," Simon said.

"If you find a way of communicating with them, let me know."

"You'll have to get Susannah to do some ferreting around."

"Miranda. But how can I tell her that her life-changing operation was phoney?"

"It wasn't the operation, though, was it?" Simon pointed out.

"I never heard anything from Lindsey," Niall said, following a different train of thought.

"I did," Simon said.

"You did?" Niall responded, choking on a throatful of beer. "When?"

"You know how it is," Simon went on. "The blind world's a small world. I met her at the Victory interview. She was going for one of their admin jobs. Which she got."

"So tell me more," Niall said. "You obviously spoke to her."

"She resigned from BAB. Loosemore went to see her. Told her she could depend on a really good reference if she agreed to go without a fuss. Apparently her boyfriend advised her to do it, and then Juliette Warwick phoned her and told her about Victory, saying she should go for it."

"So it was a done deal," Niall mused. "No wonder she didn't call me. She knew I'd accuse her of caving in. You know what this means, Simon old son? It means there's a link between BAB and Victory. It means you've inadvertently got yourself in on the ground floor of this whole investigation."

"Oh no." Simon groaned.

❧

Her head light from champagne and buzzing with Tchaikovsky, Miranda sat enjoying the seclusion of a toilet cubicle in the interval of The Nutcracker, having persuaded Daniel, eventually, that she was capable of finding the Ladies unaided. She was reflecting on Dr. Clarke's injunction before she left hospital the first time, namely that she should avoid putting herself in any situations where she might be liable to infection. And here she now was, one of an audience of goodness knows how many, carrying goodness knows what germs, and hiding out in a public lavatory, which, if everything her mother had told her since she was a small girl was true, was a kind of holiday camp for bacteria. And yet nobody had raised this point when the invitation was given, not Daniel Sullivan, not Faith, not even Niall. Shouldn't she be wearing some kind of surgical mask impregnated with disinfectant? Which would, admittedly, rather detract from the effect of her dress, hair and the make-up she had painstakingly applied with Faith's help ("Not that I'm any kind of expert," Faith had commented). But what if her currently compromised immune system were to be confronted with something it couldn't deal with? Something beyond its recuperative powers. She would feel a real fool, and she might be risking her sighted future. Belatedly, pointlessly, she held a hand over her mouth and nose.

She was enjoying the privacy of the cubicle, being away from any requirement to listen or make conversation. Since the operation her life seemed to be an endless sequence of questions requiring answers, and the answers that she gave were never quite the right ones, which meant more questions. Solitude brought the only true peace, bathrooms pretty much the only sanctuary.

She listened to the conversations of the women outside her door, criticising the costumes, criticising the dancing. She was surprised. She had found the dancing flawless, impressive, athletic, and wondered what it was that these more discerning eyes were looking for. There were also more personal conversations about partners who were there or not there with them, about other women in the audience, but these were uninteresting, except for the way that they illustrated what a visual place the world was, and how much people were judged for the way they looked. So new, so different. Literally, an eye-opener.

The bell rang, summoning people back to their seats. Miranda stood up. She could look forward to the second half with an empty bladder. She paused briefly at the mirror after washing her hands. It was very hard not to be drawn to mirrors. There she was: the bruising around her eyes had almost completely subsided. Faith had said, "'Eyes put in with the coal-man's finger,' as my grandmother used to say about dark-ringed eyes. Some would call it a very sexy look." Miranda found it hard to think that a dirty finger could be sexy, but she looked long and hard at her face, hoping it was attractive. Then another bell rang, forcing her out of self-contemplation, and she walked out into the confusion of audience members moving swiftly and seemingly in all directions.

She tried to get her bearings: she had been so adamant that she would have no difficulty finding and returning from the Ladies; had scorned Daniel's offered assistance. Now she looked round her and was baffled. Anger at her own carelessness and incompetence surged inside her, bringing tears to the corner of her eyes. She hadn't even memorised their box number, so couldn't ask for directions like some pathetic helpless fawn.

And then she saw Daniel approaching, avuncular arm outstretched.

"Was starting to think you'd got lost," he said, and she had to smile and bite her lip to conceal the surge of rage that threatened to overwhelm her. Rage because she was so relieved to see him, rage because she had allowed herself to get into a position where it was a relief to be found, rage because it had occurred to him that she might get lost and need looking for, rage because she had let herself down and felt that she had somehow broken her promise to Niall that she would remain on her guard, because in this moment of relief she had completely exposed her vulnerability.

Daniel took her arm and she allowed herself to be led meekly back to the box, where another bottle of champagne awaited her.

"Thought you'd be ready for another drink," Daniel said, raising his glass. "To arts and culture," he said, "and many more pleasant evenings such as this."

Miranda smiled weakly and drank.

❧

"Simon's got a job," Niall said to Faith as they sat drinking raspberry tea and instant decaffeinated coffee respectively, awaiting Miranda's return.

"Brilliant," Faith replied.

"With a new blind charity – Victory."

"Oh – Victory."

"You know about it?"

"Yes," Faith confessed. "They invited me to be one of their trustees. I declined."

"Because?"

"Variety of reasons. I have quite enough going on in my life without it. Computers really aren't my thing. And Vivien Loosemore is their patron. You know I never really had a great deal of time for her."

"That's interesting."

"Is it?"

"Yes," Niall said non-committally, his mind in overdrive. Vivien Loosemore. She had seemed a peripheral player at best, but now her name kept cropping up. She was moving into the frame. And she was an easy target. If he could get all the background on her, find a way to confront her, she would inevitably blunder again, and this time he wouldn't let her off the hook. He reflected on the narrow confines of the world of disabled charities, which saw people of profoundly limited capabilities hoovering up all the top jobs. Luck, accident and happenstance had seen Loosemore, a lower-division private school principal, stumble into the role of Head at the old alma mater. There the consequences of her own ineptitude had successfully been attributed to others' failings, and she had become a pillar of the establishment, treasured by BAB and sought after for the letterheads of fledgling charities. It was a small pond full of amateur, incompetent, self-important and self-satisfied fish, the disabled charity world.

He pressed his watch and it reported 11.12 pm.

"Shouldn't she be back by now?" he asked.

"Certainly the Nutcracker isn't long," Faith reflected.

"Bastard's spirited her away for a curry," Niall said.

"I don't see Daniel as a vindaloo man," Faith said, smiling. "I would say a wine bar's more likely."

"You're supposed to be looking after her."

"I am. She'll be fine. Daniel wouldn't dare try anything. He's got too much to lose."

"I can't stand the man," Niall seethed.

"Do I detect a hint of jealousy?" Faith asked.

"You're joking," Niall snapped, too quickly. "I just want her to be safe."

"Of course."

They heard a car pull up outside. Then nothing for a minute and a half. Then a car door opening and closing. Footsteps on the path. And the doorbell. Hugo leapt into action and was first to the door, with Faith some way behind.

"How was it?" she asked, as she let Miranda in.

"Amazing," Miranda said, but with a detectable lack of conviction. "I've had far too much to drink."

"Come in and sit down," Faith said solicitously, trying to feed the pair of them around Hugo, who was enthusiastically obstructing the hall corridor.

"I think I need to go to bed," Miranda said.

"I'll help you up," Faith said.

"Sullivan try anything?" Niall called from the lounge.

"Ignore him," Faith said. Miranda did. For the past hour she had been trying to say as little as possible. Words seemed to rearrange themselves and their components inside her mouth, emerging scrambled and devoid of meaning.

"G'night," Niall called out through clenched teeth.

In her room at the top of the house Miranda lay down on the bed and closed her eyes. Relief flooded through her. The second half of the ballet had become an ordeal: she had tried to focus on the dancing, but her eyes were losing responsiveness and Daniel kept breaking her concentration to force more champagne on her, which she had – in the end – quite forcibly refused. Daniel had borne it with a shrug, but she could tell that he wasn't happy about it. She was disappointed that the narrative of the ballet seemed to dry up, just to be replaced by a sequence of dances: all perfectly pleasing on the eye, but no longer telling a story. But more disappointing was the growing conviction that Daniel's intentions were to get her drunk and then presumably seduce her. It was exactly as Niall had foreseen, and she felt her own naivety in having believed otherwise. Guiding her through the crowds at the end of the performance Daniel had put his arm round her in a proprietary way which she knew she was meant to interpret as protective; he had led her down a series of side-streets to get to his car, when she had assumed they would be taking a taxi, not least because Daniel had drunk at least a bottle of champagne.

"Should you drive after drinking that much?" she had asked.

"Darling, I drive better after a bottle of champagne," had been his response.

She hadn't enjoyed his driving, or his repeated attempts to put his hand on her leg. Then he had started asking probing questions about Niall, but not questions such as a jealous admirer might ask – nothing about their relationship or what she thought about him. Rather they were questions about how she had met him, the sort of things they talked about, whether Niall had asked her questions about her operation or her medication. She couldn't help wondering whether her father hadn't set up the whole evening as a pretext for the interrogation, offering anything that Daniel was able to get from her in the physical line as bait: she had never felt close to her father, but since her operation he seemed to have become a total stranger, someone of whom she knew nothing but could believe anything.

Daniel had been irritated by the vagueness of her answers. She heard the self-control in his stale treacle pudding voice stretched to breaking point. She had been incredibly relieved when they had turned into Faith's road and pulled up outside the house. At that point Daniel had seemed to decide to cut his losses and rebuild broken bridges in the hope of securing a rematch. She responded non-committally and – she hoped – politely, although she was aware by this time that her sentences were only partly her own. She left unspoken her decision that she would never accept any invitation from him again.

❦

Sitting angrily on his own bed Niall imagined the worst. Daniel kissing Miranda, Daniel fondling her breasts telling her that they were like two choice fruits brimming with juice demanding to be sucked, Daniel running his hand up her inner thigh telling her these were experiences and sensations she needed to catch up on, even though they had nothing to do with sight.

But why did he care? What was Miranda Leman to him? A friend, a responsibility. How could he shoulder his responsibility if she kept gadding off with lecherous older men who could impress her with the size of their cars and wallets? She had ignored his advice, let him down. And Lindsey had ignored him, because she knew she wasn't going to listen to his advice. Women knew exactly how to piss you off and make you feel redundant.

EYES OF THE BLIND

It was nearly a quarter to midnight. So what? He rang Lindsey's number. She took a long time to answer and when she did it was obvious she'd been asleep.

"Hello?" she said, confused.

"Merry Christmas!" Niall said.

"Niall? Are you drunk?"

"Far from it. No festive Yuletide cheer for yours truly. How's it going? What are you up to?"

"Well, I'm up to nothing. I'm lying in bed. I was asleep, and then some idiot phoned me."

"Good job they did. Life's too short and precious to waste time sleeping."

"Mine's not," Lindsey said darkly.

"I just heard from Simon that you'd got a new job and I wanted to congratulate you."

"Thanks. But what you really want to do is give me grief over the fact that I didn't fight BAB all the way to the disciplinary."

"I don't actually. You made the right call."

"You don't mean that."

"I do. We took legal advice. You acted on it."

"OK. I'm surprised. I'm suspicious. But thanks for the vote of confidence."

"And you've got in on the ground floor of a new charity venture. Sounds great."

"It is. Don't come to the office!"

"Lindsey!" Niall complained. "It wasn't my fault that BAB decided to kick you out."

"Funny. I thought you thought it was."

"Look. Can we let bygones be bygones?"

"We always have."

"Do you see much of Vivien Loosemore in your new job?"

"Nothing at all. There's no story, no nothing. You stay in Shropshire and I'll stay here."

"And a Happy New Year to you too. Actually I'm in London."

"Staying with Simon again? I'm amazed."

"No. Frying other fish this time."

"Oh, OK. Erica will be pleased."

"Right."

"So if that's it, I'll bid you good night."

"Where is Victory's office?"

"No, Niall. Please. Just leave me alone."

"OK."

"Happy New Year. I hope things work out for you."

"Yeah, thanks. You too."

"Goodnight."

"Goodnight."

Lindsey's boyfriend stirred in the bed beside her.

"Who the Hell was that?" he asked.

"Just my ex ringing to congratulate me on my new job and trying to hook up with me again."

"Niall Burnet?"

"Well remembered. Are you jealous?"

"Where is he?"

"In London. You are jealous."

"Should I be?"

"Absolutely not."

TWELVE

The director and presenters of early evening chat show This Is Now were having a council of war. All three had serious concerns following the rehearsal for the January 29th edition of the programme. The one-time blind girl with the new eyes had said practically nothing, there was clearly some difficult chemistry between her and her parents, and the production team's third choice of 'professional' – after the surgeon, who was abroad, and the doctor in charge of the girl's aftercare, who had point-blank refused – had turned out to be an absolute nightmare, so keen to jump at his five minutes of fame that he had trampled all over everyone, including the presenters, in his attempt to ensure his place in the spotlight.

"This is in danger of being right up there with Parkinson's interview of Meg Ryan," the director, Lucy Sturmey, said. The reference was lost on both her presenters, who were too young to remember it and would have struggled to identify the Barnsley broadcaster in a celebrity line-up.

"She was so monosyllabic I was almost glad when the goon from the charity got going," Melissa McEvoy, the show's Scottish female presenter said.

"I wasn't," Sturmey said decisively. "We need to start with her, away from all distractions and with no-one to speak for her. Not Mum, especially not Dad, not the journalist, no-one. You'll have her on her own for three minutes, then we'll go to the VT of Derek's tour of British swimming pools, then we'll come back and we'll have Mum and the charity man with her."

"Don't you think a rant from Dad might be good for the ratings?" Jon Allen, the other presenter, offered.

"You could walk up into the audience to ask him for a comment," Melissa suggested.

"What I really want is for you two to make something of the girl," Sturmey said. "She's the story. Probe. Do boys look better than they sound? Get an answer. Which boy is she talking about? I don't want politics, I want human interest. Once upon a time she couldn't see. Now she can. She's a living, walking miracle. But keep off the operation because we're running this without the fucking surgeon, only don't ask me why. Keep away from the science because if you go there our audience are going to be thinking why the fuck haven't they got someone on who can answer the science questions. Keep it light, keep it personal, but get her to talk. It's your job."

"Trust us," Jon said. "We won't let you down."

"You did this afternoon," Sturmey said.

❦

Miranda was in make-up, being made to feel special by a young man who had introduced himself as Adam.

"Your skin is just amazing," he said. "I know I keep saying it but, really, I don't think you realise how amazing it is."

"I don't," Miranda said.

"Then look! Look girl! Use your eyes!" And he winked at her to show that he knew that using her eyes was a very novel experience. The trouble was that in the weeks since New Year, despite all the care she had taken with her medication, despite living a very simple life, Miranda was very aware that her eye-sight had deteriorated. Subtly at first, so that she had put it down to tiredness, but the blurring was increasing, and she had had two moments when she hadn't been able to see at all. Unable to bear the thought that she might be rejecting the eyes again, she had kept quiet about it, hoping with each new day that it would turn out to have been a blip, but she had now reached the point where it could no longer be ignored, and she had promised herself that she would tell Faith as soon as the dreaded television interview was over.

She had become very attached to Faith in the time since her trip to the ballet. Things had been awkward between her and Niall, and, although she hated it, she didn't know how to make it right between them again, so she had gravitated to Faith and found her very kind and understanding. When Daniel had called at the house proffering further invitations Faith had gone to the door and rejected them on her behalf, giving the excuse that she had been knocked out by the exertions of the ballet trip and really needed to rest and recuperate indoors. Daniel had offered to come in and 'brighten up her day', but Faith had told him that their days were bright enough.

When her agent had got in touch about *This Is Now* interview her first instinct had been to make some health-related excuse and get out of it, but Faith had persuaded her that this was something that couldn't and shouldn't be avoided, and the sooner she allowed herself to become public property, the sooner the public would be finished with her, if that was what she wanted. Niall had snarled about the interview, but he had done little other than snarl at her since Christmas; however, she was adamant that she wanted him to be in the audience on the day, and, with input from Faith, he had eventually been persuaded to attend.

The shock had come at the afternoon rehearsal, where she had found herself sharing a sofa with Daniel Sullivan, when she had been led to believe by the agent – and had really been looking forward to it as a result – that Mr. Daghash was going to be there. Daniel had treated her as his own personal accessory and allowed himself the luxury of putting his arm round her and touching her in all manner of unobtrusive but apparently intimate ways.

"You know, you couldn't've got a better pair of eyes if you'd ordered them off the internet," Adam was saying. "Beautiful, beautiful, coffee with a splash of milk. And those little flecks! Like copper stars in a chocolate sky."

"If you say so," Miranda said.

"You're not thrilled about being on telly then?" Adam went on, applying a brown mascara to her eye-lashes.

"No," Miranda said. "I'm just so ordinary."

"Hardly," Adam said. "God I'd love to be on a reality show. Anything to get noticed. I've applied five times to go on Big Brother. I'd win it, no probs, but I've never even had an interview."

"I don't want to be famous," Miranda said. "I just want to see."

"Celebrity's wasted on celebs," he said. "Most of them don't realise what they've got."

"I'm just sitting here hoping I don't muck up a live interview," Miranda said.

"Nothing you could do could possibly muck it up," Adam said encouragingly. "Everyone will love you because you look absolutely gorgeous, and because of what you've been through, and if you get stuck just get emotional. It gets me going every time."

"Thanks," Miranda said.

The producer had wanted all 'Miranda's party' to sit together in the audience, but a compromise had eventually been arrived at which saw Faith and Niall on one side of a stepped aisle and Roderick, Karin and Amelia Leman – with Matthew in tow – on the other. Hugo had also come – "He deserves his crack at celebrity," Niall had said to Faith, "and I don't want to be hanging on your arm all night like some pathetic species of parasite" – and was stationed on the aisle by Niall's feet in a position of considerable prominence, should a cameraman happen to pick him out. He looked pleased with the arrangement.

Niall had been battling demons since the night of *The Nutcracker*. His anger that Miranda had accepted Sullivan's invitation was exacerbated by the fact that she wouldn't talk to him about the evening, and compounded by anger at himself for being angry. He had also observed the growing closeness between Miranda and Faith, which had made him jealous on the one hand and anxious on the other. He believed now that Faith and Sullivan were working together: to what end he could not as yet figure out, but he couldn't think of a way to broach the subject with Miranda without sounding petty, jealous or a complete fantasist.

Hugo had been his only real comfort, but Niall could sense that even he was getting tired of listless inactivity, which had been their predominant state in the weeks following Christmas. What they both needed was something to kick-start the transplant story, and here he was sitting across the aisle from Roderick Leman, waiting for the warm-up act to get them into a responsive mood. It was, surely, too good an opportunity to miss.

"Mr. Leman?" Niall said, his head turned in what he thought must be Roderick's direction. He heard Leman pretend not to hear him, and his wife urging him from the other side to respond.

"Yes?" he said, impatience and disdain clear in his voice.

"Can we start again? I feel like we got off on the wrong foot." Niall kept his voice deliberately loud. He knew that there were a lot of other people in earshot, and their presence – and their awareness of his own blindness – would force Roderick Leman into a civility that he had no desire to show.

"I'm sorry if you thought so," Leman said. "I'm sure you can understand my surprise when we met. Susannah had never mentioned you. It came as a shock. Under the circumstances any parent would want to protect his daughter from gold-diggers."

"Of course," Niall said. "But I hope you know now that all I want to be is her friend."

"We'll see," Roderick Leman said. Niall was aware of more whispering from Leman's other side. "Yes," Roderick added.

"Shake?" Niall suggested, reaching his hand across the aisle. There was a delay, and Niall smiled to himself as he imagined the squirming distaste that Roderick Leman was experiencing, but in the end a hand grasped his in a crushing grip that managed to serve as a private warning under the charade of quaint, schoolboy manners.

"Your daughter tells me," Niall went on, thinking it best to avoid the emotive Susannah/Miranda issue, "that you're an architect."

"That's right."

"And you work for a big city firm."

"Manston Redfearn," Leman helpfully supplied.

"What do you design mostly?"

He could feel Roderick Leman seething inside as the presence of his wife, the audience and the studio staff forced him to supply polite answers to Niall's questions.

"I work a lot with renewable energy centres. Several Gulf countries are looking to build green cities, green shopping malls, green tower blocks utilising solar energy."

"Sounds fascinating," Niall said. "And incredibly important."

"Yes," Roderick said minimally.

"I'd've loved to do something like that," Niall lied. "But I don't think blindness and architecture really go together," he added.

"I certainly can't think of a successful blind architect," Leman commented.

"Although," Niall continued his own train of thought, "I suppose most of it is done on computers now, and there are plenty of blind people who are geniuses on computers."

"I'm sure," Roderick said.

"Perhaps your daughter will be able to follow in your footsteps now she can see," Niall said, pushing the envelope a little. "Keep up the family tradition."

"Perhaps," Roderick said drily. "Who knows?"

A steward called them to order and asked them to give a warm welcome to a young and up-coming comedian. Niall sat back contentedly. He had what he wanted. He could Google Manston Redfearn, locate their office, and pay Mr. Leman a visit to reinforce their new cordial relationship.

The warm-up ended. The show began. Jon Allen and Melissa McEvoy introduced each other in line with modern convention and then ran through 'What's on the programme tonight.'

"And on the sofa we've got Susannah Leman," Melissa said, "the amazing girl from Surrey who couldn't see six months ago, but now, courtesy of a brand new pair of beautiful transplanted brown eyes, can see as well as you and me."

"Probably better than you actually," Jon Allen put in, making reference to Melissa's glasses, which were a trademark part of her look.

Miranda tried to breathe deeply and tried to see herself as 'the amazing girl from Surrey.' If only she felt that way. She had allowed them to call her Susannah all through the rehearsal, and, thinking about it, she seemed to be reverting, in her slightly scared, apologetic, self-effacing attitude to everything, to the girl she had been. Quiet, invisible Susannah. Hadn't she declared to herself and everyone else that Susannah Leman was no more?

The first item ended and she was on.

"So, Susannah, welcome to *This Is Now*!" Jon said.

"Actually I'm not Susannah," Miranda said. Jon and Melissa were both too startled to think of a quick response, but – luckily, from the director's point of view – Miranda herself filled the void.

"I mean, yes, this is me, you haven't got the wrong girl," she said as Melissa and Jon looked fascinated for the cameras. "But I am just a totally different person now I can see. I realised it almost at once. I couldn't be Susannah any more. She was too tied up in the blind girl I had been. My middle name's Miranda. So, I'm calling myself Miranda now."

"Right, well, *Miranda*," (with great emphasis on the name), "welcome to *This Is Now*!" Jon tried again.

"Thank you."

"You look amazing," Melissa said.

"Thank you."

"I don't think any of us can imagine what it must feel like to be you right now," Jon went on. "Can you begin to explain it to us?"

"It is difficult," Miranda agreed. "When I was blind I had no idea what seeing would be like. I wasn't sure if I even wanted to see when people first talked to me about it. I was really lucky because just before the operation I met a journalist called Niall Burnet. He's blind but he could see up until the age of eight and he really persuaded me that sight was worth having. Nothing I can ever say or do can repay the debt I owe him. He arrived just when I really needed him. Like a guardian angel. Now I can see that he was right. The world we live in is a sighted world. I can't bear the thought of not being able to see any more."

"Why the fuck didn't we get any of this in the rehearsal?" Lucy Sturmey hissed in the control room. "And why the fuck haven't we got Burnet? I thought the journalist's name was Long."

"We have got Burnet," one of the crew remarked. "He's in the audience with his guide dog."

Sturmey groaned.

"We've been sent up completely the wrong alley on this," she said.

"The weird thing is," Miranda was saying, giving Jon and Melissa little opportunity to get a word in edge-ways, "that I feel I've learnt more about being blind and the blind world since I've been able to see than I ever did when I was blind."

"Right," Melissa said, looking to the autocue for instructions.

"That's where Miranda is so much more inquisitive than Susannah. Susannah was just this poor little blind girl wrapped in cotton wool and pity. She never tried to do anything. She never tried to be anything. Because really that was how she was encouraged to be. Passive. No trouble. Now I – Miranda – see what a pathetic specimen Susannah was. Nice enough. Harmless. But pathetic. When I see a guy like Niall who's got a decent job, got his own flat, got his own life and yet he's blind, you know I'm just – I think it's amazing."

"We need to wrap up and cue swimming pools VT," somebody said in the control room.

"Fuck swimming pools of Britain," Sturmey said. "I want to stay on this girl until she starts rambling. I want Melissa to go into the audience and get a word out of Burnet, and his dog if possible."

"What about the pompous guy?"

"Cut him," Sturmey said. "We don't need him."

"Jon mentioned him at the beginning."

"We'll get him on set to wave goodbye," Sturmey said.

◉

Rebecca Blackford's mobile phone rang. She was sitting on her bed in her parents' house reading *Grazia* magazine. The caller was Kate Newcombe, a childhood friend.

"Hi Kate."

"Have you got *This Is Now* on?" without preamble.

"No."

"Turn it on. Turn it on."

Rebecca had a small television in her room. She turned it on.

"Why?" she asked.

"It's the girl who had the eye transplant last year."

"What girl?"

"It was all over the news when she came out of hospital."

"I must've missed it."

"First eye transplant in the world," Kate explained.

"Right," Rebecca said.

"Look at her eyes. Look at her eyes when they go into close up."

Maddeningly, they didn't go into close up for a full minute, until Melissa McEvoy said 'Let's have one last close up of Miranda's beautiful eyes,' whereupon the camera obediently zoomed in.

"What do you think?" Kate asked.

Rebecca had to fight back a sob.

"No," she said.

"Got to be," Kate said.

Rebecca stared at the screen where some idiot who wasn't sporting her brother's eyes was getting excited about an open air swimming pool in Wallingford.

Pockets of pandemonium broke out like small wildfires all over the studio as *This Is Now* came to its cheery up-beat end. Lucy Sturmey sighed as she emerged from the control room to deal with them. There were members of her research team who were in for an almighty bollocking with liberal exploitation of the f-word, but there were other choice words to be had first.

"Excuse me." And there was the pompous ass from the blind charity. Shit. How could she have been so careless as to have walked straight into him?

"I know what you're going to say, Mr. – " she began, deciding to cut him off before he could start, "but this is a live show. Things happen. Unexpected things. We have to react. We have to make decisions. I have to make decisions. I made them."

"Never mind that I'm a very busy man who gave up a day on the understanding that I was to be a significant part of the interview," Daniel slavered, "you allowed a girl in a very vulnerable state and potentially with mental health issues to embarrass herself and her family in front of a huge audience and didn't lift a finger to stop it."

"She didn't sound vulnerable to me or to the viewing public, I think you'll find, Mr …" She wished she could remember his name. "She came across as self-possessed and eloquent. I grant that some of her family members and people responsible for her former life might have been embarrassed. I think that was her intention and I applaud it."

"It's well known that yours is a scurrilous organisation –" Daniel said, changing tack.

"To readers of the *Daily Mail*," Lucy Sturmey put in.

"And you have just confirmed it."

"Because I didn't let you plug your charity on air and give you a

New Year's windfall in your collection boxes."

"How dare you!"

"I know how the world works," Sturmey said. At which point it suddenly became clear that the pockets of pandemonium had resolved themselves into one large conflagration around the sofa. Lucy Sturmey pushed past Daniel Sullivan to get to it.

"Excuse me," she said.

When she got to the sofa she found everyone gathered around Miranda, who was sitting exactly as she had sat when the cameras were on her. She was also crying. If somebody had allowed one of her family to upset her – . Lucy sat beside her.

"What is it? What is it, my love?" she asked.

"I can't see," Miranda said, tears running through Adam's carefully applied make-up. "I can't see."

Lucy Sturmey panicked. She looked up in the hope of seeing someone who would know what to do and she encountered the gaze of a silver-grey-haired woman who had been sitting next to the blind journalist.

"We've called an ambulance," the woman said. "She needs to get to Moorfields as soon as possible."

"Was it something to do with the interview?" Lucy asked.

"Maybe the stress, maybe the studio lights," the woman said.

"We were told she was fine," Sturmey protested, envisaging lawsuits.

"It may be completely unconnected," the woman said. "It may be chronic rejection of the new eyes."

"Sorry," Lucy said. "You are - ?"

"Faith Hodgkiss. I'm a counsellor. I work out of Moorfields Eye Hospital. Miranda's been staying with me since she came out of there."

"Right," Lucy said, relieved that the woman wasn't some amateur do-gooder from the audience.

"You can leave her to us," Faith said. "I'm sure you've got lots to do."

"Thanks," Lucy said. "But please keep me posted. She was fantastic in the interview."

"She was," Faith said.

👁

In her darkness Miranda tried to use her old blind skills to pick out who was close to her, who was touching her. But already those skills seemed to have deserted her. Voices swirled around her head as if she were standing at the bottom of a waterfall of sound, unable to separate them into their different sources, their signature tastes. She thought this was almost certainly the end of her seeing adventure, that this blackout was the last. It had come at the end of the programme, just as the presenters were making their closing remarks. First a fog, then darkness. She had hoped it would pass. It didn't. Then people were turning to her, talking to her, congratulating her, asking questions, expecting her to get up. And she had to tell them, had to say aloud the words she had been dreading, "I can't see." Having once said them, she seemed incapable of saying anything else. She longed to hear Faith's voice, Niall's, maybe even her mother's blackberry and apple, anything to bring some kind of comfort, but the truth was there was no comfort, not if she was going back down the tunnel into the dark. Then she felt something soft pressing against her leg, and a dog's nose in her lap, and she grasped Hugo tightly, one piece of flotsam in the wreck of her blind future, as the tears ran down her face.

Niall thought it was amusing that they all prowled round Moorfields pretending they didn't know each other, all waiting for some kind of news, some kind of hope. What did he want for Miranda? Of course he wanted her to get her sight back. Of course he did. Didn't he? Or did he want to take her hand and lead her into the blind world with him? Talk about selfish. And this was the girl he had taken an instant dislike to. No it wasn't. That was Susannah. This was Miranda. And that was what he really wanted to tell her: that no matter what happened now, no matter if she never saw again, she could still be Miranda. He would help her to be Miranda. He had felt ashamed by what she had said about him in the interview, knowing how unkind he had been to her since Christmas; ashamed but also astonished. Never mind that he was actually unemployed and not the person she said he was, she had made him glow with undeserved pride and that could never be forgotten. She had given him his thirty seconds of fame as the luscious Melissa McEvoy had climbed the steps to his position in the audience, thrust microphone and cleavage into his face, and asked him how it felt to be described as a guardian angel. "Hugo's the only angel round here," he had said. "And he does most of the guarding. So I don't think I can take much of the credit." That had gone down well and a staff researcher had just been hooking up with him when it became clear that all was not well on the set. From his own professional standpoint, Miranda's blackout had been badly timed.

"Niall? Mr. Burnet?"

He felt a gentle hand on his arm. The voice he recognised as Karin Leman's.

"Hi," he said.

"Can I get you a coffee? Or a tea or anything?" she asked.

"No, thanks. But thanks," he said. And then, recognising that she was offering some kind of olive branch and not wanting to seem churlish, he explained, "I only drink raspberry tea and I don't think Moorfields is that enlightened yet."

"Can I sit here?" she asked.

"Course."

"I need to apologize to you," Karin said once she had settled beside him. "I hope you will allow me."

"No need," Niall said.

"Yes there is. We knew nothing about you. My husband jumped to conclusions and we've both been rude to you. But I am Sus– Miranda's mother. No mother can hear her daughter talk about a guardian angel without being moved. Please let me finish – " Niall had stirred himself for a disclaiming response. "I want to thank you for coming into my daughter's life when you did, Niall. Mr. Burnet – "

"Niall," Niall said.

"I believe that things are meant to be and you were clearly meant to be for Miranda. I can never thank you enough. I can probably never apologize enough for the way we spoke to you and thought about you before."

"Thank you," Niall said graciously.

"How exactly did you meet?" Karin asked.

"It was by accident really," Niall lied.

"S-Miranda said you told her you were writing an article about her. Do you work with Matthew Long?"

"No. I happened to be at Moorfields," Niall said. "I saw that Miranda's was going to be a big story. I knew there'd be some deal in place but I thought I could get in from another angle. So I chanced my arm on a meeting with her. We just hit it off, I guess."

"I wish I had known you ten years ago," Karin Leman said at length.

"You don't," Niall countered, laughing.

"I had no idea how blind people could live," Karin went on. "Even when she was a little girl I was too scared to let her do anything much. But when it got to adolescence – you know, I really needed help."

"You could have got it," Niall said. "It's out there. Someone like Faith works as much with parents as she does with kids."

"Roderick would have seen that as an admission of defeat."

"He's never liked having a blind daughter, I guess."

"No. But who could? Oh, I'm sorry."

"Don't be," Niall reassured her. "You don't have to walk on eggshells round me. Whatever you say is OK. I've most likely heard it before. And you're right. Nobody could or should be thrilled at having a blind kid. But a blind life can still be a life."

Karin didn't reply. Niall decided this was the moment to turn this fortuitous conversation to his advantage.

"So I guess it was your husband who was keen for Miranda to have the operation," he said.

"Yes," Karin replied. "Such a possibility had never occurred to me. I just assumed Susan– Miranda would always be blind, would always live with us, would never have a career. Roderick came home one night. He plays squash and somebody he plays with had told him that this operation was on the cards, and if he wanted Susie to be considered as a candidate for it he should let him know and he'd see what he could do."

"What did you think when he told you?" Niall asked.

"I told him it was too good to be true, that he shouldn't trust man-talk on the squash court or in the changing room. Men will say anything to try and impress other men with their power and influence. I'm sorry, but it's true."

"I don't disagree with you," Niall said. He heard the smile in Karin Leman's voice as she replied,

"I can see why my daughter likes you, Niall. Anyway," she went on, seemingly happy to talk, and share her side of a story she had quite possibly never been allowed to share before, "I pretty much dismissed it out of hand and told Roderick he should do the same and not get his hopes up. Because I knew what the prospect would mean for him, to have his imperfect daughter rendered perfect. Then a couple of weeks later he said Susie was on a shortlist and needed to go for a medical. I was truly amazed. And that's when I started to hope, and to pray that maybe it could happen."

She stopped, but before Niall could think of a response she continued.

"It wasn't that I didn't – don't – love her for what she was, as she was. I just thought how wonderful it would be."

"You thought right," Niall said. "So what's going on in there?" he asked, changing tack.

"I don't understand the science," Karin said. "They are doing something to try to re-establish communication between the eyes and the brain, trying to find out what went wrong and whether they can put it right. I would be so much happier if her surgeon was here. Jamal. Mr. Daghash. But he's in America. Although in fact we were lucky because one of their top men was still here, this late on a Thursday night. Duncan Clark. But Susie told us he was really spiteful to her after the transplant, claiming the whole thing was a stunt. I can't help being afraid that he'll do something now to prove that the operation could never have worked."

Niall fished up a memory he scarcely knew he possessed of Simon telling him about emails. Emails sent to a d.clark at Moorfields about meetings at Number 17. And here was a D. Clark at Moorfields and right now he literally held Miranda's eyesight in the palm of his hand.

◉

"I have two questions," Amelia said to Matthew. "One is, where did Mr. Frigging Sunshine-Arse Burnet spring from if he's a bloody journalist? You're the journalist who's got exclusive – I repeat, exclusive – rights to Susie's story. All of a sudden, blindness opens doors apparently. You need to see him off."

Matt Long made a noise that could have been interpreted as agreement or disagreement.

"The second question is, how long does a loving sister have to hang around a hospital before it's politically correct for us to leave and go home for sex?"

Matt was depressed. He'd taken a call from his editor following *This Is Now* – while he had been on his way to Moorfields with the Lemans – calling for a two-page spread for tomorrow's edition to capitalize on the interest generated by the TV interview.

"Finally we're on pole, Matt," he had said. "I want chapter and verse on life since the op, the blind guy, pick up where the interview left off. You're on, my son."

Matt knew that far from being on pole he was actually at the back of the grid, if not starting from the pit-lane. He was so far off the real story it was a total embarrassment. And all because, instead of going where the girl was going, he had hung with the family. Total, unforgivable fuck-up. Not far off a resignation issue. The only story he could write was "My Sister – Media Superstar: the embittered reflections of a highly sexed accountant" and he knew better than to suggest it to his boss.

As it was he had had to explain that since the interview Susannah – or Miranda, as he had to accept that the whole world was now calling her – had suffered a medical emergency and was being rushed to hospital.

"Yes, but you've been with her for weeks, Matt," his boss had said. "None of this is news to you."

If only that had been true. He needed to talk to Niall Burnet – at length and as soon as possible – and hope that 'us journalists must stick together – dig me out of the shit and I'll owe you one' would do the trick. But right now Karin Leman had got Burnet's sole attention and Amelia had got him – Matt – on a tight leash that he was going to have to break, and he knew that that was a conversation that could only go badly.

"So, what are the answers?" Amelia urged.

"The answer to the first question," Matt said, "is 'I need to talk to the guy to find out, and I need to do it tonight."

"Just challenge him to a duel and we can leave," Amelia said. "Pistols at 11 am. Dawn's far too early. If you can't beat a blind man in a gunfight there's something wrong."

"The answer to the second question is," Matt went on, ignoring her response, "'Just tell your Mum you need to go home because you've got to get up early for work and she'll be fine with it'. But, I can't come with you tonight, because I've got a deadline to meet."

"Crap," Amelia said.

"Have I ever tried to get in the way of your work?" Matt asked her.

"No. Why not, you bastard?"

"Because I respect you and I respect your job. Tonight you need to respect mine."

"What would you do if I started shouting and making a scene?" Amelia asked.

"I'm hoping neither of us will have to find out," Matt said.

"There are conditions," Amelia said.

"Which are?"

"Tomorrow night you're going to arrive at my place with enough champagne and vodka for us to have a bath in it. Then we're going to lick each other dry and you are basically going to pleasure me with one part of your anatomy or another all night and most of Saturday morning until I say you can stop."

"Deal," Matt said, figuring that tonight was what mattered now, and tomorrow night would take care of itself. "Now go and distract your mother with your apologies for leaving and let me get my teeth into Sunshine-Arse."

❧

Of course, everybody on the planet had seen the broadcast. Before he reached home Daniel Sullivan had taken calls from a whole raft of BAB officers, including the Director General. What should have been a triumphant lap of honour accepting plaudits from every quarter for the masterly way in which his performance would lead to a massive spike in donations had been turned into a village pillory by that idiot of a director and her two vacuous presenters in which he was taking rotten eggs and fruit by the bucketful.

All thrown most politely, of course.

"Shame you weren't given more of an opportunity to explain BAB's role in the process," Tony Strong, the Director General, had said, implying that none of it was his fault but meaning the opposite. Everything had gone perfectly in the rehearsal. He had skilfully drawn the focus of the conversation to himself and to BAB, actually to the great relief of the presenters, who were struggling to get anything out of Susannah. He had also managed to handle Susannah's bottom and her right breast, both of which had felt rich with promise. When the show finished and Susannah had her relapse he had been too angry to consider accompanying the cavalcade to Moorfields. He needed to get home and regroup, take out some of his frustration on the fourth Mrs. Sullivan and a couple of bottles of half-decent claret. It had been as he was going to pick up his car that the phone calls had started, each one making him a little angrier than the one before. Laughing-stock was not a role he was suited for, and was certainly not a role he intended to play for long. Even more annoyingly, when he tried Penny's number it went straight to voicemail.

He slammed the door of his car and crashed his way noisily into the house.

The fourth Mrs. Sullivan was in the living room watching some ridiculous reality show.

"The programme was interesting," she said uninvited. "They didn't ask you anything, though, did they? I thought that was a bit strange. And a bit unkind, after you'd been there all day. Wallingford looks like a nice place."

When he reasoned that he could put it off no longer, Duncan Clark came out to meet the family. He saw what must surely be the mother sitting with Faith Hodgkiss, a woman who had won his grudging respect for her professionalism after they had experimented with a brief romantic entanglement when he had first come to Moorfields, too long ago to count the years. It had lasted about three months and both had been equally relieved when it was over.

The father was standing in a world of his own. And two young men, one of whom was blind, were deep in a conversation which the sighted one cut short the moment Clark entered the room. The separateness of the three groups was significant but, he reflected, not uncommon. Nothing like a visually impaired child to drive a wedge into a family.

His arrival prompted an attempt to draw together, but only because all three pockets wanted to hear what he had to say.

"Well?" This was the father. Duncan Clark bided his time. He was not a man to be bullied or intimidated. He noticed the young blind man looking at him with the alert concentration that sometimes only a blind face can achieve, uncomplicated by any issues of eye-contact. He knew absolutely nothing about the private circumstances, but he assumed the reaction meant 'boyfriend'.

"Well," he said, and paused.

"Duncan," Faith said, acknowledging him.

"Simply put," he said, "the meds were either screwed up or they're not doing the job. We've got her seeing again, but the rejection is something of a puzzle. We need to keep her here for the foreseeable future in my opinion, find out exactly what's going on. Jamal will be back from America on the 26th of February and I'm sure he'll want his protégé kept safe and secure until then, so that he can conduct his own examination. It seems to me, looking at the file, that Miss Leman goes on fine when she's in hospital, but goes downhill the moment she gets out. We need to try and work out why that is. It's not beyond the bounds of possibility that such peccadilloes as appearing on early evening television programmes and pursuing a life in the spotlight could themselves be contributory factors, given the attendant stress involved."

"So in a nutshell," the father said, "Susannah can have a life in hospital with eyesight, or a life out of hospital without it."

"That is an unnecessarily aggressive and over-simplified assessment of what I just said," Duncan Clark replied. "I have had to eat several portions of my colleague Jamal's humble pie, in that I did not believe the operation he was attempting to be scientifically possible. I still wonder whether there has not been some trickery involved. Now I grant you may feel a desire to get aggressive with me, but as your daughter is currently in my care I urge you to fight it. What I can assure you is that I can find nothing within the confines of my own expertise to suggest irreversible chronic rejection of the eyes. There is something curious going on which requires investigation and discussion with other colleagues with more knowledge of organ transplantation. But I am a long way from offering you the black and white choices that you seem to be rushing into."

Duncan Clark expected a reaction, but – maybe because it was late at night and everyone's energy was at rock bottom – none was forthcoming.

"The girl is safe here and comfortable, and as well as can be expected," he went on. "Nurses will check on her throughout the rest of the night. I'm going home and I recommend that you do the same."

With that, he left them. Niall had questions he wanted to throw after him, but decided the timing was wrong. Yes, he wanted an in-depth conversation with Duncan Clark, but he needed to plan it carefully, so that the consultant had no suspicion as to his motives. He also needed time to process his conversation with Matthew Long, which had certainly been entertaining. Niall had had to fabricate a more involved career than a few years as a sports reporter for a local rural radio station, but it had been worth it, as they had been able to exchange stories of impossible editors and the stress of meeting deadlines and how that kept the adrenalin buzzing.

"So are you shagging her, then?" Matt had asked when they were properly warmed up.

"Like I want to see that in tomorrow's paper," had been Niall's non-committal reply.

"This is off the record," Matt insisted. "You're doing me a Hell of a favour."

"Nothing's ever off the record," Niall said, and they both laughed.

"I don't mind telling you I'm shagging her sister," Matt said.

"You bugger!" Niall said.

"That's about the only thing we haven't done," Matt quipped in response. "So?" he pressed.

"So no comment," Niall said. "What do you know about this transplant then?"

"Less than you."

For all that he was a fully paid-up professional journalist, Matthew Long really did seem to know less about the operation than Niall had managed to find out. In his defence, as he himself was quick to point out, his brief had never really been the operation, it had been Miranda herself.

"But you must have been curious," Niall insisted. "When you met her. Why this particular girl? Why a young girl at all?"

"No point in giving new eyes to some old bat with cataracts," had been Matthew's retort.

"Certainly not such good publicity," Niall agreed. But once he had realised that Matthew Long had nothing to share with him that would help with his story, he changed the subject. No point giving away his own knowledge and let Matthew steal it for his own purposes. He had been happy to make contact with the guy, happy to do him a favour and take his mobile number so he could call it in at any time, but that was enough. Let him go and meet his deadline, with his article which Niall had largely written for him – much of it fantasy – and get back into bed with Miranda's sister. Niall had, to use one of his favourite phrases, other fish to fry.

THIRTEEN

Rebecca Blackford stood in the kitchen of her parents' home. Her mother was unloading the dishwasher. In common with most returning twenty-somethings, Rebecca, although quite capable of turning a hand in the kitchen, fell immediately into the routine of 'let mum do everything'. This morning, in any case, she was not disposed to help her.

"Mum," she said to her mother's back.

"Mm?"

"Do we know what happened to Joe's organs?" Her mother froze. "I know you signed them away," Rebecca went on, "and I'm OK with that now. I've worked through it. But do we know what happened to them? Who got what?"

Judith Blackford turned round. Her eyes were glassy with unshed tears.

"You may have worked through it," she said. "I'm not where you are. Why do you always want to talk about it?"

"Because it keeps Joe with us, Mum," Rebecca said. "I hate the way we have to talk about everything except Joe. The three of us sit down of an evening – what are we all thinking about? Joe. Joe, and how much we miss him. But what do we talk about? Anything else. It's stupid. And I'm sorry if it upsets you, I know he was your son and that's not the same as being a brother, but he deserves to be talked about. He didn't do anything wrong."

Judith Blackford just stared ahead. It was impossible to see what she was looking at.

"I'm going back to London next week," Rebecca went on, "so you won't have to deal with me being difficult. It's been great being here and I'll come back soon but I need to pick up the pieces of my life."

"I know," Judith said sadly.

"But can you please just tell me about Joe's organs? I really need to know."

Judith Blackford sighed.

"We could've known," she said. "But your Dad and I talked about it and we decided we didn't want to know. We were told at the hospital that sometimes recipients of donated organs like to be able to thank the families in person. We didn't think we could bear that, so we said to the hospital that we didn't want to know who they were and we didn't want them to know who we were. I'm sorry we didn't ask you. But the thought of somebody turning up on the doorstep and saying thank you for Joe's kidneys or Joe's heart – how could I look at a person who had Joe's heart beating inside them without wanting to tear it out because they weren't Joe?"

"It's OK Mum," Rebecca said, going to put her arms round her. "I understand. I guess the hospitals still keep records though."

"I suppose. Why? Do you want to know?"

"I might one day."

Judith Blackford shuddered, and mother and daughter held each other in a moment of shared grief.

Rebecca started to make plans. She would go back to London. Not to her course, because they'd given her the rest of the year off, but she'd get a job as a waitress or in a bar somewhere, and that would give her the days free to try and find – or at least find out about – the eye girl. She had already had countless imaginary conversations with her; had lain awake half the night talking to her. She knew that really eyes were just eyes, that Joe's eyes without Joe's brain behind them were not really Joe or even a part of Joe. But the chance to see them again had become a burning need in her. She wouldn't be able to rest easy again until she had looked this Miranda Leman in the face.

An email was under discussion in an office at the British Association for the Blind.

"He wants to back out."

"Which we can't allow."

"Luckily, we've got him over a barrel."

"But no more emails. They're traceable."

"I'll speak to him."

"No. I will. You monitor our other problem, if you can spare the time."

"Of course."

Had Miranda heard the conversation she would have recognised one of the voices as stale treacle pudding.

"So, Hugo, how does this work then?" With the help of passers-by Niall had purchased an Oyster Card, and was now attempting for the first time to insinuate himself and Hugo through the barriers at Finsbury Park Underground Station. His internet researches had revealed that Manston Redfearn had their offices between Fenchurch Street and Tower Hill. Determined that he was going to prove that he could use public transport, Niall established that the Victoria or Piccadilly line would get him as far as King's Cross. A change there onto the Circle line would bring him – eventually – to Tower Hill. From there he would have to rely on goodwill, but it was something that had to be done. He had resisted all Faith's offers of help, not least because he didn't want her to know what he was up to. He had asked her some deliberately misleading questions about Victory, whose centre of operations turned out to be near Regent's Park, and he let her assume that he was going sniffing around there. He had allowed her to point him in the direction of Finsbury Park Station, but no more.

It didn't take Niall long to realise that the Underground was a very unfriendly place for the blind. Sound was mangled by the hollow misdirecting acoustic and opportunities for getting on the wrong platform or the wrong train were legion. Hugo seemed to be spooked by the subterranean nature of it all as well.

People on the Underground were either in far too much of a hurry or far too wrapped up in their own affairs to be helpful. It took seven 'Excuse me's before a woman stopped and guided them to the platform for King's Cross.

"If in doubt follow the crowd," the woman said. "Everybody tends to go towards town from here."

"Cheers," Niall said.

The train itself was the easy bit. Getting out at King's Cross and congratulating himself on having come so far, he rose from the bowels of the earth and became totally disorientated in his attempt to find the Circle line, especially going the way he wanted to go. He wasn't someone to confess easily to stomach-churning fear, but he wondered if any sighted person could begin to imagine what finding your way round the tube blind was like. He made a note to himself to try the buses next time.

❡

Miranda lay in her hospital bed staring at the ceiling. Here she was again. Her life had become a game of Snakes and Ladders. The first time she had got up to the second row before slithering back down to Square One. Now she had got up maybe to row four or five, and the resulting snake had been all the more depressing. They had played Snakes and Ladders as children, she and Amelia, with Amelia describing the board, although, with hindsight, she thought Amelia probably cheated, as she never seemed to win. Easy to cheat a blind opponent. 'Oh dear, you've got on another snake!' And maybe she had or maybe she hadn't. So now it was a case of throw the dice and start again.

She was surprised by the sound of a newspaper page turning, and looked to see who was in the room. She had assumed she was alone. Duncan Clark was sitting on the chair at the end of the bed, apparently reading the *Mirror*.

"Good morning," he said.

"Good morning."

"I was just catching up with your latest adventure in the paper. Didn't want to miss it. I wouldn't want you to think this was my newspaper of choice."

Miranda said nothing in response. Then decided this was Susannah-type behaviour, so said,

"I just want to see. I don't want to be famous. I don't want to be in the paper. I don't care whether you believe me or not. I know you saved my sight last night, so thank you. I wonder why you did."

Duncan Clark smiled.

"I wonder why I did too," he said. "Or rather, I wonder what it was I was saving."

He paused, and then added, "You know your relapses could be psychological."

"You'd like that," Miranda said.

"No I wouldn't," Clark rejoined quickly. "Last night would have been a complete waste of my time."

This time Miranda couldn't think of a response.

"It's not uncommon," Duncan Clark continued. "People lose the use of their eyes or legs because in some twisted psychological way it brings them attention. I'm not belittling it. It's no less real because it's psychologically induced. Just damn near impossible to treat."

"I was born blind," Miranda said.

"I know," Clark replied. "And it seems from what I know of your case which admittedly isn't much that you were a quiet, retiring creature until Jamal came along with his operation."

"Susannah was a doormat," Miranda said.

"Yes. Yes. Susannah," Duncan Clark mused.

"Why are you suggesting to me that I might be doing it to myself?" Miranda asked. "I actually really want to see."

"There are things that don't add up," Clark said. "Your body was rejecting the eyes. Why? Obvious answer, because the anti-rejection medication wasn't working. That's twice. Two strikes. And yet when you're in here it seems to work perfectly. Which suggests to me that for some reason it's not being taken properly when you're not here. Who is the one person in the best position to manipulate your medication? You."

"I have never missed or not taken my medication," Miranda said. "I know that for a fact. You're in a very comfortable position because you can just dismiss everything I say as lies or delusion."

"I can, but I don't want to," Clark said. "You don't like me, and that's fine. But I am a professional, and whilst you are accidentally in my care you'll find I leave absolutely no stone unturned in my attempt to get to the bottom of what has happened to you. You say you want to see. I see it as my professional duty to do everything in my power to help you to see. So we are actually on the same side."

"Thank you."

"So tell me about your medication. You take it religiously. Where does it come from?"

"Dr. Clarke brings it in something called a dose-it box every week. He insisted. Said that way there could be no mistakes."

"Damian Clarke," the consultant surgeon said. It might have been a question.

"I don't know," Miranda said. "He's just Dr. Clarke to me."

"Yes, yes. Good man. Nice man," Duncan Clark said. "What would you say if I suggested that you felt guilty about seeing because your boyfriend can't, and you're afraid that you being able to see might change the dynamic or even completely ruin your relationship? It could be a psychological driver."

Miranda laughed.

"He's not my boyfriend," she said. "I only met him just before the operation. And I think that's rubbish."

"OK," Clark said. He got up. "You don't have to stay in bed," he said. "I just don't want you going outside the hospital. I know it's going to be boring, but – it's winter outside. You're not missing much."

He left the room without ceremony.

�◉

It is very easy to follow a blind person. Perhaps not in the silence of night or on a quiet country lane, but in the bustle and noise of London no amount of heightened compensatory senses – if such things were not in any case a myth – can detect you, and you can stand behind, or even next to your quarry without being seen, other than by an unsuspecting guide dog. Child's play. Almost unfairly easy. You can even pretend to be helpful, respond to a request, point them in the right direction and find out exactly where they are going. Then you can actually get to their destination before they do and wait patiently for them to emerge, the faithful dog making them impossible to miss.

❧

Niall and Hugo entered Manston Redfearn. Niall was prepared for Hugo to create fuss and open doors, but he was not prepared for his dog's new celebrity status. The receptionist he spoke to had watched *This Is Now*. Of course she had: Mr. Leman's daughter was going to be on it. And she had seen Hugo, and if Hugo had possessed the ability or been in the mood to sign autographs he could have run through the whole office. Never mind, Niall thought wrily, that it had been him that Melissa McEvoy had spoken to, him that Miranda had talked about. Hugo had got on camera and upstaged him totally.

Dogs.

What it did mean, however, was that – without any questions asked and without any 'There's a Mr. Niall Burnet here says he has an appointment with you', which could have gone badly and would have warned Roderick Leman of his imminent arrival, they were both ushered directly to the lift and escorted to Roderick Leman's inner sanctum.

"Be careful Hugo," Niall admonished him as they rose in the lift. "There's probably going to be models and fragile stuff we might crash into and break, and we don't want any trouble."

The receptionist laughed.

"This way," she said, leading them out of the lift. The floor they had reached sounded as though it was open plan – a large space with few clear points of reference. Difficult to escape from in a hurry, should escape become necessary. On the plus side, there were countless casual witnesses to all conversations, so again Roderick Leman would be forced into civility.

"Niall Burnet. What an extraordinary surprise." He had been spotted. Niall would have given anything to know what thoughts were passing through Roderick Leman's mind. "I thought you'd be hovering at my daughter's bedside in guardian angel mode," the architect went on.

"Touché," Niall said amicably.

"Let's have coffee and a seat," Leman continued.

"I don't do coffee," Niall said. "But if by any chance anyone's got any raspberry tea – "

"Beverley," Roderick Leman cut in, "how are we in the raspberry tea department?"

"I don't know, Mr. Leman – "

"You're a resourceful woman. There must be six hundred people working in this building. It's a little morning challenge. Track down a raspberry tea bag."

"It might be quicker to go across to the supermarket," Beverley suggested.

"Whichever," Leman said. "I leave it entirely in your hands."

He was playing to the crowd, Niall realised. This was his work persona, and he was going to employ it while ever they had an audience. That could potentially make their conversation interesting.

"Seat just to your left," Leman said after guiding them through a maze of desks and tables. "Impossible to get out of but actually quite comfortable." Niall sat, and agreed. "Now just a pane of glass between you and a fifteen-storey drop to the street," Leman said pleasantly.

"That would be architect humour, I guess?" Niall supposed.

"I love glass," Leman said, surprising Niall with his candour. "It's solid and yet transparent. There and not there. We are quite safe and secure here, but if you suffered from vertigo there's no way you'd be able to sit where you are."

"How do you know I don't?" Niall said.

"Can blind people get vertigo?"

"You had a blind daughter."

"Doesn't make me an expert," Leman said. Niall cursed his mouth. He felt shutters coming down, and he couldn't go back to the place they had been just a moment before. "So, pleasantries aside, why on earth are you here?" Leman went on.

"I'd never seen the inside of an architect's office," Niall said. "I didn't have anything else lined up for the day. And there are things I need to know."

"Need or want?"

"Need."

"OK."

"But I've got all day," Niall added. "If you want to give me a guided tour first – "

"Sadly I can't give you the whole day. There's a lot to do here. I'm flying to Doha on Sunday."

"Nice work if you can get it," Niall reflected.

"So what is it you need to know?" Leman asked.

"It's all to do with how and why," Niall said.

"Spare me the riddles," Leman said. "I'm an architect, not a poet."

"OK. As a blind person, and speaking, perhaps, for the blind community as a whole, I really need to know how it was that Susannah – as she then was – got to be selected for the transplant. Not," he hastened to add, "because I don't think she should have had it or anything like that, but if there's a next time, another operation, you know, I'd like to think I might be able to get myself into the running."

Roderick Leman laughed.

"Is that funny?" Niall asked.

"It's the first thing you've ever said to me that's actually made sense," Leman answered. "Of course you want what she's had. I can understand that."

"So?"

"I wouldn't get your hopes up."

"Because?"

Roderick Leman didn't answer immediately.

"Let me help you," Niall said. "You're daughter's an attractive girl. I'm not. I'm a guy and I'm probably pretty ugly. From a publicity angle a girl is good. But maybe a kid could be even better."

"What makes you think it's about publicity?"

"Because everything's about money in the end, Mr. Leman. Let's not insult each other by pretending we don't both know that. The operation must have been expensive. The research required must have been even more expensive. Whoever put up most of that money is going to want some kind of return on their investment. Publicity can bring in money. Especially if BAB put up most of it, which is what the general perception seems to be. Good publicity equals donations. Somebody at BAB told me they were getting loads of donations every time there was anything about the transplant in the media."

"BAB?"

"The British Association for the Blind."

"I hadn't thought of it in those terms," Roderick Leman said. "But I suppose you're right. But don't you think a lot would depend on what eyes they got?"

"No," Niall said. "I don't think so. I think they chose your daughter and then waited for the right eyes. Unless you can tell me differently."

"I can't tell you differently," Leman said, "but that's because I actually have no idea."

"So how did it happen, Mr. Leman?" Niall pressed. "This is the mystery. This is what's intriguing. Granted it was always going to be a girl, granted it was going to be someone under the age of twenty-five. Granted it had to be someone whose eye condition was not systemic, so the new eyes would end up going the same way as the originals. That probably narrows it down to – I don't know – maybe five hundred to a thousand girls. How did it get to be Susannah?"

"If it's always going to be a girl, that doesn't look good for you," Roderick Leman observed.

"It'll be a guy next time," Niall said quickly. "Otherwise they'll be accused of discrimination."

Beverley arrived triumphantly at that moment with raspberry tea and Leman's coffee.

"Didn't prove too difficult then," Leman said.

"Nothing's difficult for a woman of my resources," Beverley replied.

"Thanks," Niall said, annoyed by her interruption. He waited for her to walk away and then said, "So?"

"What do you think happened?" Roderick Leman said.

"I'm wondering whether you made a very generous donation to BAB and whether I should take out a monster loan and do the same."

There was a silence.

"Silence implies acknowledgement," Niall suggested.

"That would certainly fit with your philosophy," Leman said at last.

"My philosophy?"

"That everything is about money."

"So tell me it happened another way."

"I don't have to tell you anything at all," Leman said, and the old hostility surged back into his voice. "I don't know what your game is, coming here," he went on in something not much more than a whisper, "but it was a mistake. Trust me. You may have fooled my daughter and my wife and the audience of an early evening chat show, but you don't fool me."

"How am I fooling anyone?" Niall asked loudly. Roderick Leman drew in a deep breath.

"All I will say to you," he said at last, "is that it isn't always what you know, it's who you know. Money can buy you a lot of things, but contacts can get you a lot more. If you want to jump the queue for the next set of eyes, I suggest you get in with the right people."

"Who are the right people?" Niall asked.

"You're a journalist. Find out."

"I will," Niall said. "I'll start by taking up squash."

When Niall Burnet was safely on his way down in the lift Roderick Leman grabbed his mobile phone and selected a name from the phonebook.

"Roderick – hi."

"Bloody Niall Burnet's been here. Just now. Just this moment left."

"It's OK. We know."

"You know?"

"We know."

"You know he's virtually asking me how much I paid to get Susannah the operation?"

"He's fishing, Roderick. Fishing in the dark. Tell him nothing, he'll find nothing. And then he'll go away."

"He's not showing much sign of going away," Leman fumed.

"Oh he will. Trust me. Enjoy Doha."

"He knows about you."

"He knows nothing about me."

"He knows we play squash."

"Does he indeed?"

"He talked about taking up squash."

"You should give him a game. You'd probably win."

"Probably!"

"Relax, Roderick. You're behaving as though you've got something to hide. And you haven't."

"If it all gets into the papers – "

"How is Susannah this morning?"

"I'm going in tonight."

"Enjoy Doha. Bring me back a camel. Or enough natural gas to power my house for a generation."

❦

Back in the street Niall took stock. It was a cold winter's day. Not actually raining, but it had been earlier and the streets were wet. Should he have pressed Roderick Leman for the squash-player's name? He didn't think Leman would have given it to him. But for now it was enough that he knew, and Leman knew he knew. Strings had been pulled. One of those strings had probably had cash attached. He did need to find out who, though. Karin Leman might know. She had described him as 'someone Roderick played squash with', but with a little gentle pushing he might be able to jog a memory. Names must have been mentioned sometime. If not, she must at least know the name of the sports club where they played.

The fact that Roderick had more or less bought his daughter the operation was nothing, really. Rich people could afford things not-so-rich people couldn't. But if he could trace the money into somebody's pocket, say, for example, the obnoxious Daniel Sullivan's, then there was a story. He could write it, and use his new contact Matt to help him sell it. He tried to imagine Daniel Sullivan playing squash. He found it hard to believe, but what did he know? Sullivan might have a really athletic body and run the London Marathon every year, raising millions for BAB.

He did worry that Miranda might see his pursuit of this corruption story as a betrayal. Of trust, of her family, of her. He wished there was a way he could get her on board with him.

Hugo walked him up to the traffic lights and stopped obediently at the kerb.

Miranda had her eyes now. Nothing that he did, nothing that resulted from what he did, could change that. Exposing the dark underbelly of how it all came about would not take her sight away from her. It was time for total honesty.

"Good to go, mate," said a voice in his ear, accompanied by a touch on his arm.

"Thanks. Go, Hugo."

Hugo was puzzled, but obeyed his master's command. He stepped off the pavement into the path of the on-coming silver BMW.

PART THREE

Then the eyes of the blind will be opened,
and the ears of the deaf will be unstopped.

Isaiah 35:5

FOURTEEN

Suddenly there were people all round Niall as he crouched on the road beside Hugo's stricken form. A tornado of concern and exclamation and at the heart of it, despite the roaring invective against the driver for speeding off, the belief that some stupid blind person had stepped off the kerb into the path of an on-coming car instead of waiting for the crossing signal.

"Didn't you hear the car, mate?"

"Should've waited for the lights. Cars come really fast up here."

"That dog looks a mess."

Somebody flagged down a taxi, but nobody seemed to have much idea of what to do. You didn't call an ambulance for a dog and Niall kept insisting that he hadn't been touched and had no need to be whisked off to A and E. There was no way he was going to let anyone separate him from Hugo. If this was the day that Hugo breathed his last Niall was going to be with him until the end.

Miraculously the taxi driver who had stopped was a dog lover and seemed to be something of a dog expert.

"Clerkenwell Animal Hospital," he said to Niall and anyone else who was listening. "I can get you there in ten minutes. Less if we're lucky. Guy there's absolutely brilliant."

"What's the damage?" Niall asked the driver.

"Front leg doesn't look too special. Probably some ribs gone too. But he's breathing nice. It's if he's bleeding inside you've got to worry."

"Yes," Niall said weakly.

"Somebody give me a hand please," the taxi driver said. "Two people, in fact. We got to lift him really gentle into the back of my cab."

While that was going on a policeman who had appeared from somewhere tried to ask Niall about what had happened.

"I've got to go with Hugo," Niall said. "I'll be at the Clerkenwell Animal Hospital. Ask somebody else. I didn't see anything."

The policeman said he was going to need a statement.

"Look mate," the taxi driver intervened, "we're going up to Clerkenwell. Emergency. Here's my number. Call me. I won't let the guy out of my sight until I hear from you."

The policeman seemed satisfied. The driver helped Niall into the back of the cab and then bustled round into the driver's seat.

"Hang in there, Hugo," Niall said, stroking his ears and listening to the dog's strained breathing. "I need you."

"You were on the telly last night, right?" the taxi driver asked.

"Right," Niall said.

"*This Is Now*."

"Right."

"Thought I recognised your face. Don't you worry mate. I'll get you to the hospital. And if anyone can fix your dog it'll be them. They did a brilliant job on my Bess."

Niall had an off-the-wall image of Bess being the taxi-driver's wife, and wondering what 'brilliant job' could have been done on her.

"You're a life-saver," Niall said. "I probably haven't got enough cash to pay you, but I'll make some calls."

"Don't even think about it," the driver said. "I'm with you until you tell me to clear off. Anywhere you need to go after we've got your dog sorted I'll take you."

"Thanks."

"My pleasure. My pleasure."

The taxi surged into the traffic while the driver used his bluetooth to call the Clerkenwell Animal Hospital.

"That's good," he said to Niall at last, opening the glass partition. "They're expecting us and they're getting an operating table ready. I told you they're good. My name's Geoff by the way. Geoff Jefferies. I think my parents were having a laugh."

"Niall," Niall said. "And Hugo."

Niall felt the taxi ducking and weaving as it fought London's clogged streets. He stroked Hugo's flank, constantly checking for the rise and fall that told him the dog was still breathing. More quickly than he dared hope they arrived at the animal hospital and Hugo was whisked away from him.

"Save him for me," Niall said.

"We'll do everything we can," one of the professionals said.

Geoff led Niall into the waiting room and they sat down.

"You don't need to wait with me," Niall said. "I'll be fine and you've got a living to make."

"I promised the police I wouldn't let you out of my sight," Geoff said.

"I don't think that's legally binding," Niall said. "I'll make some calls. Get someone to collect me from here. I'd better get them to bring you some cash as well."

"The meter's not running," Geoff said. "This is me doing me good citizen bit. Let me have me moment."

"If you insist," Niall conceded. "Thanks."

"Amazing thing, that eye transplant," Geoff went on.

"Yeah. Amazing."

"Pretty girl, too. And she's got the hots for you, all right."

"Do you think so?"

"Bloody obvious, mate. You don't need eyes to see that."

"If you say so."

Niall had been wondering whom to call. Faith was the obvious candidate. In fact, eventually, he would have to call her. But there was the fact that he no longer trusted her, and also the piece of information that only he knew – that someone had stepped up to him and told him that it was clear to cross. Not that it had been Faith: no, it had been a man; but it suggested that someone had tracked his movements and that someone had made a deliberate attempt to get him run down. As he replayed the sequence of events in his head, Niall was certain that Hugo had hesitated before obeying his command to go. Had he not done so, Niall himself might very well have gone straight over the bonnet. So, was it just the man on the pavement, or was it the man on the pavement AND the driver of the car? Had it been meant as a warning or as a serious attempt to silence him? Had Roderick Leman called for it the moment he had left him? That would have meant he would have to have an accomplice in his own office. Or had the squash player been close by? And what on earth could be going on that was serious enough to risk silencing him with a blatant hit and run? Not just a tawdry bung, surely? In which case, was he barking up the wrong tree with his story? There had to be something more imperative to be hushed up, and they thought he was on to it. Perhaps they had somehow contrived the death of the eye donor. That sounded ridiculously far-fetched, but it would certainly be something they would want to cover up at any cost. And yet, could Faith be involved in murder? He couldn't believe that of her. She was mixed up in this somehow. Perhaps more by accident than design. Perhaps she had got in at the beginning but it had all got out of hand and she now wanted nothing to do with it. He couldn't take a chance on that being the case. He couldn't trust her. But, by the same token, if he didn't call her to say what had happened she would be alerted to the fact that he was on to her, and that would not help his situation. So he made the call.

"Niall?"

"Hi, Faith. Where are you?"

"I'm at work. At Moorfields. Why?"

"Hugo's been knocked down. Hit and run."

"My God!" She sounded genuinely shocked. "Is he dead?"

"Not yet, as far as I know. I'm at Clerkenwell Animal Hospital. They're operating on him now."

"I'm tied up for the next hour but then I'll be straight over. Wait for me."

"I will," Niall said. What else could he do? Without Hugo he felt paraplegic, never mind blind.

❦

Katrina Masters, returning from her lunchtime shift at Arvo's, was astonished to see Juliette outside their house washing the car. Juliette loved her work. She loved it to the point that she spent far more hours than she needed doing it, and made it her main topic of conversation when she was at home. In all the time that they had been together, Katrina had never known Juliette to take time off. She had never had a day off sick, preferring to drag herself into the office whatever state she was in, and frequently had to be forced to use up outstanding holiday allowance at the end of the year. To be home early on a Friday afternoon was unheard-of.

"Hello," she said, walking up to the car. Juliette stopped her frenetic wiping and looked up.

"Oh, hello. Thought you'd be at work."

"I was. But I do get a few hours off in the afternoon. What are you doing here?"

"Cleaning the car."

"Shouldn't you be at work?"

"You know what I should or shouldn't be doing, now, all of a sudden?" Juliette said brusquely.

Tears stung Katrina's eyes, but she was determined not to let them fall.

"Not a lot going on at the office," Juliette went on, "so I gave everyone the afternoon off, including me."

"That was nice."

"New Year's resolution," Juliette said. "Improve the work-life balance. Maybe you should make it too."

"Yes, maybe," Katrina said. "Do you want a hand?"

"No. No thanks. You go in and put your feet up. You can make me a cup of tea if you like."

☙

By mid-afternoon Niall had spoken to the police, spoken to three local news journalists, and was tired of the sympathy. He had said nothing to anyone about the passer-by who had told him it was safe to cross, describing it to police and reporters as 'just one of those things – a mistake.' Faith had arrived, had given Geoff a large sum of money on Niall's instructions which the taxi driver had eventually accepted after prevailing upon Niall to take his phone number 'and call me any time you want to go anywhere mate', and had helped him pass the time waiting for news of Hugo.

At length the vet who had been working on him came and sat down with them.

"He'll live," was the first thing he said.

"Thank God," Faith intoned almost silently. Niall stared sightlessly at the floor.

"We'll keep him in overnight," the vet went on. "Just to keep an eye on him and because he's exhausted and traumatised. But if you come back tomorrow afternoon you'll be able to take him home, unless any complications develop."

"What was the damage?" Faith asked.

"His right fore-leg was broken in two places. We've pinned it. He may always limp but he should walk on it fine again when it's out of plaster. He's got a number of cracked ribs but his spine's fine, thank goodness. His whole body's pretty bruised and shaken up, but considering what he's been through it could've been a lot worse."

"Will he be able to carry on working?" Faith asked. "As a guide dog?"

"No idea," the vet said. "Not my field of expertise."

"I'm keeping him," Niall said. "I won't have another."

"Of course," Faith said quickly. "Can we see him?"

"We gave him a general anaesthetic and he's still out. I'd leave it until tomorrow if I were you."

Offering profuse thanks, Faith finally persuaded Niall that there was no point continuing to sit as if petrified, and the two of them walked out of the Clerkenwell Animal Hospital.

"We'll get a Number 19 bus," Faith said, guiding Niall expertly along the crowded pavement.

Niall said nothing. Ever since he had had Hugo he had never really liked being guided. There was something inherently helpless about it. You were beholden. You were at the mercy of the guide. You were totally dependent. And that was not a way he chose to live his life. But right now, what other options did he have? He had been put as effectively out of action as if the car had made him his target. Now he was thrown back onto what he actually was – a blind investigator. Incapable of going anywhere, incapable of finding anything out. Unless – he took someone sighted into his confidence. But that someone could not be Faith.

"So, Niall," she said at last when they were safely ensconced on the bus, "now tell me what on earth you were doing in Clerkenwell. I thought you'd gone to Regent's Park."

"I was following up a lead," Niall said non-committally.

"Oh, very mysterious," Faith said lightly. "Secret journalist stuff, eh?"

"Something like that."

"Right."

Niall knew that when it broke on the local news it would become clear to everyone, Faith included, that he had been at Tower Hill. And it would make the news, because of his One Show appearance the night before.

"Actually I was at Tower Hill," he said at last. "I went to visit Roderick Leman at his office."

"And you told me you were going to Regent's Park because you didn't want me to know."

"Not exactly," Niall said. "I hadn't really decided where I was going when I left the house."

"And was Roderick Leman pleased to see you?"

"What do you think?"

"So why did you go?"

And why are you fishing so damn hard, Niall asked silently inside his head.

"I was curious. I wanted to see him in a different environment."

"OK," Faith said, and then surprised Niall by dropping the

subject. Do you want to go in and see Miranda later?"

"Not tonight," Niall said.

"If it is on the news she'll see it and she'll be worried."

"She's got my number."

"Oh Niall. Come on. Think of her for two minutes. She went to Hell and back last night."

"Yeah. You're right. Sorry. I'll ring her. In a bit."

As the bus made its way sedately through the London traffic Niall drifted into a daze. He tried to re-evaluate everything that had happened from the beginning, in the light of his new, almost-outrageous suspicion. He had met Juliette Warwick on his way to meet Lindsey. Juliette hadn't liked him. But at that point she couldn't have suspected anything, so that was just an example of the natural antipathy he inspired in some women. Then he had spoken to Lindsey. He had asked her about money, and until now he had thought that that was what this was all about. But now he thought differently. In which case, Lindsey was removed from the firing line not because she could give him inadvertent access to the finance department, but *because she knew something else*. Quite possibly something she didn't even know she knew, because there was no way Lindsey Spencer would cover up anything dodgy if she found out about it. And that meant... he had to re-evaluate Lindsey. He had to go and see Lindsey. But how could he? He was to all intents and purposes house-bound. He could call her. He would wait until tonight. By then all local news programmes would have aired, and there was a possibility that she might have heard what happened to him. Which would make her sympathetic, and he would get her to agree to come to him.

But what else could she possibly know? Without knowing she knew it? He had never asked her any questions about the shadowy boyfriend. Hadn't she told him he worked at BAB? In which case maybe it wasn't Lindsey herself, maybe it was the boyfriend that they had been anxious to keep him away from. That was question one, then. Who was he? He could ask that in a very non-threatening, conversational kind of way, just pretend he was genuinely interested in her life.

Next there was Vivien Loosemore. President or whatever of the charity that had given Lindsey a job. She was involved in this somehow. He had caught her out and she had revealed her discomfort in her time-honoured way, but as Simon had said, he had lacked the facts to press his advantage home. But now her new project – only it wasn't her project – had taken Lindsey out of the gutter. As if, while whoever it was wanted Lindsey away from BAB, they still wanted her somewhere that they could keep an eye on her. And they had given Simon a job too. Was there anything in that? It did sound as though it was a perfect job for Simon, but Simon hadn't been successful in an interview since he lost out to Martin Cattermole in the battle to be Head Boy. Simon had hacked into BAB. Did they know that? Were they keeping an eye on him as well? Simon was brilliant on computers, but there was every possibility that there was someone equally blind and equally brilliant doing a job at BAB, watching out for intrusions of any kind. Had Simon got in and out without being noticed?

So they had made their arrangements to keep tabs on those two. But what had he himself done or said that had worried them enough to cripple him? In a busy London street surely it was a high-risk strategy? What if there'd been a traffic jam? The car wouldn't have been able to get away. If they were prepared to take that kind of risk, they MUST be worried. Maddeningly, he didn't know how he had worried them.

At work, Katrina Masters heard the local news on the radio. A guide dog that had been on the television the night before had been knocked down in the city of London. Eye-witnesses described a silver BMW as being the vehicle involved. The police were asking for anyone with information to come forward. Listening, Katrina over-rolled her pastry and had to throw it away.

◉

Karin Leman saw it on the South East News as she was ironing her husband's shirts for Doha. She couldn't help but notice the Manston Redfearn building in the background of every shot.

◉

Miranda Leman called Niall – he had not phoned her as he had promised – as soon as she saw the item on television in her room at Moorfields.

"Are you all right?" she asked frantically.

"I'm fine," Niall said.

"Is Hugo all right?"

"Looks like he's going to pull through."

"Thank God."

"I'm sorry," Niall said in the silence that followed.

"What do you mean?" Miranda asked.

"I've been foul to you since Christmas. I'm really sorry."

"That's OK. Are you going to come and visit me soon? It's pretty lonely in here."

"Of course. I'll come tomorrow." Niall cursed. "Well, I will if I can get someone to bring me or put me in a cab. I've kind of lost my mobility."

"I know. I keep crying when I think of poor Hugo," Miranda said. "He was there for me when I needed him at the television studio and now I'm not there for him."

"He's in good hands," Niall said.

"I'm sure," Miranda said.

"How are you doing?"

"Well I'm no more mobile than you are. But I can see. I just wish I knew why I don't seem to be able to survive outside the hospital. They all think it's the medication and I know it isn't."

"Stress," Niall suggested.

"But it's the blackouts and the fear of losing my sight that makes me stressed. I'm not stressed until it starts to go wrong," Miranda said.

"I really need to talk to you," Niall said quietly. He was in his room, which was a long way from Faith's and the communal areas, but he didn't want to take any chances on her listening in.

"What about?" Miranda asked.

"Loads of stuff. This accident. Your transplant."

"So go on then."

"Not on the phone."

"You can't just say you need to talk to me and then not talk to me," Miranda said.

"Susannah would've let me," Niall responded.

"Susannah's dead."

"Yeah."

"So talk to me," Miranda said. "I'm not going anywhere."

Niall told her about the man who had told him it was safe to cross.

"I bet he feels like a prat," Miranda said. "Why didn't you tell the police about him?"

"He won't feel a prat," Niall said. "He did it on purpose. He wanted me to get knocked down."

"Why on earth?" Miranda asked. "Not because he was jealous of your one night of fame?"

"No. Because someone wants me out of the way."

"Niall," Miranda cautioned. "Have you been reading too many crime thrillers?"

"I've never read a crime thriller," Niall said. "Too long, most of them. I prefer Braille to talking books so short stories have always had an appeal."

"I love talking books," Miranda said.

Niall realised he had come too far to back out now. In little more than a whisper, from the corner of his room that was furthest from the door, all senses on the alert for the slightest sound that suggested Faith was outside listening in, he told Miranda his reasoning for thinking first that money had changed hands behind the scenes and then, in the light of Hugo's accident, something much more sinister.

When he finished Miranda was initially silent.

"So when you first came to see me," she said at last, "it was because you were hoping to expose something dodgy."

"I didn't know you then, did I?"

"No. You didn't. I hardly knew myself."

Silence settled between them again.

"I don't really know what to say, Niall," Miranda went on. "You think my father bought my eye transplant. Or you think my father was involved in something much more sinister like the death of the donor. This is my father we're talking about."

"I'm not saying he's involved," Niall insisted. "Yes, I did think so, but I could be completely wrong. He may just be an innocent bystander. What I know is that someone knew where I was this morning and arranged for me or Hugo or both to have an accident. You don't do that unless you have something to hide."

"Or," Miranda said, "some busy-bodying do-gooder saw a blind person waiting patiently at a crossing, thought, 'Oh here's my chance to do my good deed for the day,' went up to you, looked the wrong way up the road and told you it was safe to cross, while, as fate would have it, a car was coming much too fast in the other direction."

"No," Niall said. "I'm right about this. I was there."

"OK," Miranda conceded.

"Just be on your guard," Niall said. "Keep your eyes and ears open for anything fishy."

"I suppose you think Daniel Sullivan's behind it," Miranda said mischievously.

"I think everyone's involved until I get some proof to the contrary," Niall answered.

"But HOW are you going to find any of this out?" Miranda asked.

"I'm a journalist," Niall said. It was better than saying that he currently had absolutely no idea.

"Of course you are," Miranda said.

❂

The next morning Faith drove Niall to the Clerkenwell Animal Hospital. She didn't like driving into London, but felt it was only right that Hugo should be brought back to his London home in a car that was familiar.

When they arrived, Niall noticed immediately that there was something different about the place. Instead of smelling like a vets' it smelt like a florist's, and he could hear smiles in everyone's voice as they greeted him.

"Have we come to the wrong place?" he asked Faith.

"No," she said. "It's just full, and I mean full, of flowers."

"Is it National Flowers for Animals Day?" Niall asked.

"I think," Faith said, looking to the receptionist, "that they're all for Hugo."

"What?"

The receptionist took up the story, as another florist's delivery van pulled up outside.

"They started to arrive last night," she said. "Apparently someone set up a Twitter campaign, #flowersforhugo or something. They just haven't stopped since."

"Incredible," Faith said.

Niall said nothing. He couldn't trust himself.

"So how is the celebrity?" Faith asked.

"I'm sure he'll be very pleased to see you."

A veterinary nurse took them through to where the 'in-patients' were housed.

"There he is," Faith said.

"Hugo?" Niall called, and immediately an enthusiastic bark led him to where Hugo was lying, struggling to get up.

"Keep still, mate. Keep still," Niall said, holding him tight. "I thought I'd lost you. I'll never listen to a jerk on the pavement again."

"He'll need plenty of rest, but he'll need exercise too," the nurse explained to Faith. "And we'll want him to come back for physio."

"There's physio for dogs now?" Faith asked.

"It's an underwater treadmill. Very effective for building up muscle tone after surgery. I think given that he's a working guide dog it's absolutely essential."

"I wonder if Guide Dogs will pay for it," Niall mused.

"If it's what Hugo needs, he'll get it," Faith said.

"I guess if we set up a stall and sold all his flowers that would pay for a few sessions," Niall said.

"We are NOT selling Hugo's flowers," Faith said. "Goodness knows what we're going to do with them all, but we're not going to sell them."

"We'll take a few bunches to Miranda in Moorfields," Niall said.

"Now that's a good idea," Faith said.

"Leave a load here," Niall went on. "I don't know. They should go somewhere. An old people's home or somewhere."

The hospital staff prepared Hugo for departure, checking the cast on his leg. He tried to stand and whimpered.

"We'll loan you a carrier to get him home," the nurse said. "He will need to walk in time, but it's a little soon."

"Thanks," Niall said.

"We'll come back to do something about the flowers," Faith said.

"Yes, that'll be good," the nurse replied.

Walking out of Clerkenwell Animal Hospital with Hugo a dead weight in an industrial strength animal carrier, Niall was surprised to hear the buzz of a crowd and the clicking of dozens of cameras.

"We're well and truly in the news now, Hugo mate," Niall said to the carrier. "Try not to let it go to your head."

"How is he?"

"What can you tell us about what happened?"

"What about all these flowers?"

The questions broke over Niall, Faith and Hugo like a storm.

"He needs lots of rest, but he's going to be OK. So long as you guys don't illegally tap his mobile he'll be fine."

There was a ripple of laughter.

"Niall," said a voice close by. "Matt here. Matt Long."

"Hi Matt."

"Care to give me an exclusive?"

"Bit difficult with all these people here," Niall said. "Besides, there's no story. A blind idiot walked in front of a car and instead of the blind idiot getting knocked down his dog took the hit. It's a bit like being a professional bodyguard being a guide dog. You've got to be prepared to take that bullet."

"Who started the Twitter campaign?" a voice in the crowd called.

"No idea," Niall said. "Wasn't me."

"What would you like to say to them?"

"Thanks. Obviously. And thanks to everyone who's responded. I mean it is truly fantastic."

"Who are you?" a journalist addressed Faith.

"Oh I'm nobody at all," Faith said. "Don't make me part of your story."

"She's not my mother or my lover," Niall said. "Before the speculation starts."

"But I have to say," Faith went on, "Hugo needs to get home. You wouldn't want to sit in a box like this any longer than you absolutely had to. So if you could see your way to letting us go now. We've really nothing more to say."

A reasonably respectful line to the pavement was cleared and Faith and Niall were able to start walking towards the car, although journalists kept popping up alongside them asking questions.

❂

"Niall?"

"Yes?" His phone had woken him out of a daydream.

"It's Lindsey." This was a turn up for the book. He hadn't even had to call her.

"Hello, Lindz. How are you?"

"I'm fine. But I just heard about you on the radio."

"Bizarre, isn't it? I get fired from a radio job and the next thing you know I'm back on the radio."

"Are you OK? Is Hugo OK?"

"Hugo's crap but it looks like he's going to pull through. I'm absolutely fine."

"How did it happen?"

"I thought you just heard it on the radio."

"Niall!"

"OK. Sorry. I was at some traffic lights. I thought it was my turn to go. Clearly it wasn't."

"I don't believe you."

"What?" Niall shook himself into a sharper state of wakefulness.

"I know you. That isn't a mistake you would make."

The kaleidoscope inside Niall's head shifted again. Was there anything – anything at all – in his previous knowledge of Lindsey to suggest that she had the perspicacity to figure out that he wouldn't step off a kerb before he was sure the coast was clear? It seemed utterly out of character. In which case this concerned phone call out of the blue was probably anything but. Either the shadowy boyfriend had put her up to it, or – but surely not – Lindsey herself was actually a part of this now. It was, he supposed, conceivable that they had bribed her with the job at Victory, and at that point explained what was going on and bought her loyalty, especially if the boyfriend was a key player.

"Everyone can make a mistake," he said, trying to think of ways to keep Lindsey talking whilst at the same time giving nothing away.

"You didn't hear the car?"

"No."

"Hugo didn't see the car?"

"Maybe. I told him to go so he went."

"Why did you tell him to go?"

"Lindsey I don't need an interrogation right now."

"OK. I'm sorry. I'm just – well it's all a bit upsetting when it's someone you know."

"Yeah. How's things with you?"

"Great."

"How's Victory?"

"There's not always much to do there, but it's good to be working again."

"Yeah. I bet."

"Sorry Niall. I forget you don't have a job."

"It's OK. Hugo's a celebrity now. We'll be getting our invite to go into the jungle with Ant and Dec in a day or two. Do you ever see Simon at work?"

"He's out and about a lot. But occasionally."

"What about Loosemore?"

"Vivien Loosemore?"

"Yeah. Somebody told me she was the patron or something."

"I've never seen her there at all."

"Right. How's your boyfriend?"

"Now who's doing the interrogating?"

"Sorry. It was just a polite inquiry. You never even told me his name."

"John. His name's John."

"OK. How's John?"

"Fine thanks."

"That's good."

"And you're really OK? And Hugo's really OK?"

"We're OK."

After a few more pleasantries the call ended. Niall stared sightlessly at his phone as if he couldn't quite believe what it had told him.

Katrina Masters came in from work at 2 am. She crept silently around the bedroom taking off her clothes, slipping into the bathroom to clean her teeth. Juliette was breathing steadily, but Katrina was never certain that she was actually asleep. She believed rather that Juliette pretended to be asleep because she didn't want to talk.

"Juliette? Are you awake?"

There was no response. The steady breathing continued. Katrina carried on the conversation inside her own head.

"I heard an item on the news today about a hit and run."

"Oh yes?"

"A guide dog was knocked down."

"Oh yes?"

"By a silver BMW."

"Oh really?"

"And you were cleaning our car."

"Coincidence."

"A silver BMW."

"What are you suggesting?"

FIFTEEN

"So you're back," Penny said to Rebecca.

"Yes," Rebecca said.

"I'd better clear all my shit out of your room then."

"Yes. You better had."

"Sorry," Penny said. "I thought you were gone for the whole year."

"I changed my mind."

"But haven't they given you the year off?"

"I haven't come back to go on my course," Rebecca explained. "I just need to be here. I'm going back to my waitressing job. See if they'll take me on full time."

Rebecca hoped that Penny wasn't going to suggest earning any more money at 17 Cardew Crescent. She didn't.

"Being at home didn't work out then?" Penny asked, semi-rhetorically.

"It worked fine. It was what I needed. But now – I need to be here."

"OK."

Penny shrugged and didn't pursue it. It wasn't in her nature to be overly curious about anyone else's life, being mostly wrapped up in her own.

Rebecca was glad, and more so when Penny went out and left her to her own devices. She had made some very hasty notes during the previous night's news bulletin, and from them she needed to develop an action plan – just as she might for a student with learning difficulties, she thought with wry amusement.

She went through the process of reclaiming her room, taking everything that was Penny's out and re-organising her own things. Sorting her room out had always been a way of sorting her mind out too, and as she moved and tidied she tried to process the emotions and the ideas that were wheeling around in her head.

What exactly did she think about this Miranda who had Joe's eyes? If they were Joe's eyes. Would she ever be sure, even up close? Is it the face within which eyes are set that makes them unique to their owner, or the person behind the eyes, or the eyes themselves? Because only if the last of those were the truth would she really know that she was looking at a part of Joe. A living part of Joe.

And how would that feel? She had this compulsion to go ahead and meet the girl, but if she did find herself looking at Joe's eyes alive in somebody else's face, when Joe himself was dead and burned, would that just make her want to hate her? Or love her?

Was this whole wild goose chase just a proof that she hadn't got over Joe's death?

Maybe. How did you get over a brother's untimely death? How exactly did you move on from that? This activity puzzle – find and meet Miranda – could be the perfect way. 'Keep busy' people had said. And this was keeping busy but keeping Joe in focus the whole time.

In which case, what was the plan?

The blind journalist's name was Niall Burnet. His dog was called Hugo. He was in a veterinary hospital in Clerkenwell, which wasn't an area that she knew, but surely that had to be her first port of call.

She ought to keep tuning into local news as well in case there were any updates. She didn't know a lot about dogs or Hugo's injuries, but unless she heard that he had died or gone home, she would go there and try to pick up the trail. In actual fact, she ought to do that soon, in case anything did change. She could plan further steps depending on the outcome of that visit. Further steps such as how exactly she could then contrive to meet with the man. How she would then explain her interest in Miranda without sounding like a total crank escaped from the nearest mental hospital.

In line with her thinking that time was of the essence, Rebecca put the rest of her sorting on hold and reflected that the extravagance of a taxi could be justified in the circumstances. It would be quick, and would take away any problems that she might have finding the place.

Leaving the flat she was lucky enough to flag one down before she had got to the main road, and found herself racing towards the city.

"That's where they took that guide dog," the taxi driver said conversationally.

"Yes, that's right."

"That why you're going?" he went on.

"No," Rebecca lied. "My cat's there having an operation."

"Oh right. Sorry about that."

The taxi driver didn't enquire as to why Rebecca's cat should have gone all the way to Clerkenwell when there must have been other vets closer to home. Rebecca caught herself in the act of creating an explanation before realising that she didn't have to justify her actions to someone she was paying to drive her.

It was only when she got out of the taxi that Rebecca realised she had formulated no plan for getting access to Niall Burnet or his dog. She had imagined walking in and just seeing him sitting in the waiting room, but she soon realised it wasn't going to be that simple. She needed a story. She was Niall's – what? All his family members would have his phone number. In fact in this day and age everybody had your phone number unless you didn't want them to have it. Perhaps it would have been more sensible to see if he was on Facebook.

And then, as if in answer to a prayer, she looked up the pavement and there was Niall Burnet, on the arm of a grey-haired woman, walking straight towards her. There was no sign of the dog, which meant, she presumed, that he was still in the hospital.

"This is not the moment to be cautious," Rebecca said to herself. "It's a god-given opportunity and it will never come again."

With uncharacteristic boldness she walked towards him.

"Excuse me – Niall Burnet?" she asked.

"Who's asking?" Niall responded, as Faith brought him to a halt.

"My name's Rebecca Blackford," Rebecca said. "You don't know me from Adam but I'm not a besotted admirer or a bunny-boiler."

"I could live with a besotted admirer," Niall remarked.

"And I'm not a journalist doing a piece or anything."

"OK. I now know what you're not," Niall said.

"Yes," Rebecca said, and paused. That was the easy bit over with.

"Shall we go inside?" the grey-haired woman suggested. "We've come to pick up some flowers."

"OK." Rebecca wondered if there had ever been a more surreal conversation.

"It's about your friend, Miranda Leman."

"Oh yes?" Niall said.

"I – " suddenly the truth seemed impossible. "I knew her. At primary school. When she was blind. We were actually quite good friends but then my family moved to Sussex. I saw her and you on *This Is Now* the other night and I thought then how it would be great to get in touch with her again, and then I couldn't believe it when I just saw you coming up the road. It was like it was meant to be."

"Right," Niall said, sounding unconvinced.

"I thought maybe you could give her my phone number when you next see her. Then if she did want to call me she could."

"Write it down and give it to Faith," Niall said. "I can't see the harm in that."

"Thanks. That's brilliant," Rebecca said. But if she never called it would be a dead end. "How is she?" Rebecca asked.

"She's OK. In Moorfields while they sort her out."

"Niall," Faith cautioned.

"I don't think it's a state secret," Niall said. "I'm sure Matt Long will have written it up for his paper."

Rebecca wrote her name and number down on a piece of paper she fortuitously found in her handbag, added 'friend from primary school' spuriously, and gave the note to Faith.

"Thanks so much," she said. "That's so kind. Thanks." And not wanting to draw further attention to herself she said her goodbyes and left, hoping to come across a tube station that would get her home and glad to know that Miranda was staying in hospital. That meant two things – one, she would probably get so bored that she might be reduced to phoning someone she had apparently known when she was young but had completely forgotten; and two, if she didn't, Rebecca knew where she was and could plan an alternative line of attack.

"She seemed pleasant enough," Niall said to Faith.

"Yes." Faith sounded doubtful.

"You didn't think so?"

"It just all seemed a little contrived," she said. "Not that anyone could have known we were coming here to pick up some flowers for Miranda."

"At least she didn't ask for Miranda's number," Niall said.

"No," Faith agreed.

"We can give Miranda hers and she can do what she likes with it."

"Yes," Faith said.

They collected several of the bouquets that were still arriving for Hugo, told the staff at the Animal Hospital to take any flowers home that they wanted, and then headed off to Moorfields.

"Do you fancy walking?" Faith said. "It's less than a mile away."

"No problem," Niall said.

They arrived in Miranda's room to find her looking at a magazine. Her face brightened immediately.

"Great," she said.

"We've brought you loads of Hugo's flowers," Niall said.

"Niall!" Faith said. "Where's your gentlemanly charm? These are Miranda's flowers."

"I'm a straight-talking, no-nonsense kind of guy," Niall said. "Each of these bunches probably cost upwards of twenty quid. I don't want Miranda thinking I blew over a hundred quid on flowers for her."

"No," Faith said. "She might be in danger of mistaking you for a romantic."

"They're lovely. Thank you," Miranda said. "Wherever they came from."

"Brought you something else as well," Niall said.

"Oh?"

"Faith?" Niall turned to her.

"What?"

"The phone number," Niall elucidated. "You've got a stalker," he went on to Miranda. "We bumped into her outside the Animal Hospital. Some girl you knew at primary school who said she'd seen you on the telly and thought how lovely it would be to get in touch. You were friends apparently."

"Oh," Miranda said.

Faith dutifully passed on the piece of paper.

"Can you read it?" she asked.

"No," Miranda confessed. "You know I haven't got to grips with sighted reading yet."

"You'd think they could get somebody in to do that for you while you're lying here doing nothing," Niall observed tactlessly.

"It says Rebecca Blackford," Faith said. "Do you remember her?"

Miranda thought.

"No," she said. "No. But I don't remember many people from primary school to be honest."

"She said you were friends and then she moved to Sussex."

"Oh well," Miranda said. "Nice of her to remember me."

"Just be careful," Faith said. "You don't have to call her."

"No I know," Miranda said.

When Faith went out to find some vases for the flowers Miranda looked straight at Niall and said

"So?"

"So what?"

"Have you found anything out? Are you on the trail?"

"It's not going to happen overnight," Niall said, which sounded better than the fact that he had done nothing since they had spoken on the subject. "I've got a bit of a problem with getting about at the minute."

"Me too," Miranda said.

"You keep a close eye on the people in here," Niall said. "Whatever is going on, I'm sure somebody here's involved in it."

"OK," Miranda said.

"But don't give your suspicions away," he added.

"No of course not," she said.

Faith returned with vases and a nurse, and the conversation turned to flowers.

❀

Katrina stared at the telephone number she had written down. She had started to key it in several times since Juliette had gone to work and each time had stopped before she got to the final digit. Why was she doing this? Was she just trying to get back at Juliette because their relationship was in trouble? Surely getting your partner into difficulties with the police was a bit extreme as responses went. But then there was the coincidence of the silver BMW and Juliette washing the car on a Friday afternoon, which she had never done before. And if Juliette had knocked the dog down, presumably by accident, then she should have stopped, not driven off and tried to obliterate any forensic evidence. Especially as she worked with blind people and would have known it was a guide dog. Presumably she had panicked. Not something Katrina would ever have expected from Juliette, but you never knew how anyone was going to behave in any situation until they were actually in the midst of it.

Surely she could ask the police to be confidential?

But Juliette would know at once where the tip-off had come from if they did follow it up.

And that, presumably, would be the end of their relationship. Katrina thought about women who were married to criminals. Did they admire them? Did they forgive them their way of life because they loved them? Did they like the lifestyle too much to turn their back on them?

Knocking a dog down wasn't exactly high up the ladder of criminality. What would she be doing if she had discovered Juliette was involved in drug smuggling or people trafficking? Talked to her about it, surely?

But that was the crux of the whole matter. They never talked about anything now. Not about themselves, not about each other, not about their relationships or their feelings. Not even about their working days. Any question she asked was savagely mauled and thrown back at her. Any attempt at meaningful conversation greeted with hackles and bared teeth.

When had Juliette last said a kind word to her? When – if ever, in fact – had she said that she loved her?

Juliette was a domineering woman. She wanted a partner for – it was difficult really to see what. Katrina wanted love and a partnership, and in all honesty she had never really found it. She had been lonely, vulnerable, carried along by the force of Juliette's personality in the beginning. But now...

She pressed the numbers again, all of them this time. She found herself speaking to a man who was patient and understanding. He listened to her carefully, took down every detail, asked her a number of questions related to where Juliette and her car would be now, and then gave her another number to call should she experience any unpleasantness or come-back as a result of the information she had given.

❧

Daniel Sullivan walked out of the British Association for the Blind, took out his mobile and made a call.

"The police are on to the Rottweiler," he said without introduction.

"How?" his interlocutor inquired.

"No idea. But they're talking to her now. Chances are they're going to want to look at her car."

"And what's she going to tell them?"

"God knows. She's tough. And loyal."

"Tough, yes. Have we got deniability?"

"Yes."

"I would love to know how they got on to her."

"You think somebody got the car number?"

"I don't know, Daniel. But the fact is things are not going terribly well in that area, are they? Every attempt to close down this particular problem actually seems to make it worse."

"I always said dealing with it was a mistake. We're running scared for no reason."

"The Rottweiler must go overboard."

"Obviously."

"A resignation would be good."

"I'll work on it."

Daniel walked up towards Hyde Park. He was angry. Angry because his advice had not been followed. Angry because he didn't need complications in his life when his number one priority was the seduction and subsequent energetic deflowering of Susannah Leman. Angry because it had all seemed so easy at the beginning. Ingenious. Now it was in danger of becoming a complete pig's breakfast and there was absolutely no way he was going down with the ship.

He called Penny. She was good for him at times like this.

❂

Miranda sat in her room at Moorfields. The television was on but she found it hard to be drawn into its world, and wondered why that was. Surely she should be filled with such a hunger for visual stimulation that television, with its ever-changing pictures, would be utterly compelling. And yet she felt completely detached from it. She would have liked to see a recording of her own appearance on *This Is Now*, just to see how Miranda presented herself to the outside world, but nobody had offered her that.

She reflected on Niall's suspicions about the transplant. They all seemed much too far-fetched to be true. He was understandably shaken up and distressed after his accident and it probably did help to build up a conspiracy theory. But what in the world could possibly be significant enough or sinister enough in her eye transplant to justify such a thing? She knew that Niall was no fool, and had a lot more experience of life than she did, but this time she was all but certain that he was wrong.

Not that she would say so to him. She didn't want to say anything to upset or disappoint him. She would help him in any way he asked her to, and if that meant spending time with him and being his sighted guide as he followed up various leads, so much the better. She wanted him to value her and appreciate her. To see that she could be good for him.

She looked, not for the first time, at Rebecca Blackford's telephone number. She had reviewed all her primary school memories, but there was no Rebecca in any of them. She didn't think she had ever known a Rebecca. And yet... why else would the girl have got in touch? Unless she was a part of Niall's grand conspiracy; in which case, she could follow up the lead herself and then impress Niall with having done so. But it was more likely that she had just forgotten her. Which might actually be embarrassing.

She had got as far as these conclusions before and yet she kept coming back to it. Her curiosity would not let it lie.

What had she really got to lose? She keyed in the number.

"Hello?"

"Is that Rebecca Blackford?"

"Yes. Speaking."

"It's Miranda Leman. Susannah to you probably."

"Miranda! Fantastic! Hi."

Should she admit to not remembering her? Or pretend that she did?

"How are you?" she asked.

"I'm fine. I'm great. How are you?" Rebecca said.

"Better than I was," Miranda said.

On her end of the line Rebecca wondered whether to pretend to a memory or two or just ask for a meeting.

"I couldn't believe it when I saw you on TV the other night," she said.

"Did you recognise me?" Miranda asked.

"Well it was the name first," Rebecca said, lying frantically. "I heard them say 'Susannah Leman' and I thought 'God that's a name I haven't heard in years. I wonder if it is the one I knew.' Then they said about you having been blind and I knew that it must be."

"But did you recognise me?" Miranda asked again.

"To be honest, no, not really." It was nice to be able to filter a bit of truth in amongst the lies.

"You could come and see me," Miranda said. "If you're not busy. I'm stuck here in hospital at the moment not going anywhere."

"That would be fantastic," Rebecca said. "I'm not busy. I'm doing a teaching degree but they gave me the rest of the year off because my brother was killed in an accident."

"Oh my God! I'm really sorry."

"Thanks. I'm living with it, but it's hard. That's why seeing you made a really nice diversion. Got me out of my own thoughts."

"I'm glad," Miranda said. "Come to Moorfields whenever you like. We can talk about old times."

"Thanks. Thanks so much."

Rebecca felt like a worm. The call ended and she weighed up what she had done. Lied through her teeth, with the prospect of more to come as she created some back-story for the two of them that would convince Miranda she was suffering from memory loss. And then used Joe's death to get her sympathy.

"Rebecca Blackford, you are a bad person," she said out loud.

❦

Juliette Warwick tried to analyse her feelings. Katrina's response to her righteous indignation had been an uncharacteristic outburst about a lack of love in their relationship. Then she had burst into tears, packed a bag and left. God knows where she had gone. To her visually impaired aunt, maybe.

And Juliette was left to reflect on her day.

The police had been the easy bit. She had convinced them it was all a complete misunderstanding and of course she, of all people, would have stopped if she had accidentally hit a guide dog. They were even quite apologetic in the finish.

But she hadn't expected to be called to Sullivan's office and asked to resign.

"Won't that make me something of a loose cannon?" she had said.

"We need you to be efficient and invisible," he had replied. "In this instance you have apparently been neither."

"And if I don't agree to go quietly?" she had asked.

"There are other ways," he had said, smiling.

"Don't you think it will look a bit like an admission of culpability?"

"Yes," Daniel had said. "That's exactly what it is. You knocked down a guide dog. That makes your position here untenable."

"But I'm not admitting anything."

Daniel had said nothing. She had got nothing more out of him. But she had refused to resign on the spot.

"I'll think about it overnight," she had said to him.

"Bring it with you in the morning," had been his response.

And now she wondered how she had ever allowed her fierce loyalty to the organisation she had worked in for eleven years to lead her down the path she had taken.

Still, no point crying over spilt milk. Katrina was gone. Her job was gone. It was time to think about where her loyalty lay now.

❧

"Jamal, my office."

Jamal Daghash broke stride in the corridor and looked up at Duncan Clark. He knew that Clark had few airs and graces, but he had never before addressed him as peremptorily as this.

"If you can spare the time," Clark added. "Welcome back from the States and all that."

Jamal shrugged, looked quizzical, and then followed the other consultant without a word.

Clark closed the door once they were inside.

"Is this about my star patient?" Jamal asked.

"The miracle girl? Yes," Clark replied.

"Thank you for everything you've done to keep her stable in my absence," Daghash said.

"I'm not after your thanks," Clark said, "and the truth is I've done very little. I have to hand it to you, Jamal, your impossible operation seems to have worked."

"Except...?"

"Except nothing. And that's why we have to talk." Clark settled himself back into his chair, tilted it as he leant back and put his hands behind his head. "I have driven that girl mad with my attention to her over the past several days. She thinks I dislike her and everything about her but all I've been trying to do is understand the inside of her head. Because there is absolutely no physiological reason why she should have stopped seeing, why her body should have started rejecting the eyes. We get her under observation and supervise her medication here and everything is fine. Incredibly fine. There's absolutely no need for her to be in here. So I assumed a psychological factor and I have made notes on every one of our conversations which are here and you can read them."

He tossed a manila file across the desk to Daghash.

"Like you I'm not a trained psychologist, but we get to know a fair bit about the psychology around sight problems and I also discussed it with Faith Hodgkiss, who is nobody's fool."

"Indeed not," Jamal said.

"We think the girl is sound. We don't think she is doing this to herself."

"What are you saying?"

"That somebody else is."

"What?" Jamal looked like a man punched.

"Things that can't be explained have an explanation," Clark went on. "That's the founding principle of all knowledge, and the driving force of science, isn't it? It's all about finding the one that fits. The one that makes sense in theory, and then putting it to the proof."

"What are you saying?" Jamal was floundering. "That someone is trying to sabotage Miranda's operation? What on earth for?"

"Well," Clark said honestly. "Take me, for instance. Staked my reputation on the fact that it was a stunt. Will be very embarrassing for me if it proves a triumph."

"Is this some bizarre confession?" Jamal asked.

"No." Duncan Clark laughed. "No. In the last ten days I could have finished her chances of seeing off once and for all. I'm a man of science, Jamal. Where I am wrong I patiently and humbly admit it and move on. I admit it now. You have achieved something I never thought possible. Hats off to you."

"Thank you."

"I was merely pointing out that there might be people with reasons to want the operation to fail."

"I can't imagine who or why," Jamal said, still stunned by the notion.

"You are a good man who lives in a chocolate box world where everyone's motives are good," Clark said. "How you manage that when you grew up in the Middle East is beyond me. But for now let's not fret about why or even who. Let's look at how."

"There is only one way," Jamal said.

"Precisely. If Miranda is taking her medication as prescribed and instructed..."

"Then the problem is in the medication itself."

The two men looked at each other.

"Damian?" Jamal said incredulously.

"Would certainly be worth talking to," Duncan Clark said.

It was one of those moments when Daniel Sullivan decided to review the status of everything in his life. It was a practice he enjoyed, because generally the review presented him with a great deal to feel satisfied about, but this time as he sat behind his desk having told his personal secretary that he was busy so she should hold his calls (a partially sighted woman who was besotted with him and whom he had had sex with on about a dozen occasions) he seemed to have a lot less to feel pleased about than normal. So much so that he wondered whether it might be worth making Bridget's day by calling her in and working up a sweat on her now. It had to be more satisfying than playing squash.

The Susannah Leman project was at a total standstill. She was completely unattainable whilst she was at Moorfields under the watchful eye of Duncan Clark, and the last time he had visited she had been so infuriatingly frigid that he had come close to losing his temper with her. It was clear even to a man of his ego and self-possession that she didn't find him remotely attractive, and was not swayed by his links to the famous and powerful either. The only way he was going to get to have sex with her was by plying her with so much alcohol she barely knew which way was up, and there was nothing satisfying in that. Nor could it happen while she remained in hospital.

He was still out of favour with the top brass at BAB, who felt that he had let them down on *This Is Now* and were not ready to forget about it because nothing else had yet come along to equal it for ineptitude.

Penny was starting to pall on him. Her Welsh accent irritated him. She spoke to him like an equal. She had even dared to tease him on occasion, and these were not qualities he looked for in a courtesan.

And then the Great Project, which had seemed foolproof and utter genius, was being undermined by idiotic over-reaction to a minor irritant that was now threatening the long-term success of the whole venture.

Manure whichever way you looked. He had dropped enough hints to the right people in the right places to have expected at least an MBE in the New Year's Honours, but once again nothing had materialised. The knighthood that he hankered after was as far away as ever.

Bridget knocked and walked in on him.

"I thought I told you not to disturb me," Daniel said irritably. "Holding my calls means I don't want to speak to anyone, including you, he added unpleasantly.

"I'm sorry," Bridget muttered in her wheedling, flustered tone. "Juliette Warwick is here and insisting on seeing you."

"Can't she just leave what she's brought with you?" he snarled.

"I don't think she's brought anything."

Daniel Sullivan sighed. Everyone was petrified of Juliette Warwick. It was why she was perfect for putting the frighteners on people.

"OK. I'll see her," he said, and Bridget withdrew. He composed himself and prepared for the onslaught.

Juliette walked in, making a great show of being completely relaxed, but it was only a show. If there was one thing that he was an expert at it was reading women, even women who had embraced the other persuasion and looked and acted a lot like men. "She's got bigger balls than I have," he had occasionally remarked to the Director General. Balls that he was going to enjoy crushing in the course of this conversation.

"I'm not resigning," she said without preamble. "So what's next?"

Daniel sighed and made a point of looking sad.

"This is very foolish," he said. "Nobody wants you to suffer."

"Of course not," Juliette said scornfully. "But you've got nothing on me if you're fancying the disciplinary route. And I suppose there's always a danger I might sing like a bird."

Daniel gave her a look.

"I'm not afraid of you," Juliette said.

"And I am certainly not afraid of you."

"That's good," Juliette said, reaching into her handbag and pulling out a CD-Rom. "When you've got a minute you can put this in your computer. Don't worry, there's only one file on it so it won't take you long to read. It just documents with dates and times. Every communication I have ever had from you or anyone else with regard to – shall we call them 'extramural activities' - for the Association. I have dozens of copies. Now you can dismiss them as the fabrications of a deranged and bitter lesbian when they reach the press but it will still make for a rather nasty smell around BAB, which might not suit your long-term plans."

Daniel looked at the CD on the desk in front of him. She was right. He could deny any and all of what was on it, but that kind of thing didn't matter to the chairman or the DG. Any whiff of anything and their policy was fire first for the reputation of the Association and deal with the repercussions later. And being fired would not suit his lifestyle.

"Perhaps you could arrange for me to have a tragic accident," Juliette was saying. "I'll have to take my chances. But right now I'm going back to my office. I like my job and I'm good at it."

Daniel continued to stare at the CD. He wondered whether he could persuade Bridget to level a sexual harassment charge against Juliette. Public sympathy would back a respected Blind charity over an oversexed lesbian, surely.

"We're going to let you out again," Jamal Daghash said to Miranda. She sat nervously in his consulting room, wondering why she felt nervous, wondering why Duncan Clark was also there, why he was still a part of her care now that Mr. Daghash was back.

"Will you go back to Faith Hodgkiss's?" Clark asked her.

"Well," Miranda said, "I will if she asks me."

"She's fine with it," Jamal said. "We've had a good long talk with her. It's good for us, actually, that you should be there, under the eye of a professional. We're still trying to understand exactly what is happening with your eyes. Her being on hand can only help."

"OK," Miranda said. It would be good to get out of the hospital. It would be good to get back to Niall. But now that he had put his conspiracy theories into her head she was unsure about Faith and the advantages of her being 'on hand'.

"Do you have any questions?" Mr. Daghash asked.

"Will it be the same as before?"

"Yes. Essentially. We may change the way you get your medication, but we won't do anything without checking with you first. We want you to try to live as normal a life – within sensible bounds – as you can."

"OK," she said.

"Five minutes later she was back in her room packing up the few things that were hers that had accumulated around her during her stay in Moorfields. She heard footsteps and turned to see Faith walking in.

"Hello," she said.

"Hello. I've come to take you home," Faith replied.

"Thank you. You're so kind."

"Nonsense. We started this convalescence, we had a bit of a

hiccup, now we're going to get it back on track. Niall's waiting for you back at the house. He's prowling around like a caged tiger with Hugo unable to take him out. He'll be very pleased to see you."

"I'm not exactly Hugo," Miranda said.

"Hugo is lovely," Faith said. "But he is only a dog. You're far better company."

Miranda wondered if that were really true as they travelled back to north London. Whether Niall ever thought about her in the way that she thought about him. She knew that everyone would pour scorn on her feelings, would tell her he was the first man she had ever properly met, that he was the equivalent of the boy next door, but the fact was that she thought about him almost constantly. She wanted to be with him, she wanted to listen to him talking, hear his take on the world and everything in it. People would say it was infatuation. Maybe it was. But it was a nice feeling. She liked feeling it. She had never felt anything like it before. It would be very special to know that he felt something similar about her, although she realised that was unlikely. In fact, she wasn't even sure that he really liked her that much. She had started out as a story. With his belief in dark goings-on beneath the surface of her operation she continued to be a story. Maybe that was all she would ever be to him. And yet he had been very upset when she had gone to the ballet with Daniel Sullivan. It was crumbs of comfort of that kind that kept her hoping.

❦

Niall meanwhile was puzzling over two cryptic text messages he had received from Simon. "Goings on at Victory" had been the first. Then there had been "Don't call us, we'll call you." Which had stopped him in his tracks just as he had been about to ring.

The fact that Simon now had a job was something of a pain in the arse. It meant that he couldn't be hassled on a whim at any hour of the day or night. Doubtless there were occasions when he was travelling around between appointments, but Niall never knew when those were. So now he was left in limbo, some carrot dangled tantalisingly in front of his nose and then snatched away – and Simon was irritatingly obtuse and vague at the best of times – waiting for Faith to bring him his sighted guide so that he could get back on the trail. No, that was unkind, he reflected as he drank raspberry tea. Miranda was a lot more than that. He thought of her as a friend now, a partner who was at least prepared to humour him and see this thing through.

His phone rang, but it wasn't Simon's ringtone. In fact, it wasn't anyone he knew.

"Hello?"

"Niall?"

"Maybe. Who am I talking to?"

"It's Simon, you prat."

"What happened to your phone?"

"I bought this one in case anyone was tracing yours or my calls."

"Bloody Hell," Niall said, impressed. "You're good at this cloak and dagger stuff, aren't you?"

"I have my moments," Simon said. "Don't bother to save this number because I'm going to try to get a load of SIM cards."

"You must think it's serious, then," Niall said.

"I haven't got a clue mate. I just don't want to get taken out by a car if I can possibly avoid it."

"Good thinking. So?"

"Loosemore was at Victory HQ this morning."

"Right."

"Being given the royal tour."

"OK."

"It was just some stuff she said."

"Right."

"Well I need to talk to you about it."

"And we're talking."

"Not on the phone."

"OK. Your local. This evening. All the staff know you and love you. We'll ask them to spot anyone who might be watching us. Oh, and Miranda will be there, of course."

"Is she out, then?" Simon asked.

"On her way now."

"And you've told her everything and she hasn't kicked you in the balls and told you to fuck off?"

"No."

"Remarkable."

◉

Damian Clarke sat in *Paul's* coffee shop on Marylebone station awaiting the train to Beaconsfield. He was struggling to eat a chocolate and almond croissant decorously and staring morosely at his smartphone, as if hoping it would speak to him.

In his head he was re-living the interview he had undergone that afternoon in Duncan Clark's office, the moment when the nightmare that his life had already become had reached its absolute nadir. And now, in the light of that, he wondered why on earth he had ever been tempted to step from the path of a successful and developing career; a career he had now thrown into total jeopardy, imperilling the security of his wife and young children, all of whom looked up to him as the model of perfect husband- and fatherhood. Who would sympathise with him if he said it had been for the money? Everybody knew doctors were well-paid. And yet it had been. That was precisely what he had been unable to resist. The chance to pay off their loans, the chance to improve their quality of life, buy Susan and the children nice presents, book up surprise treats.

Was that a selfish motive? When it had been his family's happiness he had been thinking of rather than his own? He had never pictured himself as someone who would or could find themselves involved in criminal activity. Was what he had done actually a crime?

The very ambiguity of that, of course, had been what they had played on. That, and the fact that it was virtually undetectable, that there would be no finger of blame, that it would all just be regarded as desperately sad, that the 'subject' would, in the end, be no worse off than she or he had been at the beginning.

Yes, those had all seemed good arguments, well supported by large amounts of cash and the promise of other 'perks' which hadn't quite turned out as he expected.

But then none of it had.

The 'virtually undetectable' had been detected by the evil genius that was Duncan Clark. The anonymous 'subject' had become a real person and he saw how Jamal Daghash's successful operation had changed and was changing her life. He had been losing heart and conviction for weeks, but they wouldn't let him go. Of course they wouldn't. He was their puppet now for the rest of his life.

And he had walked into this situation with his eyes wide open. An intelligent, educated man. In the process destroying everything that was precious and valuable in his life: the trust of his wife, the happiness of his children. For money.

He had sent emails. He had left text and voice messages. But all was silent in the ether.

He heard his train announced and got slowly to his feet. His hands were sticky and he had icing sugar down his front. These things seemed trivial, though, now.

"If what I have just suggested to you is true," he could still hear Duncan Clark saying, "your career in the medical profession is over. I shall see to that. If it is not true, you need to be able to convince me – utterly – that such is the case."

He had opened his mouth to answer, although he really had no idea what it was that he was going to say.

"No," Clark had gone on. "I don't want to hear your protestations and aggrieved denials now. Aggrieved denials count for nothing with me. Bring me some evidence tomorrow if you intend to disprove what I've said to you. Or not if you mean to acknowledge it."

With those words still ringing in his ears Damian Clarke boarded the train that would rush him back to the bosom of his family.

❧

Niall and Miranda took a taxi to Chiswick. Niall was still far too suspicious of Faith to let her know what his plans were, so just announced that the two of them were going for a drink, which she seemed to find plausible. In the taxi Miranda tried to get him to examine the evidence against Faith, because, as she put it, 'it would be really helpful if we could – what is it they say? – eliminate her from the enquiry.'

"But we can't," was Niall's response.

"Why?"

"Because she lives at Number 17."

"And what do you actually know about Number 17 that is connected directly with my operation?" Miranda asked.

Niall tried to remember.

"Daniel Sullivan," he said.

"How?"

"Sent emails about meetings at Number 17, was in on the ground floor of your operation – I even heard him speaking on the radio about it before I met you – and has pursued you ever since."

"Have you checked to see whether *he* lives at Number 17?"

"No."

"Might that be a good idea?"

"Wouldn't he have just said 'The meeting's on at my place,' or 'Meeting's on tonight. See you later,'?"

"Or 'See you at Faith's.'"

"Not if they didn't all know Faith."

"Let's try to put your theory together," Miranda said patiently. "A group of people including Daniel Sullivan plot something –"

"Skulduggery," Niall interposed.

"- around my operation – "

"Duncan Clark's involved."

"Duncan Clark?"

"d.clark@moorfields. Was told that the meeting at Number 17 was on."

"Duncan Clark hates me but he's done a decent job of getting my sight back."

"And what about the fact, going back to Faith," Niall said, "that she offered to let you convalesce at her house? Where she could keep an eye on you."

"So why did she ask you down as well? She knew you were interested in the transplant."

"To keep an eye on me. They needed to keep an eye on both of us. And Simon and Lindsey. Hence Victory."

"And meanwhile no more meetings. They must've found a new venue."

"Perhaps they don't need to meet now."

"But to get back to your theory," Miranda said patiently. "Whatever their plot is, they find you talking to this Lindsey and decide that you both need to be neutralised."

"Yes," Niall said, starting to sound doubtful. Self-doubt was bad enough, but this was decidedly worse.

"So the 'plot' – whatever it is/was – is serious enough for them to try and remove human obstacles."

"Yes."

"So what can it possibly be?" Miranda asked. "I mean, OK, your first idea about some dodgy financial dealings, maybe the odd bung or whatever they call it from my father to Daniel Sullivan. I can believe my father would do that. He thinks money is the answer to everything. But why would they need to have secret meetings at a mysterious location, well, at Faith's house, in fact? Wouldn't it be better if they didn't meet? But then, as you said before, if they were prepared to knock you down then the whole thing must be on a much bigger scale, but what? I mean, what could it possibly be? We don't know how my donor died but I cannot believe they found a perfect pair of eyes and then set about murdering their owner. That really isn't believable, Niall."

"No," he conceded.

"So," Miranda went on, "what IS the theory?"

"I don't know," Niall admitted after a brief pause. "I don't know and it bugs me. Because I do know that there is something going on. Something that seriously shouldn't be; and they think that I either know it already or am very close to finding it out. Maybe Simon will have the missing piece."

"Maybe," Miranda said.

The taxi deposited them outside Simon's pub of choice and Miranda led Niall inside, apologising for her incompetence as a guide as she failed to relay information about steps and obstacles.

"How will I know if he's here?" she asked.

"Look for a sad blind bloke with several pint glasses in front of him. Most of them empty."

"Can't we ask at the bar?"

"It's an option."

Miranda led Niall to the bar and, after asking the question, they were led to Simon's table.

"Hey," Niall said. "Simon, meet Miranda."

"Hello," Miranda said.

"Hi," Simon responded. The barman offered to sort out their drinks for them and Niall persuaded Miranda to try a vodka and cranberry juice.

"Got to start somewhere," he said.

"So?" he asked, once the drinks had come.

"I just happened to be at Victory HQ when Loosemore's royal visit took place," Simon said, refreshingly without preamble, Niall thought. "'Our patron is here. You must meet our patron,'" Simon impersonated in an awe-struck, breathless voice. "She made a bee-line for me actually. Asked me how I was liking the job, how good it felt to have a job and be doing something useful, which she managed to make sound like a bit of a threat. And then straight out she asked me whether I was in touch with you and whether you were still in London. 'Such a shame he didn't stay in Telford,' she said. 'Do you know what this crazy notion he has is?' She was really probing. I said I hadn't seen you since just after Christmas and that I didn't know what you were up to. But she's rattled, mate. Big time. It was like the old days at school when we broke into her office and found that bottle of Scotch.

She is totally panicking that whatever her secret IS, you've found it out."

"They all think I know what's going on, and I fucking don't," Niall said. "Why don't I? What the fuck is the matter with my brain?"

"Nothing's the matter with your brain," Miranda said quickly. "It's a jigsaw and you're missing a key piece. That's all."

"You've changed your tune," Niall said drily.

"There's more," Simon said, drinking beer.

"Yes?"

"She spent ages with Lindsey. In fact Lindsey showed her around."

"Is Lindsey mixed up in this?" Niall asked, semi-rhetorically.

"She wouldn't be my choice," Simon reflected. "But neither would Loosemore. Anyway, Loosemore's got an office there now."

"An office at Victory?"

"Yeah. I thought that was a bit weird. I mean, she's only the patron."

"Maybe BAB have asked her to clear her desk," Niall suggested. "What I wouldn't give to go through her office like we did at school."

"Yeah," Simon mused. "I was thinking the same."

"You guys are crazy," Miranda said, not without admiration.

"Miranda is a bloody celebrity and I'm a marked man," Niall said. "I don't think we're going to be able to walk in incognito."

"I could say I'd heard about the charity because your friend worked for them and I wanted to lend my name and face to their efforts," Miranda suggested.

"Genius," Simon said appreciatively.

"They'll know what we're doing," Niall said.

"Mate," Simon said, "they know we're doing stuff. They're watching you. They probably know you're here now."

"Not if Faith is their guard," Niall said. "It seems to me," he went on, "that going in through the front door is fraught with difficulty. You'd need to phone up, make an appointment, which would telegraph the fact that you were coming. Why would I be with you? And it might be that Loosemore is there sitting in her office the whole time. We need to get in at a time that we know she's out."

"So what are you suggesting?" Miranda asked.

"We break in. When we know the office is shut. Maybe I'll call Lindsey. Try and get some info about the layout of the place – "

"It'll be alarmed," Miranda interrupted. "We'll be breaking the law. It's different when it's a couple of schoolboys getting into the Head's study."

"You're not much help," Niall said. All three were silent.

"We have to get into that office," Niall went on eventually.

"Let me try it," Miranda said. "My way. On my own. Or maybe with Simon. If it doesn't work you can still break in."

"How would you know what you were looking for?"

"How would you?"

"What do you reckon?" Niall asked Simon.

"Worth a shout," Simon opined.

"I don't need to make an appointment," Miranda went on. "I can just turn up. If I catch them unawares so much the better. At least I can find out where her office is if nothing else so that when you two do your breaking and entering you'll have some idea where you're going."

"Yeah," Niall said doubtfully.

"I know you've got no faith in me," Miranda said.

"It's not that," Niall responded defensively.

"Yes, it is."

"Your eyesight's fragile," Niall said. "You're convalescing. You don't need excitements and extra stress."

"I won't let it stress me out," Miranda countered. "Why should it? I won't be doing anything illegal."

"OK," Niall conceded. "And when you do go I'll go to Moorfields and try to see Duncan Clark. That'll keep Faith's eyes focused on me instead of you."

"You can't just roll up and expect a consultant to see you," Miranda said.

"I'll think of something. Perhaps I'll get Faith to set it up."

Miranda's phone rang.

"This is a mobile free pub," Simon muttered.

"Who's going to be calling you?" Niall said, intrigued.

"I have a life," Miranda said mysteriously, smiling. "I'll take it outside," she added, noticing the glares from other patrons.

"She fancies you," Simon said when Miranda had gone out.

"Maybe," Niall conceded.

"But then she hasn't known many men," Simon added.

"Miranda?"

"Yes."

"It's Rebecca."

"Hi."

"I went to Moorfields. You're not there."

"Oops. No. Sorry," Miranda said. "They let me out. I forgot to tell you."

"I should've called first. Oh well. Best laid plans."

"I'm in a pub in Chiswick with some friends," Miranda said. "Niall's here. The man you gave your number to. You could come and join us if you're anywhere nearby."

"Is it anywhere near a tube station?"

"I'll have to ask. Let me go back in and find out and call you back. I promise I will."

They said a brief goodbye and Miranda went back inside. Her suggestion of Rebecca joining them was not greeted with instant enthusiasm, but in the end, "seeing as how you've already made the offer," as Niall grudgingly put it, they conceded and Simon gave Miranda the necessary instructions, which she duly relayed to Rebecca.

Forty-five minutes later, physically shaking with trepidation, Rebecca walked into the pub. This was not how she had planned it. This would not have been how she would have wanted it. All the way in the train she had cursed her own impatience that hadn't let her make an excuse and make an arrangement for another day; when the two of them could have been alone and in full daylight she could have confirmed or denied the belief that Miranda was sporting Joe's eyes. How would she possibly know in the umbered ambience of a pub? Admittedly it wouldn't be odd if the two of them went to the loo together, where the lights would be brighter, but suddenly the whole thing struck her as cruel and in bad taste. She could have passed the pub and not gone in. But curiosity got the better of her.

She recognised Niall and, after buying herself an apple and mango J2O (because the last thing she needed was alcohol), she walked over to the table, happy at least that the option to stand anonymously at the bar and compose herself had been presented by the fact that Niall – the only one of the three she had met – could not see her. Blindness had its uses, she reflected cruelly.

"Hello. Miranda. I'm Rebecca." She tried to sound calm, but her voice came out pinched and trembling.

"Hello, Rebecca." The eyes looked up at her. She looked into them.

"Are you OK?" Niall asked. "You sound rough."

Rebecca burst into tears.

Juliette Warwick answered her doorbell and was astonished to see John Holthouse, BAB Director of Finance, on her doorstep.

"Sorry to call on you at this time of night," he said. "Could I possibly come in?"

"Yes," she said guardedly. "Can I get you something?"

"No thanks," Holthouse said. "If we could just sit somewhere and talk."

Juliette showed him into the sitting room.

"Take your pick," she said, indicating the range of seats on offer.

John Holthouse sat in an armchair. Juliette sat on the sofa. There was an uncomfortable silence. In all her years with the Association Juliette had encountered John Holthouse no more than four or five times. He was a shadowy figure who seemed to remain almost entirely behind closed doors. It was extraordinary that he was in her house. It was extraordinary that he had even known where it was.

"I'm here as a friend," he began.

"I barely know you," Juliette interposed.

"I know. But if the DG had come it would not have been as a friend," Holthouse said.

"What's going on?" Juliette asked. John Holthouse sighed. He looked around the room, apparently for inspiration.

"This is really very awkward," he said. "I understand your partner left you recently."

"If it's any of your business," Juliette snapped aggressively. "Oh God," she went on, "this isn't something she's stirred up, is it?" She hadn't imagined that Katrina would be vindictive, but then perhaps she had never really known her.

"No," John Holthouse said. He paused. "I'm going to ask you

some personal questions. You don't have to answer them. But just remember what I said when I came in. I'm here as your friend. Anyone else who comes won't be."

"Go on then," Juliette said. Holthouse paused again. He breathed deeply.

"Would it be true to say that you have occasionally visited singles websites?" he enquired.

Juliette looked him squarely in the eye.

"Yes," she said.

"And that you have also advertised on these websites?" he went on.

"Yes," Juliette said. "In my own time. It's not a crime."

"Always in your own time?"

"Yes."

"And on your own personal computer?"

"Yes."

"I'm afraid that's not true, is it?" Holthouse said after a momentary pause.

Juliette looked at him. Her mind was in a whirl.

"My God. You?" she said. "You're a part of all this. Maybe THE part."

"What are you talking about?" He looked completely surprised.

Juliette laughed.

"So tell me what's been planted on my computer," she said.

"Nothing's been planted, Juliette," Holthouse said. "But we do have evidence that you have used the company's computer to place these 'advertisements', for want of a better word, and, having seen one of them, I have to say I was – well, shocked."

"One imagines ones private life is ones own affair," Juliette said.

"Not when it's conducted on the firm's time," John Holthouse replied.

"If you say so."

"I find your reaction difficult to fathom," he said. "I came here to warn you that this has been discovered."

"That's very thoughtful of you, John," Juliette said. "Now you're going to suggest I resign."

"Isn't it in everyone's best interests?" he said. "Do you really want these things to be talked about openly? The one I looked at was – obscene, in my view."

"Thank you for the warning, John," Juliette said, getting up. "It's good to know one has friends. You don't need to waste any more of your evening on me."

"If you think I'm homophobic you're quite wrong," Holthouse said, standing.

"Of course not," Juliette said. "Men like the idea of two women doing it, as I understand."

A minute later he was gone, and she closed the door behind him.

❧

In the aftermath of her tears Rebecca had explained everything. She didn't know whether she was embarrassed or relieved. Miranda had said almost nothing. Niall on the other hand was intrigued.

"Faith said you were dodgy," he said.

"Oh, I'm definitely that," Rebecca said.

"So what do you think?" he went on. "What do you see?"

"It's dark in here," Rebecca said. "It's awkward. Look, I'm sorry. This was a bad idea. I think I should go."

"No don't," Miranda said. She had been sitting quietly trying to decide what she felt, what this meant to her. Whether or not she had Rebecca's brother's eyes was immaterial. She had always known they belonged to someone before she had them, and that that someone had died before their time. Knowing who that someone was, given that it was a person she didn't actually know, made no difference to her. She could, presumably, always have found out unless the donor family had requested anonymity. She had always assumed they must have been a girl's eyes, but thinking about it an eye was pretty much an eye. 'You have your mother's eyes' was something that could be said to a man without it implying anything effeminate. The opposite must also be true. And in any case this was still all conjecture based upon coincidence. The coincidence of Joe Blackford's death and her eye transplant. Rebecca still wasn't sure, even after looking her in the face. It was the pretence of childhood friendship that was annoying her: she wished Rebecca had been honest with her from the beginning – although she could see too why the lie had been chosen over the truth.

"I suppose if you really want to know, Moorfields will have all the records," she said. "It would be a sure-fire way of finding out."

"But that's the weird thing now," Rebecca said. "I don't know if I want to know for sure. It's almost better just wondering and thinking "maybe," rather than seeing in black and white that the answer's no, even though you'd swear it was yes."

"I can see that," Simon said, surprising everyone because he had barely spoken since Rebecca had arrived.

"I mean it is good to know that Joe's death did some good," Rebecca elucidated. "It's good to know that someone's got his kidneys and his liver and his lungs and maybe his heart. It's good to know that others have moved closer to their life-saving operation because of him. I don't feel any need to track those people down. In fact I'd really rather not. And I don't believe that because those parts of Joe are still functioning, because his heart is still beating, he's still alive in some bizarre way. I really don't believe that. It was just the eyes. There is something about eyes."

"You're right there," Niall said.

"I'm sorry," Rebecca said, horrified. "That was really thoughtless of me."

"Don't shit yourself, I'm agreeing with you girl," Niall said. "Believe it or not, these were a fully functioning pair once upon a time."

"God I admire you all," Rebecca said.

"Don't," Niall said. "We don't want admiration or sympathy. We just want to be normal. But about your brother's accident, since we've entered the realm of tactless questioning..."

"Yes?" Rebecca asked willingly.

"Was there anything dodgy about it?"

"You mean other than his best friend's driving?"

"Niall!" Miranda snapped, hoping that he wasn't about to unleash his conspiracy theories on a total stranger.

"It's OK," Rebecca said, misunderstanding.

"Were there any other cars involved, suspicious circumstances?" Niall pressed on.

"No other cars as far as we know," Rebecca said. "There were no witnesses so I suppose he could have been racing someone who just buggered off. There was a suspiciously placed tree at a suspiciously sharp bend in the road which they took suspiciously fast. The police said it was all about speed and losing control."

"OK."

"Why do you ask?" Rebecca went on. "It seems a bit of an off the wall question."

Miranda was too far away or she would have given Niall an almighty kick under the table.

"I've got a theory," Niall said. "Journalist's nose," he added, in an attempt to sound mysterious and impressive.

"Sorry to knock it on the head then," Rebecca said smiling.

"Not at all," Niall said. "Just removed one possible line of investigation."

"So that could be a good thing."

"Yes."

Miranda sensed a chemistry developing between Rebecca and Niall, and she didn't like it. Suddenly she wished the girl would leave. Alternatively,

"Do you think it's time we went back?" she said to Niall.

"I don't know. No stamina," Niall said.

"I'm supposed to be getting lots of rest, remember? And we've got important things to do tomorrow."

"Tomorrow?" Niall said, startled.

"No point in hanging about, surely?" Miranda said.

"No indeed," Niall agreed. "Whatever happened to that girl I knew?"

"She met you," Miranda replied.

"Good answer. Pleasure to meet you, Ms. Blackford," he said with mock ceremony, getting to his feet. "You must catch up with Miranda in daylight sometime. I would say stay and have another pint with Simon, but Erica might not be too impressed."

Miranda guided him swiftly, if inexpertly, out of the pub and into the street.

SIXTEEN

"Oh my God," Lindsey spluttered, "you're Sus – Mary – the eye transplant..."

"And you must be Niall's friend Lindsey," Miranda said.

"First girl-friend, actually," Lindsey said, "before I came to my senses."

"Miranda wants to give her support to our work," the woman escorting her said. "I thought as you had a mutual acquaintance perhaps you could show her around and tell her what we're about."

"Yes of course," Lindsey said. "Not that there's much to show."

The woman glared.

"Lindsey's still got rather grand ideas from her days at the British Association for the Blind," she said to Miranda. "Obviously we're not on that scale. But we're proud of what we're doing."

"And it sounds great," Miranda said. "I want to see everything. And you can give me lots of gossip about Niall as well."

"You're not going out with him?" Lindsey said, astonished.

"No," Miranda said. "But we are sharing a house at the moment."

"Oh yes, Faith's," Lindsey said. "Oh well, right then. I can certainly fill you in."

The woman who had brought Miranda to Lindsey rolled her eyes. It was an expression Miranda had yet to learn the full meaning of, but she thought she understood the gist. What it meant was that her scheme was working. That playing the 'girls together' card would drive the older woman off and leave the two of them on their own. All she would have to do now to complete the plan was come over dizzy when they were in Vivien Loosemore's office and dispatch Lindsey for a glass of water. Miranda was rather impressed with her own plan, especially considering that she was a total novice where subterfuge was concerned. She smiled inwardly when she thought about what Susannah would have made of it all. Meek, mild, one-dimensional, lost-to-posterity Susannah. But she had to acknowledge that, had there been no Niall Burnet, Miranda might very well have ended up as a pale sighted imitation of her previous incarnation. And she had to admit, too, that she was enjoying playing this game of a sighted life, especially one that involved intrigue and mystery. Even though it was her own eye transplant that was the source of it all.

Lindsey chatted on in her own inimitably raucous way as she explained to Miranda that their main purpose was to raise funds in order to purchase iPads and laptops and software to help blind children access education. She explained that at the moment they had a small team of fund-raisers based in the office, of which she was one, and a small team of 'field operatives' who went into the schools to train the children to use the equipment. All their field operatives were either totally blind or partially sighted.

"There are loads of blind computer geeks like Simon," Lindsey said.

She went on to say that, if the charity really took off then they hoped to fund a department which would actually research and develop new software that would make the VI IT experience even better.

"You're going to need a heck of a lot of money, then," Miranda observed, looking around her at the less than salubrious suite of offices.

"Yes," Lindsey said eagerly. "That's why my job's so important. But we're really lucky because our patron is going to get herself personally involved, and she's got loads of experience of fund-raising."

"Is that Vivien Loosemore?" Miranda asked, careful not to sound too knowing.

"Yes. I expect Niall has given you masses of bad press about her. She was the Headmistress when we were at school, and Niall didn't exactly get on with her, but really she's brilliant. So committed. And she kept the school afloat with what she knew about fund-raising. My boyfriend says so and he's head of finance at BAB."

"Right," Miranda said. "But doesn't she have a full-time job with BAB? I'm sure Niall said..."

"Yes. I don't know how it works. I think she may have gone down to part-time there. Doing a job share, or something."

"OK."

"She's got an office here now and everything."

"Oh right. Well I'd better see that. Niall will want to know I've been in Vivien Loosemore's office."

"Too right he will. He'd want you to set fire to it."

They both laughed, and Lindsey opened the door on a small spartan room with a desk, chair, telephone and filing cabinet. There was a window that looked out over the street, but they were on the second floor, and the window itself looked as if it hadn't been opened in years. There was a calendar on the desk, a few papers, and nothing else.

"Ta-da!" Lindsey said. "Vivien's office."

"Plain and simple," Miranda said.

"Well yes. She's not had it long."

Miranda stumbled against the desk.

"Are you all right?" Lindsey asked.

"Yes. Well. I don't know. I get these dizzy spells sometimes. Apparently they're quite normal. Could you get me a glass of water? I'll just sit down for a bit and it'll pass."

"Yes of course," Lindsey said. "You do look a bit pale. I can do you water or tea if you prefer."

"Thanks. Water will be fine." She knew the tea would have taken longer, but there didn't seem to be much to take up her time here.

"Do you want to come back to the fund-raisers' office?" Lindsey asked. "I can give you an arm."

"Can I just sit here?" Miranda said weakly. "I won't touch anything."

"Of course," Lindsey said kindly. "There's nothing precious in here anyway."

She went off in search of water. Miranda sat at the desk. It had two drawers which were locked, but the key was in the lock. When she was certain that Lindsey had gone she opened the bottom drawer. It was empty. She opened the top drawer. There was a notebook and a packet of business cards. Miranda opened the notebook. It seemed to be empty apart from a list of names on the first page – conceivably possible sources of funding, although they all seemed to be Christian names and there were no phone numbers beside them. The name 'Daniel' caught her eye. Maybe these were people she knew at BAB. In which case, not likely to be sources of funding. But maybe people she had been thinking of calling to see if they had any ideas or contacts of their own. If they all worked at BAB that would explain why she hadn't added any phone numbers. It made sense. She tried to memorise names off the list, but her sighted reading was still painstakingly slow, and even as she was doing it she wondered why. Niall wouldn't know if a list of names belonged to people who worked at BAB. Faith would, if only they could trust her and take her into their confidence. She closed the notebook and picked up one of the business cards, smiling at the thought that fund-raiser extraordinary Vivien Loosemore had thought it an important and necessary expense to invest in having business cards printed. She wished she was quicker at reading. 'Vivien Loosemore. Patron, Victory. Bringing computer technology to visually impaired children.' She guessed 'visually impaired' from the v and the i.

"Has Lindsey deserted you?"

Miranda panicked and looked up with a start. The woman she had first met was standing in the doorway.

"No, no," she said weakly, smiling. "I came over a bit faint. She's gone to get me some water."

"Oh. OK," the woman said. She stared pointedly at the open drawer in front of Miranda.

"Sorry. I didn't mean to. I'm terribly nosy. It comes of only just having learnt to see, I suppose."

The woman continued to look disapproving.

"I think what you're doing is fantastic," Miranda said. "I want to help in any way I can."

At that point, much to her relief, Lindsey returned with the water.

"Here you are," Lindsey said. "How are you feeling now?"

"It's passing," Miranda said. "Thanks."

"Passing all the sooner for nosing in our patron's things," the older woman said.

"I'm sorry," Miranda said again. "It was kind of automatic. And there was really nothing to nose in."

She looked hard at Lindsey to see whether anything that resembled suspicion crossed her face, but she seemed completely unperturbed.

"Let's go back to your office," she said to Lindsey, closing the desk drawer and making a point of ostentatiously locking it. "I feel better now."

Under the fierce and watchful gaze of the older woman Lindsey and Miranda left Vivien Loosemore's office. Miranda was confident, though, that, fierce and watchful though she may have been, she had not observed one of the patron's business cards finding its way into Miranda's pocket. Something she had seen on it at the very moment she had been disturbed had struck her as potentially very important indeed.

❧

Faith sat in the room with them. It was not as Niall would have wanted it, but in the end it was the only way that Duncan Clark would agree to meet with him. They had left Hugo for his physiotherapy session at the animal hospital and walked the comparatively short distance to Moorfields, it being a grey but dry day.

"What exactly is your involvement in all this?" Clark asked. Faith had warned Niall that Duncan was an awkward customer ("As am I," Niall had quickly responded), and that he would be unlikely to agree to a meeting when there was no obvious reason for it. "Other than as Miss Leman's knight in shining armour," the consultant surgeon went on.

"I'm certainly not that," Niall said hastily.

"Right, well, I'm a busy man," Clark said. "I've got time for Faith but precious little for anyone else unless they require my professional services, which don't come cheap."

"Absolutely," Niall said. "Let's get right down to it." He was not one to be intimidated. Faith should have warned Clark about that. "A few days ago my dog was knocked down by a car outside Miranda's father's architects' office."

"Tragic," Duncan Clark said.

"It wasn't tragic," Niall cut across him; "it was deliberate. Somebody came up beside me as I was standing at the kerb and told me it was clear to cross."

"Sick," Clark commented.

"They did it because they think I'm on to something about Miranda's operation," Niall went on. He knew that he was exposing himself horribly, but if Faith was a part of whatever it was she already knew that he had suspicions, and he was past beating about the bush. Surprisingly, his statement didn't meet with ridicule. It encountered silence.

"And what is this something you're on to?" the consultant asked at last.

"I think you know," Niall said.

"And if I do?"

"I think maybe it was you who came up to me and put on some humble London accent."

Duncan Clark guffawed with what sounded almost like genuine laughter.

"I did once dabble in amateur theatricals," he said. "When I was an undergraduate. But not for a long time. Tell me upon what you base this preposterous accusation."

"I have some evidence – never mind what – " Niall continued carefully, "that you're in communication with Daniel Sullivan at BAB."

"An odious man," Clark said, "but I suppose it's not beyond the bounds of credibility that a Moorfields consultant should be in contact with the chief assistant to the assistant chief of the country's leading VI charity."

"Possibly," Niall conceded. He knew he couldn't mention the emails without risking legal complications. They had reached an impasse. "Sullivan's behind it," he said, needing something to say.

"I think that's highly unlikely," Clark said. "I suppose I would say that, wouldn't I," he added, "as I'm supposedly in league with him."

There was a pause, in which Niall wished he could see Clark's face. He heard the other man sigh.

"Mr. Burnet," he said, "your allegation against me – if that is what it is – is offensive and potentially libellous. Publish and be sued, I am tempted to say. Faith did say you were a journalist, didn't she? However, on one thing, curiously, we are agreed. Which is that all is not entirely as it should be around Miss Leman's operation. Presumably this is why Faith contrived this meeting. But I need to have some kind of idea what it is that you have put together before I decide whether I am prepared to share any of my thoughts with you. And any discussion that we do have will be completely off the record and based upon your admission that your accusation against me is groundless."

"Just tell me what Daniel Sullivan's emails were about," Niall said, risking all. He had been wrong-footed and surprised by what the consultant had said, and already wished he hadn't made his spur of the moment accusation against him regarding the hit and run. He expected a storm of outrage about illegal computer hacking. Instead Clark said

"Emails? I've never had an email from Daniel Sullivan in my life. What sort of an investigative journalist are you?"

A very confused one, Niall thought. Either that or a very stupid one who was being conned by everybody. What was he thinking?

Faith's house was Number Seventeen. Faith was sitting there. He had just revealed his entire hand to her.

"You are d.clark I presume?" he said, realising that he'd be lucky to leave the room alive, or at least not under arrest.

"Well now that is interesting at last," the consultant said. "Because suddenly you go from being an inept time-waster to someone who actually might have something significant to contribute. Whether or not the information was obtained legally."

Niall's confusion was complete.

"I am not 'd.clark', as you – logically, I have to say – surmised," Clark continued. "You reckoned without the illiteracy and lack of attention to detail that bedevils the majority of our fellow citizens. "I am actually 'duncan.clark'; 'd.clark' is the lesser of the Clark species, Doctor Damian. Whom you, intelligently, will have discounted because his surname ends in an 'e'. But, alas, I had made such a mark in my years here that our admin staff assumed there was only one way to spell Clark, so when Doctor Damian joined us, they erroneously gave him 'd.clark' without an 'e'. He did tell them about it, but they never corrected it. And so your whole edifice of a case against me collapses, under the weight of administrative incompetence."

"Right," Niall said. He felt humiliated, defeated. He wanted to crawl away into a dark corner and let everyone laugh at him behind his back. In front of Faith he had jeopardised the secrecy of their entire investigation. If they hadn't been before, they were all in danger now.

◉

Damian Clarke settled into the driving seat of the family car. His wife had gone out for the evening to play bridge. The children were peacefully asleep upstairs. Staring into space he thought back over his life, over all their lives. Saw smiles, heard laughter. Things had been good to them; life had been kind. And then had come the business with the eye transplant. How had it all begun? He remembered a meeting between himself, Jamal Daghash, Daniel Sullivan and John Holthouse. It was the first time he had met the BAB men. Jamal had explained to him beforehand that BAB had given a great deal of money to help fund the research for his 'Great Project'. These men were pushing him now to 'go for an operation' in order to catch headlines and make his work newsworthy. He resented it, but he knew he owed BAB a great deal. Without their support he would never have got to the point that he had now reached. It was still, really, too soon. But they were threatening to pull the plug from his funding if he didn't comply with their request.

"It seems to me," Jamal had said to him, "that they don't really care about success or failure for the poor person they want to be their guinea-pig. They just want it to happen."

If he had only known the truth.

At the meeting John Holthouse had explained that they had found the perfect subject for the operation. She was the daughter of a friend of his, had been blind since birth, and the man was prepared to 'make a massive donation' if his girl could be the one to have the treatment.

Jamal had rejoined that she would have to undergo a series of medical tests to assess her suitability.

"Money passes most tests," John Holthouse had rather smugly said.

The atmosphere at the meeting had been tense; at times aggressively adversarial as Jamal tried to stand up for the integrity of his work. He needed another year to be properly ready. He wanted to assess a number of possible subjects. He came up against the brick wall of the BAB men's money. To deny them would have meant a hiatus in his research while he looked for alternative sources of funding for a project that most influential eye specialists considered to be only half a step up from attention-seeking quackery.

And so he gave in. For the first time they heard the name Susannah Leman.

"I would give the operation at best a 50% chance of success," Jamal said.

"If at first you don't succeed..." Daniel Sullivan said pleasantly.

As the meeting broke up, Sullivan and Holthouse invited the two of them to a wine bar for a drink to 'celebrate'. Jamal Daghash, a practising Muslim and thus teetotal, said he didn't feel there was anything to celebrate, and declined. Fatally, he – Damian – had accepted.

Over a bottle of champagne John Holthouse had explained the delicate balance of BAB's finances.

"Make no mistake, BAB is a wealthy charity as charities go," he had said. "But I still have to give a pretty good account of myself when it comes to dishing out large sums to research projects like this one."

Damian had sipped his wine and nodded, feeling absurdly privileged to be the recipient of the other man's confidences.

"The principle for us is," Holthouse went on, "that any grant is actually a kind of investment, with the prospect – even the necessity – of showing some return. Giving sight to the blind is a hugely emotive, popular issue. When we've managed to get it into the public consciousness it has outscored Guide Dogs, and believe me that takes some doing. But, like all these things, it needs momentum. Showing the world pictures of Jamal in his laboratory isn't going to get people dipping into their pockets. And we've got to start getting the money back."

Damian, under the influence of the champagne, had said he understood. And it had been then that Holthouse had looked at Sullivan, and then back at him, and said, "There is a way that this could work out really well for all of us – REALLY well – but we'd need to be able to place implicit trust in you." And then the whole scheme had been put before him. It wasn't one operation that BAB needed, it was a series. Heroic failure followed by heroic failure would keep the topic in the news and keep the money flooding into BAB's coffers. Which in turn would give the money Jamal needed to 'get it right'. Daniel Sullivan had silenced Damian's ethical objections.

"You heard Jamal himself say there was only a 50% chance of success," he had said. "Most eye surgeons think there is none. We just want to ensure that. This girl has never seen. She'll be no worse off if, after a big burst of publicity, she still can't. But the whole blind community will be better off because BAB will have much more money at its disposal. It's about the bigger picture."

"And of course," Holthouse had added, "your importance to the whole project would be reflected in what proportion of income came your way."

Figures had been mentioned. He had asked for time to think it over. They had said they really needed to know then and there. They had exposed themselves to him by sharing their intentions. They needed to know where they stood. That had been clever. Bounced into a decision without time to think it over, he had seen what they had wanted him to see, lost sight of his principles, lost sight of the victim or potentially victims at the heart of this fraud.

He had agreed, and that road had led him here.

He turned the key in the ignition and stared into the darkness in front of him.

"I think I've put us in the shit," Niall said.

"OK," Miranda said.

Niall outlined the essence of his meeting with Duncan Clark.

"Well," Miranda said when he had finished, "Subterfuge is obviously not your strong point. But if Duncan Clark had suspected that Faith was involved he'd never've said anything to you."

"But he doesn't know about her," Niall said. "We're the only ones that do."

"Or maybe we don't," Miranda said.

"That's just what you want to believe."

"Well, I have in my possession, pinched from her desk in her office at Victory, one of Vivien Loosemore's business cards."

"You little thief," Niall said, clearly impressed. Miranda glowed. "What about it?"

"It's got lots of difficult words on it for a beginner, but it's got what's obviously an address and phone number in small print at the bottom."

"And?"

"Her address is 17, Cardew Crescent."

"My God!"

"I couldn't read the words straight away, but the number caught my eye."

"My God!" Niall said again. "Of course, it doesn't prove anything. We don't know which 17 is the one. It still could be here."

"I would say there was more than enough evidence now to give Faith the benefit of the doubt," Miranda said. "You've known her much longer than I have, but I would be prepared to bet my entire disability allowance that she's one of the good guys."

"I wonder how long you'll be able to go on getting disability allowance," Niall mused.

"Oh, Niall," Miranda said, exasperated. "Don't dodge the point."

"No, OK," he conceded. "I do agree with you, but I still don't think we should trust her."

"Duncan Clark does. And you yourself said he's no fool."

"He thinks it's your doctor."

"But why? What have I ever done that he would want to sabotage any hopes I have of being able to see?"

'Whatever his role is," Niall said, "I'm still convinced the thing begins at BAB. We ought to reel in your pet journalist. He might be able to help. And he ought to be interested."

"I thought you wanted the story for yourself. And he's only interested in my sister."

"He's probably got resources at his disposal that we haven't."

Miranda looked mulish and unconvinced, but Niall couldn't see her.

"Then there's a list of names," she said, letting Matthew Long's resources slip by.

"What list?"

"In Vivien Loosemore's almost empty office," Miranda explained. "There were basically three things. A calendar, the business cards, and a notebook. The notebook was empty apart from a list of names on the first page."

"Which you tore out."

"No."

"Great."

"How obvious would that have looked? I tried to memorise them."

"Were there numbers or anything with them?" Niall asked.

"No," Miranda said.

"So what do you think they were?"

"I don't know really. Daniel was one of them."

"Daniel Sullivan?"

"Just Daniel. They were all just first names. Gordon was another."

"Gordon can be a surname," Niall observed. "Byron's name was Gordon. And there was Gordon of Khartoum. Had she written on the calendar?"

"I don't think so."

"You don't think so. But you didn't check."

Miranda got up and walked out of the room. She knew she was about to cry and she didn't want Niall to see it. She thought she had done well at Victory. She thought she had found out at least one significant piece of information. And there had been something else, too. She went back to the kitchen where they had been sitting and stopped in the doorway.

"You might want to know that Lindsey's boyfriend is Director of Finance at BAB. Or so she told me."

"Wait," Niall said, hearing her going again, but it was too late. He sighed. He was a boor. He shouldn't take out his own frustrations on Miranda. He was the one who had majorly cocked up. Revealed all. Behaved like an idiot. She had contrived to be alone in Loosemore's office and he hadn't even thanked her, let alone praised her. No wonder he couldn't get a girlfriend. Meanwhile Lindsey had somehow found a way to appeal to the Director of Finance. How did that work? Perhaps she was gorgeous to look at (although nobody had ever suggested as much at school, where he had had friends who could see a bit). Perhaps after early floundering with him she had become a siren in bed, a mistress of the art of pleasure. He couldn't quite believe that either. If Hugo had been his normal self Niall would have engaged him in conversation at this point about the impossibility of women, but as he wasn't he found himself drawn to seek Miranda out and apologise. He called her name from the foot of the stairs but got no response. He went to the sitting room, but she wasn't there. He climbed the stairs, knocked on her bedroom door, and opened it.

"Miranda?"

"What?"

"I'm sorry. I'm a complete arse."

"Yes. You are."

"Can I come in?"

"OK." Her own resolve to be obdurate was fast evaporating.

Niall came into the room and stood, undecided and helpless.

"The bed's straight in front of you," Miranda said. "You can sit on that. There's not much else to sit on, since my clothes are all over the only chair."

"OK." Niall shuffled forward and sat. "You did really well."

"You don't have to patronise me."

"No I know. I mean it. Getting into Loosemore's office and everything."

"I was quite impressed myself," Miranda admitted, smiling.

"The question is," Niall said, "where do we go from here?"

"If my father wasn't in Doha," Miranda said, "I'd go and ask him straight out."

"What?"

"How I got to be the lucky girl."

"Yes," Niall mused. "That must be significant."

"Thanks."

"Not that you aren't the most deserving girl in the world," he added quickly.

"Yeah," Miranda said. "Sorry little Susannah Leman."

"But look what you've turned into," Niall said.

"Frankenstein's monster."

"Have you read 'Frankenstein'?"

"What do you think?"

"No," Niall said. "Nor me," he added.

"Funny, isn't it?" Miranda said. "We all make these references and sound like we know what we're talking about, but you and I've never read Frankenstein – I didn't even know it was something you could read. I thought it was just a film. We wouldn't know Frankenstein if he walked in here now."

"Probably looks a lot like Daniel Sullivan," Niall said. Miranda threw a sock at him.

"What was that?"

"A dirty sock."

"Nice."

"Meanwhile..." Miranda said, bringing them back to their immediate situation.

"Yes," Niall said. "OK. Lines of attack. Your Dr. Clarke."

"How can I attack him?"

"Don't know yet. Vivien Loosemore. Now that we know her address I could visit her at home."

"That would be a stupid thing to do," Miranda said, although I know you're longing to do it."

"Why stupid?"

"Because you don't know what her involvement is. You still don't know the right questions to ask her."

"I could ask her about the list of names."

"What about it?"

"No, OK," Niall conceded. "That leaves me with bloody Lindsey, I suppose."

"What if I agreed to go out with Sullivan again?" Miranda asked tentatively.

"No," Niall said emphatically.

"Why?"

"You know why."

"No I don't."

"Because he's a slime-ball and we know exactly what he wants."

"Which he won't get," Miranda said. "Niall, he's the only person that we're absolutely certain is involved in this and I can get him to drink masses of champagne and tell me stuff."

"He's hardly going to tell you, is he?" Niall said.

"I could use feminine wiles."

"That's what I'm afraid of."

"Why? Are you jealous?"

There was an infinitesimal pause.

"I think you're playing with fire," Niall said. "I hate the thought of him getting his hands on you."

"He won't get his hands on me."

"You don't know that."

"I don't think he'll rape me," Miranda said. "It wouldn't suit his ego."

"You've had sight for a month and suddenly you're an expert."

"Something like that," Miranda said mischievously.

"Why is it that everything we think of seems to involve you doing something and me not?" Niall asked.

"You have rather got everyone looking at you," Miranda said. "You're drawing the fire while I go under the radar. Or whatever."

"Good teamwork," Niall said, somewhat tongue-in-cheek.

"We are a good team," Miranda said, and then panicked as she realised she had almost certainly overstepped the mark. "At least I think so," she said.

"You're right," Niall said. "We are."

"You've been incredibly good for me," Miranda said.

"Don't embarrass me again," Niall said.

"No, OK." Silence descended. "Is there anything or anyone else?" Miranda said at last, in order to break it.

"Who told me to cross the road?" Niall said, after a moment's thought.

"I thought you thought it was Sullivan."

"No," Niall said. "I never thought that. He might've been driving the car although I think that's too high profile for him. No, I'm blind, remember. I've got an ear for voices. I'd've known if it was him and he'd've known that I'd've known."

"So he probably got someone to do it we've never heard of."

"You can't just go up to anybody in the street and say, 'See this blind bloke? When you see my car coming just tell him it's clear to cross, would you?'"

"No. True," Miranda conceded. "But it comes back again to the fact that Daniel Sullivan's got the information we need."

"I think you actually want to go out with him again," Niall said grumpily. Miranda was glad he couldn't see how her face lit up at even this slight evidence of jealousy.

◎

John Holthouse accepted the cup of tea Lindsey offered him. She did make a good cup of tea. When he asked himself the question as to what it was that kept him in this relationship with a much younger woman he usually concluded that it was her uncomplicated wholesomeness, the fact that she attached importance to things like making a cup of tea the way he liked it. He was not seduced by glamour in the same way that his friend Daniel was. He played the game but he was more of a pipe and slippers man at heart. He had never had much success with women, as a boy or an adult, which probably had more than he realised to do with the fact that he regarded conversation as a competitive sport, though he himself attributed it to the fact that he was 'a man's man'. Coming across Lindsey in his late forties had been unexpected on both sides, and had certainly provided him with a security upon which he had thrived.

People said he was ruthless in his work, and that was true. You didn't get to run the finances of one of the country's wealthiest charities by allowing yourself to be swayed by pity and emotional manipulation. He had revolutionised the way grants and subsidies were given out since he had been brought in to BAB, over a decade ago now, with the brief to put their finances – which were in a surprisingly parlous state when he came on board – on a secure footing. He had impressed the chairman and the Director General with his essential concept of only giving out money if you think it will make you a return – an obvious principle in business that somehow a charity had managed entirely to overlook. And the 'heroic failure transplant scheme' had been the greatest golden egg in his nest. He had sensed its emotional potential from the first. When the application had first arrived on his desk he had done some research of his own, had even spoken with Duncan Clark on the telephone, who had been adamant that the whole idea of an eye transplant was a deluded fantasy. Feeling that it might not matter, he gave a small grant and spent a lot more on publicising the fact, on getting BAB synonymous with Jamal Daghash's pioneering work. He considered it seedcorn, that he was scattering to see if it would grow. Very quickly it became apparent that his instinct had been correct. The transplant was a donation machine that paid out every time you put a penny in the slot. He agreed to up the funding, hoping to bring the research to the point of an operation. And then Daniel Sullivan had made his fatal remark.

'But John, we don't want to cure blindness. We don't want to be able to give everyone perfectly good eyes. We'd all be out of a job.' It wasn't so much the remark itself, because he had no great fears on that score, and he had already been assured that it could never succeed. But when he looked back he dated his conception of the 'heroic failure' scheme to that moment. The transplant research was a money-spinner so long as it continued. It needed to remain in the public eye, in as high profile a position as possible, without ever actually achieving the complete success that would make it old news. Heart transplants were two a penny now. He was sure raising money for them these days must be a nightmare. And whereas sabotaging a heart transplant was a matter of life and death, ensuring the failure of an impossible eye operation was not. Yes, it played with the emotions of the principals for a while – it encouraged the patient and the surgeon to hope for something – but ultimately it left everyone exactly where they started. And BAB significantly wealthier. Of course, his employers could never know, so he would have to pay himself the bonus they would have paid him had they been able to.

"You're very quiet tonight," Lindsey said, sitting down beside him.

"Sorry. Miles away," Holthouse said

"I realise that. I've already asked you twice if you wanted the news on."

"Sorry. Of course. Put it on."

"We've missed everything except the local bit."

"Put that on. We'll get the weather forecast."

Lindsey put the television on in time to see a picture of Damian Clarke accompanying a brief report on how the doctor who had been involved with the recent eye transplant operation had been found dead in his car.

Matthew Long's phone rang.

"Don't answer it," Amelia said.

"It's work."

"It's always bloody work."

"You never seem to do any bloody work."

He answered.

"I hope you're where I think you are," his editor began. Matthew doubted it.

"And that would be...?" he asked.

"That's not encouraging," the editor said. "On the scene would be good. On the way I could just about accept. I've just heard that your eye transplant doctor's committed suicide and I'm wondering why I didn't hear it from you."

"I'm working the girl, not the doctor," Matthew said, instinctively going on the defensive, his mind working overtime.

"Matthew," said his editor. "There is something going on here. Maybe there's a connection. Maybe there's not. You're on the inside. You met the man. Get to the bottom of it." He rang off.

"I have to speak to your sister," Matthew said. "Now. Her doctor's committed suicide."

"Who? The Arab?" Amelia asked.

"I don't know," Matthew said as realisation dawned. "Could be him or the tall one."

"Perhaps he couldn't face the fact that the transplant is obviously failing because she keeps having to go back to hospital," Amelia offered.

"That's what I have to find out," Matthew said.

"Seems to have been a total disaster one way and another," Amelia observed.

Rebecca had hoped that her night of shame at Cardew Crescent was something she could consign to the dustbin of history and never have to be reminded of ever again. She had been making a good job of it until now. But there, before her astonished gaze, was a picture of 'Richard', who had shared all her embarrassment, and she was being told that he had been found dead in his car. The police might argue that her 'knowledge' of him constituted evidence pertinent to their inquiry. To make things worse, it turned out that he was Miranda Leman's eye doctor, and suddenly Niall's 'something dodgy' about Joe's death and the transplant loomed in front of her like a wounded animal on a benighted road. The thought of telling anyone about that evening brought bile into her throat, but what if it was all a part of the picture? Maybe Fate had put her there for a reason and she owed it to Joe to face the worst.

SEVENTEEN

Roderick Leman had never beaten John Holthouse at squash. Sometimes he wondered why he continued to put himself through the experience, but he supposed that in some way it was good for him, physically. Though it led to regular and inevitable humiliation it had to be better than lifting weights or pounding on a running machine and going nowhere. Yet the competitor in him was far from satisfied. There was no pleasure in inevitably, relentlessly losing. He thundered after the ball, he chased down every shot, he exhorted himself to 'come on' after every rally, he occasionally won the odd point and even, once in a blue moon, took the lead temporarily, but the end result was always the same.

The two men sat panting outside the court watching the next two players knocking up, lacking the energy or the impetus to return to the changing room.

"What the Hell is going on John?" Leman asked.

"I take it you mean with Damian Clarke," John Holthouse said.

"Yes. Karin told me when I got back. It's terrible."

"I'm assuming the man had personal problems nobody knew anything about," Holthouse said.

"Nothing to do with my daughter or the transplant then?" Leman said.

"Why on earth should it be?" Holthouse inquired. "Unless he attempted to take advantage of her, got disgusted at himself and had a fit of remorse."

"I hope he didn't," Roderick Leman said darkly.

"Whatever it was," Holthouse went on, "it can't possibly have had anything to do with you. Damian Clarke had no idea how much money you put into the kitty in order to get Susannah the operation, and even if he had done that is hardly a motive for terminating ones existence."

"It's a coincidence," Leman said. "Perhaps that odious Burnet was harassing him."

"You need to stop feeling guilty," Holthouse said. "Somebody was going to get the operation. Why not Susannah? Think of it as private medicine."

Leman continued to look uncomfortable.

"I doubt we'll ever hear any more about it," Holthouse added. "His family will be left to pick up the pieces and the world will move on. It's the nature of things."

"And meanwhile my daughter has lost the doctor who was overseeing the medication that was underpinning the lasting success of her operation," Leman observed.

"I'm sure there are others equally well qualified," John Holthouse said. "Damian Clarke didn't seem to be making a particularly good fist of it. You have to face the possibility, Roderick, that it may not work in the long term."

"And meanwhile I've lost the daughter I had and acquired some changeling," Roderick Leman said.

"People don't change," Holthouse said, surprising himself with his own philosophy, "they just reveal different facets of themselves in different circumstances. The person they were is always there."

"Maybe," Roderick said.

"Try getting to know her better," Holthouse said. "She's your flesh and blood. You may find she's a chip off the old block."

For answer, Roderick Leman stood up and walked off in the direction of the showers.

◎

On the pretext of writing a freelance article about the new charity's work and aims, Niall got his entree into Victory. The woman he spoke to on the phone seemed so pathetically grateful for any publicity that she didn't ask any awkward questions. The almost truth that he was a blind journalist now working freelance having left a job on Radio Salop had been more than sufficient. Having grudgingly accepted that Lindsey was more or less the only line of enquiry he was in a position to pursue, Niall had set it up at the earliest opportunity, and had then insisted on making the journey unassisted, but taking Hugo, who was still very much convalescing and not officially working, for company.

"Hugo has a way of breaking down barriers," he had said.

And so Hugo, out of harness and therefore in theory with licence to behave as inappropriately and as much like any normal dog as possible, delightedly took his place at Niall's side as the taxi pulled up outside Faith's house. Niall had decided, on this special occasion, to give Geoff Jefferies a call and see if he was available.

"Thought you might like to see how Hugo's getting on," Niall had said.

"Be there in twenty minutes," the taxi driver had said, and had been true to his word.

"Now this is a normal fare," Niall checked as Geoff helped him into the back of the cab. "No special treatment just because Hugo is now a megastar."

"Whatever you say, guv," Jefferies said. Hugo, still heavily bandaged, hobbled in to sit at Niall's feet.

"The A team's back in business, eh, Hugo?" Niall said to him.

Their journey to Victory was uneventful, and Geoff Jefferies guided Niall as far as the door.

"Thanks a lot," Niall said.

"Any time," Geoff said. "Really glad you called. Do it again. Think of me as a mate. Good to see you up on your feet again too," he added to Hugo, messing the top of his head.

"Right Hugo," Niall said when Geoff had gone. "If we meet that fierce disapproving woman that Miranda talked about your job is to charm her. Got it?"

Hugo wagged his tail, and Niall called Lindsey.

"Hi," he said when she answered. "I'm outside the door of Victory. How do I get in and where do I go?"

"I'll come down," Lindsey said, and a minute later she was escorting the two of them upstairs to the Victory 'engine room', as she described it.

"You're going to talk to Mary, I think," she went on when they were sitting in the fundraisers' office and Hugo was soaking up attention.

"Whoever," Niall said. "I was hoping to get a chance to chat to you too."

"Wow! Privilege," Lindsey said. "About anything in particular?"

"Does it have to be?"

"No. It just usually is."

"I don't know," Niall said. "And here's me trying to be friendly and helping to do your job for you by getting you some publicity."

"Sorry," Lindsey said.

Mary, one of Victory's founders and the mother of a blind son, turned out to be excellent company and Niall thoroughly enjoyed the hour he spent interviewing her. He found himself determined actually to write the article and to try and sell it. He felt she deserved it.

"One last question," he said as they were finishing.

"Yes?" Mary said.

"Whose idea was it to get Vivien Loosemore as patron?"

"Odd question," Mary said.

"Maybe," Niall conceded.

"Or it would be," she went on, smiling, "if Lindsey hadn't told me about the history between the two of you."

"So will you tell me?" Niall asked.

"Hers," Mary said. "She volunteered. Phoned up one day and offered her services."

"And you accepted on the spot?"

"Niall," Mary said indulgently. "She might not quite be the Duchess of Cambridge but she does have a lot of contacts and kudos in the blind world. We needed a patron. She seemed a good fit."

"OK," Niall said. "You didn't think it was odd, someone phoning up and volunteering to be your patron?"

"I didn't think about it much," Mary said. "And she said she wanted to roll her sleeves up and give us some of her time too. Seemed too good an offer to turn down. And now that was many more than one last question, young man, and I have another appointment."

"Thanks a lot," Niall said.

"Just make us sound fabulous in your article," Mary said.

"I intend to," Niall said truthfully. Mary returned him to the fundraisers office, where he refused offers of coffee, tea, chocolate and water and settled down for the real purpose of his visit.

"So how's life treating you?" he asked Lindsey.

"Good," she said.

"Better than when we were standing outside the Citizens Advice Bureau in Harrow."

"Much better."

"Victory was a real turn-up for the book for you," Niall observed.

"And for Simon," Lindsey said quickly.

"Yeah," Niall agreed. "How did that happen?"

"I did put in a word," Lindsey said. "But don't ever tell him."

"Of course not," Niall said.

"They were looking for computer geeks with a human side, and I thought Simon would be perfect."

"You were right," Niall admitted. "Did it ever strike you as odd that BAB were pushing you to resign over an issue to do with dealing with a client and they then fully supported you in getting a job here where you'd be dealing with clients all the time?"

"Not old, vulnerable clients," Lindsey said quickly.

"Just rich ones."

"Are you trying to insult me as usual?" Lindsey asked, but fairly good-naturedly.

"No," Niall said. "I'm just curious. I was there, remember. Through that meeting with Warwick and the legal woman. It's like they were happy to pass the problem on to someone else, so long as you agreed to go quietly."

"Honestly, Niall," Lindsey said. "I'm a 'problem', am I? I think they saw that I didn't really deserve what was coming to me, so if I was prepared to resign they would be prepared to help me."

"Your boyfriend instrumental in it all, I guess."

"No. Why?"

"BAB Director of Finance. Impressive."

"How did you –?"

"I'm a journalist."

"Oh," Lindsey said as realisation dawned. "I told Miranda."

"I never reveal my sources."

"No, he had nothing to do with it," Lindsey said emphatically.

"So what's he like? How did you hook up with him?"

"Niall," Lindsey said with a degree of indignation, "is that any of your business?"

"Technically no," he agreed, "but as your first boyfriend I think I have some rights in that area."

"Oh really? I take it you're being ironic."

"Probably. I usually am. You just never noticed when we were young."

"I could take great pleasure in hitting you," Lindsey said.

"I wouldn't recommend it," Niall responded. "Hugo may be injured but there's nothing wrong with his bite, and trust me it's a lot worse than his bark."

"John is a really lovely man," Lindsey said.

"Good," Niall said.

"People think he's an ogre but he's as soft as a squidgy lemon underneath."

Niall wondered how the British Association for the Blind's Director of Finance would take to being likened to a squidgy lemon.

"And he was drawn to you because you saw through his Shrek persona into his squidgy interior," he suggested.

"Oh Niall!"

"Sorry."

"We're good for each other," Lindsey said.

"Great. What's he like?"

"Nice. Clever. Funny."

Niall could see that he was getting nowhere and wondered what had led him to believe that he would ever have found anything out from Lindsey. Determined, as he invariably was, to rush in where it would have been wise to fear to tread, he threw out,

"So he's not involved in the grand conspiracy, then?"

"What conspiracy?" Lindsey asked, sounding genuinely at a loss.

"I hear the word conspiracy as I pass the door, and why am I not remotely surprised to look in and see Niall Burnet, conspiracy theorist extraordinaire?"

Niall stiffened and turned his head in the direction of the voice. Vivien Loosemore! Well, he had known there was a chance, probably deep down hoped that he might bump into her. She had prevented him pressing Lindsey on her involvement in whatever was going on, but Lindsey was no actor. She would have been sounding guilty long ago if her boyfriend had dragged her into anything illegal. Now he had to turn the tables and get something positive from this unexpected opportunity.

"Nothing quite so much fun as a good conspiracy theory," he said, trying his hardest to sound affable.

"Mary told me you were coming to interview her," Loosemore said. "I warned her to be careful what she said."

"She's lovely," Niall said.

"And who are you writing this piece for?" Loosemore probed.

"I'm freelance at the minute," Niall said. "So first of all I'm just going to write it. But it's a brilliant cause and I really hope I manage to sell it."

"Simon put you on to it, I suppose," Vivien Loosemore reflected.

"It's been wonderful for him," Niall said. He wondered if there was anything more to Vivien Loosemore's persistent questioning than her natural wariness around him. He had hoped to get her to relax some of that wariness, but he saw now that that was a vain hope. Time for another throw of the dice. "But actually what I'm working on is a series of articles about different VI charities – you know, comparing Victory and BAB and Guide Dogs and the other smaller charities. I was talking to Gordon yesterday."

"Gordon?" Niall knew at once from the tone that he had scored a hit with the first name off the list that Miranda had found and tried to memorise. "Who's Gordon? I don't think I know Gordon."

"You must know him," Niall said. "I thought everybody did. He works with Adrian. You must know him. He mentioned your name."

"I think we should have a conversation about this article of yours, Niall," she said, a tremor in her voice.

"Great," Niall said. "All grist to the mill."

"Let's go to my office."

"Just like old times," Niall said, getting to his feet.

"If you've finished with Lindsey, that is."

"I can always come back," Niall said. "I know how busy you are."

Vivien Loosemore said nothing as she guided Niall down what seemed to be two corridors at right angles to each other, up a flight of stairs and through a door at the top. His senses on full alert, Niall was confident he would be able to find his way back down, in the event that Vivien was not in a mood to accompany him.

As soon as they were inside the office and she had closed the door behind them, she began.

"I don't know what you have found out, Niall, I don't know how you have found it out, but I beg you to think of the broader picture before you go public with any of it. You yourself said that this is a brilliant cause. You must see that it is doing wonders for Simon. And BAB does good work. Provides vital services for thousands of people in need. Don't let what is really just idle silliness jeopardise all that."

"You call it idle silliness?" Niall asked.

"I know it's sordid. I can imagine your delight at discovering my involvement in it and how you must be salivating at the prospect of taking me down, but there is so much more at stake."

"I can't believe what I'm hearing."

"I owed Daniel for some things that he did for me. Several quite big things. He wanted a location and he wanted discretion. I gave him those things. He can be very persuasive."

"You let your house become the centre of criminal activity."

"I don't think it is strictly criminal."

Niall snorted.

"What do you know exactly?" Vivien Loosemore asked, belatedly.

"That's for me to know, and you to wonder about," Niall said. "But I suggest that if you want me even to consider not going public with it you don't tell your buddy Daniel anything about our little conversation here, and let him go on about his normal happy business. God, I wonder if you even realise the enormity of what you're involved in. Somebody's dead, for God's sake."

"You surely don't think his death had anything to do with –"

"What do you think?" Niall interrupted. "Yes I do think. He had a crisis of conscience. He couldn't live with himself. You obviously can."

"Niall I may be a weak and feeble conniver, but I am not a doer. I promise you that."

"You disgust me," Niall said.

"Sometimes I disgust myself," Vivien Loosemore admitted.

"Only sometimes?"

She did not reply. Niall tried frantically to think of a question that would tell him more without revealing how little he actually knew. She had told him Daniel was behind it. She had told him her house was the headquarters for the 'discreet' operation. But she had described it as sordid and silly and not strictly criminal, which suggested to him that Sullivan – intelligently – had not admitted Loosemore to the inner circle of those who really knew what was going on. In which case she quite probably didn't know very much more and he should quit while he was ahead.

"So when's the next meeting?" he asked.

"It hasn't been arranged," she replied.

"I might want to know, when it is," he said.

"Why?" Vivien Loosemore asked. "What can you possibly hope to gain?"

"Just remember that I'm out there, and I may be blind but I'll be watching you. And I won't be stepping off any more pavements in front of BMWs."

"No – well I'm glad to hear that. For your dog's sake if not your own."

Her lack of reaction told Niall that she had not been involved in that particular aspect of the operation.

"I'll see you around," Niall said, turning to leave. "Lindsey's got my number."

"I'll show you down."

"No need. I'm not half as helpless as I look."

"Oh I know that, Niall," Vivien Loosemore said as he walked to the door. He put his left hand on to the wall and trailed to the head of the stairs. He was half way down when his phone rang. He half expected Loosemore or Daniel Sullivan, but it was a girl's voice.

"Hello?"

"Hello. Niall Burnet?"

"Yes."

"It's Rebecca. Rebecca Blackford. Do you remember me?"

"The tears in the pub. How could I forget?"

"Thanks for the reminder. Look, I really need to talk to you about something. Can we meet?"

"Surely. When?"

"As soon as possible."

"OK. I'm in Regent's Park. Where are you?"

"I'm sitting in a *Caffe Nero* at Notting Hill Gate."

"Right. Drink lots of coffee. I'll get a cab and meet you there."

"Niall – can it be just you?"

"It'll be just me and Hugo. He won't talk. Probably won't listen. This is all very intriguing."

"You'll see why."

❀

"And you just went and had coffee with her?"

"Yes. Is it a crime?"

"On your own."

"No. Hugo was there. And half the population of London was in *Caffe Nero*."

"And why exactly did she want to see you?" Miranda asked. "To help her through her grief?"

"No," Niall said, wondering why he was feeling guilty. "She's involved in this, Miranda, whether you like it or not, and it was actually you that roped her in, if you recall. I don't remember being incredibly enthusiastic when you invited her to join us at the pub."

"Until you found out that her brother was the eye donor."

"Which we still don't actually know. Why are we fighting?"

"I don't see why you couldn't have called me," Miranda said. "We could've all met together."

Niall realised that to reveal Rebecca's request for it to be 'just him' at this juncture would be unhelpful.

"I'm sorry," he said. "She said 'as soon as possible' and I went."

They were sitting in Faith's front room, alone in the house because Faith was at work. It was late afternoon, but the days were grudgingly starting to lengthen and, there being not a cloud in the sky, it was still light. Niall had reported his meetings with Lindsey and Vivien Loosemore, and Miranda had been delighted that her list of names had been the catalyst that had caused the Loosemore melt-down. But she had bridled instantly when Niall had mentioned Rebecca's phone call. Now he wondered whether he could possibly begin to explain what their meeting had been about, and yet he had to, because the implications for their own investigation were significant. He would leave out the fact that he had heard the tremor in Rebecca's voice as she had started to talk about it, that he had sat beside her on a *Caffe Nero* sofa and put his arm around her, that she had physically shaken throughout their conversation and that he had tried to soothe her and be understanding. He would stick to the facts, which in themselves were incredible enough to challenge Miranda's powers of belief. It had been one of those extraordinary, serendipitous moments: Gordon and Adrian had opened a door on an unknown world, and then Rebecca had come along almost at the same time to shine a light on that world and reveal it to be nothing that he had anticipated. He had tried to picture it as she described it: Loosemore the hostess, the bawd; Daniel Sullivan lolling Roman-style on a sofa being fed sweetmeats by this Penny from Wales, while other men, including the unfortunate Damian Clarke, indulged in similar pleasures. Sordid indeed, as Loosemore had said. But was that the reason Damian Clarke had taken his own life? Rebecca seemed to think so, and was now carrying the weight of his death on her shoulders along with her disgust at herself, and the still-fresh grief for her brother. Poor girl. Would a man – even a married man – take his own life because he had been invited to some sordid soiree and had a not entirely satisfactory sexual experience with a girl he had never met, either before or since? Admittedly, the guy was obviously of a sensitive disposition, but all the same... It was a bit extreme. Perhaps he had confessed all to his wife, and she had reacted badly, and had threatened to leave him and take the kids. In which case, as far as the transplant conspiracy went, it was a dead end. The whole 'Number 17' business was a red herring. They were really back to square one.

"You know what we have to do," Miranda said, when he had told her.

"Go back to the drawing board," Niall said.

"No. Think. Sullivan wants to see me in my underwear, right?"

"And the rest," Niall said darkly.

"We need to get information out of him, yes?"

"Yes."

"So we get this Penny to fix it up for me to go to one of these Roman evenings and let Sullivan think he is going to seduce me."

"No," Niall said.

"It's perfect," Miranda said.

"What makes you think he'd tell you anything, even after he raped you?"

"Well –"

"No, Miranda," Niall said emphatically. "No. I won't let you."

"Why not?"

"The whole thing's vile."

"And?"

"And what?"

"You think I can't deal with vile?"

"I'm not sure you realise how vile vile is."

"Because I'm a poor little blind girl."

"You're not blind."

"But that's how you're treating me."

"So take me through it then," Niall said, trying to be calm and rational. "It gets fixed up. Daniel gets excited. You feed him in your underwear. He carries you off to the bedroom. Then you say 'Before we have sex I want you to tell me about my eyes.' At which point he's so desperate he tells you the whole story, while at the same moment deciding that you can't leave the house alive. Don't forget the hit and run."

"You could be outside."

"Fat lot of help I'd be."

"Thanks."

The atmosphere lightened.

"Perhaps it needs some refinement," Miranda acknowledged. "But it IS a plan. Let's not rule it out."

At that moment the house phone rang and Miranda answered it.

"Hello Miranda. It's Faith."

"Hello," Miranda said, surprised.

"I hoped one of you would be in."

"We both are."

"There's going to be a press conference here in an hour. At least, 'a statement' is going to be read out," Faith said. "I think you and Niall should be here."

"At Moorfields?"

"Yes, at Moorfields."

"OK," Miranda said. "We'd better get moving."

◉

It wasn't quite a scrum. There were plenty of journalists and photographers, but plenty of empty seats too. The eye transplant had drifted off the front pages long ago, due in part to the fragile state of Miranda's health, but also to her failure to take up the gauntlet of celebrity that had been offered by the agent her father had hired on her behalf.

Matthew Long was there, and he immediately gravitated towards Niall and Miranda.

"What's this about?" she asked him.

"I don't know. They just sent a release saying an important statement was going to be made about the transplant which 'would shed light on recent events.'"

"They're rattled," Niall said.

"About what?" Matt asked.

"How did you ever get to be a journalist?" was Niall's response.

At that point three men entered the room: Jamal Daghash, Daniel Sullivan, and Duncan Clark. Looking around her at the other people in the room, Miranda was surprised to see her father slipping in quietly at the back.

The three men sat at a table which had been arranged for the purpose and it was Duncan Clark who addressed the assembly.

"Good evening. Thank you for coming. I apologise for the lateness of the hour and the short notice you received of this meeting. There was a case for putting it off until tomorrow morning, but tomorrow being Saturday there was a lack of enthusiasm for that, and there were those among us who were very keen, for many reasons, to share this information as soon as possible, before rumours emerged from other sources. I am Duncan Clark, a senior consultant surgeon of this hospital; my colleague Jamal Daghash will be known to many of you already as the pioneer behind the recent and much-publicised eye transplant operation. I notice that the recipient of the new eyes, Miss Leman, is amongst the audience. I apologise in advance to her for what she is about to hear."

Cameras flashed and clicked as Miranda's presence was noted.

"I'm going to ask Daniel Sullivan," Clark continued, "of the British Association for the Blind, to read a statement that he has prepared. As it is Friday evening, and we all have homes to go to, we are not proposing to take questions afterwards. If you want to follow up on anything that you hear now, please call our offices on Monday morning."

Clark stopped at that point. Niall was intrigued by his tone, which was that of a man who was there against his will, going through the motions for something of which he entirely disapproved.

"You are all aware," Daniel Sullivan began, reading his prepared statement, "that, with funding support from the British Association for the Blind, a pioneering eye transplant operation took place in this hospital in November of last year, conducted by Jamal Daghash. You may or may not also be aware that, on two occasions since that operation, Miss Susannah Leman had to return to hospital with complications in her recuperation process which suggested that her body was rejecting the eyes. On each of these occasions, once she was safely under observation in hospital her condition improved, and the cause of the hiatus in her recovery proved something of a mystery. It was Duncan Clark who solved that mystery, and in the light of subsequent events, we feel it is important to share the solution with you. Observing his patient, Mr. Clark realised that the only possible cause for these relapses was sabotage of the medication which was designed to ensure that the body did not reject the new eyes. There were very few people in a position to do this. Susannah Leman herself was the most likely suspect, but after numerous interviews with her he concluded that she was not compromising her own convalescence. It was then that he arrived at a painful truth. The man who was ensuring that the medication did not work was the very man whose job it was to see that it did: Dr. Damian Clarke. As you will know, Damian Clarke took his own life a little over a week ago. This was following a confrontation with Duncan, who threatened to expose him. We believe that Damian Clarke was a sick man. He seems to have been one of those doctors for whom holding the power of life and death, or sight versus no sight, was too much to bear. He did not truly believe in this operation, either in its viability or its validity. He allegedly held strong beliefs that blindness was a punishment enacted by God, and that to 'open the eyes of the blind' was a job for God and not man. Consequently, acting alone and in secret, and entirely without the knowledge of Jamal Daghash, who placed implicit trust in him, Damian Clarke determined to prevent the long-term success of the operation. When confronted with his actions he said nothing and remained unrepentant. However, we can only assume that, on reflection, he saw the enormity of what he was doing, and its implications for his career. Realising that the game was up he chose what he felt was an appropriate course, rather than face the awful consequences of his actions. There was nothing that Moorfields Eye Hospital could have done that they did not do to protect patients from Damian Clarke. All proper checks were carried out when he was appointed. There was nothing in his past record to reveal the mental condition under which he laboured. There is also no evidence that any other patients have suffered as a result of being treated by Damian Clarke. With his passing it is to be hoped that Miss Leman will make a complete and permanent recovery, and lead a full life with her new eyes. We very much hope that this particular chapter can be closed with as little pain as possible to all concerned parties."

"And the Queen is my aunt," Niall muttered under his breath.

PART FOUR

'I have a right to be blind sometimes...'

Horatio Nelson

EIGHTEEN

"I'm angry," Roderick Leman said.

"Of course you are," John Holthouse acknowledged sympathetically.

"I'm just not quite sure who to sue."

"I would strongly advise you against suing anyone. You might find yourself on decidedly dodgy ground."

Leman had surprised and shocked Holthouse by turning up unannounced at his office. He disliked anything that connected him to the transplant now.

"You must see, though," John went on, "that choosing the medical professionals was not a part of BAB's remit."

"He who pays the piper calls the tune," Leman said.

"Proverbs," Holthouse groaned. "Life reduced to its most simplistic.

"Don't insult me," Roderick Leman said. "You bank-rolled this operation with my money, and my daughter was the guinea pig."

"Roderick," Holthouse said, "I understand how you feel. I do. Believe me. But the situation has resolved itself. Clarke is out of the way. The operation seems to have been a success. Assuming everything goes OK from now on you will have got what you paid for. A daughter who can see. Nobody seems to think there will be any lasting damage from anything Damian Clarke did. As I see it, our business association is at an end. We can go back to just being friends who thrash a rubber ball at each other twice a week.

Acknowledging what Holthouse said to be true, Roderick Leman still felt somehow cheated and deceived. Damian Clarke's suicide was an entirely unsatisfactory end to the business.

❧

"Murder," Niall said.

"Oh, Niall, really," Faith protested.

"Duncan Clarke agrees with me."

"How do you know?"

"I could hear it in his voice."

They were sitting over coffee and raspberry tea in Faith's kitchen. In the wake of their discoveries relating to Number 17, Niall had told Miranda that he was "going to officially take Faith off the list of suspects." To which Miranda had retorted, "Which some of us did a long time ago."

"Number One," Niall went on, developing his theory before his sceptical audience, "this press conference was his fatal mistake. He provided us with the missing piece of the puzzle. Sabotaging the eye transplant."

"Why?" Faith asked.

"Yes, why?" Miranda echoed.

"Maybe he panicked and saw an end to all blindness and so the end of his job."

"Don't be silly, Niall," Faith said. "Even if transplanting eyes became as common as removing cataracts there would still be blind people. If there ever is a universal cure for blindness it will come about long after Daniel Sullivan has retired."

"And," Miranda added, "my father would never've gone along with it. He's absolutely furious. And it was after you went to see him that Hugo was knocked down."

"Maybe that really was just an accident," Niall offered.

"Oh Niall I could hit you!" Miranda said.

"Why," Niall ploughed on, undaunted, "did they hold that press conference? It wasn't necessary. You're old news already because you won't go on Big Brother. Damian Clarke was hardly news at all. Duncan Clark was the one person who knew and he is hardly the kind of person to go courting the press. It would've just died a death. But Sullivan was afraid that somebody might go on digging and might find out something. He was forcing a card on us. That's what it felt like. The master conjuror performing a trick and we were all obediently taken in by it. Now Matthew Idiot Long and his other cronies will go away and write a sad piece about the tragedy of Damian Clarke and how lucky it was that he was caught."

"Wasn't it only the other day that you wanted to pool resources with Matthew Idiot Long?" Miranda asked.

"I'll tell you what I think," Niall said. "I think that Damian Clarke told Sullivan that Duncan had found them out. And then Sullivan wasted no opportunity in contriving Clarke's 'suicide', at the same time using it to deflect all suspicion away from BAB. This all began at BAB. I know it. If I wasn't a bloody marked man I'd go back there."

"Isn't it possible," Faith ventured, "that you're letting your obsession with Daniel Sullivan run away with you? Isn't it possible that his 'secret' that he is so anxious to hide is these sordid evenings at Vivien Loosemore's house? Because his job certainly wouldn't survive that being revealed. And that Damian Clarke's actions were indeed his own?"

"Damian Clarke went to one of those sordid evenings," Niall replied. "He was there. We have first hand proof of that. There is a link between the two men."

"And that may have been forged when they met quite naturally in the run up to Miranda's operation."

"The voice of reason," Niall said, with a degree of bitterness in his tone. He wanted to go on arguing, but suddenly he couldn't be bothered. If Faith and Miranda decided it was time to start living happily ever after he would go it alone. Or find another accomplice. He owed it to Hugo. He wished Hugo was well enough to start working again. He felt so helpless without him. So dependent. And Miranda had positioned herself as his sighted guide cum sidekick in such a way that it was virtually impossible to do anything without her.

Later, he called Simon.

"Oh no," Simon said on answering his phone.

"That's nice," Niall responded. "There was me just phoning for a chat."

"And when has that ever happened?" Simon said.

"I'm just getting claustrophobia stuck here with two women," Niall went on. "I'm in need of some guy time. I was hoping I could trail round with you for a day."

"Because either you want to pick my brains about something or you think I'm going somewhere that might help your investigation."

"No," Niall insisted. "Hugo's not allowed to work at the minute and I feel kind of trapped. Or you could just cover for me. Pick me up in the morning and then drop me somewhere and just say I spent the day with you."

"You must be desperate."

"I am."

"OK. Tomorrow I'm going to a school in Finchley. I'll get my driver to stop off at your place and you can climb aboard. After that you can decide. Just remember I'm actually working."

"Fantastic."

"I'm supposed to be there for nine, so be ready by eight thirty. Not that I've got a clue how near you are to Finchley."

"No, nor me."

"Well, if the worst comes to the worst, I'm late. It won't be the first time. Nobody's complained yet."

◉

The next day Niall did not trail round Finchley with Simon. Leaving Hugo at home and brandishing the cane he loathed using he got into Simon's car only to get dropped off at the first underground station they passed.

"Thanks, mate," Niall said. "Sorry, and all that. Got a better offer."

"From a woman, no doubt," Simon said.

"I'm too transparent," Niall said, as he got out of the car. "Just remember, if Miranda calls I'm with you."

It was only when he was safely in the confines of the station that he called Rebecca Blackford.

"Hello."

"Hello," she said, surprised.

"Are you busy?"

"I'm in bed," Rebecca said. "I work nights in a restaurant."

"Sorry," Niall said. "I forgot. Hope I'm not interrupting anything," he added.

"Certainly not," Rebecca said. "Do you think I'd've answered?"

"Fair point," Niall conceded. "Any chance of meeting up? I want to talk over some stuff."

"Of course," Rebecca said. "I promise to try not to cry. Where are you?"

"Where are you is probably more to the point," Niall said. "It's just me and a white stick so I thought I'd just jump in a cab and turn up on your doorstep."

"This place is a tip," Rebecca said.

"I can't see it, remember."

"Good point." Rebecca gave him the address. "I'd better get up then," she said.

"Your choice entirely," Niall replied.

❧

Miranda had been disappointed when Niall had announced his intention of spending the day with Simon. She knew that in some way it was a punishment for her having not taken his latest theories seriously. He did like an admiring audience. But once she had accepted that he would not be persuaded, she had decided that his absence would give her the freedom to follow up any avenue without interference. And the avenue that she could only follow up when Niall's back was turned was Daniel Sullivan. She decided to call him on the British Association for the Blind number, so that some receptionist might recall putting her through should anything untoward happen, only to be thwarted when the message came back that he wasn't in the office. Then she tried his mobile, which he answered on the fifth ring. How lovely to hear from her, he said. He hoped everything was fine. She said it was, but she wondered if they could have lunch. He prevaricated a little – he was in Essex – but she could tell he was tempted. At last he agreed to pick her up for a late lunch around two o'clock.

"I'm curious to know what's brought this on," he said.

"Maybe I've just had time to think about things," Miranda said enigmatically.

❀

"So this is south of the river," Niall reflected. "Don't think I've ever been to this side of London before."

"It's the wild frontier," Rebecca said.

"I can tell."

They were sitting at Rebecca's kitchen table, the rigmarole of her offer of coffee or tea, Niall's tentatively optimistic request for raspberry and her apologetic negative response safely behind them. An experimental rosehip and ginger was not hitting the spot. "If I'd had any advance warning I could have got some in," Rebecca had said. "You barely gave me time for a shower."

"So," she said now, "what do you want to talk over?"

"I'm just not satisfied," Niall said.

"You're direct, I'll give you that," Rebecca said. "You'd like Penny."

"Penny?"

"My housemate, remember."

"Yes. Sorry. No. I mean the case."

"I know. I was joking. Is it a 'case' now?" Niall gave her what was meant to be a hard stare.

"Everybody's just accepting that Daniel "Is that my arse or is it the sun? I can't see because my head's inside it" Sullivan's version of events is sad but true, and it doesn't add up." Niall punctuated the last three words by pounding the table. Rebecca absorbed the frustration and the drama before she replied.

"When you say everyone, you mean Miranda, right?"

"I mean everyone," Niall said. "Including Miranda. And Faith, who has always been on my side my entire life."

"Even when you suspected her of being involved."

"I never told her that."

"No."

"But it's like she's adopted Miranda," Niall went on, unable to stop himself. "And Miranda laps it up and loves it. I should move out and leave them."

Niall heard Rebecca get out of her seat. He heard her come round the table and stand behind his chair. Then he felt her arms round him.

"What are you doing?"

"Just giving back some of what you gave to me in *Caffe Nero*," she said. "I wouldn't be much of a friend if I couldn't."

"Are we friends?"

"Aren't we?"

"I suppose."

"Miranda is besotted with you," Rebecca said. "If you can't see that you're more than just blind. You haven't lost her to Faith."

"I didn't say I had. That isn't what this is about."

"Isn't it? You feel let down by her because you want her to agree with everything you think and say. But just because she doesn't doesn't mean she doesn't care. She's probably just as upset as you are. More, in fact."

"And you know this because – " Niall said.

"I'm a girl," Rebecca said. "And an exceptionally clever and intuitive one at that," she added.

What Niall felt at that moment was the warmth of her arms around his chest, the warmth of her breath on his neck, and the consequent stirrings in his loins which he hoped were not visible to the naked eye.

"Now then," Rebecca said. "Let's review your doubts about the case."

"OK," Niall said, trying to focus. "It means talking about Damian Clarke though."

"It's fine," Rebecca said. "Since I off-loaded it all to you I've felt much better."

"You said he was like a fish out of water, nervous, apologetic."

"Yes."

"Does that fit the profile of a man who thinks he's doing God's work by sabotaging an eye operation?"

"I don't know," Rebecca said. "Advanced profiling isn't really part of your average primary teacher training course. But he could've been nervous because he thought God was watching him. He said he was under a lot of pressure at work."

"That was what I remembered you telling me," Niall said. "Between the sobs. But all that pressure was self-inflicted, if he was really working alone. Whereas, if Sullivan was leaning on him – that was another matter. And if Sullivan had influence over him, then that could explain why he was there at all. Because from what you've told me it sounds like he really didn't want to be."

"So what you think," Rebecca said, still holding him, which Niall was finding increasingly distracting, "is that Daniel Sullivan corrupted Damian Clarke and got him to sabotage Miranda's medication. If so, he wanted the operation to fail. He wanted the operation to fail badly enough to go to extraordinary lengths. Because from everything I've heard or read it sounds like there was every chance it could've failed anyway."

"Yes," Niall said. "I've thought about that. From Sullivan's perspective it was vital – essential – that the operation wasn't a success. Miranda needed to stay blind. And I'm wondering whether it's to do with Miranda, rather than the operation itself.

In which case we still don't know enough about why she was the lucky chosen one. But what I do know is that it was on the day that I pushed her dad as far as I could for information about it that Hugo was knocked down."

"Yes," Rebecca reflected. She got up and went back to her seat across the table. "I see what you mean. It's either the operation itself, or it's Miranda."

"I've thought maybe something happened that night they went to the ballet."

"You've lost me," Rebecca said.

"Sorry. He took her to the ballet one night around Christmas time."

"And you think it was only then that he decided she had to lose her sight?"

"I don't know," Niall admitted. "It's possible. It would mean I'd been wrong about a lot of other stuff, but I've got used to being wrong now. What if she saw something she wasn't meant to that night?"

"It would have been easier to do away with her altogether."

"No because he wants to shag her."

"But he needs her to be unable to see him."

"Because after he's finished he wants all his mates to have her but for her to think that it's him."

"Niall, I'm not blind, or very broadly sexually experienced, but there are ways you can tell the difference between men without looking at them."

"Yeah," Niall conceded. "You're right. It can't be that."

"It obviously bothers you that he wants to have sex with Miranda."

"Because he's a gobbet of phlegm humanity spat out."

Niall couldn't see Rebecca's smile.

"But back to the plot," she said.

"Why Miranda?" Niall said. "I'm sure it all comes back to that."

❂

Miranda waited in Faith's front room, watching for Daniel Sullivan's car. It still amazed her that she could; that she could look through a window, comprehend the transparency of glass, see the mixture of colours that resolved themselves into the solid objects she had known for years by touch alone; that the sound of a car passing on a road carried a matching image; that she – Miranda Leman – could experience both simultaneously, let one complement the other.

She had thought long and hard about what to wear. Which was, in fact, absurd, when you considered the size of her wardrobe. Not provocative, but relaxed. Not too casual – it was a lunch date she'd asked for, after all – but not formal. Luckily, it being the ambiguous season between the end of winter and the beginning of spring, it was cold, so there was no question of there being any flesh on view. She had settled on a pair of white jeans and a jumper. She still hadn't got much of an idea of what 'looking nice' meant, but she thought, following a long and still very inexpert battle with make-up, that she looked reasonably 'nice'.

As she waited for him to arrive, she thought over her plan of action. Make him believe she was taken in by his delusions of his own importance, thought he was personally responsible for her operation and for saving her from the evil Dr. Clarke. Then trip him up. Somehow. It was a bit unfinished.

His car – something dark grey and very large – pulled up outside the house. Should she go out? No. Let him come to the door. She didn't want to appear over-eager. She wanted to lead him just far enough that he would believe she was tempted by him, but that she was a good girl who was jealous of her honour. She left the front room so that he wouldn't see her standing at the window and repaired to the kitchen to await the doorbell. A minute later she heard it, and, putting on her jacket, went to answer it.

"Susannah."

"Miranda."

"Yes. I'm sorry. Stupid of me. I promise it's a mistake I shall never make again." He was standing there in what she thought looked a very expensive coat ('Why should I know what makes a coat look expensive?' she wondered even as the thought was formed). She tried unsuccessfully to gauge his mood.

"You look nice," he said.

"Thank you," Miranda said smiling.

"So. It's already late. Shall we go?" he suggested.

"Of course. I'm starving."

"Right." He led the way to the car.

"Where are we going?" Miranda asked, as he held the passenger door for her.

"Given the hour, somewhere not far away," Sullivan replied. "There's a half-decent Indian restaurant about five minutes from here, if you fancy that."

"Oh yes," Miranda said. "I always liked my mum's curries."

Daniel Sullivan selected Drive and the car moved forward.

◉

"So," Rebecca said, "what next?" They had moved from the kitchen to the living room, Niall having asked "Have you got any comfortable chairs in this house?" Rebecca had ensconced Niall in an armchair and had herself curled up on the sofa. As he had also reported that he was "ravenous" she had phoned for a pizza, which had not, as yet, arrived.

"That's the million dollar question," Niall said. "A bit like "Are they your brother's eyes?""

"I think they are," Rebecca said. "Part of me doesn't want them to be, but really I don't think I care any more. Only it certainly pisses me off that any operation involving one or more of Joe's organs could have been deliberately sabotaged. So I do still feel a part of this, Niall."

"Good," Niall said. "I'm glad."

"So?"

"So. Roderick Leman. Who does he play squash with? Have you ever seen Daniel Sullivan?"

"Not so as I would recognise him."

"I wonder if he looks like a squash player."

"Ask Faith."

"I don't want to involve her any more."

"Take me to him then," Rebecca suggested. "Or get me a picture."

"Then there's still the question of who knocked Hugo down. That's all gone very quiet. The police have never come back to us."

"No leads, presumably."

"Presumably."

"If you could find out where Mr. Leman plays squash I could go there," Rebecca said suddenly. "Pretend to be finding out about joining. I'm guessing it's some kind of sports centre. I don't play squash but I do play badminton."

"OK," Niall said.

"Have you ever talked to the surgeon?" Rebecca asked.

"Jamal Daghash?"

"It's a great name. I don't know. He might have his suspicions. And he probably knew Damian Clarke better than anybody."

"You're bright, aren't you?" Niall said appreciatively.

"Unquestionably," Rebecca said.

"Do you want to go out with me?" Niall asked.

"I think Miranda would have something to say about that," Rebecca said.

"I've had more physical contact with you than I've ever had with Miranda."

"Because she probably doesn't know how."

The conversation dried up.

"Sorry," Niall said eventually. "Forget I said it."

"If things were different, Niall, who knows?" Rebecca said. "Let's just be friends. I'm liking that."

"Me too," Niall said, truthfully.

"So how about talking to the surgeon?"

"I'm sure I could. He's a bit of a jet-setter by all accounts. I'd have to pin him down."

"Which would be no problem to a tireless newshound like you."

"Course not."

"And you can be pretty certain that he wanted the operation to succeed," Rebecca said.

"True enough."

"So we've got a plan," Rebecca said. "You go after the surgeon. Of course, there's someone else we haven't even thought about."

"Who?"

"Penny."

"What's it to her?"

"Not the operation or the sabotage," Rebecca explained. "Daniel Sullivan. She knows him. In the Biblical sense. Well, in the Mary Magdalene sense, anyway. We should ask her about him. No. You should ask her about him."

"Does she know anything about the eye transplant, and his connection to it?"

"I don't know what he's told her. We don't really talk about her extra-mural activities. She knows that I got upset because I thought I saw my brother's eyes in Miranda's face, and she knows I've been in contact with her and with you. More than that I couldn't say."

"You're right, though," Niall said. "He may talk to her about stuff when they're together. God, what a revolting thought."

"I know," Rebecca agreed. "Penny's extraordinary, but I think you'll like her. And I don't think her opinion of Daniel Sullivan is very different from yours."

"Understandably."

"I never know when she's going to be around, though. Between her shifts at the hospital and her 'private work'."

"If you can find out her shift pattern I can try and fit in with it," Niall said.

"OK. I'll do that," Rebecca said. "Should I tell her you want to speak to her?"

"No," Niall said quickly. "I'd rather just bump into her by accident. If she knows I'm looking for her she might in all innocence mention it to Sullivan, and, based on what happened to Damian Clarke, that would not be a good thing."

"My God!" Rebecca said, soaking up the implication.

❧

"Excuse me."

Faith looked up from her computer where she was making notes on one of her 'charges' – she didn't like to think of them as patients. She saw a large-framed woman filling her office doorway.

"Yes?" she said. "Can I help you?" She assumed the woman was lost and seeking directions. There was certainly nothing the matter with her eyesight, so she wasn't in Moorfields for an appointment, but she might be a carer or a relative.

"You are Faith Hodgkiss, aren't you?" the woman asked.

"Yes," Faith said, scrapping her original analysis of the situation.

"I would really like to talk to you, in confidence, if you have a moment," the woman said.

Faith sensed that presenting herself as a shrinking violet, as the woman was trying to do, went against the grain. Humility did not sit comfortably on this woman, whoever she was. A parent, most probably, of a blind child, who had been given her name by someone she knew; a parent who was unhappy with the provision her child was getting from the local authority, and had been told that Faith was a useful ally if one wanted to take on the authorities for the sake of one's child.

"Come in, please," Faith said.

The audience granted, the woman's manner changed. She became immediately bolder as she strode to the chair opposite Faith's desk.

"Thank you," she said, sitting. "My name is Juliette Warwick."

Faith tried to place the name. She knew she had heard it. She scrapped her angry parent scenario.

"I've just resigned as Human Resources Manager at BAB."

"Good Lord!" Faith said involuntarily. Niall's descriptions of the woman from their encounters the previous autumn leapt into her head.

"Yes, I'm sure you've heard all sorts about me," Juliette said.

"Well, not really," Faith said. "How can I help you?"

"I need to tell you something," Juliette said.

"OK," Faith replied, intrigued.

In a booth deep within the incongruously named Michael's, Miranda chewed garlic naan bread and contemplated the array of dishes that had been ordered and put before her. Though she had never seen one of her mother's curries, she felt sure they looked nothing like any of these.

"Nothing too hot," Daniel had said when ordering. "We want to taste what we're eating, not blow our heads off." In different company he might well have ordered the hottest dish on the menu, but Indian food had that range: choose wisely and it could be Leporello to your Don Giovanni, a positive aid in seduction; at the other end of the spectrum it could be the statutory twenty paces of a duel.

"Now then," Daniel said. "To what do I owe this unexpected pleasure?"

"Well," Miranda said, calling up the script she had pre-planned, "you made lots of very kind offers at the beginning of all this, and I wasn't really in the right mental state to appreciate them then. And lately I've been thinking about them a lot. You talked about showing me round BAB, you talked about even getting me a job. Then the other night all that business about Dr. Clarke came to light and I wanted to ask about him."

"I don't know much about him," Daniel said, "but by all means ask away."

Miranda helped herself to some spiced vegetables and pretended to think. "Was he always going to be the doctor in charge of my aftercare?"

"Jamal Daghash would be more likely to be able to answer that," Daniel said. "By the time I was involved, Damian Clarke was a part of the team. They were a double-act, Daghash and Clarke."

"Right," Miranda said. "So," she went on after a short pause, "had I already been chosen when you were first involved?"

"No," Daniel said. "When Jamal was looking for money from BAB there was a meeting involving the two of them, myself, and BAB's director of finance."

"So do you know how I came to be chosen?" Miranda asked.

"I'd love to say it was all down to me," Daniel said, "but hand on heart I don't have a clue. Again, Jamal might be your man."

"He never invited me for lunch."

"I rather think, my dear, that you invited yourself."

"I suppose I did. Sorry."

"I must say," Daniel continued, "I'm glad to see you stepping out of the shadow of your minder, Mr. Burnet."

"Yes, well, he's got his agenda," Miranda said, "but I'm tired of that now. I'm not blind anymore. Suddenly we haven't got so much in common."

"Trust me, you have NOTHING in common," Daniel Sullivan said warmly.

"I was just wondering," said Miranda, returning to her theme, whether it might've been Damian Clarke who suggested me for the operation. I wondered whether he had some grudge against the family."

"My dear," Daniel interrupted, "you mustn't think it was personal. The man was sick."

"But why become a doctor if you didn't believe curing people was man's work?"

"Who can enter the mind of the insane?" Daniel offered. "I imagine there was a huge difference in his mind between healing and ameliorating suffering on the one hand and opening the eyes of the blind on the other."

"It all seems so strange," Miranda said.

"I'm sure," Daniel agreed. "But that's all over now. You can start to think about a real future."

"Yes," Miranda said. "And that's why I want you to show me round BAB and get me that job."

"Well," Daniel said. "One thing at a time. I'll certainly give you a guided tour of the place. But to be honest, the best thing you could do for BAB at the moment is to raise your profile a bit. Agree to the interviews. Allow the photographs. Go on a few more chat shows. Recognise on air that without BAB there would never have been an operation."

"And the money will roll in," Miranda concluded.

"That could ultimately pay your salary, if BAB offers you a job," Daniel added.

"Fair enough," Miranda said. "It's funny to think of charities as being hungry for money, but they all are, I suppose."

"Because they want to do good with it."

"And paying your salary is doing good, is it?"

Daniel smiled.

"Would you rather we all worked for nothing?" he asked.

"No. I wouldn't be getting a free lunch then," Miranda said coquettishly.

"I will make it my personal mission," Daniel declared, "to demonstrate to you that my salary is money well spent."

"OK," Miranda said.

She ate for a while and then asked,

"Why did you decide to hold the press conference?"

Daniel was in the act of swallowing red wine as the question was asked, and the choking that followed stripped him of any dignity he had managed to amass up to that point.

"I'm sorry," he said. "Went down the wrong way."

"I hate choking," Miranda said.

"Yes," Daniel said. His voice had not yet recovered its timbre and his eyes were running. "You were asking about the press conference."

"Was I?" Miranda asked. "Oh yes."

"It was Duncan Clark who thought it was necessary," Daniel said. "He thought it would put an end to gossip and speculation and draw a line under the whole business. I'm just relieved the whole sorry saga is at an end and you won't have to go through any more trauma." He reached across the table and put his hand over hers.

"Thank you," Miranda said.

❡

Niall was surprised to find Hugo disgruntled and alone when his taxi deposited him back at Faith's. He had not given much thought as to how Miranda would spend her day, but he had certainly never factored in the possibility that she might have gone out. He had come to something of a decision during the ride from Rebecca's: she was right – whether he liked it or not he did fancy Miranda. He did want a relationship with her. It was up to him to initiate it, and he had planned to get straight into that initiation before Faith got home from Moorfields.

"Best laid plans," he muttered to Hugo as he made himself a raspberry tea. Hugo, however, was not particularly responsive. He was still sulking because everyone had seen fit to leave the house without him. The habits of training and a lifetime and a generally forgiving nature meant, though, that he followed Niall into the living room and dutifully put his head on Niall's lap.

"So where's she gone?" Niall asked, ruffling Hugo's ears. He was tempted to phone her, but he was supposed to be out having a fun day with Simon, so to be calling her at three o'clock would destroy that illusion. On the other hand, it might show that he was missing her (which he was), and that might prepare the ground for what he hoped to achieve later. Then again, he would be pretending that he was out and thinking she was in, and if she then started to pretend she was in, what would he do then? And she would be bound to ask him how his day was going and what he was up to and, then, what, in fact, was he going to say? What was he going to say anyway? That he had been to Rebecca's? That he was planning to keep going there until he bumped into Rebecca's housemate? How could he? Miranda was very sensitive on the subject of Rebecca. He needed to get her past that, but that wasn't something that could be achieved on the phone.

"Let's have a think," he said to Hugo. "Number One, she went to work with Faith. Faith's a sensitive soul and the two of them are joined at the hip at the minute, so she probably offered, knowing that otherwise Miranda would be alone all day."

Hugo didn't respond.

"But Miranda was showing no signs of getting up at 8.30, and Faith was already up and about and getting ready to leave not long after I did. And there was no talk of it last night."

Hugo sighed.

"Number Two, she called her mum. Hasn't seen her for a while. Suggested they spent the day together. Or, Two (A), her mum called her. Missing her. Her blind daughter is suddenly her sighted daughter and now she never sees her."

Niall paused as he processed these thoughts. It sounded a plausible scenario. Why had he just assumed that she would stay at home? Why hadn't he even asked her what she was going to do with her day? Because he had been angry with her then and wanting to punish her for not agreeing with him. So it was his own fault.

"Number Three – there is no number three," he declared conclusively.

He picked up his phone. If she was shopping with her mum it would be OK to call her. He could say he'd got bored with Simon's school in Finchley and got a taxi home. He selected her number and rang it.

The phone was switched off.

"Or maybe she's just got no signal," he said to Hugo.

He sat, at something of a loss. He didn't have Karin Leman's number, or he would have tried it. Perhaps he should call Faith at Moorfields. Either she would know where Miranda had gone, or, as her sort of temporary guardian, she ought to know that her charge had disappeared.

"Yes," he said to Hugo, convincing himself.

Faith's mobile went to voicemail. He didn't leave a message.

He tried Miranda again. If she and her mother were in and out of shops or tubes they would pass in and out of pockets of reception.

Still nothing.

He called Simon.

"You're missing a great day," Simon said as he answered.

"Has Miranda called you at all?" Niall asked.

"Don't worry," Simon said. "I know what to say."

"It's just that she's not here," Niall said.

"Where?"

"At the house."

"You went out. Maybe she went out," Simon observed.

"Genius," Niall said.

"She may've left a note."

"She's only just learning to write. Why not call and say she was going?"

"Because she was probably pissed off with you for leaving her."

"Yeah. Maybe," Niall acknowledged.

"She probably told Faith."

"Faith's not answering."

"No, well, some of us work," Simon said.

"So you do. Sorry mate," Niall said, hanging up. He had been one of the world's workers six months ago. Would those days ever come again? Once you fell off the carousel (or got pushed off, in his case), could you ever get back on it again? The news was full every day of the millions of unemployed. With all those millions to choose from, what employer was going to be drawn to a blind man? A blind journalist. It was a joke, when you thought about it. He should eat humble pie and see if he could get something at Victory. He could write copy for their promotional material.

Victory. Might Miranda have gone to Regents Park? What for? He could call Lindsey. No, he couldn't face that. He would just have to sit, bored, and wait.

❧

Alone in her office, Faith reflected on the extraordinary interview that had just ended. She had got used over the years to confessions of one kind or another – the confessions of parents who felt guilty and inept, the anguished confessions of blind adolescents following questionable paths in their search for warmth and meaning in their world. But Juliette Warwick's was unique, in both matter and manner. It had been entirely devoid of emotion and, really, of explanation. Just a litany of barely credible facts, and she didn't know, even now, if she was in possession of them all.

And what was she going to do with it now?

"I just want someone to know," Juliette had said. "I'm not

looking for action or sympathy or even understanding. None of that matters, but it matters to me that the knowledge is out there."

Which was all fair and fine, but given the nature of the knowledge, the enormity of the secret empire building Juliette had described –

Most of it, though, was about BAB and its own internal workings. That three people had stopped at nothing to make BAB their own personal gravy train was really none of her business: she wasn't a BAB employee. Only BAB did cast a huge shadow over the lives and expectations of many of her charges, and where these Machiavellian plots impacted the lives of vulnerable others – then there was a case to answer.

Niall's 'journalist's nose' had led him to the tip of an iceberg. She could imagine how triumphant he would be, armed with what she now knew, what cages he would ill-advisedly and unsubtly rattle.

All of which made a very good case for not sharing any of it with him.

❡

Apart from the occasional wandering hand, the lunch had passed off uneventfully. Miranda did not feel that she was much further forward in terms of the investigation, but Daniel had definitely thawed. He exuded confidence and ease. Now she needed that confidence to tip the balance into over-confidence, and then, she was sure, she would start to find things out. It was a relief to escape from the dark intimacy of the restaurant, and the prospect of accompanying Daniel to his office and having a look round at BAB, where there would be people, and lights would be on, was actually quite exciting.

"What pathetic things I find exciting," Miranda told herself.

Daniel spent the drive from north London to Knightsbridge trying to impress her with the various shortcuts and rat-runs he knew that could avoid the worst of the traffic trouble-spots, but in truth she was left confused and cold. She would rather have followed major thoroughfares and seen famous landmarks that she had never been able to see before.

"I don't usually go in the main entrance," Daniel said to her after they had parked, "but it's much more impressive and this is something of an occasion. Our own celebrity coming to pay us a visit."

"Well," Miranda said, trying to sound flattered and at the same time not to feel it.

Daniel put a proprietary arm around her shoulder as they approached the imposing porticoed entrance, where a woman was standing in a light blue raincoat.

"Excuse me," the woman said, as Daniel and Miranda prepared to pass her. "It's Daniel Sullivan, isn't it?"

Daniel stopped. Miranda looked at the woman. She appeared pale – drawn and exhausted.

"Yes," Daniel Sullivan said.

"I've been waiting here all day in the hope of catching you," she went on.

"Then you're very lucky," Daniel said. "I very rarely use this entrance."

"God is good," the woman said, and spat in his face.

Miranda felt Daniel stiffen, and then relax as he calmly removed a handkerchief from his pocket.

"That's for my husband," the woman said. "Yes, that's right. Look confused. You don't know me from Adam. Which is why you couldn't care less. I'm Theresa Clarke. I've heard your disgusting and libellous allegations about my husband, that he was some deranged killer, some wolf in sheep's clothing. He was a good man, a lovely man, a family man, and I don't know what awful place he ended up in that caused him to do what he did and leave me and the children but it must have been truly awful and I can't help thinking that maybe you or one of your ilk had something to do with that. But then to have the effrontery to claim to the media that he was trying to ruin the operation that he had been so excited about – oh, and look, you've got the poor brainwashed girl on your arm now. My husband did nothing to damage your recovery, Miss, he cared about you and he cared about his job and he cared about us. And you, Mr. Sullivan, are a vile man."

Miranda could see that Theresa Clarke was shaking. Tears were running uncontrollably down her cheeks.

"Madam," Daniel Sullivan said calmly, "I understand that it is a shock –"

"How dare you!" she shrieked. "How dare you give me that and try to pacify me. I am his wife. I know him. Far better than you ever can or will."

"Of course you are upset –" Daniel began again. Theresa Clarke ignored him and turned to Miranda.

"How can you bear to stand next to him?" she asked. "You think it's all thanks to this man that you can see?" she asked. "It was the doctors that made you see. Jamal Daghash and my husband. My dead husband. He'd've probably given you his eyes if he thought you'd stand a better chance with them. That was the kind of man he was. Oh but no because he was secretly on some mission to do God's work which was apparently to make sure brilliant pioneering scientific endeavour was an utter failure. You're all vicious and evil and vile."

BAB security had clearly communicated quickly with the police, as a female officer materialised as if by magic and started to escort Theresa Clarke away.

"It's very hard to defend yourself when you're dead," Theresa Clarke called out as she started to walk away, "but I've not finished with this. I'm telling you."

Miranda watched her walk angrily up the road, the police officer keeping pace with her and trying to talk to her.

"Shall we?" Daniel Sullivan said, indicating the door.

Suddenly it was the last thing she wanted to do. All she could see were the tears streaming down Theresa Clarke's face as she spoke. She wanted to go home, to get away from all the unpleasantness. But she had come this far. She should see the day through to the end.

NINETEEN

Disaster. Was perhaps the politest, the kindest, the least emotive way of putting it. Debacle. Catastrophic cock-up. They were other options.

Niall lay in bed reflecting on the point at which his evening had gone off-plan and descended into chaotic, humiliating failure. Wasn't there some poem by Robert Frost about a road forking in a wood and going one way or the other? He had thought he was on one path but he had ended up on the other and it had led down and down into a hideous swamp. Where he was now wallowing.

Of course it was all his fault. But was it though? Yes. No. Yes.

Miranda had come home at last. He heard her getting out of a taxi and went to meet her at the door.

"Hello. Where have you been?" he asked in what he meant to be a friendly and not peremptory tone.

"Out," she said. "Like you." He could tell at once that something was wrong.

"What is it? What's happened?" he asked.

"Oh Niall," she said, and burst into tears. Clumsily he took her in his arms and held her, which felt surprisingly good. Hugo came to see what the commotion was and leant affectionately against their legs.

Niall steered Miranda into the front room and sat her down, still with his arms around her. He kissed her damp cheeks and then turned her face towards him so that he could kiss her mouth. Though her lips were trembling, he could feel the eagerness of her response. Even as a beginner, her kissing was more advanced than Lindsey's. Without a word having been spoken, they seemed to have got to where he wanted to be. If he could rewind his life to that half hour or however long it was that their lips were locked together, then he would.

But the moment had come when they had paused for breath and he had asked her what it had all been about.

"Promise you won't get angry," she had said.

"I promise," he had replied.

Then when she told him he had got angry. He couldn't control himself. And yet two minutes before he had been tasting the passion in her lips. It seemed she had done the one thing that would be calculated to spite him, and though she claimed it had been for the good of their research, she had actually found out nothing. Too busy lapping up Sullivan's odious attention. By the time she got to Damian Clarke's wife he had totally lost interest, and had deliberately trumped her by saying "Well while you were sharing fingerbowls with Daniel Sullivan I was having a pizza with Rebecca Blackford."

"I thought you were spending the day with Simon."

"I spent the day with Rebecca Blackford."

"You lied to me."

"No I didn't." Yes he did. "And you weren't honest with me."

"You never asked."

By the time Faith came home Miranda was shut up in her room and Niall was sitting disconsolately in the kitchen. He had snapped at her when she asked if anything was wrong, and she had then suggested that perhaps it was time for him to go home.

"I don't think you're doing any good here anymore."

"What about Hugo's physio?"

"There are vets in Telford."

"Fine," he had said, "I don't want to outstay my welcome," and had promptly got on the internet and booked himself a ticket for the following day.

So an evening that had begun with Miranda in his arms without a word having been spoken, an evening that had 'dream come true' written all over it, had ended up as a nightmare in which his friendship or whatever it almost became with Miranda had come to an end; he had fallen out with Faith, his oldest ally, the one person who had stood by him in his life when others hadn't; and he found himself on the eve of walking away from the newly discovered love of his life, and the whole Daniel Sullivan eye transplant case that he and Rebecca had made plans for.

Sometimes he wished he could cry.

He heard soft footsteps on the landing outside and then his bedroom door opened.

"Niall, are you awake?" Miranda whispered.

Was he going to be awake?

"Yes. What is it?"

"Ssh. I don't want to wake Faith. Can I come in for a minute?"

"Yes. Of course."

He heard her come in, close the door, and walk to the bed, which she sat on.

"I can't sleep," she said. "I can't bear it when things aren't good between us. So I've come to say sorry. I don't care whether it was my fault or not. I'm sorry. I don't want us to stay upset and angry with each other."

"I accept your apology," Niall said, meaning to sound comic, but actually coming over a little pompous. "But you know it was me. So I'm the one who should be sorry."

"Well, are you then?" Miranda asked, and he could hear the smile in her whisper.

"Yes."

"Not for kissing me, I hope?"

"No. Not sorry for that."

"When I decided to come along to your room I was rather hoping you might kiss me again," Miranda admitted.

"Were you now?" Niall asked. He reached out to where he knew she was sitting and gently pulled her towards him.

After ten minutes of steadily increasing passion he asked, "Why don't you get under the covers so I can kiss you properly?"

"Do you promise you won't take advantage of me?" Miranda asked. "Because I don't think I'm ready for that."

"Promise."

"So long as you mean it." Niall felt her stand up and then slide under the duvet beside him. "Hello," she said.

"Hello," he answered, turning to her and running his hands up under the jersey night-shirt she was wearing. When had he last felt a girl' skin under his hands? Too long ago to even remember. How different Miranda felt to the likes of Lindsey. Lindsey had been generally soft, her breasts large and malleable; Miranda was firm. Her legs and buttocks were firm, he could feel the bones of her back, and then, when he tentatively explored her breasts, they were small and firm too.

"Nothing special, I know," Miranda whispered.

"Very special," Niall breathed in her ear.

They kissed for another acre of uncharted time.

"I'm sorry," Miranda said then.

"What for now?"

"For not being ready. I know what you want."

"It's fine, really."

"I'm going to go back to my room now," Miranda said. "Just promise me one thing."

"What's that?" Niall asked.

"That when we meet in the morning we won't be all awkward and pretend this never happened."

"It happened," Niall said. "And I'm glad."

"Me too," Miranda said. They kissed again and then she extricated herself and slipped out of the bed.

"Goodnight, Niall," she said.

"Goodnight," he answered. Then he heard her go. Niall lay on his back reflecting on the switchback nature of the evening. The disaster scenarios had been premature. Miranda had dragged him out of the swamp and given him another chance to choose the right road. Bless her. Suddenly, life was good. As good as it had ever been.

But he still had a ticket to Telford. Shit. Faith had still told him to go and he wasn't going to plead with her or let Miranda plead on his behalf. She didn't even know that he was going. He should've told her. He hadn't thought about it. His mind had been on other things. But he needed her to know. And before morning really because his train was at eleven. Would she be asleep yet? Oh, bugger it.

He got out of bed and trailed through the dark house to Miranda's room. Although he still had light perception it was as easy wandering around in the dark as in the light.

To knock or not to knock? No. Knocking was the kind of noise that might wake anyone. He opened the door gently.

"Miranda? Are you sleep?"

"No," came the reply. "Hardly, after what just happened. But you're very naughty."

"I just need to come in for a minute."

"I haven't changed my mind," Miranda said.

"No, I know," Niall said. "I just need to tell you something."

"If it's some confession about Rebecca Blackford I don't want to hear it."

"It's nothing to do with Rebecca Blackford."

"Good."

Niall decided the Rebecca Blackford bridge could be crossed another day.

"Faith asked me to move out," he said, sitting on the bed. "After you'd come upstairs."

"Oh, Niall. Why?"

"I snapped at her. I was under stress."

She stroked his arm.

"And now I've got a ticket to Telford for tomorrow."

"Where is Telford?"

"You don't want to know."

"Do you want to go?"

"No. Of course I don't."

"Then come and stay with me. It's time I went home."

"Your dad will never have me in the house."

"My mum will."

"Without warning?"

"Niall, I'm offering you the chance to come and stay at my house. Try to sound pleased."

He kissed her.

"I'm pleased," he said.

"Now go to bed. And leave me to sort it out in the morning. You can concentrate on getting the money back on your ticket."

After one more lingering kiss, Niall left and went back to his own room.

❂

"So this is Surrey," Niall thought, as he, Miranda and Hugo travelled south in Geoff Jefferies' cab. "I've really arrived."

Faith had been shocked and surprised to find Miranda packed and ready to leave as well as Niall in the morning.

"Are you going to Telford?" she had asked Miranda.

"No, I'm going home," Miranda said, "and Niall's coming with me."

"Oh," Faith had said. She had sounded genuinely lost for words and Niall had felt sorry for her. He realised that Faith's house, without them in it, would be large and dark and mostly empty. She would actually miss them a good deal more than they would miss her.

Niall had suggested seeing if Geoff Jefferies was free.

"It'll be bloody expensive," he had said, "but I promise it'll be the last cab I ever take and you don't really know your way round the trains."

"OK," Miranda agreed. "And I need to call my mum."

Which she had done and, yes, Karin Leman was home and was delighted that Miranda was coming back. She had accepted the addition of Niall with a surprisingly good grace.

"Although," she had added, "I'm not at all sure what your father will say about it."

"No, well, we'll deal with that between us," Miranda had said confidently.

Now they pulled up in the drive of the Leman house, Geoff's SatNav having delivered them flawlessly to the door.

"It's just weird that I've lived here so long but I hardly know the place," Miranda said. "To look at," she added. "I'm sure if I close my eyes it will feel far more like home."

Hugo got out and sniffed the air.

Niall heard Karin Leman coming out of the house and decided to let mother and daughter have their reunion while he paid the taxi driver.

"Thanks for everything," he said to Geoff. "The gods were watching when they had you arrive on the scene after Hugo was knocked down."

"Don't know about that," the driver said, "but it was certainly lucky for you. And for me too. I've felt a better person since I've met you and your dog."

"Look after yourself," Niall said.

"You too," Geoff replied. "And take good care of that dog, or you'll have me to answer to."

"I will," Niall said.

"And if ever you're in town –"

"Of course."

They made their farewells and Niall stood on the drive, waiting for directions.

Faith sat with Duncan Clark in his consulting room.

"And it's been going on for how long?" he asked.

"Nearly ten years, from what Juliette Warwick told me. This is just the latest in a string of schemes, each more outrageous than the last."

"And she was their piratical maid of all work," Clark reflected. "Why?"

"She never really explained," Faith admitted. "It was a case of 'Here are the facts, don't ask me any questions.'"

"Was she besotted with Sullivan, or something?"

"I may be very wrong," Faith said, "but I don't think Juliette Warwick could ever be besotted with a man."

"And they held that over her?" Clark scoffed. "In this day and age?"

"I don't know. BAB is a rather conservative organisation."

"I have to confess I know very little about it," Clark said. "The more I'm learning the happier I am that that's the case."

After a pause he added, "And now she's had enough. Jumped ship. But instead of going to the police she's gone to you."

"I'm guessing," Faith said, "that she has done things in the course of her 'work' that might not play too well in a police station."

"God it makes you sick," Clark said suddenly. "I mean, we all accept that bankers and businessmen have no ethics but we naively imagine that people who work for charities have some kind of altruistic guiding principle that attracted them to the work in the first place."

"Which, I suppose, makes it a good career for the unscrupulous," Faith said.

"I don't see what you can do," Clark said. "I don't know what she hoped you would do."

"No," Faith agreed. "She must've known I was hardly likely to start gossiping about it."

"Other than to me," Clark said, smiling.

"Being another person who knows how to keep his own counsel."

"Something must have precipitated her attack of conscience."

"Money, maybe."

"Yes," Clark agreed, "it usually is money. She wanted more, they said no, and she said 'Enough.'"

"In which case," Faith reflected, "she may have wanted to tell someone in the event of something happening to her."

"That's a little melodramatic, surely?"

"She implied that they were behind Damian Clarke's death."

"If you ask me, Damian killed himself because he allowed himself to be sucked in somehow to this odious conspiracy." Clark seethed. "Damn it, the man was a good physician, why didn't he come to me or to anyone when they exerted whatever influence they had over him? It certainly stuck in my craw letting Sullivan tell the world Damian was a dangerous lunatic."

"I did wonder why you let that happen," Faith admitted.

Clark paused, and straightened items on his desk.

"Whatever the root cause, it was my confronting Damian that led directly to his death," he said at last. "I have to live with that. I didn't know him well. When Sullivan came up with his story I allowed myself to believe it momentarily because it mitigated my own guilt to some extent. If the man was on a mission to do harm, then conceivably the world could be better off without him. Shameful, I know. If I'd taken Boy Wonder a bit more seriously maybe I wouldn't have allowed any of it to happen."

"Yes. Niall," Faith said. "You didn't allow it to happen, Duncan. You discovered a serious breach of medical ethics and you confronted the perpetrator. You acted entirely properly."

"I know what I'm like, Faith," Clark sad. "I'm acerbic, sarcastic, a bully. I don't always mean to be, but it always comes out that way. If it had been you confronting him, you'd've been trying to find out why, trying to support him at the very moment you were threatening him. I can't do that. I'm a blunt instrument. He wouldn't have gone away from a meeting with you and killed himself."

"That's idle speculation. And it smacks of self-pity, which I wouldn't expect from you, Duncan," Faith said. "There's a coldness at the heart of our business. There has to be. It's how we protect ourselves. It's even part of the training. I would have been just as clinical as you, in my own way. And the result, I am absolutely sure, would have been the same. It's the ones who got to him first and put him up to it that we should go after now."

"Yes," Clark said thoughtfully. "Just because a disease kills a patient doesn't mean you stop searching for a cure to the disease."

"Very medically put," Faith said.

"And how do you propose to 'go after' them?" Duncan Clark asked.

Well," Faith said smiling, "I do have one other piece of information that might come in useful."

❦

It was when Niall was comfortably ensconced on the Leman's sofa forcing himself politely to drink a cup of coffee that Rebecca called him.

"It's Rebecca," he said before answering, glad that Miranda's mother was in the room to prevent a potential outburst. Blind, he had no difficulty fielding Miranda's look and sigh.

"Hey," he said to the phone.

"Hi, it's Rebecca."

"So my phone told me."

"Yes of course," Rebecca said, a little flustered. "How are you?"

"I'm good," Niall said. "I'm in Surrey. I'm staying with Miranda at her parents."

"Things have moved on, then," Rebecca said mischievously.

"You could say so," Niall replied.

"I'm glad," Rebecca said. "But I'm calling about Penny, if you haven't lost interest in Daniel Sullivan. I can see that you might've."

"Of course I haven't lost interest," Niall said. "What about Penny?"

"She's on nights this week. I figured mid-afternoon might be a good time to bump into her. She's usually getting up around then."

"Superb," Niall said. "What about tomorrow?"

"No time like tomorrow," Rebecca replied.

"Can I bring Miranda?"

"Of course. We'll have a party."

"Where is it you live?"

"Tooting."

"Oh, well. We'll find it."

"Of course you will. You're you," Rebecca said. Niall suspected irony, but he liked the implication all the same.

"Friend of a friend," he said to Karin Leman by way of explanation as the call ended.

"You have a lot of friends, don't you?" Karin said.

"Not really."

"I found it so hard," Karin went on, unburdening herself, "when S- Miranda was young – trying to find the children who would want to play or be friends with her."

"I bet," Niall said.

The day spent with Miranda and her mother passed remarkably pleasantly, Niall thought, but as evening drew on, the imminent return of her father seemed to cast something of a shadow over them all. It was a "squash" night, so the moment had been delayed. There had been a discussion about whether to let him know Niall was in his house before he returned home, but Karin Leman hadn't had the stomach for the call, and Miranda had promised to meet him herself at the front door and tell him. Conversation became sporadic as the tension mounted, and it was almost with relief that they finally greeted the sound of the garage door opening automatically. Without a word, Miranda got up and went out.

"She's so fearless," Karin said admiringly. "Where has this person come from?"

"It's who she is," Niall said. "It was always there, just obliterated by circumstances."

"By us, you mean."

"You're too hard on yourself. You needed help. You didn't get it. My dad ran away faster than a speeding bullet when I lost my sight. People genuinely don't know how to deal with it. At least you guys stuck by her."

"We turned her into a second-class citizen, though," Karin said.

"You did what you thought was right."

"You're trying to be kind, but I don't think you really mean it."

"You should know enough about me by now to know that I always say what I mean."

They fell silent, and in the silence they could hear voices in the garage, but the tone wasn't angry or aggressive.

"Roderick should be thanking you, really," Karin said. "You've given him the kind of child he always wanted. Feisty, fearless, determined. Like him."

"It's not me, it's the eyes," Niall said.

"It's you, and the way she feels about you."

"I'm not going to hurt her," Niall said. "I'm not going to let her down."

"I believe that," Karin said. "I hope she doesn't end up hurting you. This is all so new to her."

"Occupational hazard," Niall said.

At that moment the door opened and Miranda and her father walked in. Niall got to his feet.

"Don't get up," Roderick Leman said. "Good evening. Welcome to our home."

"Thank you," Niall said.

"Look at you all," Roderick went on. "The three conspirators looking desperately guilty." But his tone was light.

"Sorry," Niall said.

"My daughter has been a passionate and persuasive advocate," Roderick said.

"She certainly has a mind of her own," Niall said.

"Hang on," Miranda interrupted. "I'm not blind any more. You don't have to talk about me as though I'm not in the room."

They passed a relaxed and convivial evening. Roderick Leman made a number of jokes at Niall's expense, which annoyed Miranda but which Niall seemed almost to enjoy, and for his part Niall kept off inflammatory topics such as squash, money and the eye transplant. By unspoken mutual consent nobody broached the subject of Damian Clarke and sabotage either.

Later, lying in bed in "the guest room", Niall contemplated his situation. That he was sleeping under the same roof and eating at the same table as Roderick Leman was bizarre. However, seeing how much the man was enjoying his newly sighted daughter did reveal another side of him. While he remained convinced that Leman had made a significant donation to BAB to secure the operation for Miranda, a bribe brokered by the squash partner and probably now mostly in his pocket, he no longer believed that the father's involvement went any further. You didn't pay a lot of money for something and then help it to fail.

❧

The next afternoon saw Niall, Hugo and Miranda walking down Upper Tooting Road while Rebecca, on Niall's mobile, tried to pilot them in. A lift from Karin Leman to the end of the Northern line and a train to Tooting Broadway had done the rest. Aside from a biting wind that seemed to be in their faces whether they turned left, right, or went straight on, Niall was glad to be out of the inevitable taxis, and irrationally proud of himself for using public transport.

"OK, I can see you," Rebecca said finally. "I'm coming down to let you in."

"We're here," Niall said to Miranda, ending the phone call. Miranda gathered Niall into a proprietary arm and saw his smile.

"She needs to know you're off limits," Miranda said.

"She knows," Niall said. "She knew before you did. You're safe with me. Girls just aren't that interested."

"Rubbish," Miranda scoffed.

"Hi." Rebecca came out to the pavement and welcomed them. "Penny's in the shower but I told her you wanted to meet her. She's fine about it. Didn't even ask why. That's just what she's like."

They went inside.

"Be impressed," Rebecca said to Niall. "I went out this morning and got some raspberry tea."

"I'm impressed," Niall said.

They settled in the living room, Niall and Miranda on the sofa this time, and Rebecca in the armchair that Niall had previously occupied. She found that she couldn't help being drawn to Miranda's eyes. They were striking, whether they were Joe's or not, but also so like his that she felt it was almost impossible for them to have belonged to anyone else. It was more disturbing than upsetting. Disturbing because Miranda looked nothing like Joe. His eyes didn't make her face his face, and somehow she had expected that they would.

"I'm sorry for staring," she said.

"It's OK," Miranda said. "I understand."

"I'm so pleased for you guys," Rebecca went on. "You make a great couple."

Niall felt Miranda's body relax a little beside him.

Penny burst into the room in a dressing gown, with her hair in a towel.

"Hello," she said. "Anybody make me a drink?"

Two minutes later she was back with a large mug of instant coffee.

"Well now," she said, sitting down. "One of you's a journalist apparently, and so I'm assuming you want to interview me about the NHS."

"Not exactly," Niall said. Penny winked at Miranda. It annoyed her.

"Cute dog," Penny commented.

"Hugo," Niall said. "He's still recovering from being knocked down."

"By DS," Rebecca added.

"No!" Penny said. "Prosecute the bastard."

"It might not've been him," Niall said.

"He's the sort who'd think someone should go ahead of him to clear the road," Penny said. "A self-important twat, in short."

"Couldn't've put it better myself," Niall said smugly. "And he's trying to get Miranda into bed."

"Let's take it back to the beginning," Miranda suggested, trying to get control of a conversation that was starting to annoy her.

"Right," Niall said.

Penny listened wide-eyed as the story unfolded, soaking up the facts and the suspicions.

"So now you want to sting him," she said when they had finished.

"Bearing in mind he may not be afraid of stinging us," Niall said.

"You know," Penny said, "I can't see him as a murderer. I mean, yes, I can well believe he'd knock over a dog and not stop short of much to get his own way, but he's really not very dynamic. He just thinks he is."

"What about a Roman evening?" Miranda said suddenly.

"What do you mean?" Penny said, at the same time that Niall was saying "No!"

"Hear me out," Miranda said. "You said we wanted to sting him. Penny could arrange it so that we were the three girls for the evening. The chances are that whoever else is in this thing with Daniel also goes to these parties, because poor Dr. Clarke went to one. It was probably meant to be his reward for going along with their plans. We can threaten to reveal the whole story about the sex nights if they don't tell us the truth about the transplant."

"And none of you might ever be seen again," Niall said.

"You could be outside the door with your friend Matt, the great reporter," Miranda said. "I could ring you before we went in and just leave the phone line open. You could hear everything that went on. If I scream you know it's time to call the police and knock the door down."

"I don't like it," Niall said. "You keep suggesting it and you know I don't like it," he added, turning to Miranda.

"I think it's brilliant," Penny said. "But," she went on, "there is one problem which is that there hasn't been a Roman soiree for months."

"If he knew that Miranda was an option..." Rebecca started.

"No," Penny interrupted before Niall could. "He'd suspect something then. You might have to leave this with me and trust in our 'special relationship'. I'll see what I can do."

"If we expose the sordid sex nights, we'll never get to the bottom of the transplant," Niall said. "They'll get fired but they won't go to prison and then they'll be after us for ruining them."

"Whatever they are up to would end, though," Miranda said.

"Because they wouldn't be in those positions."

"We owe it to Dr. Clarke to nail them for what they did to him."

"So what's your plan?" Penny asked Niall.

"I don't have one," he admitted. "I hate to say it but I am reluctantly starting to think we've got as far as we can and it's time to hand everything we know over to Matthew Long and the might of the *Mirror*."

"That is a way to go," Rebecca said.

"But?" Niall said, adding the word Rebecca's tone implied.

"It doesn't strike me as the Niall Burnet way."

"No," Miranda agreed.

"No, well, sometimes you just have to accept your limitations," Niall said with a hint of bitterness. "All part of the 'happy to be blind' package."

"You've got these guys rattled," Penny said, filling the uncomfortable silence. "They've lashed out at you and your dog, they fired your friend, they're all over the place. Right now, they know you're on to them, but they don't know anything about Becky and they certainly don't know about me. Imagine what DS is going to think when Miranda rocks up with me, unannounced, for a Roman night. The message is going to be loud and clear: "We're onto you, you bastard, all your dirty little secrets are ours and we're going to humiliate you massively." He's going to react, and his reaction will be his downfall."

"You watch too much TV," Niall said.

❧

On the way home Miranda tried to lift Niall out of the gloom into which he had descended.

"If you'd never got involved in this I'd be a blind girl again and the whole operation would have gone down as a heroic failure. Jamal Daghash would think he had failed and Duncan Clark would be feeling smug and Daniel Sullivan – "

"If I hadn't got involved in this," Niall interrupted, "Lindsey would still have her job at BAB, Hugo wouldn't've been knocked down, your eyesight would still have been saved by Duncan Clark and the sabotage would still have been exposed. I haven't done anything good. Mr. Blundering Blind Investigative Journalist. I'm just a joke really. Daniel Sullivan's probably pissing himself."

"You made me want to see," Miranda said. "I would have been perfectly happy to stay blind if it hadn't been for you. I would've accepted failure and played into their hands. Do you know what, Niall? I don't care whether we bring down these people or not. What I care about is, one, I met you through all this and, two, you changed my life. You changed me. You changed me into someone I really like. And I know you'll say it was the eyes, but without you I would have been timid little Susannah with eyes she didn't know what to do with. I would never have been this person I am now. So I give thanks for you, Niall Burnet. You don't have to prove anything to me. You're a hero as far as I'm concerned."

"You want us to just ride off into the sunset?"

"Why not?"

"Then why did you suggest the Roman evening?"

"Because, idiot, I'm trying to impress you. Trying to be as fearless as you. Trying to do what I think you would do if you were me."

"Let's tell the whole story to Matthew Long," Niall said; "put it in his hands and get shot of it."

"OK, if that's what you really want," Miranda said.

TWENTY

"Staying at his HOUSE?"

"Apparently. He didn't know until he got home one evening and, hey presto! He was the lucky winner of a blind man and his dog."

"Shit."

"You may as well mothball your seduction plans."

"No. She was definitely interested. She may be playing a bit of a game but she was definitely interested. If Damian's demented wife hadn't butted in on the steps of BAB our last meeting could have ended very differently."

"Tony wants you to let her go."

"Tony doesn't need to know."

"He'd see it differently, I fancy."

"Tony owes us a lot."

"He wants a clean break."

"He's an ass."

❧

Matthew Long felt like an emancipated slave. And even as he felt it he reflected on the curious nature of relationships: how one could be drawn into something that seemed utterly compelling and felt wonderful, that gave meaning to life, and then the very fabric of what had been compelling became at first an irritating pattern and ultimately as destructive as that shirt that some Greek hero or other had put on and been killed by. If he had been contracted to a women's magazine he could've written a very interesting piece about it. Life with Amelia had been amazing, and then it had got boring, and then it had become completely stultifying and he had stepped back and seen that his own personality had been totally subsumed in the relationship. He had become, at best, an on-demand plaything or, at worst, a genuine sex slave. It took him a week and a half from realising that he was in the wrong life to pluck up the courage to face Amelia with it, and there had indeed been an ugly scene with crockery thrown and other behaviour that he couldn't help feeling was learned or copied from TV soaps; but now it was over. He was free. He had escaped from the rubble of the Leman Disaster.

As he ran on Wandsworth Common with the guilty pleasure of Justin Bieber in his ears he started making plans for a better future. He would take time out. Travel. He had done the Thailand down to Australia thing after university, much to his parents' annoyance, but now he had a bit of a hankering for Latin America. Mexico, Panama, Venezuela, Peru. He could take some Spanish classes before he went and blend in with the natives. You'd see more that way. Being honest with himself, he had been too young in his previous gap year. He had followed the crowds and taken the photographs, but he had next to no idea of what life in those countries was actually like. It would be different, this time.

He sat on his regular bench and went to select another playlist on his phone. It was then that he saw he had a missed call from Niall Burnet.

"Shit" mingled with the early spring birdsong.

Niall Burnet had done him a massive favour. Which he had promised to return. And this was probably about calling it in. But Niall was a part of everything he had just consigned to the landfill part of his life.

"Shit."

He liked the guy. They had got on. When he'd said he'd return the favour he had really meant it. If he didn't call back, Niall would know he was ignoring him.

But if it was about the Lemans... He could tell Niall the truth. He'd just dumped the oversexed sister and really didn't want to go there.

He made the call.

"Good morning," Niall said.

"Hi Niall. You rang me."

"I did."

"For a reason, I'm thinking."

"And you're thinking right. How are you?"

"I'm great. You?"

"I'm great too."

"Great. So?"

"I've got a story you might be interested in. I'd like to run it past you."

"OK."

"Not on the phone."

"OK. Where are you?"

"I'm at the Lemans' house. I think you know it. You could kill two or more birds with one stone."

"Hi Simon."

Simon jumped like a child caught in the process of finding hidden Christmas presents. He told himself it was the voice.

"Hi Lindsey."

"You don't often pass by the office these days."

"No," Simon admitted. "I'm pretty busy out and about. I'm here for some meeting or other. I'm hoping it's to do with writing software."

"I haven't got a clue," Lindsey said. "Come and have a cup of tea while you're waiting."

"OK," Simon said, realising that he had no viable reason for saying no.

Lindsey guided Simon into her office, dealt with the business of refreshments, offered him a custard cream, and then said "So what's this I hear about Niall moving in with Miranda's parents?"

"How do you know about that?" Simon asked.

"Oh I keep my ear pretty close to the ground," Lindsey said.

"Are you jealous?"

"Hardly!" Lindsey shrieked. "I know he's your friend but he's on a par with pondlife in my book."

"That seems a little harsh when he tried to help you."

"After he lost me my job."

"I thought that was down to a meltdown you had with a client on the phone."

"If Niall had never come to ask me questions about the eye transplant it would never've happened."

"So you're saying there was something dodgy about the eye transplant?"

"No I'm not," Lindsey said, a little flustered. "I think people were just worried that I might not be as discreet as I should be working in that department."

"You're in the same kind of department now."

"They realised they'd made a mistake and tried to help me out. But what about Niall, though?" Lindsey went on quickly. "I presume he's wormed his way in with the Lemans because he still thinks there's something fishy going on. Even after that doctor committed suicide."

"I thought it was more about finally getting a girlfriend," Simon said.

"Why did they leave Faith Hodgkiss's?" Lindsey asked.

"Why do you even care?" Simon said, mildly irritated.

"I wouldn't want another girl to get hurt by him," Lindsey said. "I'm sure he's just using her."

"You're just sounding bitter and twisted."

"You're just too loyal. He's still digging around the transplant, isn't he?"

"Lindsey," Simon said, exasperated, "I have absolutely no idea. Other than being besotted with Miranda, I know nothing about what's in Niall's head at the moment. He's not calling me."

"You should find out," Lindsey said. "Stop him making an ass of himself."

"God you're weird," Simon said.

❦

Jamal Daghash looked down into his lap; then back at the man sitting on the other side of his desk.

"The Association is going to stop all funding?" he said, trying to make sense of what Daniel Sullivan had just told him.

"Not all," Sullivan clarified. "You'll still get something in the general dole out. But the director general wants a different flagship. He thinks Damian Clarke tainted the concept of eye transplants in the public perception. He's looking for something that helps more than one person at a time."

"Without BAB's support there will never be another transplant."

"There must be a ton of money for this kind of thing in the Gulf. Why not go to Moorfields in Dubai?"

"I wish I had recorded the conversation a couple of years ago when you talked about prestige for London."

"I'm sorry, Jamal," Sullivan said, suddenly conciliatory. "This wasn't a decision taken by me, and what I think is immaterial. You can make representation to our funding wing, but I can tell you it will be a waste of time."

"It's certainly a disappointment to find that a major V.I. charity is more concerned with its own image and marketing than it is with helping the people it is supposed to serve."

"All charities rely on the public," Sullivan said. "Public image is everything."

"Would the public be happy to know you'd pulled the plug on eye transplants?" Daghash asked.

"They would if the case for using the money differently was well-made, and our marketing people are very clever."

Jamal Daghash said little more, and within ten minutes Daniel Sullivan had said his goodbyes and was on his way back to Knightsbridge. Daghash waited for a gap in Duncan Clark's schedule and then called in to his office.

"I'm not surprised," Clark said, when Daghash had reported the conversation.

"I feel as though I've been played for a fool," Daghash said.

"You got what you wanted," Clark replied: "the chance to prove that the impossible was possible. You weren't going to be looking at what they wanted. It was a scam, but only in the way they intended to ensure failure. Look on the bright side. Had it not been caught, you would have got more transplants but every one would have ended in baffling failure. Instead, your first patient is still seeing and doing very well. Better than that, she seems to have enough personality not to want to be a celebrity. Congratulations on your choice. And you will get more funding. Not from BAB, maybe, but you know the whole world wants a piece of this now."

"I led Damian to his death."

"No you didn't."

"I've had Theresa Clarke in my office – "

"So have we all," Duncan Clark interrupted. "She is adamant about Damian's innocence but she's wrong. He was sabotaging the aftercare, and I'm sure he was being paid handsomely to do it. We can never really know why. Maybe they were short of money. Maybe he just wanted them to have more than they had. He was tempted and those bastards found a way to convince him. Neither you nor I nor anyone else is responsible for him making that decision. Or, ultimately, the decision he took when he was exposed."

Jamal sat in a brooding, frustrated silence.

"And as for the bastards," Clark went on, "I'm not going to let them walk away untarnished."

"How?"

"It's a work in progress."

"Can I help?"

"I'll let you know."

"Wow," Matthew said. He was sitting in the Lemans' lounge, soaking up the story that Niall and Miranda had told him. Having railed at himself all the way there for agreeing to go, he was now very happy that he had.

"It is a story," he acknowledged, "but unless we can get some pretty substantial evidence my editor's not going to run it. Big charities are basically untouchable. They do good works and shouldn't be undermined. All these guys have to do is deny it and we're in court and destined to lose big time."

"Can't you tap their phones?" Niall suggested.

"You're joking, right?" Matt responded.

"Niall thinks the sordid sex nights are a red herring," Miranda said, "but I think if we can get them on that then they'll lose their jobs anyway."

"Which is true," Matt agreed, "and if you're thinking that the big story will put them away, it probably wouldn't, so either way they're going to be out there. Wounded tigers."

"That sounds very melodramatic," Miranda said.

"I want them to know they were nailed," Niall said. "I don't care about anything else."

"If we expose them for the sex nights," Matt said, "someone may well come out of the woodwork to corroborate the fraud. People love kicking people when they're down. I'm thinking maximum humiliation. Get the word out across the media. They walk out of their bordello into a blaze of flash photography."

"What about the girls?" Niall asked. "We don't want the press turning on Penny and Rebecca and calling them sex workers."

"Sounds like that's exactly what this Penny is," Matt said. "But she could sell her exclusive to us and we could spin it so that it's really about the scandal of nurse's pay. A nurse can't survive in London without supplementing her income."

"If Penny told her story," Miranda said, "wouldn't that do the damage without a big sting?"

"No," Niall said.

"No," Matt said less forcibly. "They'd have deniability. And she doesn't know most of their real names. We'd have a string of allegations by an embittered prostitute, no matter how detailed."

"I admit I don't know the law," Niall said, "but these Roman evenings behind closed doors aren't actually illegal, are they?"

"Legal or not," Matt said, "I can't see BAB enjoying a two-page spread in a tabloid about some of its top people paying girls for sordid services."

"I think they'll get out of it," Niall said.

"They'll be like rabbits in headlights when they're caught," Matt said. "You'll be there. You ask the tough questions. Keep firing and they'll crack."

👁

"Grateful though I am for the free lunch," Daniel Sullivan said, "I do hope Jamal hasn't unleashed you to try to put pressure on me about his funding."

Duncan Clark laughed.

"I'm not sure which of us should be more insulted by that suggestion," he said. "If you think I'm Jamal's dog then you're very much mistaken, and if you think I'd choose the monkey rather than the organ grinder if chasing funding were my aim, then you have very little knowledge of the way I operate."

Daniel Sullivan sipped Tio Pepe and decided to let silence swallow his opening gambit. Duncan Clark's emailed invitation to lunch had been a shock as well as a surprise, given that the only time they had worked together on anything had been the press conference on Damian Clarke's demise. Curiosity had led him to accept, but he was annoyed at himself for feeling nervous about it. He couldn't remember the last time he had felt nervous. Convincing himself that Clark was running an errand for Jamal Daghash had been a way of conquering those nerves. He now wished he hadn't put it up to be shot down so early in the proceedings.

"Let's begin again," Duncan said. "I didn't invite you here for a slanging match. Nothing could have been further from my mind."

Daniel relaxed and took a long pull at the sherry.

"I felt," Duncan Clark went on, "when our paths crossed recently, that you and I were two of a kind. Men who have risen high in their chosen fields of endeavour through genuine merit and hard graft, but also men with a taste and appreciation for the good things in life."

"I can't disagree with you there," Daniel said, as foie gras was set before him.

"I felt sure that we shared the same enthusiasms," Clark continued, "and I confess I did a small amount of discreet research – "

"I'm flattered," Daniel interjected.

"And a very small bird told me about something that I must confess set my mouth watering."

"Intriguing," Daniel said.

"Involving high quality food, excellent wine, and high class exclusive service from diaphanously clad young women."

"I cannot imagine what little bird could possibly have sung such a song," Daniel said, his mind racing.

"Shall we just say the late lamented Dr. Clarke was not as appreciative as he should have been of the favour you bestowed on him. He chose a confessor at Moorfields who kept his secret until after his death. Then she felt moved to share it with me."

"I see," Daniel said.

"Don't look so worried, man," Duncan said. "You look as though Damian Clarke's ghost were standing at your elbow. He isn't, I trust?" the consultant added, smiling.

"No, no," Sullivan said quickly.

"That's a relief. No, I was fascinated. Envious, even. I realise we didn't know each other, but now that we do, I was wondering whether I might push for an invite of my own to one of your soirees. I assure you I should be far more appreciative than Dr. Damian."

Daniel Sullivan smiled inwardly. Why had he allowed himself to get dragged into self-doubt? He knew human nature. He knew men particularly, especially men after his own heart, and Duncan Clark was clearly one such.

"Well," he said.

"I realise it should be you doing the inviting," Duncan Clark said, "but I hope you will think of me the next time you're planning one."

"I certainly will," Daniel said. "We haven't held any for a while. I shall need to speak to a few people and then let you know."

"Excellent," Duncan Clark said.

❧

"Niall Burnet knows about them," Vivien Loosemore said when Daniel broached the subject in her office at BAB.

"Because you told him," Daniel snapped. "Niall Burnet is an overgrown blind schoolboy. It's absurd to live your life in fear of him. You obviously did when he was at school and now you are again."

"I am certainly not afraid of him and never was," Loosemore said hotly. "And I bitterly resent your accusations that I told him anything. The point is that he knows, and it seems utter folly to me to take the risk."

"Number one," Daniel said, "life without risk is no life at all. Number two, whatever Niall Burnet does know, he can't possibly know the date of the next evening because we never set one. If his informant was Damian Clarke, he won't be learning any more through that channel. If you and I set a date and he still finds out, I shall know where he's getting his information."

Vivien Loosemore opened her mouth to respond but Sullivan swept on.

"The boy's got other things on his mind. He's shacked up with Transplant Girl and it's all systems happy ever after. There's no reason why you should ever see him again. Meanwhile, I have friends who have certain expectations of good times I can provide for them, and my stock is already starting to fall because of your groundless cowardice. Do I have to remind you about the dirty linen I washed for you? Now you are a patron of one charity and you head up the education division in another. Nice work if you can get it."

"Very well, Daniel," Loosemore said after a pause. "Give me time to check my diary. I'll give you a date before the end of the week."

❧

For Niall, life settled into a new routine. His days were spent alongside Miranda, talking, walking, kissing, establishing their relationship. In the evenings the pair of them skulked upstairs or went out to give Roderick and Karin Leman breathing space.

"I don't want to be in their faces," Niall said, "and Hugo isn't everybody's cup of tea."

Hugo healed himself and got back into harness. Ease and happiness seemed to settle around them like a comfort blanket.

It was when he lay in bed at night that the clouds gathered. He felt the danger of sinking into the kind of life so many of his former schoolmates had succumbed to. Giving up the fight for a career and settling for disability living allowance. Curling up in a corner and letting the world go by. He didn't want that. He wanted independence. He wanted a job. He wanted something that gave him some status in the eyes of the world. He definitely wanted the relationship with Miranda, but he wanted it to be more grown-up. They were living like a couple of early adolescents in her parents' house, and he could understand that in many ways Miranda was going to be immature. It was inevitable. But he wasn't. He felt as though he was slipping back into childhood.

And then there was the whole question of BAB. Daniel Sullivan and the rest. As the days lengthened and the air warmed towards late spring he felt that everyone else was happy to let sleeping dogs lie. It had been an adventure but now it was over. They had heard nothing from Penny or Rebecca, nothing from Matthew Long. The trail was going cold and nobody seemed to mind but him. He sensed that Miranda no longer wanted to talk about it. She didn't want to be reminded of the dark days because now her sight seemed secure. The operation had been a triumphant success. So he couldn't talk to her about it. Couldn't talk to anyone.

Clutching at straws – as he acknowledged to himself – he emailed Lucy Sturmey and Jon Allen of *This Is Now*, asking if they knew of any media opportunities that were coming up, explaining that he was looking to move in a new direction. He had a bland but friendly response from the presenter but nothing from Lucy Sturmey. He was yesterday's man before he had even been today's.

"How do you feel about us getting a flat together?" he asked Miranda one evening.

"Shouldn't one of us get a job first?" she said.

"Neither of us is exactly galloping towards that, though, are we?" Niall said.

"Why not ask the woman at Victory?" Miranda suggested. "You said you really liked her."

"I will never get a job anywhere that Vivien Loosemore has any influence," Niall responded. "What about you?"

"You know about me. I've got absolutely no training or experience in anything. I don't even know what I want to do."

"Perhaps you should've gone for celebrity after all."

They sat in an inconclusive silence.

"I can't stay here for ever," Niall said. "It just isn't right. Your father'll get to the point where he kicks me out."

"I know," Miranda said. But she was enjoying life too much to want anything to change.

Niall's phone rang.

"Hi?"

"Hi Niall. It's Rebecca."

"Hi Rebecca."

"I thought you'd want to know that Penny's got a date."

"Good for her."

"No. A date for a Roman Evening."

Niall sat up straight.

"Right!"

"There are going to be four men. She needs three girls. If Miranda's up for it, she and I could be two of them."

"You know what I think about that."

"Strength in numbers, Niall. It'll be fine."

"When is it?"

"Friday week."

"So we've got time to meet and discuss it."

"We have."

"I'm glad about that. I'll get in touch with Matt Long and fix something up."

"OK. This is it, Niall. Payback. For Miranda and Joe and the insult to both of them."

"Yeah," Niall said doubtfully. He relayed the information to Miranda and sensed her excitement. "Why do you actually want to strip off in front of these guys?" he asked her.

"I don't," she said. "But I want this whole business over with, and this seems to be the only way."

"As soon as he sees you he'll know the game is up."

"I could disguise myself. Dye my hair. Have it cut."

"Who's talking like she's been sighted for ever now?"

"Even blind girls dye their hair, Niall."

"It won't work."

"Don't you think his excitement that I'm there will override everything else?"

"No. He's not a fool."

"Then we have to move fast and flush them out into the waiting arms of the press."

"It's a mess," Niall said.

"So kiss me and let's talk about something else."

TWENTY-ONE

Vivien Loosemore tried to crush the feeling of foreboding that engulfed her when she thought about the evening ahead. She had never enjoyed these soirees, lived with herself only because she convinced herself no real harm was being done and the girls involved were being well paid for their services. She had been adamant from the beginning that she would not countenance anything that caused physical pain or injury, and Daniel had conceded the point, saying that as far as he was concerned there was no pleasure in pain and he wouldn't issue an invitation to anyone who thought there was. Tonight, however, she sensed a different atmosphere, one that she couldn't trust. There was something discordant about the whole event. Was it just that it had been such a long time since the last evening? Was it that one of the last guests had subsequently committed suicide? Was it Daniel's insistence that the numbers be increased from three to four when it had always been three, which suggested to her that he was no longer fully in control?

She acknowledged her debt to Daniel. Her career had been on the precipice and he had been in a position to save her and steer her into the secure and prosperous waters that she now enjoyed.

But now – she had an astronomical pension: she could retire and take the risk that Daniel would blacken her name retrospectively. Would it matter anymore? She could free herself at a stroke from his power over her. The trouble was – as it had always been – she liked her life, liked the trimmings of her status, and all that would be lost. What would she do? Retirement held no attraction. She liked having purpose and influence, and using it to do good. She *had* made a difference in the V.I world. She knew it, even if others didn't, and she could still do more.

She checked the delivery from the caterers and turned up the thermostat on the central heating.

❧

"Why do you want to go?" Lindsey asked John Holthouse. He was out of her shower and dressing.

"It's something Daniel's organised and I can't really get out of it."

"Of course you can," Lindsey said. "Be ill."

Holthouse was tempted. Why did he need to go out for dinner and sex when he could get it all at Lindsey's? Lindsey always let him do exactly what he wanted in bed, or did what he asked, and he couldn't deny that her large breasts and buttocks were more to his taste than the skinny girls who came to Number 17. Add to that Daniel's 'extra guest' and the whole evening was shaping up to be something best avoided.

Yes, he had enjoyed them on occasion. Had gone along with Daniel quite enthusiastically when he had first come up with the idea and they had been buoyed up by the success of his pocket-lining schemes. But what Daniel seemed incapable of understanding was that the secret of continuing success was to lie low when your peace and security were threatened. And while ever Niall Burnet was close to the Leman family Holthouse felt the threat. It was a time for quiet retrenchment, and if what Vivien Loosemore had said, as reported by Daniel, were true, then tonight's meet was insane.

He stood indecisively, wrapped in a towel.

"I could serve you dinner topless," Lindsey said. "You could pretend you were in some dodgy lap dancing club." As she spoke she pulled off her jumper and unhooked her bra with the unselfconsciousness of the nearly blind, letting her large creamy-pale breasts spill into view. "That's got to be more fun than some boring BAB dinner."

"What's got into you tonight?" John asked, impressed.

"I read some stuff in a magazine," Lindsey said, "about how to spice up your sex life."

"Does ours need spicing up?"

"It can't hurt, can it. I'd much rather you wanted me for sex than for what I can find out for you about Niall Burnet."

"Which, let's face it, wasn't very much."

"I don't know why you're so bothered about him," Lindsey said. "I refuse to believe it's because he was my first boyfriend."

"You'd be surprised."

John was finding it hard to concentrate. It was as if he was in two conversations, one with Lindsey and one with her breasts, and it was her breasts he was mostly listening to. He made only token resistance when she pulled his towel away and let it fall to the floor.

"Looks like you do want to have fun with me," Lindsey said, rubbing his penis against the very breasts he had been trying unsuccessfully to ignore.

Two minutes later they were having energetic but very conventional sex on the bed.

Duncan Clark carried two glasses of wine over from the bar.

"Cheers," Faith said when he sat down.

"Cheers."

"So what is your plan exactly?" she asked him.

"I've got a better than average recording app on my phone," Clark said. "I'm going to try to get Sullivan into conversation about the whole business and record everything he says."

"You don't think he'll be on his guard?"

"I'm not going to accuse him of anything. Just try to draw him out by being nauseatingly sycophantic."

"My flesh creeps when I think about the whole degrading..." Faith struggled for the word – "...scenario. I don't know how you're going to be able to hide your disgust. I couldn't."

"I shall be focusing on the conversation and not on the girls," Clark said. "And as soon as I've got what I'm going for, I shall cry off."

"If they let you leave. Remember Juliette Warwick and everything she told me," Faith cautioned.

"Juliette's not with them any more. And they won't be expecting trouble so they won't have anything set up."

"These people are odious, but let's not make the mistake of thinking they're not cautious and clever. And dangerous."

"It will be refreshing to know that you're worrying about me. After all these years."

"Oh Duncan."

"We shall convene in my office in the morning and I shall be able to tell you all about it."

"I shall look forward to that."

It was cold in Matt's photographer's car, parked up inconspicuously around twenty-five yards from the front door of number 17 Cardew Crescent. They had stopped off at a kebab shop for sustenance on the way and now the car stank. Niall suspected that some chilli sauce had found its way onto his jacket as well, which was annoying.

"What's going on?" he asked.

"Nothing," the photographer – Ed – replied. Matt's plan for a paparazzi storm outside the house had fallen by the wayside, partly because they hadn't wanted to risk spooking any of the key players in the event of some photographers arriving too early, and partly because Matt wanted the exclusive.

"It is early yet, though," Ed added.

"According to what Penny said, the girls are always the first to arrive," Matt said, "and we know they haven't even left yet."

"I'm freezing," Niall observed. He had never given his blessing to the plan for the evening. He felt frustrated because he wasn't going to be the one carrying the battle to the enemy; he was sure the girls were going to mess up and the moment Miranda was recognised, despite that morning's expensive new hairstyle and colour, the game would be up and God knows what might happen.

There had been a very disconcerting moment in the middle of the day when Roderick Leman had called home to say that something had come up and he was going to stay in town for the evening, making himself a candidate for the Number 17 guest list. Annoyingly – ridiculously – they hadn't discussed it, although Miranda had gone very quiet as soon as she found out and he knew for a fact that she was thinking about it. Why hadn't he said something? Why hadn't she said something? Instead they had inhabited a vacuum of near silence until it had been time for her to go to Penny and Rebecca's.

In Niall's considered opinion, the evening had 'disaster' written all over it. He knew a bit about disasters.

Matthew Long's phone buzzed.

The girls are on the way," he announced.

❦

The girls were in a taxi, tense for a range of reasons. Rebecca had said nothing against the plan from the start, nor asked to be excused from it, but the thought of returning to Cardew Crescent and the memories of everything that had happened there made her feel sick inside. The fact that this time there would be no sex of any description really didn't help. Everything about the house just filled her with horror. And telling herself that she was doing it for Joe wasn't helping as much as it needed to. It was the only thing that had got her this far, but she knew that every time the taxi stopped in traffic there was a real danger she might make a run for it.

Penny was surprised to find herself a little on edge. Normally she took everything in her stride, but tonight was going to be different, and it was going to mark the end of the Daniel Sullivan chapter of her life. Not, in all honesty, before time. What had begun as a convenient arrangement had become tiresome, yet still lucrative. This was, perhaps, the moment to call a halt to all her 'extramural activities' and claw back some self-respect, because, despite herself, the 'geisha lifestyle' – as she thought of it – had taken its toll. And in that case tonight would be a watershed – an end and a beginning.

Beth, Penny's trusty partner in crime, was tense only because she sensed it in all the others and realised there was something going on to which they were all party but she was not. When she asked if there was anything she should know, they all said 'no'. And she knew they were lying.

Miranda was focusing all her attention and energy on stopping herself from shaking. She wished she had never suggested using this evening as the means to expose Daniel Sullivan and whoever else was involved. She wished she had allowed herself to be talked out of going in herself – her presence in the building seemed to be an unnecessary risk that wouldn't add anything to what they were doing. She wished she had gone out before her father's phone call in the afternoon – the thought of him being there brought bile into her throat. She wished she had suggested moving back to Telford with Niall and starting a new life. Leaving her entire past behind. Even if Daniel didn't recognise her, it would be very obvious to her 'partner' that she was out of her depth. She just hoped that somehow, although she had no idea how, it would all be over quickly.

❧

In the watching car they saw the taxi arrive and the girls go in.

"If Loosemore recognises Miranda this is where it ends," Niall said.

"Shouldn't think she'll even look at her," Matt said. "And I don't think many people would recognise her with her new spiky blond hair. It's amazing. And it suits her."

Niall grunted.

The house was dark and quiet.

❧

Inside, Miranda took a card from the infamous box and became Elaine. It was a name she had never seen and she tried to flash it discreetly to Rebecca, but Vivien Loosemore herself said, "Elaine. Welcome. Go upstairs with the others." She looked Miranda full in the face but showed no sign of recognition, ("Well, she does hardly know me," Miranda reminded herself, as she had reminded Niall several times already), and the four girls made their way upstairs.

"It's just so creepy," Miranda said when they were safely behind a closed door.

"Tell me about it," Rebecca agreed.

"Will someone tell ME what is going on?" Beth asked bluntly, stopping in the act of stepping out of her jeans.

Penny ended the silence that followed.

"My friends here have a slightly different agenda for tonight," she said.

"Meaning what exactly?"

"Meaning things may not all go according to the usual script."

"Why didn't you tell me?" Beth asked angrily. "Don't I matter? What is going to happen?"

"It's my fault," Miranda put in. "Some of these men did something pretty vile and I persuaded Penny to help me get them back."

"You weren't even supposed to be here, Beth," Penny said. "It was only because they needed four of us – "

"So now I'm bottom of the ladder?" Beth said bitterly.

"No – "

"And if I hadn't just forced the issue now," she went on, "would you have said anything to me? Or would you just have carried on and let me play catch up?"

"You were safer not knowing," Rebecca said.

"I can't believe you're here," Beth said savagely. "After last time."

"I've got a reason," Rebecca replied.

"We should be talking about what we're going to do," Miranda said.

"Oh fine, yeah, I don't matter," Beth said. "Just leave me in the dark. What if I went downstairs and warned Mary that something was brewing and she should call the whole thing off? At least she might give me my money, which it doesn't sound like I'm going to get otherwise."

"Beth if you knew what this was about you'd agree with us," Penny said.

"So tell me. Show me that much respect."

"I was blind," Miranda said. "I had an eye transplant and now I can see."

"She's got my brother's eyes," Rebecca said. "He died in a car accident."

"These men were all involved in it and they tried to fix it so it didn't work," Miranda continued. They wanted me to stay blind and the gift of Rebecca's brother's eyes to be wasted. It was all about money to them. We want to expose them to the world for what they are."

❧

Daniel Sullivan chose an Armani suit. He didn't usually push the boat out that far on a Number 17 night, but he felt sure that Duncan Clark would dress to impress and he was determined not to be outdone. The shirt and tie had required long deliberation; so long that the fourth Mrs. Sullivan had come upstairs to see if anything was amiss. With his extravagant eating and drinking and his delight in taking no exercise at all if he could help it, she lived in constant fear of his suffering a massive heart attack.

"I'm absolutely fine," Daniel had hissed at her, and she had retreated.

Finally dressed to his satisfaction, Daniel left the house and got into his car. He had missed nights like this, and tonight was going to be a particularly pleasing one. John's scepticism and groundless fear would be exposed for exactly what it was. He – Daniel – should have backed his own judgment and taken this step a long time ago. Though he said it himself, the future was looking particularly rosy.

◉

Roderick Leman saw Daniel Sullivan get into his car, and the grey Mercedes pull away from the kerb. He started his own engine and followed. He wished it were a little darker, but the nights were light now and it wasn't even dusk.

"Now then," he said to his passenger. "Tell me again what all this is about."

"It's about that odious man in the car in front," Theresa Clarke said.

Roderick made no response, concentrated on the Mercedes.

"He made a public statement about my husband that was a total lie," Theresa went on. "You knew Damian. You saw how he was with your daughter. He would've done anything to help her. He was a good man."

"Yes I met him," Roderick said. "Yes he seemed all those things. But we can't get away from the fact that before he died Miranda's eyesight failed twice. Since he died, she's had no more trouble. I'm only stating the facts," he added quickly as he heard Theresa's sharply indrawn breath ready for an angry riposte.

Instead she said nothing.

"This is what I know," she said at last. "These are my facts.

Damian was incredibly excited when he knew he was going to be involved with the aftercare of your daughter's operation. He was like a small boy on Christmas morning. He hero-worshipped Jamal Daghash and he used to say "Nobody believes him but he's a genius. It really could work. It will work." Why would he have said that if he was secretly – on his own, which was what they claimed at the press conference – planning to derail the whole thing?"

"Misdirection," Roderick Leman hazarded.

Ignoring him, Theresa Clarke went on.

"What I do know is that he changed in the last six months of his life. It was as if someone had sucked all the joy out of him. I mean he tried to hide it, but we noticed at home. The children noticed. They asked me if something was the matter with him. I couldn't believe it was his work, so I thought it must've been me." Tears started to strangle her voice. "I thought he'd met somebody else but I couldn't bear to ask. I wish I had."

"And so you think," Roderick said, filling the space because he knew Theresa couldn't speak for crying, "that Daniel Sullivan and Duncan Clark had some hold over him and made him do it. That's what you said in my office this afternoon. But I still don't understand why or what."

Theresa made a supreme effort to compose herself.

"Duncan Clark went on record with his opposition to the operation," she said. "He said it was impossible and that it was a huge waste of money. His credibility would have been destroyed if it had worked."

"When Miranda's sight failed on *This Is Now* it was Duncan Clark who restored it," Roderick countered.

"Very clever," Theresa said; "turn himself into the hero of the hour safe in the knowledge that Damian would ensure that it continued to fail."

"But why Daniel Sullivan?" Leman asked. "It was BAB who put up most of the money in the first place."

"I wish I knew," Theresa said. "But as soon as he said that about Damian having some religious conviction I knew he was in it up to his neck. It was an incredibly convenient lie, impossible to disprove because he was dead, but anyone who really knew Damian would have known. He was an atheist. His whole life. My family are churchgoers and when we first started going out we had some quite heated discussions about it. Well, I got heated. He never did. He used very calmly and rationally to lay out all the 'evidence' as he described it and then say, "So you see, my darling, I would love to be able to give in to you, and the idea of God is a lovely one, but it just can't be true." I stopped going to church. For him really. But I've never stopped praying. And I pray every day for justice to catch up with that evil man."

"OK," Roderick said. He had heard most of this story when she had surprised him at his office when he got back from lunch. "And this evening?" he asked. "What are we doing this evening?"

"I knew very little about Damian's dealings with Daniel Sullivan," Theresa Clarke said. "But there was an occasion when he was invited to some kind of do. It was called – pathetically, in my opinion – a "Number 17 Night". When he told me I laughed. It sounded like something a group of adolescent boys might have come up with. He told me absolutely nothing about it beforehand other than that it was an honour to have been invited, and even less about it afterwards. I thought it might have been the freemasons or something. But I do know from the way he behaved when he came home and afterwards that he really didn't enjoy it. Then I was speaking to Jamal Daghash yesterday and he let slip that Duncan Clark was going to a Number 17 Night tonight. Which means they're both going to be there, and I'm going to walk in and confront them."

"And you want me there."

"Because they were stringing you along too," Theresa said. "And I know they're not going to take notice of threats from a woman like me, but they will from you. And the police will listen to you."

"OK," Roderick Leman said. Yes, he had at first been irritated and surprised by Theresa's arrival at his office But when he had heard her out he found himself acknowledging that she was not just a crazy widow, but a woman presenting reasoned cogent arguments. He was moved by her understanding of her husband and persuaded by the total disconnect between her knowledge of him and the story postulated by Sullivan and Clark. Thinking on, he had then become angry. And angry most of all with John Holthouse. On Holthouse's recommendation, he had handed over a large sum of money to ensure that his daughter got the operation. Some of that money, he was sure, had ended up in Daniel Sullivan's pocket. And all the time one if not both of them had known that the whole thing was a scam. That his daughter would never get her sight. Presumably when Miranda's operation was deemed a total failure, some other unsuspecting parent with the means to pay would be targeted. And then another. It was in the throes of that rage that he had agreed to join forces with Theresa and called home to say he would be out late. The rage had now subsided, but a controlled anger at having been played for a fool simmered under the surface. He was looking forward to confronting the perpetrators. To letting them know that he was on to them, that he would do everything he could to ensure there was never another sucker to follow in his footsteps.

Beth was causing problems.

"I don't want any part of this, Pen. I wish you'd left me out of it," she said. "I need this money and I'm not part of your crusade."

"What do you mean, you need this money?" Penny snapped. "This is the first of these nights we've had in months. They used to be quite regular but they've gone down to nothing."

"And they might have got back to being regular but they won't after this," Beth retorted.

"Just be glad it happened at all," Penny said.

"I should be glad, should I? Grateful to Auntie Penny for giving me this great opportunity?"

"Beth. We're a couple of part-time prostitutes. Face it. It's nothing to be proud of. We've made a bit of money and sometimes we've had a laugh. But there are actually things that matter more than us, and rich bastards playing god with people's lives is one of those things. We've both had clients that needed a bit of caring for, but these twats aren't them."

"Suddenly Penny is a champion of social morality."

"Oh Beth. Do you enjoy what we do? Because I don't. And if there are any who do I take my hat off to them."

Beth said nothing. Rebecca looked at Miranda. Miranda looked back. She kept hearing Niall saying the plan for the evening was a mess. He was right, and here they all were sitting in the middle of it.

Here's what you can do," Penny said. "You can go downstairs and tell Mary you're ill and you can't stay. Then when all this is over and Daniel gets desperate for extra-marital sex I'll give him your number."

Beth continued to sit in silence, her right leg twitching ceaselessly up and down.

"I'm not going to walk out now," she said at last.

"Thank you," Rebecca said. "I'm really sorry."

"I should've known as soon as I saw you in the cab," Beth said.

"Yeah," Rebecca admitted. "I'm generally bad news."

"So *now*," Beth went on, "tell me quickly how and when exactly this is going to break."

"Penny thinks we should wait until after the meal," Miranda said, "but Rebecca and I want to get straight on with it. Daniel Sullivan will probably recognise me."

"He'll only have eyes for Penny," Beth said. "Wait till you see the way he looks at her. And she's right. The moment they think they're about to get their pricks into us they'll be at their most vulnerable. When Gordon says it's time for dessert we say "No sex until you tell" or words to that effect."

"I don't know if I can carry it off for that long," Miranda said.

"You will," Beth replied. "They hardly notice us while we feed them. Just the odd wandering hand."

Miranda shivered.

"I think we have to play it by ear," Rebecca said. "We just don't know how things are going to go."

"Obviously," Penny said.

They heard the doorbell down below.

"It begins." There was a hint of excitement in Penny's voice.

◉

"Good evening, Mary," Daniel said to Vivien Loosemore. "Any of our guests arrived yet?"

"No," she responded.

"Not even Adrian? He's usually keen."

"No, not even Adrian."

"The girls are here, I trust?"

"Yes."

"How did they look?"

"I can honestly say I didn't notice."

Daniel walked through Vivien's house as if it were his own. He reached the lounge where a sideboard was set with a range of drinks and mixers and made himself a gin and tonic.

"Cheers," he said, and drank a large mouthful. "Are you going to look like a cross between death and a terrified rabbit all night?" he asked.

"I don't like these evenings," Vivien said. "I've never made any secret of that."

"What's not to like?" Daniel said, sitting. "All you have to do is get the food in. You don't even cook it."

"I don't like anything about them. You exploit the girls upstairs. You exploit me. Right-thinking people would find the whole idea disgusting."

"The girls enjoy it. Ask them. The calibre of men they get to be pleasured by here is far above anything they're going to meet in their daily lives – "

"You know absolutely nothing about their daily lives."

"And I'm sure they enjoy spending the money."

Vivien Loosemore wanted to tell him that this was the last time, but the words wouldn't let themselves be said. She retreated to the kitchen. Daniel took out his phone and checked his emails and messages. He saw there were two from Theresa Clarke and deleted them unread. He had an email – presumably spam – from an address describing itself as Nemesis4DS@gmail.com. His finger hovered over the delete icon but then curiosity got the better of him. The message had come to his BAB email, so whoever it was hadn't got to his private account. He opened it.

The message was three words long:

"Tonight's the night."

He stared at it. In many ways tonight was the night, but Nemesis? There were two things about Nemesis. One was that she was the classical goddess of comeuppance. The other was that whoever had created the email account knew that. They also knew something about tonight. He doubted that Penny's education stretched to the more obscure classical deities, and she was the only one in her party who could have found his BAB email – the others didn't know his name or his place of work. Penny might not be the sharpest tool in the box, but she was unquestionably discreet. That left the guests and Vivien, and anyone that they might accidentally or deliberately have told. John had gone flaky recently, jumping at shadows. Could this be him, anonymously making some tongue-in-cheek prediction? Lining himself up to say "I told you so." No, not the John he knew. And Vivien would never have scraped up enough gumption, but of course she could have leaked the information to someone else, although he had always felt that her distaste for the whole thing and her own involvement in it acted very efficiently as a muzzle. Which brought it down to Duncan Clark and the director general. The eye consultant – he went back over their lunch together and their conversations before and after the press conference. No. Although Duncan Clark would certainly know who Nemesis was, an anonymous email wasn't his style, and it made no sense.

What did he know about Tony Strong? Tony Strong OBE, curse him. Soon, no doubt, to be Sir Tony for services to the visually impaired. For somebody in such a high profile role, Tony was a shadowy figure. He was always busy doing something else when you needed him, but somehow, without ever making his presence felt, he seemed to know everything that was going on, and he had a reputation for ruthlessness from his previous incarnation as a

CEO in the business world. He had panicked John by spotting his financial wizardry very early on, but then seemed to share John's view that it equated to the bonuses a big company might pay, and that they were well-deserved. They continued, so long as he got his share and he had a say in what happened. He said, "I didn't get where I am today by being a saint. But the golden rule is, the business always comes first. If you're thinking of the business as your cash cow, you're going to work a damn sight harder for the business."

What annoyed Daniel about Tony Strong was that his admiration was all for John. He tolerated Daniel because John thought highly of him and he had been at BAB for twenty years, but he didn't value what he had to offer. It was time for that to change. Daniel had started to feel that Tony was calling more of the shots than he and John were. He was acting like someone who had joined the board and was suddenly trying to buy a majority shareholding and get control. Inviting him tonight was about wresting back some of that control. He had put it off for years , for a number of reasons, but in the aftermath of the eye transplant business it had seemed like the right move, and Tony had been very excited to be invited. Or had that excitement been at an opportunity to hang Daniel out to dry?

The email was a bore, because it was now going to be at the back of his mind all evening. Where the Hell was Holthouse? He needed someone to talk to and take his mind off it. He thought about firing off a quick message of the "Where are you?" variety, but decided against. It would look panicky, which was the last thing John needed at the moment. Instead he downed his gin and tonic and made himself another.

"So do we go in?" Roderick Leman asked.

"What do you think?" Theresa threw back at him. Roderick was a little uneasy because they were in residents' only parking and he was reluctant to leave the car.

"Well," he said, "you did say that – when Damian went – he told you it started at eight. It's only quarter to now. So I doubt that the other guests will have arrived. We don't want to go off half-cocked. I say we wait until five or ten past eight. Longer if Duncan Clark hasn't arrived by then."

"OK," Theresa agreed.

Just before eight o'clock a taxi pulled up and dropped its passenger outside the house. The light was fading and their view was partially obstructed, and neither of them could positively identify the passenger as Duncan Clark.

"Too thin," Roderick said.

"You've seen him more than I have," Theresa conceded.

◉

Vivien Loosemore opened the door to Tony Strong. Despite having been warned to expect him, she was flustered, both by the circumstances and by the fact that she had thought the next arrival would be John.

"Vivien," Tony Strong said confidently. "Not too early, am I?"

"We don't use our real names on these occasions," Vivien said. "I thought Daniel would have told you. To preserve our anonymity."

"I see," Tony said, grinning like a small boy. "Who am I, then? Who are you? Who's Daniel?"

"I'm Mary," Vivien said, feeling ridiculous. "Daniel is Gordon." Tony Strong burst into a loud laugh. "How do you feel about Charles?"

"Charles?" Tony Strong mused. "Heir to the throne. Posh name. Works for me. So long as it wasn't the dead doc's name. I don't want a hand-me-down."

"No. Oh no. He was Richard. You knew about that?"

"I make it my business to know, Mary. That's why I'm good at what I do."

Vivien ushered him through to the lounge. Daniel looked up, also expecting Holthouse, and then leapt to his feet, hand outstretched.

"Gordon, this is Charles," Vivien said quickly.

"Charles, delighted to see you," Daniel said, noting that Strong was also wearing a designer suit and congratulating himself on his own choice. They would be an elite and high-class gathering tonight. John would let the side down, when he finally condescended to appear, in his inevitable jeans. "Let me fix you a drink," he went on. Charles asked for vodka, straight, with a single ice cube, and slightly disconcertingly downed it in one.

"Another?" Daniel suggested.

"Why not, Gordon, why not?" Charles said, smiling.

"I hope you'll enjoy the evening," Gordon ventured.

"I hope so too," Charles said. "I take it we have to talk about the weather and the state of the nation, as our work might give away who we are."

"Don't worry. You'll find conversation flows well enough."

"Shame we can't talk about work, though," Charles reflected. "There are a number of things I was hoping to get the chance to go through with you, away from the office."

"Well, while it's just the two of us of course we can," Daniel said. At that point they heard the front door open and a minute later Mary introduced Clive to them.

"Good evening, Clive. I'm Gordon and this is Charles."

Daniel looked Duncan Clark up and down. He was wearing black motorcycling leathers and boots.

"Came on the bike," Clive said, noticing his gaze. "Best way to beat the traffic."

"What is it?" Charles asked.

"I have something of a stable," Clive confessed. "Tonight it's the Honda NC700. My pride and joy is a 1966 Norton Atlas, but it was more about expediency tonight."

"I'm rebuilding a Triumph Thunderbird," Charles said. "Been into bikes since I was six."

Daniel felt himself reduced to the role of drinks waiter as Tony Strong and Duncan Clark sat down and talked motorbikes, a subject he knew absolutely nothing about. He was further disconcerted by Duncan asking for sparkling water ("Never drink when I'm on the bike"), which he had had to get Vivien to provide from the kitchen. Had Clark not appreciated that the purpose of the evening was to enjoy good wine and food as well as the girls? Where was John? It was time to get things moving and there was still no sign of him. Deciding to call him, he pulled out his phone, only to be distracted by another email from Nemesis4DS. He opened it.

"Not long now," it said.

What the Hell?

John Holthouse's phone went to voicemail. Daniel sent him a text. "We're waiting for you."

◉

"What's going on? What are we waiting for?" Miranda asked. It was a quarter past eight and they could hear voices down below.

"We have to wait till we're called," Beth said.

"Somebody's late," Penny said. "It happened before once. DS will be livid."

Miranda was shivering, despite the warmth of the room.

"Put your coat on till they call for us," Penny said.

"I'm not cold," Miranda responded.

"It'll be fine," Rebecca said, wishing she meant it.

❂

"When is something going to happen?" Niall said from the back of the car.

"Penny said she would message us when they were going down to the banquet," Matthew said. "We know there should be four men and we've only seen three. They're waiting for someone."

"Shit."

❂

"Do you think that was Duncan Clark on the bike?" Roderick Leman asked.

"I don't know. You can't recognise anyone under a helmet."

"Did your husband ever say anything about Duncan Clark having a motorbike?"

"No," Theresa said. "Damian really didn't know him."

"We're a bit stuck then."

"We'll go in at half past."

"OK."

❂

At twenty-five past eight, furious, Daniel told Vivien to bring the girls down and start serving food. The spare girl would just have to help out and provide an element of choice. Vivien went up and spoke to them, explaining that one guest had not yet arrived, so they were all to be especially attentive to the other three. Penny discreetly sent her pre-written message to Matt, and they followed 'Mary' down the stairs, trying to smile and look relaxed.

Miranda was hoping that it was her father who hadn't arrived. She didn't know why she was so sure he had become a late addition to the guest list, but it was fixed in her mind. But maybe now he had thought better of the whole thing and gone home instead. She followed Rebecca into the lounge, last of the four, and her eyes took in the buffet set out on a table to one side, the array of bottles of presumably alcohol on a piece of furniture against another wall, a large mirror over a large fireplace where coals were flaming, the chairs and sofas and their occupants: Daniel Sullivan, whom Penny was trying to distract so that he wouldn't notice her; a thin-faced, dark-haired man whose eyes looked – in her limited experience – as if they had been set too close together in his head; and – she recognised the voice with shock and astonishment before the face – Duncan Clark. What could he be doing here? Niall had said he had turned out to be one of the good guys, but now...? Had they all just walked into a trap? It felt like the press conference all over again. Ranks of the enemy closing like water over their heads.

She realised she was doing nothing and she should be doing something. Penny was monopolising Daniel – who seemed to expect nothing else – but Beth and Rebecca had each picked up a plate of somethings and were offering them to the other two men, who were engrossed in conversation, although she didn't hear the words, only noise. She went to the buffet and picked up a plate. She had no idea what was on it. She walked towards the man who wasn't Duncan Clark and he took one of whatever they were off her plate without looking at it or at her, or breaking the flow of what he was saying. She walked on to the sofa where Duncan Clark was sitting. She offered the plate at arm's length, but he broke off his conversation, reached out, and took hold of her around the waist in a sudden, strong movement, pulling her proprietorially towards him.

"Sit here," he said, indicating the space beside him.

Miranda felt she couldn't say no.

"Profiteroles are delicious," he said quietly when she had sat down, "but would normally be served after the savoury dishes."

"Sorry," Miranda said. "I wasn't thinking."

Duncan Clark watched until he saw that both Gordon and Charles were engaged with other girls. Then he said,

"Interesting hair colour. What's your name?"

"Elaine," Miranda said hesitantly.

"What's in a name?" Clark mused. "Some girls seem to change theirs at will. More often even than their eyes. I don't forget the eyes I work on," he continued. "I am astonished to encounter yours here. If you're hoping for some physical intimacy with our mutual friend it looks like you're going to be disappointed."

"Are you involved in all this?" Miranda said directly. "Just tell me. Because you're all about to be exposed."

"Involved in what?" Duncan said.

"Dr. Clarke's death," Miranda whispered.

"Absolutely not," Clark said. "My God, what on earth are you up to?"

"Why are you here?"

"I could ask you the same."

"We're going to expose the truth."

"We? Oh God, you haven't got Niall tucked up your sleeve

somewhere ready to blunder in and cause trouble?"

"I haven't got a sleeve."

"Touché. But this is not a place for you. You don't need to do this. I'm here on the same mission and I want you to leave it to me. Now I'm going to stroke your leg. I apologise in advance, but I have to look as though I'm here to enjoy your wares and we're being watched."

"OK."

"Don't freeze. You took a Hell of a gamble with your attempt at a disguise."

"I know."

❦

Daniel started to relax. Penny was good for that. Also, the other girls seemed to be charming his first-time guests. Duncan Clark had made a big play for a very blond spiky-haired boyish-figured girl he'd never seen before, and the other two were engaging Tony Strong OBE's attention. Presumably John would explain all in the morning. This Number 17 Night was oddly different. Usually the men carried on a conversation amongst themselves with the girls as something of a sideshow during this part of the proceedings. Tonight they were drawing the girls out, almost as if they wanted to know who they were. The girls seemed different, too. The one that normally partnered John looked a little lost and there was a tension about the others. The blond had picked up a plate of profiteroles, which one could charitably put down to nerves, but was more likely to do with her hair colour. He needed to speak to Penny about sourcing a certain quality of recruit.

The doorbell rang, which meant John had finally arrived. There would be a tale of traffic or car trouble, no doubt.

For some reason Vivien kept him talking in the hall. There were raised voices, including a woman's. All Daniel's relaxation went. Who was this? Mrs. Tony Strong OBE? Mrs. Duncan Clark? Had one of the men been fool enough to let slip where they were going? For one awful moment he envisaged a vengeful Juliette Warwick wielding a machete, having already dismembered John and dined on his private parts. Then, to his complete amazement, the Clarke woman who had spat at him walked in with Susannah Leman's father, despite Vivien Loosemore's best efforts to keep them out.

Everybody froze.

"Disgusting," Theresa Clarke said at last.

"And you have trespassed into a private function because?" Daniel said, fighting back rage.

"There are things to talk about," Roderick Leman said. "Urgently. And both the principals are here." He looked from Daniel Sullivan to Duncan Clark, for the first time taking in the girl sitting beside the latter. "No. Oh no. What the – ? Your hair – . What the fuck are you doing here? In your underwear? I cannot believe this."

Everybody looked at Miranda.

"No," Daniel half-whispered, as he saw, finally, through the disguise.

"We're not leaving until we hear the truth," Theresa said, not recognising Miranda and not realising why her co-conspirator appeared to have run out of steam.

"Daniel," Tony Strong said, getting to his feet, "I think I'm going to leave you to it. Thanks and all that, but you seem to have matters to deal with that are no concern of mine."

"No you don't," Daniel said quickly. "Vivien do something useful and lock the door."

"Excuse me?" Tony Strong said, with an inflexion that reinforced the roles of their working relationship.

"We're not boss and underling here, Strong," Daniel said.

Roderick was staring at his daughter, nearly naked on a sofa next to Duncan Clark, trying to make any kind of sense of the world he had just walked into.

"You lied about my husband, about Damian," Theresa Clarke said, addressing Daniel and Duncan.

"We did, and I'm sorry," Duncan Clark said quickly. "I needed time to get to the truth."

"What are you talking about?" Daniel snapped.

"Money," Miranda said, wishing the cavalry would arrive, not really knowing who was on whose side any more. Everyone seemed surprised that she had spoken. The girls were just window dressing.

"A great deal of it mine," Roderick Leman said. Daniel laughed.

"You call that a great deal?" he asked derisively.

"If there are allegations to be made against British Association of the Blind employees," Tony Strong said, "I urge you to make them through the proper channels – our own complaints department. I assure you they will be treated with the utmost seriousness, and I will personally – "

" – ensure that no dirt sticks to me," Daniel interrupted, "having first lined my pockets."

There was a furious knocking on the front door. Vivien inched towards it.

"Don't," Daniel said.

"Police," was shouted from the other side of the door. Despite his own agitation, Daniel was still able to relish the look on Tony Strong OBE's face as he heard the word. It was as if he had stooped to pick a flower and realised he had put his hand down in dogshit.

Vivien opened the door and a man with a camera burst past her, taking pictures all the while. Two men started to walk in after him, neither of them police officers.

"Niall," Vivien managed to say in strangled tones. "You're not the police."

"Not exactly," he said. "But if I'd said Nemesis you might not've opened the door. Now where's the orgy?"

Tony Strong assumed control when journalists and a photographer entered the fray.

"You are a long way outside your legal parameters," he said to Matt.

"The front door was opened to us when we knocked," Matt said.

"I shall call the police if you don't leave now," Tony Strong continued. "And I shall make sure these pictures never get into any papers."

"There's always YouTube," Niall said. Strong seemed to take in his presence for the first time. The front door slammed and Vivien Loosemore's quick footsteps could be heard fading into the distance. "The rats are leaving the sinking ship," Niall said. "Cerberus has quit."

"Nobody's leaving until I hear the truth about my husband," Theresa Clarke shouted. "Then you can get back to your depravity for all I care."

"The best place to have this conversation will be at the Association in the morning," Tony Strong said. "Then if there is a suggestion of wrongdoing we have a procedure – "

"Here will do," Roderick Leman said.

"Damian Clarke committed suicide because I confronted him with the knowledge that he had been sabotaging the aftercare medication for Miranda's eyes," Duncan said suddenly. "At a press conference following his death we headed off suspicion with a fabricated tale about his being a religiously motivated nutcase. I shall be going to the police in the morning to tell them that that was a convenient speculation. I shall also be telling them what I suspect to be the truth."

"I'll be coming with you," Theresa Clarke said.

"And what is this truth you suspect?" Daniel asked. He had meant to be contemptuously silent, but he couldn't resist the question.

"Damian Clarke did what he did at your behest."

"Why?"

"And you rewarded him," Rebecca chimed in to everyone's amazement including her own, "by inviting him to one of these evenings. To show him he was part of your crew. And he hated every minute of it."

"Before we get into the business of defamation and slander," Daniel said, "I would still love to know why."

"It's always money, isn't it?" Niall said. "I was told by someone at BAB way back that any publicity for the eye transplant brought a massive spike in donations. She lost her job for telling me. So here's a theory. Eye transplant a success – patient swans off into a happy future or a celebrity future – operation forgotten – no more donation spikes – each new transplant less newsworthy than the last – public lose interest. Eye transplant a heroic failure – public engaged, give more money: more money equals better chance of success – each failure brings a bigger windfall."

Briefly, nobody spoke.

"If this is true, Daniel," Tony Strong said, "although I applaud your commitment to the Association, I'm afraid you're going to have to resign. I'll give you that much dignity."

"What do you mean, 'if'?" Daniel snarled. "You've made more out of this than anyone."

The next day the *Mirror* ran a two-page exclusive about extraordinary goings-on at a house in northwest London. The reporters credited were Matthew Long and Niall Burnet. Significant figures in a major national charity had been embarrassingly caught in the throes of some kind of sex party which had then disintegrated into a battle of incredible allegation and counter-allegation. There were pictures of the house, of Tony Strong OBE and of Daniel Sullivan, director general and deputy director general of the British Association for the Blind, with scantily clad girls whose faces were pixellated or out of shot. There were lengthy interviews with Theresa Clarke, widow of the eye doctor whose recent suicide had shocked his profession, and with Roderick Leman, father of Miranda Leman, recipient of the world's first binocular eye transplant. There were detailed biographies of Tony Strong and Daniel Sullivan, and of the owner of the house, pictured in the act of opening the front door, Vivien Loosemore. One of the girls present, Rebecca Blackford, had agreed to be named and gave salacious details about what took place on these exclusive gentlemen's evenings, of which this was her second.

Under the circumstances, Carl Fisher, chairman of the British Association for the Blind, felt he had no option but to ring the changes at the top of the organisation.

Niall was frustrated. The police showed massive reluctance to go after a major charity and dig into its finances. It was exactly as he had predicted. The real crime remained unpunished.

"But it's over," Miranda said. "And you've got lots of money from the *Mirror*."

"True," Niall admitted. "Do you fancy a holiday?"

"Yes! Where?"

"I was thinking maybe Telford."

"Sounds perfect."

"You've got a lot to thank me for," Lindsey said to John Holthouse.

"Did you know?" he asked her.

"I'm not just a pretty face," she said.

"No," he mused. "But I'm wondering how – "

"Wonder on, Mr. New Deputy Director General."

THE END

ALEX TRESILLIAN

Alex grew up in rural England with a dream to write for a living which never quite came true. He has enjoyed incarnations as a theatre publicity officer, restaurant manager, teacher, teacher trainer, and curriculum developer. Along the way Alex wrote five plays that were performed by students including one, Never Mind the Rain Forests, that was enthusiastically reviewed (3 stars) at the Edinburgh Fringe. Another, Gavin's Kingdom, received a professional workshop production at the Birmingham Rep. Plays Into Shakespeare, a book for English and Drama teachers that introduced students to the characters in Shakespeare's plays through short modern-English 'additional' scenes, was published by First and Best in Education in 2007.

Alex moved to Abu Dhabi in 2008 with a Lebanese international education company that had a contract to train English teachers and develop curriculum materials. Latterly moved to their Academic Development office in Beirut and wrote two series of books for students from ages eight to sixteen – one on grammar and one on the art of writing.

He is now living with his wife of many years in Worcestershire, his children pursuing careers in education, fashion, charity fundraising and web development in places as disparate as Beijing, London and Chesterfield. Alex also enjoys writing stories for his young grandchildren.

Urbane Publications is dedicated to developing new author voices, and publishing fiction and non-fiction that challenges, thrills and fascinates.

From page-turning novels to innovative reference books, our goal is to publish what YOU want to read.

Find out more at
urbanepublications.com